The Secret Life of
Miss Mary Bennet

THE SECRET LIFE OF MISS MARY BENNET

A Secret Life of Mary Bennet Mystery

Katherine Cowley

TULE
PUBLISHING

Praise for *The Secret Life of Miss Mary Bennet*

"Beautifully written, masterfully plotted, meet a Mary Bennet every bit as fascinating and twice as daring as her more famous sisters."

—Gretchen Archer, USA Today bestselling author of the Davis Way Crime Capers

"Cowley's creative continuation of the story of one of literature's famous forgotten sisters into a world she could never have dreamed possible, broadens her horizons and ours. Following the pedantic Mary Bennet in her adventures after the conclusion of Pride and Prejudice was a delight that Jane Austen and mystery fans will embrace and cheer."

—Laurel Ann Nattress, editor of *Jane Austen Made Me Do It*, and Austenprose.com.

"In *The Secret Life of Miss Mary Bennet*, Katherine Cowley takes the least interesting sister from Jane Austen's *Pride and Prejudice* and turns her into the heroine of her own story. It's very fun to watch Mary transform into a competent spy, but the true delight is how Cowley masterfully keeps Mary true to her pedantic, socially awkward self from Austen's original while making her a whole person we can root for."

—Molly Greeley, author of *The Clergyman's Wife: A Pride and Prejudice Novel*

"A delightfully fresh take on Miss Mary Bennet. A story I didn't even realize I was waiting for until I read it."

—Jess Heileman, author of *A Well-Trained Lady*

"An intriguing historical mystery that fans of *Pride and Prejudice* will find compelling."

—Tina Kashian, author of the Kebab Kitchen Mysteries

Dedication

to my mother

for giving me a love of words

and helping me achieve my dreams

CHAPTER ONE

*"Bonaparte is still flying from [region to region], review-
ing his troops, fortifying his positions, improving his
garrisons, collecting provisions, and, in short, doing everything that can give him a permanent hold upon
Germany."*

—*The Times*, London, August 3, 1813

M ISS MARY BENNET could do nothing to stop her life
from shattering to pieces, so she played the pianoforte.

Her cousin, Mr. Collins, had arrived to take possession of
Longbourn before her father, Mr. Bennet, was even in the
grave. As Mr. Collins and the men he had hired swept
through the house, removing items he had sold, Mary
attempted to drown out the commotion by playing faster and
faster, louder and louder, until her younger sister, Kitty,
exclaimed, "Can you please stop, Mary!"

Mary pulled her fingers off the keys and sniffed.

Their eldest sister, Jane—known as Mrs. Bingley since her
marriage not quite a year before—cleared her throat. "What I
think Kitty means to say is it might be more appropriate to
play that funeral march with a little more solemnity."

Mary tried not to take offense. It was she, of all her sisters,
who had applied herself most to the pianoforte over the years.
Should she not be able to choose the manner in which she

played?

A sticky summer scent blew in through the open window, and the breeze disturbed Mary's music. She carefully rearranged the pages.

Kitty, Jane, and Elizabeth were seated at a nearby table assisting with the funeral preparations. They answered letters of condolence and sorted the black gloves for the funeral guests. In a few minutes they would organize the mourning rings. Mary had assisted them for a while, but she was more inclined to pass the time on the pianoforte. However, if they would not appreciate her playing—

"Oh, here is a letter from Lydia," said Elizabeth.

Lydia was their youngest sister and had been the first to marry, to a Mr. Wickham. Elizabeth's husband, Mr. Darcy, had purchased him a new commission, and his regiment was currently training so they could travel to the continent and fight against Napoleon Bonaparte.

Mary did not leave the pianoforte, but she did lean forward to better hear the contents of the letter.

Dearest Mother and Sisters,

I am devastated by the death of Father, and I have not stopped shedding tears since I heard the news. While I would love to return to Longbourn, my dear Wickham must remain here, and I find myself unable to part from him for even a few days. Surely you understand what it is to be newly married and in love.

I have used the money that you sent to purchase clothes of mourning. Have you seen the advertisements? In London some women are wearing burgundy for mourning instead of black. I went to the dressmaker and chose out a fine fabric. I intend to be the envy of all the mourners.

I will be thinking of each of you with fondness. Know that you and Father are in my heart.

With love and tears,
Lydia

The four sisters sat in shocked silence.

After a moment of reflection, Mary felt prepared to speak. "A duty to one's spouse is paramount, but in this case, a duty to one's parents should take precedence. To spend the money meant for travelling costs on expensive mourning clothing instead—that speaks of focusing on matters of little worth. Hannah More wrote, 'A life devoted to trifles not only takes away the inclination, but the capacity for higher pursuits.'"

"Thank you, Mary," said Jane.

"How could she write such a letter at a time like this, with such disregard for our father?" said Elizabeth. Elizabeth was often the most rational of Mary's sisters, which was an admirable trait, and she generally managed to express her sentiments in a concise yet compelling manner, a skill which Mary wished she could imitate.

"Even if I were married to a man like Wickham," said Kitty, "I would come for a funeral."

Jane reached across the table and took the letter. She would probably say something altogether too kind, and more forgiving than Lydia deserved.

"Oh, surely she is prevented for some reason from coming and is using this excuse as a mask for her emotions. See this line, 'I have not stopped shedding tears since I heard the news.' Do you not hear the real sadness there?"

Mary did not sense any sadness on Lydia's part. Of course, she had never understood her youngest sister. She tried to withhold judgment, for various sermons said it was not man's role to judge, yet she often found herself condemning Lydia's follies. Jane and Elizabeth had come when their father had taken ill; all his daughters had been there with him in the moment he took his last breath. All except Lydia. And now she chose not to attend his funeral.

A man entered the room without the courtesy of a knock or warning, and they silenced and turned back to their work. It was best not to discuss overly personal matters in front of servants, and this seemed especially true for the men hired by Mr. Collins.

Due to the entailment, which was unalterable, as each of the daughters tried to explain to Mrs. Bennet time and time again, the estate and most of its possessions went not to any of Mr. Bennet's daughters, but rather to his closest male relative, Mr. Collins.

Mr. Collins had been serving as a clergyman, but upon Mr. Bennet's death a week before, had decided to renounce the living and devote himself to the running of Longbourn. After his arrival, his first task was to follow the advice of his esteemed patroness, Lady Catherine de Bourgh, and to immediately, without any delay, make the estate match his personal expectations of taste and comfort. Mr. and Mrs. Collins intended to use some of the existing furniture at Longbourn, but they also planned to bring some of their own pieces, and so Mr. Collins had arranged to sell the excess. Mary wondered how a mismatched collection of furniture would serve them, but it was his furniture, and he could do with it as he liked.

He had stated that Mrs. Bennet could remain at Longbourn until she chose a permanent place. In the meantime, she could even maintain possession of her bedroom, which he admitted was the best in the house and would be within his rights to occupy (though of course his sense of duty to Mrs. Bennet would not allow him to take it from her). All of Mr. Collins's actions and words seemed, on the surface, very rational to Mary, yet somehow his mannerisms left her feeling that he should be doing more to accommodate their family.

Despite Mr. Collins's insistence that his goal was to make the situation agreeable to everyone, Mrs. Bennet had declared that she would not be a guest in her own home. She had wanted to vacate the premises immediately, but Mary and Kitty had convinced her that they should not leave until several days after the funeral. Mary could not abandon her father's body to the care of Mr. Collins; she and her sisters would watch over it. Meanwhile, Mr. Collins's haste in selling the existing furniture did make living here during the funeral preparations more difficult. She could not even play a funeral march uninterrupted.

The hired man passed rather closely to where Jane, Kitty, and Elizabeth were seated. A loud noise, perhaps some sort of bird, came from outside; it was louder than a typical bird, and not the sort of sound one normally heard in these parts. They all turned to look, but there was nothing to be seen, so after a moment they returned to their tasks. The hired man was examining an upholstered chair. He paused and looked briefly at Mary with the sort of focused attention that disconcerted her. His eyes then turned to Kitty before returning to the chair.

"Will you be sitting with Father tonight, Mary?" asked Jane.

"Yes, I am prepared to do my duty." She considered saying more, but she was distracted as the man lifted the chair.

As he passed her on the way out of the room, Mary could

not help but notice that his clothes seemed a bit crisper than those of the other hired men, and his cravat was a slightly different shade of brown. She did not recognize his face, though it was a very normal face, with no distinguishing characteristics. He must have arrived later than the other men, or maybe he had been sitting with the wagons until now, but still, something about him unsettled her.

"Did anyone notice something strange about that servant?"

Elizabeth and Jane shook their heads, quizzical expressions on their faces.

Kitty leaned forward and said, in a conspiratorial whisper, "Did he do something untoward?"

"Of course not," said Mary. "But I was certain Mr. Collins only brought eight men, and he was not one of them." Not only had she sensed that he did not belong, but she felt like he had been evaluating her.

Kitty gave a brief, derisive laugh. "You counted the men he brought?"

Mary looked down at the pianoforte's keys. Kitty had spent a lot of time mocking her lately. Mary ignored it with practiced indifference, but still it grated on her.

For the most part, she had liked it better when all four of her sisters had been at home. But of course, it was impossible for things to always stay the same. She had lost Elizabeth, Jane, and Lydia to marriage. Elizabeth lived at Pemberley, Lydia with Wickham's regiment, and Jane and Mr. Bingley had recently given up Netherfield Hall and bought their own property near Pemberley. With her father's death, she had only her mother and Kitty to look forward to for constant company. It still had not been decided where they would live permanently after the funeral, but once they vacated Longbourn, they would live, for a time, with Mrs. Bennet's sister, Mrs. Philips, in Meryton. Mrs. Bennet had been bedridden since Mr. Bennet had taken ill, and they could not possibly travel farther until Mrs. Bennet's health improved.

If only Mary were married to Mr. Collins. When Elizabeth had rejected Mr. Collins's offer of marriage, Mary had hoped that he would propose to her. But he had not, instead wedding their friend Charlotte Lucas. Mary still looked on the incident with some regret: Mr. Collins was a religious man, full of profound statements and insights, and if she had married him, the Bennets would not be losing their home and possessions.

Mary breathed deeply, then set her fingers back onto the keys. She resumed the funeral march from where she had left off, this time playing so solemnly and slowly that no one could possibly complain. If she were of a more curious nature, perhaps she would make further inquiries after the servant, but it was a matter of little import.

"I have a mind to join the funeral procession," said Elizabeth.

Mary paused, and Jane and Kitty looked up. What a strange idea. Of course, there was nothing that prohibited a woman from joining the funeral procession, or even the service in the church if she desired, but it defied tradition and was not part of a woman's duty.

Mary resumed her music but paid close attention to the words of her sisters.

"Are you sure?" asked Jane. "You will be the talk of the region."

"What does it matter to me what the people of Meryton think?"

"That is easy for you to say," said Kitty, "with ten thousand pounds a year."

"If I do not attend the procession, the closest blood relation to father will be Mr. Collins," said Elizabeth. "I cannot imagine our father wanting that."

"If you go," said Kitty, "I will accompany you." Every morning since their father's death, Kitty's cheeks had been raw and tear stained. Her outward expressions of grief seemed, for her, a necessary demonstration of her love for their father. Mary tried to keep her sentiments—which were just as strong—more contained within herself.

"What about you, Jane?" asked Elizabeth.

"I had best stay with Mama. She will need my support." Jane's voice sounded tired.

"And you, Mary?"

"It is not part of a daughter's duty," said Mary stiffly. She continued to play as she spoke, unwilling to stop, and unwilling to admit that the idea of joining the funeral procession had a certain appeal. "And besides, between the two nights I have already spent and tonight, I will have passed three nights watching his body. That is enough."

"I think, in this situation, any of our choices are justified," said Jane. She stood. "Now where were those mourning rings?"

The mourning rings needed to be sorted so they could be distributed as part of the funeral, one to each family member and friend who attended. It was a small token of appreciation, and something they could wear in remembrance of him.

"I put the case next to the gloves," said Kitty. She and Elizabeth also stood. They lifted gloves, shifted letters, and examined every nearby surface.

"Did we leave them in the downstairs parlor?" asked Elizabeth.

"I know I carried them up," insisted Kitty. "Mrs. Hill must have moved them." The housekeeper had been in the room not long before.

But Mary suspected that Mrs. Hill would not know. She re-examined the last few minutes in her mind: the servant entering the room, the strange sound, the removal of the chair, and now the missing mourning rings. It was too much of a coincidence. Yes, they could find Mrs. Hill or Mr. Collins and assemble the hired men, but that would take time. And why require someone else to solve a problem when you could solve it yourself?

Without a word to her sisters, Mary stood and exited the room. The men would be taking the unneeded furniture out the back of the house and loading it into wagons, and so she headed that direction, in a manner that was a bit faster than was normally appropriate for young ladies (though she took care not to run). She rushed down a staircase and out the door. Her heart pounded and her lungs felt short of air.

The chair was strapped to the back of the first wagon. The wagon's wheels began to turn.

Mary stepped onto the gravel. She hesitated, for it was never ladylike to raise one's voice. But this was an urgent matter. "Stop! Wait!" she cried, waving her arms.

The wagon stopped, and one of Mr. Collins's men stepped down from it. He was one of the original eight. "What do you need, miss?"

"I need to examine that chair."

The man removed the ropes and lifted down the chair. She ran her hands over the back and sides and noted that the cushion was slightly dislodged. Beneath it she found the black velvet case. She undid the latch, opened it, and saw that it still held the rings.

By now her sisters had followed her outside. "I found it," she called to them, holding up the case.

Mr. Collins exited the house. "What is all this commotion?"

"Someone tried to steal the mourning rings," said Elizabeth.

"Yes," said Kitty. "It was one of the servants. He placed them in that chair."

Mr. Collins puffed up his chest. His hands closed tightly and then opened again, as if he was trying not to clench them. "How dare you accuse me of stealing the rings? I, who out of generosity and Christian benevolence, have allowed you to remain at Longbourn when I would have been justified in casting you out."

"We are not accusing you in any manner," said Jane, her voice a little strained. She worked so hard to help everyone feel better when she herself was in mourning.

"You accused one of the men I hired." His eyes fell on Elizabeth.

Before Elizabeth could reply with something scathing, Mary interrupted. "It was not, in fact, one of the men you hired. You brought eight men, and we saw them at the start. This man, while he tried to imitate their dress, did not quite match the others, and was an impostor."

Elizabeth and Jane spent several minutes reassuring Mr. Collins that he was at no fault, that he had been taken advantage of by the criminal, and that they placed no blame on him whatsoever. Finally, once he was properly appeased, they assembled all of Mr. Collins's men and the household servants outside, underneath the warm, languid sun. Mary was the only one who was able to give a decent description of the man. But besides the four sisters, not a single person had seen the man who had moved the chair, and no one knew his identity.

"This chair is not even one that I have sold," declared Mr. Collins. "Return it to the house at once."

Eventually everyone was back in their places—Elizabeth, Kitty, and Jane carefully sorting and labeling the mourning rings, choosing which would go to which families, since their father had given only minimal details in his will. Mary tried to help them, but despite having solved the mystery, her heart continued to pound, and she could not focus on the rings. She returned to the funeral march on the pianoforte.

"How did you infer what happened?" asked Kitty with wonder.

"It seemed to be the only logical conclusion," Mary replied. "First there was the servant I did not recognize, then a noise from outside which distracted us, and then he removed the chair, and not long after we noticed the mourning rings gone." She felt warmth inside, a joy at being of assistance. Yet the fact that they had not found the thief troubled her. Where was he now? And what crime would he commit next?

After a few minutes, Mr. Collins entered the room with four of the men. Mary was surprised when Mr. Collins spoke to her rather than her sisters.

"Miss Bennet, I find it necessary to address you at this time."

She stopped playing and rested her hands on her lap. "You have my attention, Mr. Collins."

"It is quite unfortunate, especially in light of you clearing up the matter of the mourning rings, but I need to remove the pianoforte."

Mary stared at him, disbelief on her face. "But I...but I need it."

"However, I do not need it. The esteemed Lady Catherine de Bourgh, who has always been so generous to our family, recently gifted us with our own instrument. It is a much finer pianoforte and should arrive within a few weeks."

Mary did not move from the bench. Her hands instinctively reached out to the pianoforte, and she gripped the instrument as if holding on for dear life.

"I have found someone willing to pay forty pounds for this pianoforte as it is rather old and does not have the best sound. But, as you are family, if you are willing to pay thirty-five pounds, you can keep it and take it with you."

Thirty-five pounds. The amount was impossible. At the moment, she had only a few pounds of her own. Mrs. Bennet's remaining fortune was five thousand pounds, which, invested in the four per cents, gave them only two hundred pounds a year to live off of, a drastic decrease from the two thousand pounds a year provided by Mr. Bennet. When her mother died, Mary would only inherit one thousand pounds, which would give her only forty pounds a year with which to maintain herself. She could not possibly purchase the pianoforte, no matter how dear.

"Let go of the instrument, Miss Mary," directed Mr. Collins.

Her fingers tightened further. She could not let go of this pianoforte that she played for hours every day—this instrument that made her life tolerable even in the hardest of times.

"But Mr. Collins," said Jane, "surely the pianoforte could wait two days to be taken."

"Lady Catherine de Bourgh told me that it was best to arrange all of my affairs as quickly as possible when I arrived, and I intend to do so."

"Can you not see that Mary is distraught?" said Elizabeth.

"And you claim to be a gentleman."

"I suppose Miss Bennet's unseemly behaviour may be excused due to the loss of Mr. Bennet. If it were possible, I would delay the removal of the pianoforte, but I have only hired the servants for today."

Mary pressed her lips firmly together, determined not to succumb to an outward display of emotion. The pianoforte was the only thing she had found in the past week to keep her sorrow in check. Yet she would find a way to move forward without it, even as Mr. Collins cast her out of Longbourn, adrift and without anchor, into the world.

"I will do no more to embarrass you, cousin," said Mary. She stood and collected the music sitting on the pianoforte, then sorted it into two piles, one large, one small.

She handed Mr. Collins the larger pile. "This music belongs to the estate and is now yours." She picked up the smaller pile. "But this music is mine, and I will bring it with me."

Ignoring her sisters' attempts to comfort her, Mary turned and marched out of the room with whatever semblance of dignity she had left.

Chapter Two

"HERTFORDHSHIRE—A funeral will be held today for Mr. Bennet of Longbourn, in the town of Meryton."

—*The Morning Post*, London, August 4, 1813

MARY SET ASIDE her book of sermons. She rubbed her fingers under her eyes, trying to keep herself awake. The clock read four in the morning, and the candles serving vigil around Mr. Bennet's body grew low. The smell of decomposition made sitting here less than pleasant, but death was not pleasant, so she found it fitting.

She considered trying to read again, but her eyes were too weary. This book belonged to her—not to Mr. Collins—and she would take it with her when they left to stay with her aunt and uncle, the Philipses. She only had a handful of personal books, and Mr. Philips's library was not much to speak of. Without books and a pianoforte, she wondered how she would pass the time. Hopefully their mother would continue their membership at Meryton's subscription library, but Mrs. Bennet might not see it as a necessary expense. Mary could not picture how she would occupy her life in the coming months, for she had no interest in endless days of needlework and gossip.

Mary twisted the mourning ring around her index finger. Traditionally, the rings were not dispensed until the funeral.

They were gifted to the men, who brought them home and gave them to their wives to wear. In his will, Mr. Bennet had specified that each of his children should receive a ring. For his married daughters, the matter was simple—give it to Mr. Darcy and Mr. Bingley, and if he were here, Mr. Wickham, and Elizabeth, Jane, and Lydia would receive theirs. But for Kitty and Mary, who would it be given to? Mr. Collins? That was certainly not an ideal solution. Perhaps one of their uncles, Mr. Philips or Mr. Gardner. But they would also receive rings for their own wives.

Elizabeth and Jane had decided it made the most sense to give both Mary and Kitty their rings in advance, to ensure there would be no confusion or difficulties.

Mary's ring was more expensive than she thought necessary, but it had been too late to argue with her older sisters—the purchase had already been made. Yet despite the extravagance, she found herself liking the ring. In the bezel, encased under a thin layer of crystal, was a miniature painting of a broken column, shaded by a weeping willow. Written on the column in tiny black lettering were Mr. Bennet's name and date of death.

Mary removed the ring from her finger and twisted the bezel so it faced the inside of the ring, revealing another thin piece of crystal, this one with a small lock of her father's hair underneath. She flipped the bezel around and around, revealing painting, hair, painting, hair, painting, hair, finally stopping on painting. She liked that she could keep her father's hair next to her finger, that she could keep her longing and sorrow close, yet hidden from the world.

Her eyes were a touch watery, so she blinked them rapidly, then gazed at her father's body, lying on a table, surrounded by flowers. She had never learned any painting or drawing, but if she had, she would attempt to create a likeness of her father, with his profile in recline, surrounded by the room draped in black. Even in death, there was a certain lightness of spirit in his features.

No one had expected his sudden illness or his passing only a fortnight later. Death was, as Mary's sermons taught her, a natural part of life, but part of her had assumed she would always have her father.

She had never been his favorite. That position, of course, belonged to Elizabeth. But he had encouraged Mary in her studies and listened to her philosophical discoveries. In the last year, with Elizabeth, Jane, and Lydia gone, they had spent far more time together. Sometimes he had even shared his humor with her, and though she did not always understand it, she appreciated the gesture. Yet perhaps the additional time she had spent with him had not been enough; she should have asked his opinion more often, done something more—anything more—to demonstrate that she cared. She spun the mourning ring around her finger. At least she had been able to do some small service for him by finding the rings.

A sudden noise startled Mary.

She looked immediately to her father's body. The flickering candlelight sometimes played tricks on her eyes, made it difficult to tell if she saw life or death, so she stood and walked slowly around her father's body, laid out on the table. Nothing had changed. There was no movement, no life.

The sound came again, several times in a row. Someone was knocking at the front door. How strange to have a visitor at this hour.

"Sarah," she called.

The kitchen girl did not respond. She was supposed to be sitting right outside the room, in case Mary needed anything.

Mr. Bennet's body had been laid in the front parlor, directly off the main hallway. The room's windows faced the front of the house. Mary pushed aside some of the black drapery and the curtains and peered into the night.

She could make out the faint outline of a carriage and horses. At the door stood a servant or driver holding a large lantern. Behind him stood a regal-looking older woman with a younger man at her side. Their dress marked them as distinguished visitors. It almost looked like Lady Catherine de Bourgh.

If it was Lady Catherine de Bourgh, she best open the door immediately and then wake the others. Lady Catherine de Bourgh was Mr. Darcy's aunt and a prominent individual. The one time Mary had met her, she had observed that Lady Catherine was not the type of person who liked to be left waiting. Besides, though the summer meant it was not cold, one still could catch a chill from exposure to the air in the middle of the night.

There were more knocks at the door. Mary stepped out of the room into the main hall and found Sarah slumped on a chair, fast asleep. Mary nudged her on the shoulder. "Wake up, Sarah, we have visitors."

Sarah startled awake.

"Someone is knocking," said Mary. "Would you open the door and let them in?"

Sarah nodded quickly. She almost tripped as she stood, and then righted herself and picked up a candle. She stepped to the front entryway. Her fingers fumbled on the locks and finally Mary helped her pull open the door.

The visitor was not Lady Catherine de Bourgh.

The woman's hair was a fierce grey, and even in the low light, her eyes were piercing. The man next to her was only slightly taller than the woman, and was young, probably in his twenties. He flashed a smile that would have caused Kitty and Lydia to giggle but did nothing to impress Mary.

The woman cleared her throat and looked expectantly at Mary.

A terror seized Mary: she did not know this person, who was obviously her superior, she could not speak to someone unless she was introduced, and there was no manner by which they could be introduced. The housekeeper, Mrs. Hill, would know exactly how to handle this situation, but Sarah did not and stood there as dumbfounded as Mary.

The woman scrutinized her, and Mary self-consciously looked down at her dress. She owned several new black dresses for mourning, but she had chosen, tonight, to wear one of her older dresses. It had been taken apart at the seams, dyed black, then stitched back together by a servant.

She swallowed and tried to curtsy. The woman raised her eyebrows. The man's smile diminished.

"You are a Miss Bennet, I presume?" asked the woman.

Mary nodded.

"I am Lady Trafford, and this is my nephew, Mr. Henry Withrow. I am a relative of your father, and I have come to pay my respects to him." She leaned towards Mary, her chin jutting forward. "Well, are you going to stand here, or let me in?"

Mary did not know the social protocol for accepting distant relatives in the middle of the night, but she supposed letting them in was a part of it. "You may come in."

As Lady Trafford and Mr. Withrow stepped inside, their servant returned to the carriage. Mary closed the front door.

"Sarah," said Mary, "would you wake Jane? And...Mr. Collins?" Waking Mrs. Bennet at this hour would do no one any good, but since it was now Mr. Collins's house, she supposed he must be woken.

"That will not be necessary, Sarah," said Lady Trafford. "There is no need to wake anyone else at this time of night. But it would be excellent if you could prepare tea for the three of us."

Sarah hurried down the hallway to obey Lady Trafford's directions as if their visitor were the mistress of Longbourn.

Unsure of what else to do, Mary led Lady Trafford and Mr. Withrow to the sitting room. Mr. Withrow's nose wrinkled and Lady Trafford raised her handkerchief to her mouth. Even after being away for only a moment, the smell was almost overpowering. Piles of flowers surrounded Mr. Bennet, and new ones had been added daily, but they did not mask the scent of death. It had been over a week since his death, and with each progressing day, the odor grew stronger.

Mary walked around the room, lighting more candles to provide greater illumination. Lady Trafford stood at Mr. Bennet's side and whispered a prayer. Mary could not hear the words, but the woman's facial expressions testified of her sincerity. Once she finished with the candles, Mary waited, unsure whether to sit or stand. She glanced at Mr. Withrow. He nodded at her and said, "I am sorry for your loss."

"Thank you." Mary looked away, and again twisted the ring on her finger. After a few minutes, Lady Trafford stepped away from the body.

"You are welcome to take a seat," said Lady Trafford, as if this were her sitting room and Mary was the visitor.

Mary sat in the middle of the room, facing her father. Lady Trafford sat in a chair to her right. Instead of sitting in one of the chairs next to his aunt, Mr. Withrow sat to Mary's left.

Unsure of the best way to start a conversation with the

guests, Mary said the first thing that came to mind. "You should have come during the day." Elizabeth would have found a better way to say the same thing. Something like, *we expected most of our visitors to come during the day*. But Mary had already spoken, and it was too late to change her words.

"I was passing by this way, and I had read about it in the paper, so I decided to stop. Unfortunately, we have business in another village and will not be able to attend the funeral, but we wanted to pay our respects."

Lady Trafford's words did not make sense. To Mary's knowledge, her father's death had only been published locally and in one of the London papers, *The Morning Post*. In their announcement, *The Morning Post* had neglected to publish the information about the funeral, but they had promised to do so in today's paper, which had not yet been distributed. Mary blinked her eyes and stifled a yawn. "In what paper did you read about his death?"

"I do not remember. There are so many."

She supposed it did not matter how Lady Trafford had heard the news. It surprised her, though, that she had never heard of Lady Trafford before, given that she was a relation.

Sarah came in with the tea and poured it for each of them, and then she left to sit in the hall. Mary hoped that Sarah did not fall asleep again, for doing so would embarrass their entire family in front of this great lady.

Mary sipped her tea. It did not do much to help with her fatigue. She looked to the right, to Lady Trafford, then to the left, to Mr. Withrow, unsure where her attention should fall now that the conversation had gone silent. She decided to compromise by looking at her feet.

After a few agonizing minutes in which Mary searched her mind for a suitable topic of conversation, Lady Trafford spoke again. "Now which daughter are you?"

"I am the third daughter."

"And what is your given name?"

"Mary."

"It is a pleasure to make your acquaintance," said Mr. Withrow smoothly. "The third daughter. How many sisters do you have?"

"I have four."

"It must have been wonderful, to always have so many companions," he said with sincerity.

"I…suppose so."

"You suppose?" he asked with such attention that she felt obligated to give a more detailed response.

"Well, my two elder sisters are such dear friends, as are my two younger, and I have always felt a little…" She trailed off, not wanting to express how it sometimes made her feel alone.

"It is always a challenge to be in between groups of people," said Mr. Withrow. "Who are your elder sisters?"

"My eldest sister is Mrs. Bingley," said Mary, grateful to move away from a discussion of her emotions. "She lives in Derbyshire with her husband. They recently purchased an estate there. The next eldest, Mrs. Darcy, lives near there as well."

"I know Mr. Darcy," said Mr. Withrow. "He is a good man. What about your younger sisters? Are they still at home?"

"My sister Kitty—Catherine—is at home still, but my youngest sister, Mrs. Wickham, lives with her husband and his regiment."

"I see," said Mr. Withrow. "You mentioned a Mr. Collins to your servant. Is he a relation?"

Mary was beginning to find it unusual for someone to ask so many questions of her, but she supposed Mr. Withrow was simply trying to make conversation. Yet she had no obligation to divulge her entire life story. "He is a cousin."

"A cousin?" he prodded.

She nodded.

"Has he come for the funeral?"

"Because of my father's death, he has inherited Long-bourn." It seemed Withrow would pry out whatever information he wanted.

Concern filled his face. "And what will happen to you? To your mother? And your sister?"

"For now, we will stay with my uncle and aunt, Mr. and Mrs. Philips, in Meryton."

"And then where will you go?"

"Why does it matter to you?"

"As a relation, I am naturally concerned about the well-being of you and your mother."

She felt guilty for acting so resistant to his questions. "We can always stay with my aunt and uncle in London, or with one of my sisters in Derbyshire."

"I see," said Mr. Withrow. Then suddenly, all his concern seemed to disappear, and his voice became critical, almost cold. "You give a lot of personal information to people whom you know so little."

"Thoroughness is typically seen as a virtue," said Mary. "And you asked a great many questions." She knew her statement could be seen as impertinent, especially to someone above her station, but she was bothered by Withrow's behav-iour and the way in which he pretended to care about her family and then withdrew all sympathy. She turned towards Lady Trafford just quickly enough to catch what might have been a brief smile, though it was difficult to tell in the candlelight.

Lady Trafford leaned towards her. "I am sorry if my nephew gave offense. We genuinely care about your well-being."

The woman looked at Mr. Bennet's body, and only when the silence felt full and heavy and uncomfortable to Mary did Lady Trafford speak again. "If Longbourn goes to Mr. Collins, then would I be correct in assuming that, in addition to the good will of family, you, your mother, and your sister must rely entirely on your mother's fortune? Is it three or four hundred pounds a year for the three of you?"

Mary looked down at her lap. "Not nearly that, Lady Trafford." She found herself heeding Mr. Withrow's advice and not revealing everything. Their family had been living off of two thousand pounds a year, which, admittedly, included the running of the farm and the estate, but two hundred pounds was a pittance in comparison. Mary suspected Lydia and Wickham would still demand a portion; Mr. Bennet had promised them one hundred pounds a year. Even if Mrs. Bennet lowered the amount given to Lydia to fifty, Mrs. Bennet, Kitty, and Mary would truly be at the mercy of others for their very sustenance.

"Have you considered making something of yourself?" asked Lady Trafford.

Mary shook her head.

"There are things a woman of your standing can do to make herself independent. For instance, you could become a governess."

Mary had not considered that possibility. Mrs. Bennet had always placed her entire focus on marrying her daughters.

"It would bring me great satisfaction to assist you," said

Lady Trafford. "I could provide you with tutors and additional training, which would make you more qualified for future opportunities."

Mary sniffed. It had been said, several times, that she was the most accomplished girl in the neighbourhood. "I have applied myself sufficiently to all of my studies. If I were to become a governess, I would not require any additional training."

"You think rather highly of yourself," observed Mr. Withrow.

"There is no virtue in false modesty," asserted Mary. "I know my strengths."

"I see," said Lady Trafford. "How familiar are you with the classics? Are you well versed in Milton, Shakespeare, Donne, Alexander Pope, and Samuel Johnson?"

Mr. Withrow stood and began to pace the room, yet he managed to keep Mary always within his line of sight.

Mary gave her attention back to Lady Trafford. While it was common for visitors of the deceased to make conversation with their hosts, this was an unusual subject of discussion for the occasion. "I know Milton and Shakespeare, and a little Pope."

"And the others?"

"I found Donne rather objectionable when I read the commentaries on his work. I have no interest in Samuel Johnson."

"It is the duty of the governess to teach more than just the texts she likes the most. Do you speak French?"

"Only a little, Lady Trafford, but I can read it fluently."

"You can read it but not speak it—however is that possible? What sort of French teacher would teach you only how to read French?"

"I had no teacher. I taught myself."

Lady Trafford reached her hand out towards Mr. Withrow. "Pass me that book you were reading earlier."

He stopped next to her, removed a small book from his pocket, and handed it to her. The words on the cover were too small for Mary to make out.

Lady Trafford opened the book, took a minute to choose a page, and passed it to Mary. "Read this for me."

Mary could feel the pressure of the woman's eyes, as if she were being evaluated for some grand, mysterious purpose and found lacking.

She forced her eyes to the page. It was difficult to read in the candlelight, and her eyes were tired, but she would do it. She did not attempt to read the text aloud, for she knew her pronunciation would not stand up to any scrutiny, but she read a few lines to herself and attempted to translate.

"It is a political text which argues that the people who make laws should not be the ones to carry them out. Yet the normal person should not carry them out either. And there is the risk of corruption, by people letting their own interests influence public ones, and—"

"That is enough, child. Have you read this text before?"

"I do not believe so."

"It is Rousseau's *Du contrat social; ou, Principes du droit politique.*"

Mary tried not to betray the fact that she had not understood a word of Lady Trafford's French.

"You truly cannot speak French," said Lady Trafford. "The text is called, in English, *On the Social Contract; or, Principles of Political Rights.*"

"I am not familiar with it," said Mary, self-conscious about her lack of knowledge on the subject.

"I see," said Lady Trafford. "But your translation was adequate. French is such a useful language in these dreadful, dreadful times. What are your feelings on Bonaparte?"

Mary pressed her lips together. She glanced at Mr. Withrow and then back at Lady Trafford. It appeared to be a serious question.

"Your father read pamphlets, and the papers, I presume. How do you feel about Napoleon Bonaparte?"

She had never met a woman who spoke like this. Normally, politics was not seen as an issue for women, though it was often spoken of by men, behind closed doors, when the women were elsewhere.

"I oppose him, of course," managed Mary. She took a large gulp of tea.

"Why?"

Lady Trafford's question hung in the air while Mary attempted to prepare a suitable response.

"Is it not the duty of an Englishwoman to do so?"

Lady Trafford waited, as if to ask for more. Mary turned her head to see if Mr. Withrow's eyes were also on her, but he was examining his pocket watch, so she turned back to her questioner. She had read some of her father's pamphlets, but people typically did not ask for Mary's opinion on matters such as this. She was both gratified and overwhelmed by the request for her thoughts, so it took her a moment to formulate a better answer.

"Bonaparte would have us all be French. He would take the whole world. But more than that, he seems to, he wants to…" Mary paused, having lost the force of expression that she had intended. Finally, it came back to her and she spoke quickly. "He seems to threaten the British way of life." She breathed deeply, pleased with her answer and the way it had come out.

"You are well-spoken, and clearly an intelligent woman," said Lady Trafford. "With training in a few areas, you would be quite prepared to be a governess."

Somehow Lady Trafford managed to compliment her and point out her inadequacies in the same breath. Mary looked down at her hands and twisted the mourning ring around her finger. She liked the idea of being useful and independent, of solving problems, and being able to direct her own fate. Yet this woman had barged into her home—actually, Mr. Collins's home—in the middle of the night and planned out a future for Mary without even consulting her.

"As a relative, I feel it my duty to provide you with some assistance. You could come to my house and I could train you for several months, provide you with tutors and such, and then help you find a place in a good household."

Mary sat up a little more stiffly and looked at her father, laid on the table. He appeared dignified, even in death. Did Lady Trafford really think so little of her and her own resources?

"I do not need your charity."

Both Lady Trafford and Mr. Withrow looked affronted. Maybe she should have phrased it differently, more like Elizabeth would have. Elizabeth, her father's favorite daughter. She pictured her sister in her mind, then knew the words to say.

"I mean no disrespect, but I would not impinge on your generosity in such a manner."

"But you would rely on the generosity of your other family members?" asked Lady Trafford.

"That is different," said Mary.

"How?" asked Lady Trafford.

Mary tried to answer, but words seemed inadequate for her sentiments. They would be completely reliant on the goodwill of the Philipses and the Gardiners, the Bingleys and the Darcys. Already, she did not like knowing that her entire future depended on them, though it was their familial obligation to support her, Kitty, and their mother. Deep down, though, it felt wrong to take the assistance of a complete stranger—even if a relation—who had found her so lacking, so inadequate for even the position of a governess. She could not consider such a proposition. Furthermore, for Lady Trafford to ask Mary such a thing, without consulting Mrs. Bennet, seemed illogical.

"I have no desire or need to become a governess."

"I see," said Lady Trafford, setting down her cup of tea. "If you change your mind, please send me a letter. I live at Castle Durrington, near Worthing, in Sussex."

Mary did not deign to respond. She had no reason to change her mind once she had made it up.

Lady Trafford turned to her nephew, who stood, emotionless. "As much as I would love to stay longer, it is best we leave now. We have much travel left before our business in the morning."

He helped her to her feet.

"Thank you for allowing us to interrupt your vigil," said Lady Trafford. "Your father was a good man, and I respected him."

Mary nodded, unsure how to respond to the compliment. At this time of night, it was difficult to remember all the proper courtesies, and the conversation had taken such strange paths that she felt a bit lost.

Lady Trafford placed her hand on Mary's shoulder. "I can tell that you loved your father very much."

Mary looked away. She could not respond to this statement either, not when it brought her own feelings of inadequacy so close to the surface.

Lady Trafford removed her hand.

"It was a pleasure to meet you, Miss Bennet." Mr. Withrow's charm from earlier had returned, as if it was a habit he could not shake.

Mary was not certain the visit had been pleasurable for anyone involved, so she did not return the approbation, but she did have something else prepared for this sort of statement. "Making new acquaintances is always a worthwhile activity."

Withrow cocked his head and his brows pinched together.

Mary led them out of the room. Sarah had indeed fallen back asleep, and to make matters worse, she was snoring. Mary wanted to shake her awake, but that would be improper, so she pretended not to see Sarah and opened the front door herself. Lady Trafford and Mr. Withrow entered their carriage and drove off into the night. That was by far the strangest visit she had ever received. With the now-empty road, it was almost as if they had never been here.

She returned to the room with her father and sat, watching his body, for several minutes. She felt very alone and unsure of her future. She removed the mourning ring from her finger and rotated the bezel so the side with her father's hair faced out. She walked to her father's body and placed her hand on top of his dead hand, now dry and cold.

Mr. Bennet had passed on a night like this. His breath had grown labored and weak, and he reached his hand out to Mrs. Bennet. "You have been a good companion, my dear. And so have your nerves."

Everyone chuckled.

Then he had turned to Jane. "You are so good, and so kind."

His eyes met Kitty's. "I hope you remain silly, and keep all your vigor."

He looked at Mary. She swallowed, wondering what he would say to her.

Mr. Bennet coughed horribly, a deep, rattling, wheezing sound.

And then his hand had reached out to Elizabeth. "I will miss you. I will miss you ever so much."

He breathed in, once, twice, three more times. He gazed up at the ceiling and his body went still. He was dead. He was dead, and Mary was the only one he had not spoken to.

That thought had crept through her mind again and again in the last week. Maybe he had nothing he needed to say to her. Maybe they did not have the sort of relationship that merited a final statement.

Logically, Mary knew that her self-pitying reflections were selfish. The cough had stolen whatever he had planned to say, and at least he had managed to say something to almost everyone before dying. Yet still she was filled with guilt and regret for what she did not have with her father, and for what she now could never have.

She forced her mind to the present, here, in this parlor, holding vigil for a corpse, for memories tied to the remains of flesh. She withdrew her hand from her father's, but she did not sit down.

"I miss you," she whispered into the night, and she stood in that position in a sort of trance until morning when she was relieved of her duty.

CHAPTER THREE

"During the last week, the French fleet have been observed to venture farther out to sea than they have ever been in the habit of doing before; but as soon as the English fleet stands in towards them, a few of their ships lie-to, until we arrive within gunshot and a half of them."

–Extract from a letter about the fleet off Toulon, in
The Times, London, August 4, 1813

DESPITE HER EXHAUSTION, Mary attempted to be an example of dignified mourning. She sat, back straight and head high in her chair, focusing on needlework. The key was to regulate her emotions, to consider her actions before taking them. She would not disrespect her father by having an outburst. She would not feel sorry for herself. Restraint was essential.

On the other hand, her mother did not rein in her emotions at all. She sat in the finest seat in the room, somehow looking as if she would collapse even though she was not standing. At the moment she was focused on berating Elizabeth. "You must not be allowed to attend the funeral. How could I have such a daughter? If your father were here, I would make him stop you. And Kitty, why must you go along with her? Why will you not stay home, like Jane and Mary?"

"I feel I must go, Mother, to do my duty to him," said

Elizabeth.

Kitty looked conflicted, so Mary thought it appropriate to add her opinion. "The best way to honor your parents is to follow their advice in all things."

"Why must you always be so certain that your way is the only right way?" asked Kitty as she glared at Mary. "I am going with Lizzy."

Mrs. Bennet let out a sound that rather resembled a wail. "Mary is the only one with sympathy for my poor nerves."

"I am sorry, Mother," said Elizabeth, "but I will bring honor to both of my parents by attending the funeral today."

The discussion was cut short; the time had come for the funeral procession. The family moved to the parlor, still draped in black, and watched as Mr. Bennet's coffin was closed. Mary strained her neck to the side in order to see one last glimpse of her father's face, but there were too many people in front of her, and all she saw was the case as it closed with an irreverent thud.

The coffin was carried outside, followed by the family. Mary pushed ahead so that in this, at least, she would have a better view. The six bearers, dressed in black, placed the coffin in the long black carriage designed for such a load. Everything was black and solemn as it should be. In addition to the coffin bearers, they had hired a man who was a mute and six page boys, all dressed in black. Even the horses were black; on their heads had been placed tall, glossy ostrich plumes, dyed a deep black and lending the group an extra measure of dignity.

First the family entered the carriages. In the position of honor, as children and spouses of the deceased, Elizabeth and Mr. Darcy, Mr. Bingley, and Kitty entered the first carriage. Mr. Collins, Mr. Philips, and Mr. Gardiner entered the second. All the other guests—her father's associates, people from the village, even a few friends from London—entered the rest of the carriages.

The women, excepting Elizabeth and Kitty, stood on the steps and watched as the funeral procession left the house and made its way towards Meryton. The carriages travelled at a slow pace as they were led by the mute, the bearers, and the pages, who were all on foot.

As soon as the procession was out of sight, Mary's shoulders tensed. Maybe she should have joined Elizabeth and Kitty. She pushed the thought aside; it was not her duty, and attending the funeral would not eliminate the hollow feeling she felt inside. Besides, they had already left; it was too late to change her mind.

The women repaired inside and instantly Mrs. Bennet began to lament. "What will I ever do without Mr. Bennet? We shall be on the streets, with nothing to sustain us."

"We have sufficient means, Mother," said Mary. "Frugality is a commendable trait which will help us develop more sympathy for the less fortunate around us."

"No one will think of us, and our misfortunes!" said Mrs. Bennet.

"Remember, dear sister," said Mrs. Philips, "that you will be staying with me. You also have two well-established daughters who will surely see that no ill comes to you."

"Of course, Mother," said Jane. "You are always welcome in my home. And if Elizabeth were here, she would say the same of Pemberley."

"But it is so very far away. I cannot possibly travel such a distance while I am in mourning. I wish you had not bought an estate, and that you still lived at Netherfield."

"We understand that travel would be quite difficult for you at this time," said Mrs. Gardiner. "But when you have recovered your nerves, you are also welcome to stay with me and your brother in London at any time."

Mrs. Bennet nodded her acceptance of everyone's offers, but then turned to other complaints. "I feel so alone. No one understands my sorrows."

Yet Mary *did* understand her mother's sorrows. And while she knew she should try to comfort her mother, she mostly wanted to ask her to be silent. Everyone else was in mourning as well, everyone else was in pain. Perhaps, though, she could both comfort her mother *and* provide her with a better way of thinking.

"It is important," said Mary, "to recognize that the state of sorrow can be beneficial. Laurence Sterne speaks quite eloquently on why the house of mourning is more useful for our salvation than the house of feasting. He begins by quoting the book of Ecclesiastes, where it says—"

"I think that at this moment your mother needs rest more than anything else," said her aunt, Mrs. Gardiner.

"But it is a very uplifting sermon, and it is short," said Mary. "I have it memorized, and I think it would be beneficial for all of us."

"You best save it for later," said Mrs. Gardiner. "Your mother is exhausted."

Mrs. Bennet let out a theatrical cry, as if to emphasize the validity of Mrs. Gardiner's statement.

"You must be exhausted as well," said Jane. "You did spend all night with Father."

"I feel fine," said Mary. "I do not need any rest." She had the beginning of a headache, but that could occur even with a full night's sleep.

"Then perhaps you might be benefited by taking a short walk," said Mrs. Gardiner.

"It is such a lovely day," said Jane. "I can take care of Mama. It will be several hours before they return from the funeral."

"Very well. I will leave you to it." Mary had always been able to tell when she was not wanted, and clearly no one wanted her presence right now. She turned around and walked out of the room slowly, counting her steps and focusing on her breathing so no one would notice her irritation, or worse, how much their dismissal stung. She always seemed to be least wanted when she tried her hardest to be involved: her family often shut her out when she tried to help them or show them that she cared.

Once outside the room, she leaned against the wall. The mourning ring felt tight around her finger. She took it off, rubbed her finger a little, and then forced the ring back on.

She almost went up to her room, but decided, at the last moment, to leave the house. Perhaps Jane was correct, and a walk would do her good. As she stepped into the sunlight and fresh air, it felt, suddenly, as if she had left a bit of the gloom behind.

Typically, she only walked if there were a particular purpose or an errand she needed to complete. It was not often that she walked for the sake of walking. There were always so many more important things to do.

Out of habit, she walked towards Meryton. The funeral procession had taken this same path, and if she continued through town, she would pass by the church. Despite her regrets at not joining, she would not, of course, interrupt. It might be permissible for a woman to ride in a funeral procession and to attend a funeral service, but an interruption would be grievous indeed.

As she walked, she considered the events of the previous

night. Lady Trafford's visit had been as strange as a dream. She was surprised that no one had asked her about it this morning. She was certain all the servants had heard word of it from Sarah. But perhaps, because of the funeral, none of the servants had mentioned it to any members of the household.

Mary entered Meryton, nodding to people as she passed. She held her arms tight against her body. She felt vulnerable, walking here, without Kitty or someone else to accompany her. Instead of people's eyes turning to her sisters or her mother, they turned to her, and she was not accustomed to their focused attention.

Down the road she spotted an elegant carriage, brown with an ornamental mahogany trim. There was a man behind the carriage, unlatching one of the cases that was attached to it.

The carriage was parked in front of a shop. Out of the shop exited Lady Trafford and Mr. Withrow. How peculiar. They had specifically stated that they would not be in Meryton today.

Mary was not prepared for another conversation with Lady Trafford, so she paused at a nearby shop, pretending to consider the hats on display. It was the sort of action Lydia took when she saw someone she did not want to meet. She shifted her head slightly so she could see the man tampering with the back of the carriage. He removed something from the case and put it in his pocket. His build and his height looked familiar, though not his clothes. Unable to stop herself, she abandoned the display of hats and took a few steps closer. The man's face turned to the side, and she recognized him as the man who had been in Longbourn the day before, the one who attempted to steal the mourning rings.

Distress filled her entire body. With the angle the carriage was parked, as they exited the shop and entered the carriage, Lady Trafford and her nephew must not be able to see the man. Because of his quality clothing, the townspeople must believe he was working for Lady Trafford instead of stealing from her.

He had almost managed to steal the mourning rings, and, as unusual as Lady Trafford was, Mary would not let him rob the woman. Like the mourning rings, she could solve this problem herself.

"Thief!" she cried. "It is a thief!"

The thief looked at her with a ferocity she found frightening.

Some of the townsfolk also turned to her, but a few headed towards the man and started shouting. The thief took off at a run.

She pointed again. "That man is a thief!"

Mr. Withrow jumped out of the carriage. "You rascal!" he shouted at the thief, and then ran after him at a great speed. Several other men followed but were quickly outpaced by the thief and Withrow. The thief turned down a side street and soon they were both out of sight.

The townsfolk surrounded both Mary and the carriage. There were cries of, "Miss Bennet, are you all right?" and endless questions which blurred together as they pounded into Mary's head. She could not say a thing as the people pressed closer and closer to her. The only time she liked the attention of large groups of people was when she performed on the pianoforte or demonstrated another accomplishment, but that was a planned, practiced, and controlled situation. She felt small under the people's stares.

Lady Trafford exited the carriage. She spoke loudly and with such poise that the crowd instantly quieted. "Thank you, everyone, for your concern. Miss Bennet has performed a great service for me today, and now you may all go back to your business." She gestured for Mary to follow her into the carriage.

Mary obeyed her without question. She would rather be in a carriage with Lady Trafford than surrounded by the people of Meryton. There would be talk of this incident, and people wondering why she was not at home during the funeral. She should have walked in a different direction or stayed back at the house.

Mary's hands shook from the second encounter with the thief, and she wondered that Lady Trafford could be so composed. She climbed into the carriage, stooping awkwardly as she considered the available seating. She could sit at Lady Trafford's side, but it would be rather cramped with the woman's full skirts, so she sat in the middle of the seat opposite. She could not still her hands, so she tucked them under her legs. The theft yesterday had been discreet, but today was very public. It was a touch too much excitement for her. Lady Trafford watched Mary, but thankfully did not say anything, which gave Mary a moment to compose herself.

Mr. Withrow climbed into the carriage. His face was sweaty, and he was out of breath. "I chased him all the way to the edge of the village, but then I lost him." Withrow lowered himself onto the same seat as Mary. She shifted farther down the seat to put some distance between them.

Mary smoothed out her dress. This morning, she had put on a new, black dress. It was of quality material, but a plain design, which Mary always preferred, and in her opinion was more appropriate for mourning than the more stylish gowns of her sisters.

"Did you know that man?" asked Lady Trafford.

"No," said Mary. "But yesterday he tried to steal all of the mourning rings."

"How dreadful!" Lady Trafford said. "The audacity of such an act." She rubbed her pearl necklace with her fingers. "Are you certain it was the same individual?"

"I would not make such an accusation if I were not certain," said Mary. "It is essential to never judge in haste, lest that judgment come back upon you."

"That is wise," said Mr. Withrow. "How could you tell it was the thief?" He asked the same way he had last night when he was questioning her, as if her answers were the most important thing in the world.

"I have a skill for remembering faces."

"Well, Miss Bennet, I find myself beholden to you," said Lady Trafford.

Mary wondered what that meant. Some people took a debt like that very seriously. Lydia had always managed to extract a gift or trinket in situations like this, but Mary had no interest in such trifles.

Both Mr. Withrow and Lady Trafford considered her, and so Mary tried to fill the silence. "I thought you were travelling farther, for business."

"My business was cut short, so we attempted to return in time for my nephew to join the funeral service. I regret that we were too late." She leaned forward. "I had hoped to meet your mother."

"If you had come during the day to view my father's body, you would have received the opportunity."

"What my aunt really wants," said Mr. Withrow dryly, "is to know if she can visit Longbourn right now."

Mr. Withrow said it as if Mary should obviously have come to that conclusion, but Lady Trafford had not been direct in her communication. Mary did not appreciate Withrow's attitude: charming one moment when he wanted information, and almost disdainful the next. But it did not matter how Withrow treated her, so she pushed thoughts of him aside and considered Lady Trafford's request. There would be plenty of people at Longbourn after the funeral, and Lady Trafford was a relation—albeit a distant one—so she could see no harm in it.

"We are having a funeral meal for family and friends. I believe everyone would view it as acceptable for you to join us."

"That would be lovely." Lady Trafford tapped the side of the carriage and said, "Thomas, if you would do us the kindness of taking us to Longbourn."

The carriage turned around, and Mary thought it was a very good thing that she had been walking for the sake of walking, rather than for a purpose. If she had possessed a true reason for visiting Meryton, Lady Trafford's overwhelming sense of purpose would have left no room for it. Mary did regret that the carriage had not gone a bit farther, to the other side of Meryton, for then she would have seen the exterior of the church where they were holding her father's funeral.

She gazed out the window, and then pulled herself back so she would be less visible from the outside. There was no point in having the rest of the villagers wonder what a young Miss Bennet was doing in the company of her ladyship.

"It would have been terrible if you had not arrived at that moment and spared us from that thief," said Lady Trafford. "Do you not agree, Henry?"

"Of course," said Withrow. "Your assistance was invaluable. The thief even dropped the handkerchief he had taken." He withdrew it from his pocket, so Mary could see. He glanced at his aunt and then added, "I do hope you will let us find a way to show our appreciation."

"I suspect that you care less about material items than things of intellectual or moral worth," Lady Trafford mused. "But surely there would be other demonstrations of gratitude you would not be opposed to. You seem to value knowledge and accomplishments. The very fact that you taught yourself to read French speaks highly of your intelligence and dedication. I know that you are not interested in training to become a governess. But is there anything that you *would* like to learn, Miss Bennet? An opportunity you would like to have?"

Mary remembered her desire, in the night, to be able to draw.

"I can see there is something," said Lady Trafford. "Please, do tell us."

"I regret never having drawing lessons," said Mary.

"That is an admirable desire. Are there any masters in Meryton?"

Mary shook her head.

"That is regrettable. Most of the masters live in London. But I do know one, a friend who lives near my home, in Worthing. If you were to come and stay with me, I am sure he would agree to train you. I also know a French teacher who could teach you to speak as well as you read."

The thought did tempt Mary. She had never had a private tutor, never received instruction in anything (besides dance lessons, which Mrs. Bennet saw as an essential skill for obtaining a husband). Jane and Elizabeth had, at times, received private lessons on various subjects, but by the time it was Mary's turn to ask for lessons, Mrs. Bennet had insisted that it was an unnecessary expense. Mr. Bennet and Elizabeth had at times given her a sentence or two of instruction on various topics, but a private tutor would do so much more.

"I will consider your offer," said Mary. "I will need to ask my—" She stopped herself. She had been about to say father.

If she asked her mother, Mrs. Bennet would agree without hesitation. To find Mary a situation with a woman of wealth and influence, even for a short time, would please her very much. She would probably hope it would throw Mary into the arms of an eligible suitor.

While a suitable suitor would be welcome, Mary's purpose was not to find a husband. Yet staying with Lady Trafford would have certain advantages, such as being out in society without being overshadowed by any of her sisters. Each of her sisters had made trips on their own, but Mary had never done so. Before she seriously considered such a thing, it would be expedient to make inquiries about Lady Trafford and ensure she was a woman of character.

"Take whatever time you need to consider."

They sat in silence the rest of the carriage ride to Longbourn. Mary had never felt the need to fill silence with idle conversation and was grateful that her companions did not press her to do so. Yet silence gave time for contemplation, and contemplation made way for a sense of dread, a dread for how her mother might act in front of Lady Trafford.

CHAPTER FOUR

*"The private letters from Paris, contrary to the spirit of
the Journals, which would indicate a general peace, spec-
ulate diffusely on a Continental peace, under the
supposition that Great Britain will not be included in
the arrangement."*

–*Hereford Journal*, Herefordshire, England,
August 4, 1813

MARY DID NOT like making introductions. She felt this
strongly, even though it was quite possible that she had
never made an introduction before. There was always someone else who was a much more logical person to make
introductions. But as she was the only one who had made
Lady Trafford and Mr. Withrow's acquaintance, it was not
possible for someone else to shoulder the responsibility.

The housekeeper led Mary, Lady Trafford, and Mr.
Withrow to the drawing room where the family was gathered
as they waited for the funeral party to return. As they stepped
into the room, everyone quieted, immediately looking at the
guests and getting to their feet. Mrs. Bennet did not stand,
but she did study the guests with care.

Mary smoothed her dress, trying to remember a passage
she had once read about the most proper methods of introduction. It was a solemn day, so she spoke with solemnity.

"On this sad day, we have been blessed with the presence of distant relatives who have come to pay their respects. This is Lady Trafford, of Sussex, and her nephew, Mr. Withrow."

More quickly, she pointed out everyone in the room. "This is my mother, Mrs. Bennet. And my aunt, Mrs. Philips. And my aunt, Mrs. Gardiner. And my sister, Mrs. Bingley. This is Mrs. Collins, a friend of our family who married my cousin. This is her mother, Lady Lucas. And this is Lady Lucas's other daughter, Mrs. Blankenbeckler."

"What a lovely family you have," observed Lady Trafford.

After a moment's pause, everyone returned to their prior conversations.

"Do you not have three other sisters?" asked Withrow.

"Two are attending the funeral party, and one was unable to travel at this time."

"Please, come speak to me," said Mrs. Bennet loudly. "I would stand and greet you, were it not for my poor nerves. I am completely undone with my husband's death. It is a miracle that I was even able to rise from my bed today."

Mary led Lady Trafford and Mr. Withrow to her mother's side.

Mrs. Bennet clutched Lady Trafford's hand. "It is so good of you to come. To what do we owe this visit?"

"As Miss Bennet explained, I have come to pay my respects to your husband. I knew him only briefly in my youth, but I greatly admired him."

"He was a great man," said Mrs. Bennet. "But now he is gone and due to the wretched entail, I am left with nothing. It has all gone to Mr. and Mrs. Collins. They are happy to leave me on the streets. Happy, I say." At this she frowned at Charlotte Collins, who grimaced for only a moment, betraying that she had heard the words. Charlotte had made herself scarce since she had arrived and had spent the majority of her time overseeing the household staff.

"It is not as dire as you say, Mother," said Mary. "The Collinses are not forcing us to leave—that is your choice—and the rest of our family will take good care of us."

"Oh, but we are poor," lamented Mrs. Bennet. "And when I die, Mary will be left even more poor and helpless. My fourth daughter, Kitty, may yet marry, but no one will ever ask for Mary's hand. She cannot help that she is plain."

Mary felt herself go red in the face. She could not even bring herself to glance at Lady Trafford to see her reaction. Mrs. Bennet had said things like this before, spoken of Mary's plainness and lack of marriage offers, but had done so less since Elizabeth, Jane, and Lydia had married last year. While Mary normally did not place much importance in how others viewed her, she realized she desired Lady Trafford's good opinion.

"Mother, I think we…should speak of other—"

Mrs. Bennet cut her off and continued her tirade about how she was being forced out of her own home. Mr. Bennet had often been able to stop Mrs. Bennet from embarrassing them, and Elizabeth and Jane could sometimes manage as well, but Mary had no such skill. Instead she looked at the floor, trying to block out the sound of her mother.

At the sound of Lady Trafford's voice, Mary raised her head.

"I am so sorry for your loss," Lady Trafford was saying. "It appears that you have a beautiful family, and many wonderful friends in Meryton to offer you comfort in this time of great need. Would it be too much of an imposition if I borrowed Miss Bennet? I had hoped that she could help me become better acquainted with other members of your family."

"Of course, Lady Trafford," said Mrs. Bennet. She looked around briefly before calling out, "My dear sister!" Mrs. Philips immediately came to her side.

As she reflected on her mother's behaviour, Mary's face burned and her dress itched against her skin.

"Do not feel bad, my dear," said Lady Trafford once they reached the other side of the room. "Everyone mourns differently."

"Thank you."

Mr. Withrow was notably silent, his blank face a mask over whatever emotion or judgment he felt.

They joined in conversation with Mrs. Gardiner and Lady Lucas about the different merits of the city and the country. Lady Trafford praised both, and Withrow used his skills at asking questions to encourage both women to give elaborate answers. Mary spoke very little, still embarrassed by the earlier conversation with her mother.

After a while the funeral party returned, one or two people trickling into the room at a time. The room became fuller and fuller, louder and louder. The last people to enter were Kitty, Elizabeth, and Mr. Darcy. Mr. Darcy looked in their direction, nodded, and to Mary's surprise, smiled.

"Oh, I see Mr. Darcy," said Lady Trafford. "I knew his parents well. I will have to speak to him later."

While Withrow had mentioned his connection to Mr. Darcy, it surprised Mary that Lady Trafford had not mentioned her own connection before.

After a minute, Withrow asked, "Is that one of your sisters?" Kitty was headed in their direction, her hands clasped together, a smile on her face.

"Yes," said Mary. "That is Catherine. I can introduce you

and your aunt."

"That would be most agreeable," said Lady Trafford. "Thank you, Miss Bennet."

Kitty reached them and clasped Mary's hands as if they were the dearest of friends. "Oh Mary, I am so glad I went. It was beautiful and solemn to attend the procession, and then Lizzy and I joined the funeral. It was the most lovely tribute to Father."

"I am glad to hear it."

"And who are your friends?"

"This is Lady Trafford, and her nephew Mr. Withrow. They are distant relations, come to visit us from Worthing, in Sussex."

"Then you have travelled a long way to see us. I have *always* wanted to visit Brighton. Do you live far from there?"

"About fifteen miles," said Withrow. "It is a trip I make regularly. But we have our own view of the ocean in Worthing. In fact, if the sky is clear, you can see it from the house."

"I have never seen the ocean before," said Kitty. "Can you believe that?"

Kitty engaged in a vibrant conversation with both Lady Trafford and Withrow. She drew people to her in a way that Mary never had.

Suddenly, over all the voices in the room came that of Mrs. Bennet. "Why is the food not ready?"

And then Mr. Collins. "It is Lady Catherine de Bourgh's opinion that a company must always have the opportunity to converse prior to eating, so I instructed the staff to have the meal ready thirty minutes after we returned from the funeral."

Trapped in between them—and suffering the frustrations of both—was the poor housekeeper, Mrs. Hall. Quickly both

Mrs. Collins and Elizabeth crossed the room and joined the fray in an attempt to appease both parties.

Normally Mary could ignore this sort of debacle, but today she could not, maybe because of her lack of sleep or all the forced pleasantries. It was as if the unpleasantness floated up from the argument and over the room until it landed on Mary and enveloped her in its uncomfortable embrace.

After a dismissive smirk in their mother's direction, Kitty resumed her conversation. At a convenient pause, Mary said, "If you will excuse me, I need to step out for a moment."

"Are you feeling well?" asked Lady Trafford.

"Quite well," said Mary, though her statement did not sound convincing even to herself.

"I hope you will still be dining with us."

"I will," said Mary, and then before anyone could say another word, she slipped out of the conversation and up to her room. Or, to be more factual, to one of Mr. Collins's rooms that she was borrowing.

She lay on top of her bed, staring up at the ceiling. The room was stuffy and smelled faintly of damp fabric: the maids must not have dried the clothes out properly before putting them away several days before, causing them to slowly develop an odor.

Mary had an urge to leave Longbourn, to go far from Meryton and leave all of this behind. To do something entirely new. She wanted the lessons; she wanted to learn. Yet at the same time she wanted things to stay as they had always been, though that was not possible. In her mind, she compiled a list of possible positive and negative consequences of accepting Lady Trafford's offer.

After a while, she thought it best to make her way back to the group, in case one of the maids forgot to fetch her for the meal. As she walked down the hall, she heard a faint noise from her parents' room. She paused outside of it. The door was cracked open. She pushed it open a bit farther and peered inside. Someone stood at her father's clothes press, lifting up his clothes and looking beneath them. The person was not one of the servants. She considered his coat, and the cut and shade of his hair. It was Mr. Withrow.

Fear paralyzed Mary. She wanted to confront Mr. Withrow. She wanted to tell him it was not his place to handle her father's things, and yet the thought of speaking to a man alone in a bedroom, even if it were not her own, seemed highly improper. It might be even less proper than whatever he was doing. Even if she were to speak to him, she would not know what to say or do. She had never been in a situation like this before.

Mr. Withrow stilled, and then he turned towards the door. Mary fled back to her bedroom, heart pounding, unsure if Mr. Withrow had seen or recognized her.

She waited next to her doorway, listening, but heard nothing from the hallway. There were no footsteps, and no one to accuse her of prying. After a minute, she left her room again and went back down the hallway, worried that Mr. Withrow would still be there, but determined to yell for a servant if he was.

The door to her parents' room was wide open, and no one stood inside. Nothing seemed to have been touched or disturbed. Her father's clothing press had been closed, and she reopened it; while the clothes were a touch disheveled, nothing appeared to be missing, and she could not understand what Mr. Withrow had been looking for.

Mary walked down the stairs to the crowd, trying to interpret Mr. Withrow's behaviour. But the time had come for the meal, and with all the bustle, there was little room for thought. She was relieved to be seated between Lady Lucas and her daughter, Maria Blankenbeckler. She was even more relieved that while Lady Trafford was seated near her mother, she was not immediately next to her, and Mr. Withrow was on the opposite end of the table, in between Mr. Darcy and Kitty.

Maria, the second daughter of the Lucas family, had wed six months prior and moved with her husband to Brighton. After the first course was served, she turned to Mary.

"I have missed you," said Maria. "There are no sensible women in Brighton, at least none near my age."

"But you do like it?"

"Oh, I like it very much. You should come visit me."

"I would love to come stay with you in Brighton!" Staying with a friend would be much better than living with strangers.

Maria's face scrunched up in discomfort. "I think I misspoke. Unfortunately, I do not have the space to host anyone for any extended period of time. However, I would love if you came and visited for a day."

Mary set down her fork and pretended to laugh. "Of course that is what you meant. I apologize for misunderstanding your words." This was not the first time this had happened between her and Maria.

"Do not apologize! The fault is mine." She patted Mary's shoulder. "Someday you will leave home and have your own adventures."

"I do not know if I am much suited to adventures." Mary took a slow drink and considered her food. None of it looked very appetizing.

Maria put her hand on Mary's. "You must be very sad about your father."

Mary nodded, but could not bring herself to say anything.

"He was a good man. I am glad that I am visiting my parents, so I could be here today."

"Thank you," said Mary. She had never felt extremely close to Maria, but she felt as close to her as anyone, and they had spent much time together as children. It was a comfort to be seated next to her.

"I assume you are taking solace in the scriptures?" In her letters at least, Maria had become much more interested in the Bible since her marriage.

"Yes, I am."

"One of my favorites is from Proverbs: 'God is our refuge and strength.'"

Mary tried to resist correcting her, but she could not. "That is actually a verse from the Psalms."

Maria laughed. "I always mix them up. You have a much better mind than I."

After that, their conversation stayed on pleasant topics. Yet it was not to be a peaceful meal. A few minutes later, Mrs. Bennet was heard, her voice carrying above everyone's conversations and down the table.

"I had my heart set on a night funeral."

The rest of the conversations silenced, so Jane's much quieter, conciliatory response could be heard. "Night funerals are almost never held out of London, and even there, it is not the standard."

"No expense should have been spared," insisted Mrs. Bennet. "You are not lacking, nor is Lizzy. Mr. Darcy is worth 10,000 pounds a year, and Mr. Bingley 5,000 pounds. Yet you mock me in my grief."

Mary pushed her food around her plate with her fork, not eating any of it. It was important to be able to control one's speech and emotions and make them appropriate for the situation. It was one thing for Mrs. Bennet to make these sorts of comments in private; stating them in public was entirely uncalled for.

The conversation resumed, perhaps to help cover everyone's embarrassment, but a few minutes later Mrs. Bennet's voice once again drifted down the table. "And the funeral only had one mute, when Mr. Bennet deserved at least two!"

It was a good thing, indeed, that women did not normally attend funerals. If Mrs. Bennet had, she would have been hysterical, and detracted from the proper solemnity of the occasion.

In fact, Mary suspected that Mrs. Bennet would be hysterical for months. Normally, Mary could tolerate, and even enjoy her mother's presence, but not when she went on like this. If she could, Mary would travel by herself to stay with Jane or Elizabeth or the Gardiners. But no one had made her that offer. Everyone's invitation was for Mrs. Bennet, and Kitty and Mary could come along as well. No one wanted her for herself. No one, except for Lady Trafford.

She was silent for the remainder of the meal. As everyone stood, the men to gather in the parlor and the women in the drawing room, she stopped in front of Mr. Withrow.

"Mr. Withrow."

"Yes, Miss Bennet?"

She tried to gather up her courage to ask him her question. At least, now, it was not improper for her to speak to him. "I thought, a few minutes ago, that I saw you in my parents' room, handling my father's things."

He seemed genuinely confused. "I was not in your parents' room. When did this occur?"

"Immediately before the meal."

"I was speaking with your sister, Catherine, until it was time to be seated. However, I would love to be of assistance to find out who you actually saw."

He was smooth of speech and flawless in his denial. If Mary did not have confidence in herself and her perceptions, she would have doubted her memory of the event. Yet she knew what she had seen: it had been Mr. Withrow. Accepting his assistance to look for a supposed other person would not lead to any answers and would distract from the purpose of the occasion.

"Thank you for your offer, but it will not be necessary."

He went on his way with the other men, and Mary found a quiet spot in the drawing room. Likely his lies covered some trivial transgression, but she disliked lies and wished she knew the truth of the matter. If she accepted Lady Trafford's offer, it might put her in a position to find out. She felt some moral obligation to find and share truth, and yet, it was not her responsibility. What would her father recommend she do? She did not know.

Mary rotated the mourning ring around her finger, thinking of the way her father spoke, the way he stood, the way he looked intently on something, trying to remember and memorize every detail. She was seated only a few feet away from where the pianoforte had stood. She wished she could play a song in her father's memory, one of his favorites. Whose pianoforte would she borrow when they stayed with the Philipses? Perhaps they had a neighbour. Or surely Charlotte Collins would allow her to come back to Longbourn and use the new pianoforte, once it was installed. It would be a mile walk both directions, which was very manageable, but it also meant it was unlikely that she would be able to play every day.

Mary looked around the room. Although Longbourn was filled with family and friends, she felt alone. She regretted not attending the funeral with Elizabeth and Kitty, for perhaps the words spoken would have given her strength.

All of her sisters seemed to be coping with their father's death. Elizabeth sat with Charlotte Collins, conversing, Jane seemed a little strained, but continued to comfort Mrs. Bennet, and Kitty was engaged in an animated conversation with Lady Trafford. Mary was apart, and no one sought her out.

The men rejoined the women in the drawing room. Kitty gracefully detached herself from Lady Trafford and met her nephew, Mr. Withrow, next to the fire. He acted as if everything were normal, as if he had not searched her father's things and then spoken falsehoods.

Kitty flirted with him, even touching his arm once, in a manner that made it appear as if it were accidental, though Mary knew it was not. Mr. Withrow was the sort of man who would like a girl like Kitty. Mary wondered what sort of man would like a girl like her. Of course, emotional sentiment had only a small part to play in marriage, so if Mary ever did marry, it did not matter whether the man she married liked her or not. And marriages always came with their own sets of problems and difficulties. She watched Mr. Collins and Charlotte. They seemed to tolerate each other well, but it was not a situation of ease. Her parents' marriage had been much the same way. Most of the young ladies Mary knew sought for marriage as a way to complete or fulfill themselves. Yet that was not the purpose or effect of matrimony: one needed to find meaning elsewhere.

If she stayed with her mother, marriage or relying on her sisters were her only possible paths, and she would not even know how to begin seeking for marriage. It would be better to focus on something she could obtain with certainty: a broader education. The thought of venturing out on her own frightened her a little, but today she had confronted a thief. Surely she could do this as well.

Mr. Darcy and Elizabeth stood nearby, so Mary rose from her chair and joined them.

After a minute or two of inconsequential conversation, Mary decided to broach her real purpose.

"Mr. Darcy, how well do you know Lady Trafford and Mr. Withrow?"

"Lady Trafford and her late husband were friends with my parents. I saw quite a bit of her during my youth, and I spent ample time with her son. I know Withrow as well."

"I see," said Mary. "Lady Trafford has offered that I could come stay with her and take lessons in French and drawing."

Darcy raised his eyebrows. "That is very generous of her."

"Before I accept, I wanted to ask your opinion on Lady Trafford's character. As well as Mr. Withrow's."

"No harm would befall you at Castle Durrington. They are trustworthy and reputable in all their dealings." He paused. "She can be a bit unusual at times, but she is a good woman. If you want to go, I can see no reason why you should not."

"Thank you," said Mary, reassured by his words. "What about Mr. Withrow?"

"He is a respectable gentleman, and a good man."

She thought of mentioning that Mr. Withrow had been in her parents' room, but she did not know what he had been doing, and she had no proof beyond her word, so she decided against it.

Mrs. Bennet gestured to Mary from across the room,

where she reclined in a large comfortable chair and spoke with Lady Trafford. "Come here, Mary," said Mrs. Bennet loudly. "We are speaking of you."

Lady Trafford gave Mary a knowing smile. Mary excused herself from the Darcys and joined her mother and Lady Trafford.

"I have told Mrs. Bennet of my offer to train you."

"You should have informed me at once," said Mrs. Bennet. "And to think, you could stay at a castle!"

"I was still trying to make my decision. I do not desire to be an inconvenience to Lady Trafford."

"It will be no inconvenience at all, Miss Bennet."

"Surely it is owed to us, Mary, for you to have such an opportunity. Especially as you are not beautiful like your sisters, and you have had no suitors."

"I have already made up my mind, Mother."

"You cannot possibly think to turn down Lady Trafford's offer! What an inconsiderate child you are."

"I did not say how I had made up my mind."

"What do you say, Miss Bennet? Will you join me at Castle Durrington?"

"How big is your library?" asked Mary. "And do you have a pianoforte?"

CHAPTER FIVE

"[Bonaparte] did not think it prudent to attempt any pursuit [of the enemy army]. 'The rain fell in torrents—never was the French army assailed by such bad weather.' Bonaparte always [blames] the weather [for] any disaster he meets with."

—*The Courier*, London, September 8, 1813

MARY DESPISED CARRIAGES, especially public ones. She had spent a full day in travel from Meryton to London surrounded by tedious strangers, young and old. This had been followed by two days with the Gardiners in London, enjoying the company of her young cousins, which unfortunately was only a brief respite before another miserable day in a public carriage with an old woman who had no sense of proper morals or manners, and a constant rain pounding on the roof. The inn in Horsham had left much to be desired, and then she had taken yet another public carriage for the thirteen miles to Washington.

Now she waited on a bench, still miles from Worthing, with her luggage piled on the ground behind her. She removed Lady Trafford's letter of instructions.

At the carriage station in Washington you will be met by one of my servants, either Thomas Parker or Joseph

Tubbs. He will drive you the remaining seven miles to Castle Durrington, where I will be pleased to greet you and welcome you for your stay.

The letter's wording implied that the servant should have arrived in Washington first, so she would not have to wait. But there had been no carriage waiting for her, and those at the station had seen neither Mr. Parker nor Mr. Tubbs. She supposed she could hire her own carriage to take her to the castle, but she had never hired a carriage before, so she hoped it did not come to that. She tried to sit tall and be an example of long-suffering for the men at the carriage station.

After a few minutes, a shiny black carriage approached and stopped in front of her. The driver, a jovial man with peppered hair, spoke to her. "Are you Miss Bennet? I am Mr. Tubbs. I work for Lady Trafford."

"Yes, I am Miss Bennet. I have been waiting for at least half an hour. I thought Lady Trafford had a brown carriage, not a black one."

"She has two carriages, miss. I am sorry that I forced you to wait. The carriage from Horsham must have been fast today. Normally it is late." He laughed. "You can never predict these things."

Once they had exited Washington, Mr. Tubbs took the horses at a trot. The countryside did not appear markedly different than what she had already seen, so Mary leaned back in her seat and closed her eyes, trying to ignore the bumps in the road.

Before this, she had only left Hertfordshire a handful of times in her life, and that had been as a child. Travelling seemed overrated, with endless inconveniences and only small benefits.

But at least she would be able to use a pianoforte and a library when she arrived. The past month at the Philipses' home had been tedious without either. She raised her hands as if she were seated at a pianoforte and played the beginning of a song in the air, hearing the melody in her mind.

She let out a sigh and set down her hands. She could wait a few more minutes.

It occurred to her that it would be proper, as a guest, to express her gratitude to Lady Trafford upon her arrival. She composed a short speech in her mind, making sure her phrases were crafted to her satisfaction.

After a little over an hour, the carriage slowed, and Mr. Tubbs tapped on the wall. "We are here, miss."

All thoughts of her speech disappeared as she saw Castle Durrington for the first time. She had not expected something nearly as grand or magnificent as this. It looked like an illustration in one of the books she had read to her cousins in London, about King Arthur's castle.

The central mass of the castle consisted of grand, square stone towers, topped by parapets. The right section of the castle was edged by rounded stone towers with parapets, and the left section, while it did not have true towers, had a two-storied tracery window, which she could confidently say, based on her architectural readings, had been constructed in the Gothic style. Though the edges of the grey stones looked sharp and new, she could picture medieval soldiers standing behind the parapets and shooting arrows at an attacking foe.

She leaned forward in anticipation as the carriage came to a stop in front of the main doorway. Outside stood five servants waiting for her arrival, but there was no sign of Lady Trafford.

As Mr. Tubbs helped Mary out, one of the servants

stepped inside and returned but not with Lady Trafford. He led Mr. Withrow. Yet the letter had clearly stated that Lady Trafford would be here.

Withrow stepped forward and gave a practiced bow. "Lady Trafford sends her regards. I apologize that she is not here to greet you. While she had every plan to be here today, she was called to Brighton for urgent business and will not return until tomorrow or the following day."

What type of business was so urgent that it could not wait a single day? How peculiar. And what sort of business would preclude sending her nephew or a trusted servant instead? It was very peculiar indeed.

Mary twisted her hands together, unsure of how she should act until the mistress of the house returned. Admittedly, she felt less welcome here with only Mr. Withrow. From their brief interactions, he did not seem as approachable as Lady Trafford, and there was the matter of him searching her father's things and then lying about it.

"Are you going to respond to what I said?" asked Withrow. "Or have you gone mute?"

She opened her mouth and out came the words she had prepared to deliver to Lady Trafford. "It is a great honor for me to be invited to stay at Castle Durrington. My gratitude stems from both my commitment to my education and my willingness to expand my spheres of interaction. I feel that during my stay—"

"Your gratitude is appreciated," interrupted Mr. Withrow, making it impossible for her to finish the speech. "Would you care for a brief refreshment? This is Mrs. Boughton, our indomitable housekeeper. After we have tea, she will provide you with a tour. I have obligations to the estate today and will be unable to join you, but you can trust that you will be in very capable hands."

Clearly, he did not want her company. She had no particular need for his either. "I do not need any refreshment," said Mary. "I feel refreshed already. You may return to your work so I can immediately begin the tour."

"Very well," said Mr. Withrow. "I will see you at dinner." He seemed relieved that she did not demand his attention and stepped into the castle.

Mary pressed her lips firmly together. This was not the welcome she had envisioned. She had prepared for Lady Trafford, she had not been able to give her speech, and she did not particularly want to be thrust into the care of a housekeeper, no matter how capable. She was a little thirsty and hungry, but she had no desire to drink tea and chat with Withrow.

Mrs. Boughton curtsied to Mary. She was a tall, greying women, with sharp edges to her facial features, and to her elbows. "It is a pleasure to make your acquaintance, Miss Bennet. Throughout your stay, please let me know if there is any way I can be of assistance to you."

"I am sure my stay will be quite suitable, thank you. Before the tour, I would like to see my trunks up to my room."

"No need to worry yourself over that, Miss Bennet. The footmen will bring them up." Mrs. Boughton nodded at several of the servants.

Mary watched with consternation as they removed her trunks from the carriage. She was accustomed to servants handling her things, but she did not personally know these servants and did not know what care they would give her belongings. Her entire life was in those cases: almost all of her worldly possessions, her books and her music, her black mourning clothes, and her normal ones, too, as she did not know how long she would be a visitor here. She watched the men as they carried the case into the house, memorizing their faces, their heights, their builds.

"Now shall we begin?" asked Mrs. Boughton.

"Yes. I have never toured a castle before."

Mrs. Boughton smiled. "Which raises the first point of interest. Castle Durrington is not, by strict definitions, a castle. Construction began twenty-three years ago, in 1790, by the late Sir George Trafford. While this north side does use a Gothic, castellated style, its fortifications are visual only, and not designed to withstand an assault. I pray every night that fortifications never become necessary, especially because we would need them on the south side, not on this one. Should Bonaparte cross the channel, he could choose to land in Sussex. We would be overrun by French soldiers before we had time to flee."

Mary's visions of the castle withstanding an attack disappeared like morning mist. She hoped she never saw Bonaparte, or any of his troops. He had not yet dared to land on the British Isles, but there was always speculation as to when or where he might attack, if the British forces did not do well enough in battle.

Yet despite Mrs. Boughton's purported fear of invasion, she seemed quite able to forget her concerns and redirect her attention to the tour. She pointed to the right section of the castle. "That section, with the rounded towers, is the stables, and there, on the left, is the kitchen and dairy and servants' quarters. As there is a cool breeze today, we best go inside."

The last remaining servant opened the door, and Mrs. Boughton gestured for Mary to enter first. Mary stepped inside and immediately stopped. Despite herself, she found herself impressed by the grandeur.

The entry hall was a round room, and at its centre was a grand staircase that seemed as if it was suspended in the air. The stairs had a slight curve and drew her eyes upwards, to a glass dome far above their heads.

Mrs. Boughton cleared her throat, and Mary stepped forward so the door could be closed.

"The entirety of Castle Durrington was designed by the architect John Biagio Rebecca. It is said that this dome is the only of its kind in a private residence in Britain." As Mrs. Boughton pointed out the different kinds of pillars used in the entry hall, Mary could not help but conclude that this was a rather pompous display of wealth. Not only was there a grand staircase in this main entry area, but a smaller spiral staircase as well.

Mrs. Boughton led Mary through the rooms on the main floor which were off of the entry hall—first two dining rooms, then two parlors. She pointed out a final door. "And this is the library." She put her finger to her lips to indicate that silence was needed, then gently twisted the door handle. It was locked. "Mr. Withrow must not be able to spare time for an interruption, so you will be shown the library later."

Mary swallowed her disappointment. The library was one of the rooms she most wanted to see. Withrow had *known* Mrs. Boughton was giving her a tour, he had *known* that Mary loved books, and yet he had locked the door.

They left the main floor behind, ascending the grand staircase to the first floor and to what Mrs. Boughton called "the rotunda, or domed balcony room." It was a large, circular room directly below the dome. It contained a series of different alcoves. Some were covered by curtains; of these, some were simply decorative, covering blank paneled walls, and one hid the small spiral staircase which led both downstairs to the main floor and upstairs to the second floor. The other alcoves contained doors with hallways to the rest of the rooms.

Mary wanted to sit and rest, but she did not say anything. Fortitude was a virtue to be prized in the face of great odds. She lagged half a dozen steps behind as Mrs. Boughton showed her a long gallery filled with paintings that could be used as a ballroom, and four grand drawing rooms. One hallway led to Lady Trafford's and Mr. Withrow's rooms, but they did not visit them. The housekeeper kept pointing out the way different architectural styles had been combined. But Mary was not here to learn about architecture. If she wanted to learn about it, she would read a book.

Many of the rooms faced the back, south side of the house, and featured large windows, from which you could see the ocean, a faint blue line on the horizon. As they stepped into another drawing room, which also had a view of the ocean, her attention was drawn instead to the pianoforte.

"May I play this instrument?" she asked.

"Lady Trafford enjoys music, and I am certain she will encourage you to increase your skills."

Mary sat down at the bench and rubbed her hands together.

"Perhaps it would be better if you played after the tour. There should be time before dinner."

"I have not had the opportunity to play these past five weeks. I should not neglect it now."

Mary did not have many pieces memorized, but she had been working on one before her father's death. She set her hands on the keys and relaxed in a way that she had not been able to at any point during her long journey here. This pianoforte had a different sound than she was used to, a little deeper. The first few measures brought her pleasure, but after five or six she stumbled to a halt. She could not remember what came next. She started anew, hoping it would come to her, and she managed an extra measure, but the notes after that were jumbled and dissonant.

Mary took her hands from the keys and stood up promptly. "I need to see my music."

"There will be plenty of time for that later," said Mrs. Boughton, as if Mary's desires should be remedied and corrected. Elizabeth would take such a tone with her at times, as would her father, when alive. They said these sorts of things politely, but it always seemed that Mary was getting in the way of their plans, the way they envisioned the world best working.

"Very well," said Mary stiffly.

"And now," said Mrs. Boughton, "for my favorite part of the tour: the south terrace and the lawns."

Mary did not want to continue the tour with Mrs. Boughton, but she knew it would be impolite to refuse. People like Elizabeth always managed to do things that were impolite, yet in a way that did not give others offense. Perhaps Mary would try it. She pictured her older sister in her mind and decided on the proper phrasing.

"I would truly love to see the terrace, but I am feeling great fatigue from my long journey. Perhaps we can continue it another day."

"It is well worth seeing the back of the house. I can make it a short excursion."

Mary had seen plenty of backs of houses. They were typically a duller version of the front.

"I need to lie down," Mary said flatly.

Mrs. Boughton looked like she was about to protest but

then thought better of it. As the grand staircase did not lead to the second floor (it was covered by a dome) they went up the smaller spiral staircase. Even though Mrs. Boughton had agreed to continue the tour another day, she would not stop talking. There were over a dozen rooms, with one section reserved for visiting relatives. Mrs. Boughton pointed out her own room ("it is close to yours, and I will act as a chaperone until Lady Trafford returns"), and the nursery ("should Mr. Withrow ever choose to marry and produce heirs"), and then she finally brought Mary to the room that would be hers during her stay. Her room was on the north side of the house, the side from which the carriage had approached. From her windows, besides the clearing in front of the house and a glimpse of the road, all Mary could see were trees, some with a few leaves turning their fall colours.

After Mrs. Boughton verified that all of Mary's cases had been brought up, she left so Mary could rest.

As soon as the door was closed, Mary opened the case with her music and found her error. It was an easy part—how could she have completely forgotten the opening movement? She wanted to return to the pianoforte but stopped herself short of the door. She had used the excuse that she was tired to free herself from the rest of the tour, but now that prohibited her from using the pianoforte. Next time, she should come up with a different polite reason. And next time, she would not decline refreshment after travelling.

Mary lay down on the bed, holding her music to her chest. This castle—no, house—was grander even than Netherfield, where Mr. Bingley had lived for a time. And compared to the residence of the Philipses—well, she should not compare her aunt's house to this place. Perhaps she should have stayed there, in a place that was familiar, with people who were familiar. At least there she knew her place in the world. Here, more seemed possible, yet it also made her future feel more uncertain. But there was no use in looking back. Her decision had been made, and she would make the best of it.

She set her music to the side and tried falling asleep, but too much afternoon light shone through the window. She rose and walked to the window; instead of closing the curtain, she gazed outside at the walk and the trees. She removed her mourning ring. She read her father's name and date of death, then flipped the bezel to reveal the clip of hair. She pressed the translucent stone to her lips. Change was inevitable, and death, as the philosophers liked to say, was but a natural part of life. While she would suffer through it with resolve, that did not mean she had to relish her suffering.

A movement—or perhaps a light—caught Mary's attention. She peered out her window. There, in the trees, a red light flashed, two more times. A minute later the light flashed again, three times. What even made a red light, strong enough to be seen through trees in the daytime?

She waited, but the light did not flash again. Yet a minute or two later, someone walked away from Castle Durrington, towards the light. She recognized his clothes and hair. It was Mr. Withrow.

She tightened her fingers around the fabric of the curtain. Withrow could be engaged in business for the estate, but then why the mysterious red light? It seemed like a signal, a secret signal that most people were not meant to understand.

What he did was none of her concern, yet she could not stifle her curiosity. This was the man who had searched her parents' room, after all, and she still did not know why he had done so. She might never learn why, but at least she could discover what occupied him now. If Mrs. Boughton questioned her leaving her room, she would simply state that she had received sufficient rest.

Mary took the small spiral staircase down two flights, all the way to the main floor. A servant stood at attention in the front entryway.

"Would you please open the door?" she asked.

He did so, asking, "Where are you going, miss?"

"I need a bit of fresh air," said Mary. She should not need to justify her movements to Lady Trafford's servants.

"Are you in need of any assistance?"

"No. I am quite independently minded."

As she stepped away from the castle, she realized that the servant might report to Withrow that she had left the house. She did not want the servant to know that she was following his master, so she veered to the left, as if she was headed to the side of the house. After a minute she turned back, towards the place in the trees where she had seen the light.

As she neared the trees she slowed. She stepped over branches and around fallen logs, keeping as quiet as possible. She heard voices, not truly audible, and as she neared them, she crouched down into some shrubbery.

She pushed aside a branch and peered at the two figures who stood a bit farther forward. One was unmistakable: it was Withrow. The other took her a moment to place, in part because his presence was so unexpected. The man had a mustache and a beard, which changed the look of his facial structure, and his hair was now a darker colour, but despite these changes, Mary recognized him.

Mr. Withrow was meeting with the man who had attempted to steal her family's mourning rings.

CHAPTER SIX

An extract from a letter from a British officer in Spain, to his friend in Glasgow, written after a British victory: "There was a great deal of plunder taken, and a considerable number of prisoners, among whom, as I went along, I observed two French officers, as I thought, a young one who was wounded, and a middle-aged man, unhurt, with his arm round the young one's neck, and comforting him the best way he could. The soldiers observed that they must be brothers; but it turned out that they were husband and wife—the woman dressed in men's clothes."

–The Courier, London, September 8, 1813

MARY HAD ALWAYS felt that thoughts were like feet: a lady should keep them at a steady, controlled pace. But now Mary's thoughts were running in all directions, and she could do nothing to stop them.

Mr. Withrow was talking to the thief. Did he know the man was a thief? He must. It would be too great a coincidence for the thief to be here at Castle Durrington *and* back at Longbourn. He clearly knew the man, and he *must* know of his business.

The thief was quite animated in his discussion, and Mr. Withrow laughed, loud enough that it carried to Mary. She could not hear their conversation, but it was clear that they were comrades.

Mary's breath sounded loud in her ears, and she feared that at any moment they would notice her. This man was a criminal, and who knew what bodily harm he would do to her if she were discovered? She had read several descriptions in the newspapers of evil men forcing their way into dwellings, dragging women off, and, though the papers never actually stated it in words, raping the women. Mary shuddered at the thought of that awful word. She did not know that the thief was that type of evil man, but he did look strong, and there were plenty of other descriptions in the papers of highway robbers and men causing physical injuries to their victims, breaking bones and the like. She tried to breathe quietly and slowly, and to keep her body from shaking, but it was difficult to do.

Perhaps only Withrow knew the thief, and Lady Trafford was ignorant of the whole affair. Mary found herself disappointed in him. Withrow knew Darcy, and Darcy respected Withrow. Their acquaintance should have prevented something such as this.

When Mary had caught the thief in Meryton, fiddling with Lady Trafford's cases, she had assumed he was trying to steal them. She reconsidered the events of that day, drawing up the details in her mind. He must have been helping them with their cases. But when Mary had called him a thief, Withrow had chased him. Of course, Withrow could have chased him for the show of it, to maintain a facade. During their conversation in the carriage after, neither Withrow nor Lady Trafford had made mention that he was their acquaintance or servant. They must have already known that he had stolen the mourning rings, and perhaps even tasked him with it. They would not have expected Mary to walk to Meryton at that moment.

Mary's legs began to cramp. She watched impatiently as Withrow and the thief traded letters. The thief wrote something in a small notebook, and then placed it in his jacket pocket. Withrow said something, the thief responded harshly, and for a minute, Withrow gesticulated angrily. But then their faces and their mannerisms became cordial again.

She looked down at the mourning ring on her hand, considering how abruptly Withrow and his aunt had come into her life. While the theft of the mourning rings could have been orchestrated by Withrow alone, the middle of the night visit was clearly led by Lady Trafford, and she had put a great amount of effort into persuading Mary to come to Castle Durrington for lessons.

But what benefit would Lady Trafford and Mr. Withrow gain from stolen mourning rings? They would not be able to use them, and they certainly did not need the money that could be made by selling them. Had she foiled their plan by finding the rings? Or had she performed the exact part they had hoped she would play?

Mary's thoughts led her in endless, futile directions until Withrow and the thief finished their conversation, embraced, and left the trees in opposite directions, Withrow towards the castle, and the thief towards the main road. There was a brief moment of panic as Withrow paused not far from her hiding place, but then he was gone.

MARY RETURNED TO her room, collapsed into her bed, and fell into a restless, uneasy sleep. A knock on the door jolted

Mary awake. The door was pushed open a crack, and a voice came from outside. "Excuse me, miss, but Mrs. Boughton has sent me to help you prepare for dinner."

"I do not need someone to wait on me." Mary never needed the help of maids to dress, not even for a ball.

The door pushed opened the rest of the way, revealing a pretty girl with dark skin and a smiling face.

"Don't worry," said the maid. "You are not my only task. But this is a big house with many expectations, and you are rather short on time, and it's no trouble at all."

Mary tried to come up with some way to stop the maid but could not find the words.

The maid was opening all of Mary's cases, examining the clothes. "I'm Fanny, by the way. Fanny Cramer." She settled on the nicest black gown, the one Mary had worn on the day of the funeral. "Now this one will be just right, unless you want to leave mourning behind and put on some colour for tonight."

"I am not one of those young ladies who is in mourning for only a week or two. I plan to wear black for my father for at least three months."

"Whatever suits your fancy," said Fanny. "It is a bit unusual though. I have never heard of anyone wearing it for more than a month or two."

Before Mary knew it, Fanny had disrobed her and put on the new gown. She was efficient and friendly, keeping up a constant chatter, and fortunately, did not seem to expect Mary to respond.

"Do you need help going down?"

"I was given a tour of the castle."

"It will be the smaller dining room tonight, the one on the left. While you're there, I will put away the rest of your things for you."

Normally, Mary did this sort of thing herself, but she was tired, and Fanny seemed the sort who would do it even if told not to. She owned nothing overly private that Fanny could not see.

"Be careful with the music. And with the family names chart. I spent a long time copying everything down and would not like to see it wrinkled."

"I always treat everything with care," said Fanny. "Don't you worry over it." She squeezed Mary's arm in a manner that felt rather familiar for having just met. "Now go and eat. It will help you feel better."

Mary was feeling quite well and had not said anything that would have indicated otherwise, so she wondered at Fanny's statement. But she was hungry, so she went down the two flights on the small spiral staircase and entered the smaller dining room.

Mr. Withrow was already seated, but he stood when she entered.

"Good evening," said Mr. Withrow.

"Good evening," said Mary.

The servants brought out the food, course by course, and Mrs. Boughton stood on the side, a watchful chaperone. Mr. Withrow appeared to be thoroughly engaged in his food and did not speak. Mary wondered if he disliked her so intensely after such a short acquaintance, if he simply found her so far beneath his notice, or if he was treating her this way because of her previous accusation.

"What business called Lady Trafford to Brighton?" asked Mary.

"One of the charities she is involved in, I believe."

"Oh really?" asked Mary, trying to draw out more details.

"What did they need her for?"

"I am not aware of the particulars."

She wondered if he did not know, or if he was simply being evasive. If a family member of hers went off on urgent business, she would have found out the particulars before they left.

"Does Lady Trafford do a lot of charity work?"

"A reasonable amount. She does what she can and never feels she has done enough." He took a very large bite of food, apparently not wanting to elaborate.

"I think that is very commendable. A soul that is turned towards others does some of the most important work."

He nodded but did not respond.

"What charities does she assist?"

"A large number, both in Worthing and other nearby locations. I cannot keep track of all their names."

He really did not want to give her any information. "I would like to do work for the benefit of the poor and the needy as well. Is there any society that might be able to use my skills?"

He sighed. "I am not personally involved in any of them, so the best thing to do would be to wait and ask my aunt when she returns."

There were other things Mary wanted to ask, such as how exactly their families were related, how often she might expect to visit Worthing, and most especially, Withrow's connection to the thief, but Mary suspected he would deflect her questions, so she did not verbalize them. They sat in silence for a few minutes until Mary asked, "May I use the library?" Mrs. Boughton had already implied permission to use the pianoforte but had not been clear about the library.

"Lady Trafford will, without doubt, grant you a full run

of the house."

It was an indirect permission, but she would take it.

Then he added, "When I am working or reading in the library, you are welcome to procure a text, but I prefer not to be disturbed."

Her father had been much the same way. He preferred if the library was kept a place of quiet contemplation. "I will not disturb you."

They finished their food in silence. Mary stood to leave.

Withrow raised his hand to stop her. "Tomorrow the servants will serve you breakfast in this room at nine thirty. Unfortunately, I have other commitments and will not be able to join you. Your lessons will begin at eleven in the parlor next to the library. You will have drawing for an hour and a half, followed by an hour and a half of French. Hopefully my aunt will have returned by that point."

Mary nodded. She hoped so as well, for she was certain Lady Trafford's company and conversation would offer a great improvement over Withrow's.

WITH DINNER COMPLETE, Mary went directly to the library. She turned the door handle, which was unlocked, and stepped inside. She paused for a moment at the entrance, taking in the smell of paper and leather binding, and smiled.

The walls of the room were covered with bookshelves of beautiful dark brown wood. She let her fingers trail along the well-polished surface as she explored. In addition to the shelves on the walls, there were several additional rows of shelves, of half the height, in the middle of the room. Based on her mental calculations, Lady Trafford owned at least twice as many books as had been in her father's library, if not three times as many.

Ladders were spread throughout the room. She tried sliding one, but it did not slide. She noted a ledge at the top of the shelves that the ladders seemed to hook onto. She lifted one of the ladders, shifted it, and placed it in another position on the shelves.

Every single book had high-quality bindings, even a novel she found. Lady Trafford must have a proficient craftsman who bound all of her books. Mary removed a few books at random but could find no rhyme or reason to their organization. Surely a library of this size *must* have a logic to it, but if it did, she could not find it.

Mr. Bennet's library—now Mr. Collins's—had four general categories: religion, natural history, politics and world history, and other. Within these categories the books were organized by a combination of size, colour, and purchase date. Mr. Bennet had created a catalogue which recorded all of his books and assisted in finding them. He also knew his books well, so if Mary had a question, she simply had to ask him. Her father would sit for a moment, thinking, then stand and go directly to the book Mary sought.

Mary searched for a catalogue of books but did not find one. She supposed she could ask Mr. Withrow or Mrs. Boughton, but she did not want their help; she preferred to explore places on her own, at her own speed.

One section of the library had no shelves, but rather paneled walls of various materials and textures, a very fine desk, and other seating—several chairs and sofas. The desk was covered with papers, and one of the pages caught her eye. She did not mean to read it, but once her eyes fell upon the words, she could not unsee the meaning of them. It was a list titled "Tasks for September eighth." It appeared to be items Mr. Withrow had hoped to accomplish today. "Greet M. Bennet, give apologies" was crossed out, along with five other items: "Update ledgers," "Check harvest," "Trade letter D. Ray," "Newspapers," "Check on mine investment." There were fourteen other items on the list that he had not completed.

Withrow must be very busy indeed. It seemed to her almost futile to create a list of that length; it was better to keep one's life simple and meaningful than to fill it with endless tasks. She had never had more than one or two things she needed to do on a given day, and some days she did not have any.

There was a large detailed map of the region, and she studied it for a moment. Then she turned back to the books, looking for something she might borrow. Finally she found a book of sermons. Next to it on the shelves were other sermons and religious histories. Even if she could not get a sense of the library's organization as a whole, at least the religious books were all grouped together. She chose two collections of sermons and one history of the Anglican church, then found a small piece of paper on Mr. Withrow's desk and wrote herself directions on where to replace the books once she was finished. She wrote another note listing the books she was borrowing, which she set on the desk, then sat down in one of the chairs with her new reading.

Halfway through the first chapter of the Anglican church history book, Mary paused. Lady Trafford must have a family Bible which included the family records. Mary could figure out their direct relationship on her own, even before Lady Trafford returned.

On the shelf of religious books, she found commentaries

on many of the books within the Bible, but no Bible. Puzzled, she stared at the shelf for a minute. Then she walked around the room, step by step, peering at each and every shelf. Surely Lady Trafford owned a Bible. She could not imagine what kind of person would not.

Mary had begun to question the potential for the salvation of Lady Trafford's soul when she found the Bible and quickly repented of her hasty judgment. It had been placed on a shelf with other books that appeared to be prized or rare.

With care, she removed the Bible from the shelf and returned to her seat. She opened the book and inhaled its pleasant, musty smell. Inside she found page upon page of family records, written in dozens of different hands over the years.

She closed the book and set it on the chair, then went to her room and retrieved the family names chart she had prepared. Once she had returned to the library, she laid both the book and her chart on Mr. Withrow's desk—on top of his papers, as she did not want to move them—and studied name after name, searching for the point of convergence.

The records in the family Bible were very thorough, containing every child, spouse, and connection for every single family line for the past one hundred and fifty years. Mary compared each name to those on her chart, wondering if they might be third or fourth or fifth cousins, either directly or through marriage.

Finally, Mary leaned back in the chair and rubbed her temples with her fingertips. She was getting a headache as she tried to sort out the significance of the evidence before her. Based on the records in the family Bible, Mary was not, in fact, related to Lady Trafford.

CHAPTER SEVEN

A bulletin published by the Crown Prince of Sweden to his people, after the failure of the armistice: "Soldiers! It is to arms then... The same sentiment which guided the French in 1792 and which prompted them to assemble and combat the armies which entered their territory, ought to animate your valour against those who, after having invaded the land which gave you birth, still hold in chains your brethren, your wives, and your children. Soldiers! What a noble prospect is presented to you. The liberty of Europe, the reestablishment of its equilibrium, the end of that convulsive state which has had twenty years' duration; finally, the peace of the world will be the result of your efforts. Render yourselves worthy, by your union, your discipline, and your courage, of the high destiny which awaits you."

—The Bath Chronicle, Bath, England,
September 9, 1813

MARY ATTEMPTED, FOR the first time in her life, to draw a still life. The master, a Richard Linton who resided in Worthing, had arranged several items in the centre of a table, given Mary a piece of paper and a pencil made of graphite encased in silver, and instructed Mary to draw.

In this she found herself anything but proficient. She

could not even force a straight line when she desired a straight line, or a curved line with a proper curve.

Mr. Linton stood a few feet away, looking out the parlor of the window towards the sea, which was hardly visible because of the rain. After a few minutes he returned to stand behind Mary.

"Have you ever had any drawing instruction before?"

"No, sir," said Mary, sinking a little in her chair.

"Have you spent much time drawing on your own?"

"No, sir," she said again, feeling a little smaller.

"Then you have no bad habits to correct. You are a blank canvas." He pulled up a chair beside Mary. "May I use the pencil?"

He took it and began drawing on top of Mary's picture. She felt an initial surge of resentment but then forced it back down. Mr. Linton was a master, after all, and it was not as if her fruit or the flowers had turned out well in any case.

"The key is to draw not what you know is there, but instead, only what you can see from a particular vantage point." He paused. "What you have done is look at the outside of the forms. Blocking your arrangement onto the page can be quite useful because it helps you lay out your image and keep the correct proportions between objects." He made her apple a little larger and rounder and sketched a new outline for the vase.

"In the coming weeks, I will give you other supplies—graphite of different hardnesses, charcoal in different shades. But for now, I want you to master this pencil, and do all that you can with it."

Mr. Linton demonstrated how to form a thick or a thin line by adjusting the sharpness of the pencil or the angle used. He made darker and lighter lines depending on how hard he pressed the pencil on the paper. And he showed how to use lines not only on the outer edges of an object, but on the inside, to create depth, give an appearance of shape and shadows, and make it seem as if the picture depicted more than a flat object on a flat page.

"You should write a book of these techniques," said Mary. "I am sure many individuals would find it invaluable."

"Perhaps," said Mr. Linton. "But there is only so much one can learn from a book. There are many things that are best taught by a teacher, or by experience itself."

"My best teachers have always been books," said Mary.

"I will see if I can teach you to draw better than they did." He directed her attention back to the page. "Now try with the apple. You need to create depth and curve."

She tried to do as he said, adding shadow on one side of the apple, and suddenly, the sketch seemed more like the real thing.

"Add a little shading near the stem—a little bit darker, if you will. And now perhaps a few very light lines where the light is hitting the apple right here."

She followed his direction as best of as she was able and was surprised by the results. She congratulated herself on learning from him so quickly.

Mr. Linton guided her to add lines and texture and shadow to the flowers, then gave her a second piece of paper and a mirror.

"Now take the next fifteen minutes and draw a self-portrait of your face. Think about blocking, think about light and shadow, consider how all the parts of the face relate to each other, and how each is required to make a whole."

Mary swallowed but she lifted up the pencil. She sketched an oval very lightly, in case she needed to change it later, and then stared at her face in the mirror. Two eyes, a nose, and a mouth, how hard could it be? Yet she found herself at a loss for where to begin. Her features were normal, unremarkable. She did not consider herself ugly or unattractive, but she certainly was plain.

After a minute, she began work on the nose, but the curves were challenging. She moved on to her eyes, which were much easier, then stared at her lips in the mirror. Mr. Linton sat across from her, drawing furiously, with only an occasional pause and glance in her direction. She wondered what he drew. Finally she drew her own lips. She had just started on her hair when Mr. Linton said, "one more minute," so she hastily sketched her hair in a bun.

She breathed out and considered her work. It was not perfect, but for her first attempt at drawing a person, it certainly had some merit.

Mr. Linton stood and examined her drawing. She waited for some praise of her effort, but instead he said, "Your proportions do not match that of a real human face. For instance, the eyes are much too high on the head, well into the area where the forehead should be."

He took a fresh paper and sketched an oval. He then drew a slightly curved line at the halfway point. "If you study the human body, you will find that the eyes always fall at the midpoint between the top of the head and the bottom of the chin. I recommend blocking those first and then positioning the nose and the mouth beneath them." He demonstrated the positioning and moved on to show the placement of the ears, eyebrows, and hairline. "Children's faces are proportioned a bit differently, but we will cover that another day."

Mary looked at his sketch of proportions and then back to her self-portrait. Suddenly it seemed woefully inadequate, like something drawn by a young child.

"Why did you not teach me this before I drew my face?"

"Because then you would not appreciate the knowledge, and you would be less likely to remember it."

Mary sniffed. That was, to her, not the ideal teaching method. Why force a student to fail before providing proper instruction? She almost said as much, but an image of Elizabeth and Jane appeared in her mind. They would look down on such a comment, consider it improper even, and perhaps they were right.

"While you were drawing, I did a quick sketch of your face. Ideally, I would spend an hour or two more, but it does provide a resemblance."

Mary took in a quick breath of air. The portrait was absolutely marvelous, the work of a true artist. She had not even been sitting still, and yet in fifteen minutes he had managed to pin her to the page. She could not possibly imagine what he would improve if he spent an hour or more on it.

"If you apply yourself with diligence, in a few months you should be able to draw a self-portrait that satisfies you."

"One's commitment to hard work is a reflection of the value one places on one's own soul." If there was anything Mary knew how to do, it was to apply herself. And if she had the potential to draw anything like what Mr. Linton had, she would do all that was required.

"Keep every page you sketch on. It will be a record so you can see your own improvement, and so I can give you specific feedback on what is and is not working. Please date and sign each of your pages." He then gave her instruction on what he wanted her to complete before her next lesson: three still lifes; a page each of ears, noses, mouths, eyes, and hands; and three landscapes. She was to have drawing lessons twice a week, on

Tuesdays and Thursdays, and as today was a Thursday, that gave her five days to complete the task.

Mr. Linton packed up his things.

"Can I keep the portrait you drew of me?"

"If you would like." He signed the page. "Maybe someday I will draw a better one."

As he left, Mary studied her portrait. It was excellently done, but on closer consideration, she looked scared and timid. There was nothing noteworthy about her appearance; it was the sort of face that people would ignore and dismiss as unimportant. Yet a real artist had found it worth drawing, worth putting in pencil on a page.

Mary's ruminations were interrupted by the housekeeper, Mrs. Boughton, who announced the arrival of the second tutor, a Madame Dieupart.

Madame Dieupart was a small woman with dark, curly hair and pronounced cheekbones. She wore simple, dark-coloured clothing, a style Mary approved of.

She curtsied to Mary. "*Bonjour.*"

Now that was a word Mary did know how to say. "*Bonjour.*"

Madame Dieupart clucked. "*Non, non, non. Bonjour.*"

She looked at Mary expectantly, but Mary did not know what she expected her to say.

"*Quand je dis quelque chose, il faut écouter bien et répéter. Bonjour. Répétez.*"

Mary understood *bonjour*, but Madame Dieupart spoke so quickly that Mary had no idea what any of the other words meant. Reading had truly not prepared her to speak the language.

Madame Dieupart pointed at herself and said, "*Bonjour,*" pointed at Mary and said, "*Bonjour. Répétez.*"

Mary supposed the woman wanted her to repeat. She must have said the word inadequately.

"*Bonjour*," said Mary. They went back and forth saying *bonjour* to each other until finally Madame Dieupart said, "*Enfin!*"

What did that mean? Mary had not the least idea.

"*Asseyez-vous.*"

Vous meant you, but Madame Dieupart had spoken very quickly, and Mary could not figure out how the first thing her teacher had said was spelled, so she did not know what it meant.

"*Asseyez-vous.*" Her teacher gestured at the chair, so Mary sat, and Madame Dieupart followed suit.

The next hour continued in a similar manner, Madame Dieupart saying a word or a phrase in French and insisting Mary repeat it back dozens of times. Mary wondered if Lady Trafford had employed someone to teach her French who did not speak a word of English. She also questioned whether this would actually teach her French. If she was forced only to repeat words without understanding them, how would she ever learn to speak?

Mary wanted to tell her that she could read French. She wanted to ask questions and learn something about the language. But instead it was just this endless repetition. Every time Mary attempted to say something in English, Madame Dieupart ignored her.

She began repeating the words with a defiant tone. It was not her fault no one had ever given her lessons before. There were several French speakers her parents could have hired, or they could have sent her to London for a true education.

Finally, when Mary was about to abandon Madame Dieupart and the endless repeating in the parlor, Madame

Dieupart said, with only a light accent, "Very good. That is enough listening and sounds practice for the day."

"You speak English?"

"Of course. I fled France during *la Terreur* and have been living here ever since." Her eyes turned to the window. "I like to imagine that I can see past the ocean and back to my home. I have never returned, and with things the way they are, I could not."

Mary did not know much about French politics or what would lead a French person to either sympathize with or oppose Napoleon Bonaparte.

Madame Dieupart passed Mary a book titled *An Introduction to French Phrases and Grammar*. "Lady Trafford said that you can read French?"

"Yes, Madame Dieupart."

She instructed Mary to read a few sentences of a text and then translate them. Then she explained the general rules for pronouncing the sounds.

"Why did we not start with this?" asked Mary, annoyed.

"You have to be able to listen. You must be able to understand and create the sounds. This book will make it easier for you to study and practice on your own, but I do not want you to be overly attached to the page." She paused, considering Mary. "You are much older than my normal beginning students."

"I am only nineteen."

"It is easier to learn the sounds when you are young. But we will manage. Lady Trafford has asked me to teach you for an hour and a half a day, five days a week."

Mary was surprised. She had expected French to be like her drawing lessons, only twice a week. Seven and a half hours was an enormous portion of time spent with a single teacher.

Apparently when Lady Trafford decided to do something, she did it thoroughly.

"In addition to your lessons, you should spend at least an hour every day practicing. You can practice the sounds and phrases from the book. Or, if you have a French speaker to converse with, that is even better." She raised her eyebrows dramatically. "Mr. Withrow is fluent in French."

"I do not think Mr. Withrow would agree to practice French with me."

Madame Dieupart laughed. "Perhaps you are right. Or perhaps you would be surprised." She paused. "I taught him, you know. And Lady Trafford's children, Anne and James."

"Where are they?" Mr. Darcy had mentioned Lady Trafford's son, but besides that brief reference, no one had spoken of him. Mr. Withrow seemed to be responsible for running the estate, which meant Anne and James must either be absent, or have passed on. She rather suspected the latter.

"That is not my story to tell."

Madame Dieupart left, and Mary rubbed her face with her hands. Her head ached from the lessons, particularly the French. Why ever had she told Lady Trafford that she wanted to learn French?

"Excuse me, miss," said a voice. Mary lifted her face and saw the maid, Fanny, carrying a platter of food and drinks. "I thought you might like some light refreshment."

Mary had not thought she needed anything—she would not have asked for anything—but suddenly it was exactly what she wanted. "Yes, thank you."

Mary began on the tea and the pastries, eating more quickly than was normal for her.

While yesterday Fanny had been full of talk, today she stood quietly, waiting to be of assistance.

Mary finished the food, yet did not want Fanny to leave, so she spoke. "I do not know if I can do this. Drawing and French; it's all rather overwhelming."

"Things are harder when you are new," said Fanny. "I have only been here three months, and the first fortnight was dreadful, trying to figure out my place and learn everything. But my mum always said you have to stick with something for long enough to give it a real chance. And things often start hard, don't they?"

It was good wisdom, even though it was not expressed in the most sophisticated fashion.

"Has Lady Trafford returned?"

"Not yet, miss, and there has been no word on when she will."

Fanny gathered the tray. Mary desired company, but she had no excuse to make Fanny stay.

It was strange being in such a big house, with only Mr. Withrow for company, and him not even here today. She was certain there were many servants, but she had only seen a few so far. At home, no matter how many of her sisters were gone, it had never felt quiet or lonely with Mrs. Bennet in the house.

Mary did not desire to draw or practice more French just yet, so she went upstairs and played the pianoforte until her fingers remembered what they were doing. Her fingers would be sore on the morrow.

She decided she best start on her drawing assignment, for diligence was the key to mastery. She wanted to start with a landscape, and so she wandered about the floor, looking out the windows for the most interesting view. Some of the spaces and proportions and sizes of the rooms surprised her, but she could not pinpoint what was off. She supposed it was due to the use of a circular room for the staircase and balcony inside of a rectangular structure. Each of the rooms were square or rectangular, which meant that there must be large gaps in the walls between the round landing and the rooms.

She thought she heard voices from the smallest drawing room, so she stepped towards that door. They were both voices she recognized—Mr. Withrow and Lady Trafford. She had returned. It surprised Mary that she had not sent a servant to find Mary and apprise her of the arrival—Mary was, after all, her guest, and they had not seen each other since Longbourn. Of course, this was also the woman who claimed to be a relative when no connection between them was apparent, and who surely must know of Mr. Withrow's friend, the thief.

These thoughts made her wary, so Mary stepped towards the room quietly, hoping to hear what they spoke of. But before she could hear anything of their conversation, Lady Trafford said loudly, "Miss Bennet, please come in."

Apparently she had been louder than she thought.

As she stepped inside, Lady Trafford passed Mr. Withrow a paper which quickly disappeared into his jacket.

"Miss Bennet! What a pleasure to have you join us here at Castle Durrington."

"I am glad to be here and grateful for this opportunity." She tried to remember the words of her speech, but Lady Trafford gestured for her to be seated.

"And how was your trip? Not eventful, I hope."

"Nothing unusual occurred. How was your trip to Brighton?"

"Very brief, but necessary."

"Mr. Withrow said you were there for some charity work?"

"Yes, I am on the board of Brighton's Society for Literacy and Improvement of the Poor. There was an incident with one of the teachers we hired, and so I thought it best for me to resolve the problem myself."

The answer was satisfactory, though still a little vague. But Mary supposed it was better for Lady Trafford to not disclose the particular details about the incident, in order to protect those involved.

"I wish I had been able to go with you to Brighton. My friend from Hertfordshire, Mrs. Blankenbeckler, lives there now."

"I do not visit Brighton very often," said Lady Trafford, "but if I visit again, I will make sure to bring you with me."

They engaged in polite, trivial conversation—or at least, Mary and Lady Trafford did. Mr. Withrow looked on, not saying anything unless prompted by his aunt. There was nothing strange or unusual in the conversation, unlike the night that they had met. Everything was exactly what you would expect from a woman of Lady Trafford's position. Mary kept wanting to bring up the issue of the family Bible, but she needed to do so delicately. She did not want to be accusatory, for she had only arrived and would rather not endanger her stay.

"How were your lessons?" asked Lady Trafford.

It was only the first day, Mary reminded herself, thinking of Fanny's words. And she did not want to appear ungrateful. "They were not quite what I expected. But I really enjoyed the drawing."

"I agree that French is challenging," said Lady Trafford. "But I suspect you will find the effort worth it, in the end."

Mary had said nothing about French, and so wondered at Lady Trafford's rather accurate surmise.

Mary summoned up her courage, and said, in as polite a tone as she could, "I brought a detailed family chart of names with me. I know you said that we are related, and I was hoping to discover our connection, and so I—"

"That is quite a natural desire," said Lady Trafford, cutting her off and thus preventing her from mentioning the Bible. "I believe one of your great uncles or aunts married one of my cousins. I have my own chart which contains all of the details. I need to find it, and once I do, we can compare."

Mary supposed the records in the Bible could be incomplete, but before she could reflect on it, Lady Trafford moved to a new topic of conversation.

"Mrs. Boughton said you did not finish your tour of the house."

"I had seen sufficient."

"Oh, it is much better to be thorough. Come, take a stroll with me on the back lawn."

"But it is cold." It was only September, and yet already the temperature was dropping.

"I presume you have a shawl. And if not, I insist that you borrow one of mine." She did not wait to see if Mary agreed, instead turning to her nephew. "Will you be joining us, Henry?"

"Unfortunately, I have matters of the estate to attend to," said Mr. Withrow, all courteousness. "But perhaps we can take a walk together later."

Lady Trafford rang a bell and called in Fanny, who carried Mary's drawing supplies up to her room and returned with her black shawl.

From what Mary had observed, there were two ways to exit the house to the back lawns—from the parlor downstairs, and from this parlor, on the first floor. They exited and found themselves on a large terrace. Lady Trafford led the way down the grand marble steps. Mary followed her closely, keeping her eyes fixed on the older woman in case she started to fall, but Lady Trafford's steps were deliberate, and she had no trouble. She guessed that Lady Trafford was about the age of her mother—maybe a few years older—but more physically able. When they reached the bottom of the staircase, they walked out onto the lawn, which was rather plain with an undeveloped landscape.

"Do you often take unexpected trips?" asked Mary.

"From time to time. I like to keep myself busy and involved in many worthwhile endeavors, which means there are always many places to go and things to do. When possible, I travel farther afield. There are always so many new experiences, so many possibilities that the world has to offer."

Mary had never had a desire to see the world. She had always been able to experience plenty of the world through books. And people were more understandable in books than in life.

Lady Trafford turned back to face the house, but Mary continued to look out across the lawn. It was difficult to tell if she saw the sea or only storm clouds. She would need to attempt a drawing from this angle; it was a worthy view.

"Why did my lessons start so quickly?"

"Would you rather wait a week or two? I thought it best to begin immediately, for both myself and Mr. Withrow can be rather dull company. Besides, there is always so much to learn." Lady Trafford gave her a sharp look. "Really, Miss Bennet, you should turn around and look back at the house."

Mary did so and could not stop a gasp. If she had not known better, she would have thought she had been instantly transported to another house somewhere else in the countryside, for the back of the house did not look anything like a castle. Gone were the turrets and towers she had seen on the front of Castle Durrington. There was no grey stone, nothing at all castle-like. Rather, she felt like she had stepped into an Italian painting. The house was grand, with yellow facing and beautiful, tall white pillars.

"I had asked Mrs. Boughton not to tell you in advance about the two styles of architecture of the estate. I much prefer if guests experience it for themselves."

"I did not expect…" said Mary, but she found herself at a loss for words.

"My husband and I conceived of it together. He did not live to see it finished. It has taken twenty-three years, and there are still some improvements I would like to make."

"What happened to your husband?" asked Mary. "And to your children?"

"You will find that it is not always best to ask extremely personal questions of new acquaintances," said Lady Trafford. Despite giving correction, she did not look angry or ruffled. Instead she continued as if Mary had never asked. "I have always enjoyed architecture that combines very different styles in new and intriguing ways. To me, it is true to my experience of life, of people.

"I think sometimes we look at a person and we assume we know everything about them. We think we know all of their sides. Yet often there is more to a person than meets the eye. There is a side we have not seen, and until we see it, we cannot know them.

"The real reason I have brought you here, Miss Bennet, is I think there is more to you than meets the eye. I think people underestimate you, and so they do not see you fully. But I have confidence that you will surpass everyone's expectations."

No one had ever spoken like this to Mary before, and the words made her feel warm and hopeful inside. Whether or not they shared a familial connection, Lady Trafford had seen something in her, something of worth.

But it also made Mary wonder. Yes, Lady Trafford had been speaking of Castle Durrington and of Mary, but surely it must apply to the lady herself. What was hidden beneath the surface of Lady Trafford? If there was more to her, Mary was determined to find out.

Chapter Eight

"May the Cydads glide smooth, and the party be free
From that cursed of maladies, sickness at sea."
　　　　　–The Sussex Weekly Advertiser, Lewes, England,
　　　　　　　　　　　　　　　　September 13, 1813

L
ADY TRAFFORD UNFOLDED a large piece of paper and laid
it on the table in the parlor, nearly covering the entire
surface. Her finger trailed along the fibers of the paper until it
came to rest upon her own name.

"Here is where I am located on the chart. And this is my
dearly departed husband." Her finger traced upwards to his
parents, and then down to a woman's name, "Susan Trafford."

"My husband's sister married a Mr. Charles Withrow.
You, of course, know their third child, Henry Withrow, who
will inherit Castle Durrington and the estate."

Mary nodded, eager to move past these basic facts and see
how she and Lady Trafford were related. After all, it had been
four days since Lady Trafford had promised to show her their
familial connection, and Mary found herself growing impatient. Despite her lessons and meeting some of Lady
Trafford's friends, Mary would feel more firm in her position
at Castle Durrington if there was a substantial connection
between them.

Lady Trafford moved back to her own name. She traced up to her great-grandparents and then down to a second cousin once removed. She tapped on his name. "I believe this is where the connection occurs. Let us see your chart."

Mary spread out the pages of her own family chart. They went through Mary's records and discovered that Mary's cousin's aunt—who was an aunt by marriage and shared no blood with Mary—had married the man that Lady Trafford had pointed out on the chart.

Mary had been wrong. She had examined these relationships—and even remembered looking at this aunt's name—the other night in the library. Yet in the family Bible, she had not seen her aunt's name, and truly could not remember seeing her husband's name. She must have missed his name and missed this connection even though it was really quite simple. The failure felt as strong and sudden as knocking over a shelf full of books.

They *were* related, tangentially. But it was clear that Mary did not have a strong claim on Lady Trafford as a relation and that Lady Trafford taking her in and providing her with lessons was truly an act of benevolence—and a supposed act of gratitude for preventing the thief from interfering with her cases. Mary must have made their day much more difficult by recognizing him, forcing Withrow to pretend to chase him.

"May I copy some of this information, for our family records?"

"Of course," said Lady Trafford.

Mary fastidiously wrote out name after name, date after date. As she did so, Lady Trafford read newspaper after newspaper. Several seemed to be local, regional papers, like the *Kentish Gazette*, while others were from London—*The Times*, *The Courier*. There even appeared to be one from

Scotland and another from Ireland.

She took a minute to consider the names closest to Lady Trafford's. Her husband, Sir George Trafford, had died in 1805. Her daughter, Anne, in 1808, at only fourteen years old. And her son, James, in 1810, at the age of twenty. Mary twisted the mourning ring on her finger. Death could come to anyone, at any time, without warning. She was struck by a sudden sadness. She blinked quickly to keep her eyes clear and dutifully copied down the names and dates for Anne, James, and Sir George. That was a large amount of personal loss for Lady Trafford to suffer in a period of only five years. But why would both Madame Dieupart *and* Lady Trafford refuse to give any details? Was there something unusual or strange about their deaths?

Speculations besieged her mind as she continued her work. Finally Mary finished—not the whole chart, for there was no reason to copy *all* of the information—but enough that she had the relevant details.

Armed with this new knowledge, Mary decided to return to the library. Lady Trafford was engrossed in a newspaper, so Mary did not interrupt her reading as she left. She wanted to find these names in the Bible so she could see how she had missed them before.

She went down the grand staircase, pausing briefly to look at the dome above her head. It was a cloudy day so only a dull light shone through it. She continued down, crossed the round entry room, and entered the library, her new chart with supplemental information in hand.

Only a few steps into the library she heard her name. "Miss Bennet!" It was Lady Trafford; she must have followed her out of the room and down the stairs. "You must be looking for a book. Has anyone explained the library to you?"

"I gave myself a tour the first evening," Mary admitted. "I managed to find the section of religious books, but I cannot make sense of the library as a whole." She was about to say that she had also found the rare books and examined the family Bible, but something made her hold back. It was embarrassment, perhaps—if she was going to talk about the family Bible, she should have done it hours ago, when Lady Trafford first showed her the chart. And she did not want to admit her failure at finding their connection on her own.

Lady Trafford gave her a thorough tour of the library. There were twelve different sections—twelve! how could one possibly have twelve categories of books?—and within each section the books were organized chronologically by publication date.

As they passed by the rare book section, which was the only section organized visually, rather than chronologically, Mary glanced at the family Bible, but, as Lady Trafford was watching her, she did not allow her eyes to linger on it. Yet she was certain that something about it had looked a little different, as if it had a slightly different shade of binding. Mary pressed her top teeth to her bottom lip as she tried to remember the exact details of the Bible from her first time in the library.

"You seem deep in thought," observed Lady Trafford. "What troubles you?"

Mary stepped away from the rare bookshelf. If something was different about the book, she needed to figure out what it was before she asked about it. And she needed to do so privately. If possible, she preferred figuring out things without the watchful eye of others. She gestured around the library with a bit of a sour taste in her mouth for not truly answering the question asked of her, and said, "Why organize the books by the publication date?"

"Knowledge is something that builds, something that is growing and evolving. Every new text is written in reference to other texts, whether intentionally or not, and so a chronological organization allows one to see *where* something occurs within a conversation."

Already, Mary could not remember all twelve categories.

Lady Trafford seemed to guess her struggle to understand the library and showed her the catalogue, a massive handwritten tome with many extra pages to accommodate the purchase of more texts. The beginning of the catalogue was organized by section and had each of the library's books listed within its section; the middle of the catalogue had an alphabetical list by author and a chronological list of all the books; the end of the catalogue contained each book title by purchase date, with a list of relevant details, people, and events contained within. All of the sections in the catalogue cross referenced each other.

"Has Mr. Linton assigned you Alberti's *On Painting*?"

Mary shook her head.

"He asked me to purchase it for my daughter, Anne. I am certain he would like you to read it as well."

"But I am not learning how to paint."

"It has a great deal on other topics that will be relevant to you—perspective, the history of art, and ways of thinking about art."

Lady Trafford showed her how to find the book within the catalogue and its corresponding spot on the shelves. She gave *On Painting* to Mary.

"Thank you. I appreciate the recommendation and am certain it will give Mr. Linton and me more things to discuss."

Lady Trafford smiled. "Now I do believe I should find

something for *me* to read."

Mary excused herself and put the book about painting in her room, as well as her family chart and the additional pages she had created. She would return and search for the family Bible later, once the library had been vacated. She wanted to rest or work on her studies, but an unease, both in her stomach and her head, prevented either. Was it wise to stay in a castle with two individuals who knowingly associated with a thief? And why was she so hesitant to accuse them?

Perhaps she simply needed fresh air to clear her head, so she left the castle through the front doors. She would use the time to learn about the rest of the estate.

She vaguely knew that east of Castle Durrington were cottages for the estate workers and other buildings, but she wanted to see for herself. She walked east on the main road that passed in front of the castle on the north. She passed a patch of forest, and then she saw the cottages, but there were not just cottages—there was a granary, a sawmill, a brickyard, and another stable, this one for the work horses. This explained why Castle Durrington was much larger and grander than Longbourn; the estate and holdings were much more expansive.

Once she reached the end of these buildings, she considered where on the estate she would visit next. Quite a ways southeast was a barn, but she had seen barns before. From here she could also see all the land south of the castle. The castle was more elevated than the land south of it, which explained why, though several miles away from it, you could see the beach. The area south of the castle had a long, sloping plain, but the plain was interrupted by a rounded circle of forest—which looked intentional enough that it might be a Roundel—as well as an orchard and a strange walled structure.

Mary walked across the plain, down mild slopes and around occasional rocks and oak trees until she reached the walled structure. It was made of red brick with regular pilasters breaking up its flat surface and was a little over two times her height. She walked slowly around the perimeter of the space, dodging the occasional shrub and counting her paces. It was rectangular, and a huge area—approximately 300 feet on the long side and 180 on the short side.

On the north side, facing Castle Durrington, were several flues, as well as several other structures jutting out whose entrance must be on the inside. There had been a door on the south side, facing the orchard and far beyond it, the beach. There was also a door on the north side. She leaned with her ear against it. She could hear noises—unknown things hitting other things, grunts and moans, some talk and even some laughter. She wondered what could possibly be the source of all that, and why it was on Lady Trafford's land—for she must still be on Lady Trafford's land. It was such a strange walled space, and she suspected that if she had paid more attention, she would have been able to see it from the house. Even stranger was the fact that no one had mentioned this wall or what was housed within.

She pulled her ear from the door and, wondering if it was unlocked, put her fingers on the handle.

"Miss Bennet!"

Mary cried out in alarm. Her shoulders bunched up, involuntarily, towards her ears.

She whipped around towards the sound of the deep, sharp voice.

It was only Mr. Withrow. She breathed in and out slowly, attempting to calm herself. "You startled me," she managed to say, with a bit less dignity than she intended.

"I can see that." Mr. Withrow chuckled.

"Are you laughing at me?"

His emotion slid from his face like water off a roof. "I would not attempt to laugh at someone as serious as you, Miss Bennet." He scratched his ear. "What are you doing next to the garden?"

"This is a garden?"

"Yes. What did you think it was?"

"That was what I was attempting to ascertain when you came upon me without any warning."

"Do you make it a habit of prying about other people's property?"

"I thought I was a guest here," said Mary. "I have done no wrong. And I believe it is quite appropriate to familiarize oneself with one's surroundings. As long as curiosity is kept within certain bounds, it can be quite a productive character trait."

Withrow shrugged noncommittally. "If you will excuse me, I need to open this door."

Mary felt anger rise within herself, but she could not pinpoint why or justify the emotion, so she stepped aside.

He pushed open the door and stepped inside a space brimming with green. The smell reminded Mary of home, of Longbourn and the fields behind the house. Withrow turned back to her. "I am going to check with the workers on their progress. If it would please you, you are welcome to join me."

"I would like that," said Mary as she followed him inside.

Withrow walked quickly through the space, pausing only when he saw one of the workers. He would stop for a moment, check if they needed anything, and ask about their progress. He would often give them a few words of encouragement. They appeared to be collecting some of the final harvest of the crops—beans and onions and tomatoes.

Withrow did not speak to Mary, which she found preferable. It let her lag a little behind and experience the garden at her own pace. As a young child she had spent some time in her father's fields, but as she had grown older she had stopped, though she could not remember why. This area seemed about half the size of her father's—no, no longer her father's—Mr. Collins's crops at Longbourn.

"Would you like a tomato, Miss?" asked one of the women, holding out a small, yellow tomato in her hand. Mary was still feeling a bit jumpy, so she had to bite back her surprise.

"I think I will be fine," Mary began to say, but then she saw Withrow shaking his head with his lips pinched together. "Actually, I *would* like it, thank you."

She knew that tomatoes were not poisonous, as had long been believed, so she took the tomato and, as the woman watched her, rubbed off a bit of dirt with her finger and put it into her mouth. She had never particularly liked the texture of tomato seeds, but she chewed and swallowed, as that was clearly expected of her. "Thank you."

Withrow gestured for her to join him and led her around the rest of the garden. "Why is this space walled?" Mary asked him. "Will that not prevent the plants on the outer perimeter from receiving as much sunlight?"

"Unfortunately, this is the only area of the estate with the ideal soil and light for crops. In the first few years there were incidents of animals and vagrants getting into the crops. Because this area is so far from everything else, the most practical solution was to build a wall."

"Why not build the workers' dwellings next to here?"

Withrow answered with not a little impatience, "First,

many of their cottages were built *before* planting the gardens. Second, it is easier for the workers to live near the road. And third, we have no desire to disrupt the entire view of the ocean from the castle. Even this mars the view a little, though there was no helping it."

They left the garden from the south door, emerging into the apple orchard.

Withrow examined his pocket watch. "Have you been to the beach?"

"No," she said. "Not once in my entire life."

"You have been here for five days and you have not visited the water?"

"I have had no opportunity or reason for doing so."

"I had planned a short visit, and you may accompany me." He began walking south, through the trees.

"I do not know that I want to visit the ocean—it is a long way away!"

"It is only a mile, Miss Bennet, and you have no choice in the matter," he said without turning around.

She was not sure what he meant by that. But, after he had walked a few steps, she decided to follow him. It might provide her with more insight into his character and motives.

The walk to the beach, in Mary's estimate, was actually *longer* than a mile. As they approached, she saw the tiny village of Goring-by-Sea—a cluster of houses, really—off their path, further east. The smell of the sea gradually increased, plants and fish and salt all mixed together. Gulls squawked to each other, and several flew overhead. The closer they came to the ocean, the larger it looked. Water extended in all directions, farther than the eye could see, a rolling, shifting, unstable backdrop. Its immensity made her feel very small and insignificant. It could carry her away in a moment and no one would notice.

She peered out across the water. If her understanding of geography was correct, this was not actually the full ocean, but rather the English Channel. "Can you see France from here?"

"If it is a clear day, you can see it from the cliffs at Dover. But not here. Yet even though it is never visible, France is only a few miles away." Withrow continued his walk forward and she followed him.

There was not an exact moment when the grass shifted to sand and pebbles, but as the sand overtook the grass, Withrow stopped. He crouched down, untied his shoelaces, and removed his shoes and socks.

"What are you doing?" asked Mary, feeling rather scandalized. She had never seen a gentleman with bare feet before—not even her father.

"I have no desire for my shoes to fill with sand. You could remove yours as well."

She looked away so she did not see his feet. "I will be fine as I am."

"Suit yourself," he said, and he walked down into the sand, not bothering to see if she followed.

He turned and walked parallel to the water. By the time Mary caught up with him, her shoes were indeed filled with sand. Grains of sand had somehow crept within her stockings and ground between her toes. With every step her feet sank into the sand, and with every step she had to fight against the sand to pull them free again. Withrow, with his bare feet, did not seem to have the same difficulty, though she could not tell whether it was due to the lack of shoes or to the fact that he walked on damp sand, lapped at by the waves.

She looked at Mr. Withrow's profile against the backdrop

of the ocean. His face seemed less guarded than she had ever seen it. They walked in silence for a few minutes before Withrow spoke.

"I would always come here, as a child. Sometimes I would visit for a few months, other times for a year. Whenever the opportunity arose—or whenever we ran away from tutors— my cousins and I would come down to the beach and play in the water."

He rolled up the fabric of his trousers, exposing the bottom portion of his legs. Mary felt that if he had not before, now he had certainly overstepped the bounds of propriety. It struck her that they were unchaperoned and that she did not, in fact, know Mr. Withrow very well.

He stepped out into the water.

It was not very deep—the water only came to his ankles. But then he stepped out farther.

A sudden gust of wind bit through Mary's clothes. The day went from feeling mild for September to very cold. The wind seemed stronger here than at the house. She walked away from the ocean and sat on a grassy patch. She watched as Withrow stood in the water. He always seemed to be in motion, even when seated at a desk, and yet now he embodied stillness. Mary did not know what to make of it, could not imagine how something as tempestuous as the ocean could calm him so.

A wave approached, much larger than the others. It rushed towards the shore, yet Withrow did not move. Maybe his eyes were closed; maybe he did not see it.

"Mr. Withrow!" she cried out in alarm.

The wave hit him, and she closed her eyes. When she opened them, he was still standing. She breathed a sigh of relief.

He turned around. His trouser legs were wet a little above the knees, but besides that he seemed unharmed. "Whatever is wrong now, Miss Bennet?"

"That was a huge wave! I thought it would carry you away, and I did not know what I would do."

He laughed again, and this time he did not stop when she glared at him.

"Do you know anything, Miss Bennet?"

Her cheeks flushed in anger and she felt her jaw drop. She began preparing a rebuttal, but she was never as good at a quick response as her sister Elizabeth and before she could speak, he spoke again.

"That was a little wave and could do no harm to anyone." His voice was less sharp, but she still took offense.

"So the ocean is not a thing to be afraid of?"

"Not today. It can be frightening. It can be dangerous. You have lived a very protected life, Miss Bennet, but everything and *everyone* can be dangerous, given the correct circumstances. You would do well to remember that."

Mary swallowed. The way he said *everyone* made her think that he meant even himself. Yet he did not know that she had seen him with the thief, so why would he want her to fear him?

"Do you know how to swim, Miss Bennet?"

"No."

"Then you would do well to take especial care and not go into the ocean alone. Even a strong swimmer can be carried away by a powerful current." He gave her a disdainful look and then stepped out of the water and headed back towards his shoes.

Mary stood quickly and brushed the sand off her dress. She turned away from the ocean, but then looked back.

Withrow thought she was a fool; he thought she was fearful. Neither was true: she simply lacked knowledge in certain areas, and maybe she was a little fearful, but she could overcome her fears.

She walked slowly up to the ocean, contemplating the pattern of how the water moved up and down, then leaned down and dipped in her hand. It was bitingly cold, yet pleasant somehow, and she liked the movement and the energy of the water around her fingers.

After standing, she wiped her hand on her dress. Withrow was still walking towards his shoes. She did not think Withrow had seen her touch the water, but she had not done it for him. She had done it for herself.

She managed to catch up to him as he finished putting on his shoes. He had been more relaxed at the water, and they had spoken more to each other than they normally did, so she thought she might ask him about Lady Trafford's chart and tell him about how she had looked in the family Bible and initially thought they were not related. She wanted to observe and analyze his response.

"Mr. Withrow—"

"I apologize, Miss Bennet, but I have no more time for conversation or amusement. I have lost too much already. If you will excuse me, I must be going. Can you find your way back to the castle by yourself?"

"Of course," said Mary. He inclined his head towards her and then set off at a jog.

Mary watched him go but did not immediately follow. Madame Dieupart had sent word that she was ill, so Mary had no lessons today, and no reason to rush back to the castle.

Mr. Withrow ran quite quickly. He was one of the most unusual people she had met: cordial and almost charming one minute, and then harsh and abrupt the next. She still could not make out his character.

Rather than return to the castle, she walked farther up the beach, staying at least ten feet from the water; she had touched it once, but had no need to do so again. There were some larger rocks, boulders almost, though she had no notion of how they had gotten there. Surely the ocean was not strong enough to move a boulder! But then again, maybe it was. She needed to find a book on the subject. Past the boulder was the larger part of a tree, a downed tree, stripped of leaves and smaller branches. The bark looked as if it had all been rubbed off, and the surface felt smooth beneath her fingers. In the distance was another boulder, and beyond that, something else that she could not make out.

As she approached, she was filled with a sense of foreboding. It seemed like she should recognize the shape in front of her—it was a familiar shape—and yet her mind refused to put a name to it as she stepped closer, closer, closer.

A few feet away, she finally recognized what was before her, or at least she recognized parts of it. The back of a shirt, a man's shirt. There was no coat on top of it. She recognized breeches, men's breeches. And hair, short brown hair. But the shirt, the breeches, the hair, these were not discrete objects. They were part of something larger.

It was a body.

The water lapped at the body's feet—the man's feet. He must have been washed ashore.

She knelt in the sand. Perhaps he was still alive, perhaps he simply needed his face out of the sand so he could breathe. She tugged on his body, flipping him over, and then scrambled away.

The man was dead. His face was discoloured, a dark greenish colour. His eyes were gone, missing entirely, and his empty eye sockets seemed to stare up at the cloudy sky.

CHAPTER NINE

"On Saturday last as Mr. Snasdale, a shopkeeper of Creake, and his apprentice, son of Mr. Samuel Cocksedge, of Larling, were walking out in the afternoon, they met with a boy who was keeping off crows. Mr. S. borrowed his gun to shoot at a rabbit, and whilst in the act, his apprentice crossed at the time, and received the contents of the charge in his head. He languished but a few hours after the melancholy accident. The young man was only in the fifteenth year of his age."

—*The Sussex Weekly Advertiser*, Lewes, England,
September 13, 1813

MARY COULD NOT take her eyes off the body; it both revolted her and commanded her attention. Since she could not look away, she would at least not dwell on the empty eye sockets, or the question of what had happened to the eyes. She focused instead on the mustache and the short beard, and then on the clothes, which led to the realization that she recognized the man.

It was the thief.

The dead man was the thief who had stolen her family's mourning rings, who she had seen with Lady Trafford's carriage in Meryton, and who had met with Withrow in the forest on her very first day at Castle Durrington. She had seen him, alive, a few days before, and now he was dead.

A morbid sense of curiosity overcame her. She approached the body again. Yes, his mustache and his beard were exactly the same as they had been when she had seen him last, and despite the discolouration of the skin and a certain puffy appearance, perhaps due to the time in the water, his facial structure was the same. His clothes were the ones he had worn that day in the forest with Withrow. He might have even died that very day.

A possibility struck her: could Mr. Withrow have killed the thief? She shook her head. Of course he would not kill someone. He was a gentleman. But even though he and the thief had parted with an embrace, Withrow had seemed severe, angry even, for a portion of the conversation. Perhaps they had met again, and things had escalated between them.

Part of the thief's shirt was ripped—no, it had been cut. It was a long, straight cut, and beneath, the skin appeared as if it had also been cut open, though the time in the water had clearly caused further damage: at the top of the wound, the flesh was peeled back, and lower down, pieces of skin and muscle were missing.

He had been stabbed.

Someone had stabbed the thief with a knife in the side. She considered possible sequences of events and concluded that he must have been stabbed before his body entered the ocean.

Her stomach felt a touch indisposed, but surprisingly, Mary did not feel a sense of panic. She rubbed her hands on her skirt and stood tall. She could not stand here next to the body all day, hoping that someone would come along and solve this problem for her.

Two possibilities presented themselves before her: she

could return to the castle and alert Mr. Withrow, Lady Trafford, and the servants; or instead of taking the path back to the castle, she could walk a little to the east of it, to Goring-by-Sea. With the length of time she had spent walking, she suspected it was several miles back to Castle Durrington, so she headed towards Goring.

After a few minutes, she reached the handful of houses, which were set a little farther back from the shore. Mary rapped her hand on one of the doors. No one opened it, so she tried the next house. Once again, there was no one there. These were working-class people, and they must be at work. She tried the third house, and finally someone answered, a woman with her baby.

Mary told the woman of the dead body, and the woman sighed, as if this was yet another annoyance in her day. The woman yelled into the house for her daughter. A nine- or ten-year-old girl with carefully plaited hair appeared and was sent off to Worthing to find help. Meanwhile, the woman made Mary a cup of tea.

"I don't 'ave a place for a lady like yourself to sit," explained the woman, and so they stood, outside, drinking from clean but chipped cups. Mary watched with fascination as the woman cooed and talked to her baby, and then sat on the steps and fed the child at her breast. People of Mary's station did not raise their own children until they were two or three years old; Mary had spent the first several years of her life in Meryton, cared for by a woman such as this, and visited regularly by her parents. Mary twisted the mourning ring on her finger, struck by a longing for her family and the weight of her loss.

After a second cup of tea, Mary wished she had gone all the way to Worthing herself, rather than letting the woman send her daughter.

The woman attempted to offer Mary a third cup of tea, but her voice was muted by the sound of horses: six horses carrying six men, five of them in military uniform. Not far behind them followed another man, driving a wagon.

The men dismounted and approached. One of the officers, a kindly looking man with curly grey hair, bowed.

There was no way to avoid it; Mary would yet again need to meet someone without a formal introduction. She curtsied and said, "I am Miss Mary Bennet. I am a guest of Lady Trafford's, staying at Castle Durrington."

"I am Colonel Coates, the head of the regiment here in Worthing, and I am at your service." He paused, and then addressed the subject as if it were a delicate matter. "I greatly apologize that you were the one to discover the…" He trailed off, as if afraid to use the word.

"The corpse?" asked Mary.

"Yes, the corpse," he said gravely.

"It is probably best if I show you where I found it." It was, after all, why they had come, and there was little point to excessive pleasantries over such an unpleasant matter.

"Oh, no, I cannot allow you to go to such trouble," said Colonel Coates. "If you simply describe the location, we will be able to find it."

"It will be easier to show you." Mary knew perfectly well that they would be able to find it on their own, but it was the body *she* had found, and even though the man was a thief, she now felt a certain responsibility for him.

"If it really was a murder," said Colonel Coates, "there is no reason to subject yourself to such an ordeal."

"Miss Bennet seems as if she is spirited," said the man not in uniform, an older gentleman with thinning hair and a

French accent. "Come, Colonel Coates, let her lead us. I am sure you will have more questions for her."

"Very well," said the colonel.

Mary led the way. Colonel Coates walked by her side, the Frenchman close behind, and the others farther back, leading the horses and wagon.

"Were you alone when you found the body?" asked Colonel Coates.

"Yes."

"Did you come to the beach by yourself?" He seemed surprised.

"No," said Mary. "Mr. Withrow was showing me the beach." Her face reddened at the tacit admission that a chaperone had not accompanied them. "He returned to Castle Durrington, and I walked a little more on my own."

"Has word been sent back to Castle Durrington?"

She shook her head.

"Then I will see that it is done." He sent one of the other officers to Castle Durrington to speak with Lady Trafford and Mr. Withrow.

"On the matter of the body," Mary said slowly, unsure of the best way to raise her suspicions, "I believe I recognize the man. I do not know his name, but I saw him speaking to Mr. Withrow on the day I arrived here."

"What day would that have been?" asked the Frenchman, catching up with them.

"The eighth of September," said Mary. "It was my first day here, so I remember it distinctly."

"That is extremely useful," said Colonel Coates. "With Mr. Withrow's help, we may be able to identify the victim."

As they approached, part of her wondered if she had only imagined the corpse. But Mary did not suffer from an overactive imagination, and the body was indeed on the sand where she had left it, the ocean still lapping at its feet. The men immediately blocked her view of the body and engaged in whispered discussions, probably so as not to offend her feminine sensibilities.

After a few minutes, the Frenchman came to her side.

"I am afraid we have not been properly introduced. I am Monsieur Corneau, formerly of a small village north of Paris. I am now a resident of Worthing, and a good friend of Colonel Coates."

"*Je suis enchantée de faire votre connaissance,*" said Mary, taking advantage of the opportunity to converse with a native French speaker. Madame Dieupart would be pleased.

"Ah, *vous parlez français?*"

She understood his question, but when she tried to think of the words to reply, they escaped her. "I only speak a little, I am afraid. But I am learning."

"That is commendable."

The Frenchman pursed his lips and studied her. He had deep wrinkles on his forehead and around his mouth—friendly wrinkles—and she wondered at his age. After a moment, he spoke. "You seem the sort of woman who would like to know more about what happened to the man who died."

She nodded, surprised. "Yes, I would."

"We believe he was stabbed, but that did not kill him. Ultimately, he drowned. When a person drowns, their lungs fill with water and they sink, but sometimes, after a while, the body floats back to the surface. It likely washed ashore last night, and today you found it."

"I see," said Mary. "Thank you." She appreciated that he did not attempt to shelter her, and that he treated her with respect. Maybe he treated her differently than other men did because he was French. But despite his explanation, something else still bothered her. "What happened to his eyes?"

Monsieur Corneau hesitated, but after a moment, he said, "They were eaten, by a fish or other animal of the sea."

Bile filled Mary's throat. She had always believed that knowledge was superior to ignorance, yet in this case, ignorance might be preferred. She pushed that thought aside: surely it was better to know than to always wonder. Yet what must Monsieur Corneau and Colonel Coates think of her? She had not behaved at all like a young lady was meant to behave. She probably should have screamed and fainted, required much consoling, and allowed someone to carry her to a sofa.

"Is there anything else you know about the dead man, anything at all? Any details that might help us?"

She hesitated, for answering his question properly required making an accusation of sorts, not only against the thief, but against her hosts. But he was working with Colonel Coates on the investigation, and a serious, irreversible crime had been committed; she needed to disclose what she knew.

"There is one thing that I should tell you." Mary explained how the man had visited Meryton and attempted to steal her family's mourning rings. She decided not to mention that it was possibly on Lady Trafford's or Mr. Withrow's orders, as she had no evidence for that claim.

"That is very serious indeed," said Monsieur Corneau. "I will make sure Colonel Coates knows of it."

It was not long before Mr. Withrow arrived at the scene on horseback. He dismounted, rushed over to Colonel Coates, and after a few brief words was permitted to see the body.

After a minute or so, he stepped away from the body, clearly distraught. His jaw was visibly clenched, and he ran his fingers through his hair, tugging on it.

Monsieur Corneau approached Colonel Coates, and they had a brief, whispered conversation, after which Colonel Coates addressed Mr. Withrow.

"We are hoping that you might help us identify the body. Miss Bennet said she saw you with this man on the eighth of September."

Mr. Withrow gave her a brief but calculating look, which frightened her a little. He now knew that she had followed him into the forest.

"Miss Bennet is correct," Mr. Withrow said smoothly. "This is Mr. Frederick Holloway, and I spoke with him at Castle Durrington. He is… He *was* a clergyman in Crawley."

"Thank you," said the colonel. "I will make sure word is sent."

"His parents will appreciate that," said Withrow.

"I apologize for the question in advance, but what were you speaking about with Mr. Holloway?"

"He was acting as an intermediary for me for a potential business deal with several gentlemen in Crawley. After our conversation, he was headed to Worthing on other business, I know not what. Perhaps what he did there was related to this unfortunate circumstance."

Colonel Coates nodded. "It seems quite likely that Mr. Holloway met his unfortunate end within a day or two of when you spoke with him. Do you know anyone here, or in the surrounding area, that would mean him harm?"

"He had many acquaintances in Worthing, but I am not aware of any who meant him harm." His eyes strayed to the body, and then returned to Colonel Coates. "I apologize, but

I do not think I know of anything more that will be useful to you or to the magistrate. You have sent for Sir Richard Pickering, I am sure?"

"I had meant to," said Colonel Coates. "I shall do so now. Oh—I do not have quill or paper. It shall have to wait until I return to Worthing."

Colonel Coates directed his men to prepare to move the body, and Mr. Withrow took it upon himself to make sure the job was done properly. The wagon was brought up the beach, and it seemed quite likely, with the men's handling, that Mr. Holloway would lose a limb, in addition to all he had already lost.

At one point, Monsieur Corneau took Colonel Coates aside. After a brief conversation, the Frenchman once again approached her.

"Miss Bennet, I have what may seem a peculiar request. Since Colonel Coates and this regiment arrived in Worthing six months ago, I have been assisting him in his work, particularly in keeping him informed about this community." He paused, and Mary wondered if he was attempting to be dramatic. "We would like you to observe if anything unusual might occur at Castle Durrington, whether it be the behaviour of the servants or the actions of Mr. Withrow and Lady Trafford."

"Have they done something wrong?" asked Mary.

Corneau looked meaningfully at the body, which was now mostly in the cart, and largely covered by a blanket. "I do not know if they have or have not. But in case they have, we need to know. We need you to be our spy in their midst. It is of utmost importance."

"A spy?"

Corneau nodded.

Mary looked at the body, then to Mr. Withrow. To spy on her hosts, that was a serious request indeed. She looked out to the sea, to the water that had changed everything in a moment, when it had washed the body ashore.

As a guest at Castle Durrington, she was uniquely suited to perform this task. Yet merely being in the right place was not enough to be successful in this sort of endeavor. She swallowed, attempting to rid herself of a sudden sense of inadequacy, but she could not escape the feeling. She was just Mary Bennet, an unimportant middle child in a normal family. Who was she to be a spy—who was she to do something of import? If she was honest with herself, she had achieved nothing of consequence her entire life. It was preposterous to think she could do so now. If her family were here, Kitty and Lydia would laugh at her delusions of grandeur. Elizabeth would make some clever comment but would not think her capable. Jane would say something kindly and supportive but would then attempt to dissuade her. Mrs. Bennet would express vocal disbelief, and her father… Well, if her father were alive, he would call her silly.

She opened her mouth, about to make excuses as to why she could not do what Monsieur Corneau and Colonel Coates asked of her, but then she stopped herself. Why could she not be something more than she had always been? Corneau and Coates obviously thought her capable. She pictured herself: confident, intelligent, driven to discover the truth, unravelling key clues that would lead to the apprehension of the murderer. Suddenly, she wanted to accept, wanted it more than anything.

She had left her home, she had left her family, and now she must leave behind her previous roles and become something more.

Mary looked confidently into Monsieur Corneau's eyes. "I will do it."

"Thank you, Miss Bennet." The Frenchman smiled and returned to the colonel's side.

Finally, the corpse was secure and the wagon ready.

"Come, Miss Bennet," said Mr. Withrow. "If you stay much longer in the elements, you may catch a chill. It would be best if we returned to the castle."

"Very well," said Mary, smoothing out the skirt of her black dress.

"Wait one moment," said Colonel Coates. "I need a brief word with Miss Bennet."

He led her farther down the beach, and they watched the waves. Strange, to think that a few hours ago she had stood like this with Mr. Withrow. How quickly everything could change. Once again, her thoughts went to her father, to her loss that was ever present, never ceasing.

Colonel Coates looked at Mary with kind eyes. He reminded her of her grandfather on her mother's side. "This must be such a terrible way to start your visit to Worthing," he said. "Do you still feel safe here?"

Even though she had been asked to spy on Mr. Withrow, Lady Trafford, and their servants, Mary could not bring herself to believe that anyone at Castle Durrington or in Worthing meant her harm. "I feel safe."

"I trust that Mr. Withrow and Lady Trafford will do everything they can to keep you safe and comfortable, and ensure a pleasant stay, but if at any time you feel threatened by anyone or anything, please come immediately to me, and I will help you with all the powers at my disposal."

"Thank you, Colonel. I appreciate it."

"You are a very brave young woman," he said. "Remember that."

Colonel Coates and his men went on their way to Worthing, and Mr. Withrow walked next to Mary back to the castle, holding the reins of his horse. During the long walk, Mr. Withrow said not a single word to her, not even when it started to rain. She did not know him well, but he seemed upset, and she could not help but wonder: Was Mr. Withrow upset about the death of Mr. Holloway because they had been friends, or was he upset that Mr. Holloway's body had not remained deep in the sea?

CHAPTER TEN

"WORTHING—The body of Mr. Frederick Holloway was found on the beach east of Worthing on Monday. Mr. Holloway had been stabbed with a knife and drowned. Mr. Holloway was a well-respected vicar in Crawley, where he had served for twelve years. He was thirty-six years of age, in healthy condition, and known to visit friends and acquaintances in Worthing on a regular basis. Local authorities have offered a reward of five pounds for any knowledge of Mr. Holloway's death which would lead to the apprehension of the perpetrator."

–The Kentish Gazette, Kent, Surry, and Sussex, England, September 14, 1813

"INCOMPETENCY," DECLARED SIR Richard Pickering. "Incompetency on all sides."

The magistrate from Brighton had come to assist with the investigation into Mr. Holloway's death. He was a stern man, and, based on his terse greeting and the manner of conversation, did not appear to be friends with either Lady Trafford or Mr. Withrow. Lady Trafford seemed to find him amusing, while Mr. Withrow responded to his remarks with a touch of defensiveness.

"Do not blame Colonel Coates's incompetence on me. I

did everything in my power to encourage him to leave the body where it was, and to contact you quickly."

"I am certain that you could have done more," said Sir Richard Pickering. "There were injuries to his arms, and it is impossible to tell when these injuries were sustained, whether it was before his death, or during the handling of the body."

"I did all that I could during the loading of the wagon," said Mr. Withrow. "But I had no justification for accompanying the body after that point."

Sir Richard Pickering turned to Mary. She almost shuddered, knowing that he would surely find something to criticize about her as well. She wished she could escape from the parlor, make her way up the stairs, and play the pianoforte to calm herself.

"Tell me what you noticed when you saw the body, Miss Bennet. Mr. Holloway was on his back…" He waved his hand, inviting her to elaborate.

"Actually," said Mary timidly, "when I found Mr. Holloway, he was on his front."

"Why on earth did you turn him over?" said Sir Richard Pickering. "No one teaches or possesses a bit of common sense these days."

Mary's chest rose and fell as she tried to control her breathing. His condescension was unwarranted, so she responded in a way that Elizabeth might. "Dealing with corpses is not typically considered part of a lady's education. Besides, I did not realize at first that he was dead. His face was in the sand, and I thought he needed air."

"I am quite impressed with the way you immediately acted in what must have been quite a difficult moment," said Lady Trafford. "I believe the action you took was commendable."

"Given Miss Bennet's understanding of the situation, it is justifiable," said the magistrate. "Now describe the body—it was on its front." The magistrate watched her attentively, quill ready to take shorthand as she spoke.

"The feet were closest to the sea, and the water was lapping at them. His face was completely in the sand, and his arms...were limp at his side. I do not remember anything wrong with his clothing, from the back side, though he was not wearing a jacket, and he had worn one when I saw him before. I did not notice the discolouration of his skin until after I turned him over."

"Did you see anything else nearby on the shore, anything that could have washed ashore with Mr. Holloway?"

"I walked the whole section to the east of the body and there was nothing there, except boulders and a tree. I did not walk west of the body, but I was faced that direction for several minutes, and I do not recall seeing anything at all on the sand for at least fifty or a hundred feet."

"When you turned Mr. Holloway to his back, what did you notice? Besides the discolouration, was there anything on his body? Any objects or remnants of anything or blood?"

"There was sand on his shirt and his face. I was surprised at his missing eyes. But there was no blood really, or at least I am not sure that there was blood, and the wound in his side had discolouration."

"Was there anything in his pockets?"

It was a peculiar question, but Mary tried to remember the body and its appearance. "I did not check, but his trousers lay flat. It did not appear that there was anything in his pockets."

He made another note on his paper. "You reported that you saw Mr. Holloway speaking with Mr. Withrow on the eighth."

She nodded.

"Please answer verbally, yes or no."

"Yes, I saw them speaking."

He turned to Mr. Withrow. "Where and when specifically did this conversation occur?"

"At about three in the afternoon, here on the estate." Mr. Withrow gave Mary a quick glance and then continued. "In the patch of trees in front of the castle."

"The front entrance?" asked Sir Richard Pickering.

"Yes, the north side."

"Can you confirm Miss Bennet's statement that he was wearing the same clothes that were then found on his dead body?"

"I believe so."

"Why were you meeting in the forest?" asked Mary.

"A very good question, Miss Bennet," said Sir Richard Pickering. "I myself would like to know the answer."

Sir Pickering was not as friendly as Colonel Coates or Monsieur Corneau, but the longer this conversation lasted, the more she appreciated his thoroughness and perceptiveness.

"Mr. Holloway has always been rather theatrical," said Mr. Withrow. "Though he had a comfortable living as a vicar, at several points he considered running away to perform on the stage in London. Sometimes he insisted on living life in a theatrical manner—staying at out-of-the-way inns, conversing with unsavory characters, trying out different accents and clothing. For him, life was always a bit of a game, a bit of a performance. He did not like to sit still; he would rather have a brief meeting in the forest than over a cup of tea in a comfortable room."

Withrow's description painted a very different portrait of

a man who Mary knew only as a thief and a corpse.

"What did you speak about?" asked Sir Pickering.

Despite some of the unfriendliness of demeanor between them, Mr. Withrow gave the magistrate a more detailed response than he had given Colonel Coates.

"I had interest in several potential business dealings with men in Crawley, people seeking investments to develop new technological inventions in horticulture. Since Mr. Holloway knew them well and was soon coming to Worthing, I had asked him to speak with them on my behalf. Often, in a conversation, one can gather more than a letter. He had come to Castle Durrington to tell me what he had learned. I can collect my notes on the matter if you are interested."

"That would be useful," said Sir Pickering. "Did Mr. Holloway mention what he planned to do after the conversation?"

"He said he planned to meet several people in Worthing. He seemed anxious, but when I asked who he was meeting and why, he did not say, and grew rather upset." Withrow paused, in thought. "Holloway did have a small notebook and a pencil with them. He placed them in his jacket pocket. If you find the notebook, it may give some indication of who he was meeting and why."

Withrow turned to Mary. "What were you doing in the forest, Miss Bennet, when you saw me with Mr. Holloway?"

"I was in my room, looking out the window, when I saw strange lights in the forest. I wanted to see what it was."

"I see," said Mr. Withrow. "When you saw us, why did you not call out or approach?"

"I did not want to disturb you."

Sir Richard Pickering cleared his throat, drawing their attention back to him. Mary expected him to ask if she had seen Mr. Holloway before and was prepared to disclose the full details about his theft of the mourning rings. But Sir Pickering did not. Mary was certain that Colonel Coates and Monsieur Corneau had informed Sir Richard Pickering of that key detail, so Sir Pickering must have his own reasons for not bringing it up now.

"Mr. Withrow, can you account for your whereabouts for the remainder of the day on the eighth?"

"Of course," said Mr. Withrow. "But some might construe your question as making a rather unpleasant accusation."

"I am making no accusations," said Sir Pickering. "I am certain that you would agree that it is best I be thorough as I gather information."

"Of course," said Mr. Withrow. "I apologize. I took care of other matters of business at Castle Durrington, mostly in the library. I ate dinner with Miss Bennet, chaperoned by Mrs. Boughton. Then I retired to my room. You may speak with the servants and verify my whereabouts."

Sir Pickering turned to Mary. "What about you, Miss Bennet?"

"I retired to my room and slept. Fanny woke me, then I dined with Mr. Withrow. Following dinner, I spent a significant amount of time in the library, and then I retired again to my room."

"Lady Trafford?"

"I was in Brighton, seeing to matters of various societies I am part of. I will write you a list of all of the particulars, and since you live in Brighton, it should be simple for you to verify them."

"That concludes my questions for now," said Sir Pickering. "Though please, gather your relevant papers, Mr. Withrow. Do any of you have any questions for me?"

"I do," said Mary. "Are you working with Colonel Coates and Monsieur Corneau on this investigation?"

"Yes," said Sir Pickering. "The militia is tasked with keeping the peace, and so Colonel Coates and I will pass information back and forth until this mystery is solved. Monsieur Corneau has also proven himself useful in the past."

After a few more minutes, Sir Pickering departed. Mary hoped that she too would prove herself useful. Due to Sir Pickering's visit, her lessons for the day had been cancelled, which gave her time to begin gathering information.

Once Mr. Withrow and Lady Trafford had gone upstairs, Mary entered the library. She sat for a minute in a chair, waiting to see if anyone would interrupt her again, like the previous morning, but no one did.

She went straight to the shelf with the prized books and took down the Bible. While it was similar in appearance to the family Bible, it was *not* the book she had held her first evening at the castle. It contained no family records whatsoever. She spent the next hour searching the library for the family Bible but found not a trace.

SEVERAL HOURS LATER, the Shaffer family arrived for dinner. Mrs. Boughton led them into the drawing room with the pianoforte where Lady Trafford, Mr. Withrow, and Mary were waiting.

Mary recognized Mr. Shaffer from the sermon he had given at church two days before. Lady Trafford introduced him, as well as his wife, Mrs. Shaffer, who was blind in one eye, and his daughter, Miss Shaffer, who appeared to be approximately Mary's age.

"It is so kind of you to invite us," said Mrs. Shaffer to Lady Trafford. "I hope we have not been a burden on your kitchen staff, what with the last-minute notice."

"It is no trouble at all," said Lady Trafford. "It simply occurred to me that it had been too long since our last dinner engagement, and I decided that I best act quickly upon my realization, for sometimes if I do not, my best intentions go to naught."

"That is a laudable approach," said Mr. Shaffer. "So many people have endless good intentions. I firmly believe that every single person has the potential to do and be good, but intentions *must* be put into action."

Miss Shaffer smiled at Mr. Withrow, but then she spoke to Mary. "I heard that you are at Castle Durrington in part to pursue your studies."

"Yes," said Mary.

"Please, tell me about what you are learning."

Miss Shaffer was attentive to Mary's answer, so Mary described her French and drawing lessons in detail. Everyone in Worthing seemed much more apt than those in Meryton to listen to Mary with their full attention. At one point Mary paused for breath, and Lady Trafford inserted herself into their conversation.

"It makes me very happy that you are so appreciative of your studies," said Lady Trafford, effectively ending Mary's description. Lady Trafford must not have realized that Mary had more to say. "Now tell me, Miss Shaffer, how are your own studies progressing?"

"I have not been doing as much as I ought—I spend much time assisting the less fortunate—but I have taken several more painting lessons from Mr. Linton, and I feel like my work is progressing."

"That reminds me," said Mrs. Shaffer, "you still have not shown me your newly acquired painting, Lady Trafford. I have been rather expecting an invitation to see it, and it has been a month since it arrived at Castle Durrington."

"I apologize for neglecting to show it to you," said Lady Trafford. "Come, there should be time to view it before the meal."

Lady Trafford led everyone to the hall that could be used as a ballroom. The large room, which was often left dark, was already aglow with candlelight; Lady Trafford must have predicted that they would visit the painting, or maybe it was lit anytime that guests were expected. Mary stayed near the end of the group, with Miss Shaffer. As they entered the ballroom, Miss Shaffer paused for a moment at the portrait of a man who had the same nose as Lady Trafford. Miss Shaffer spent longer gazing at the next portrait, a young lady not more than twelve or thirteen years of age, with a pleasant face and a warm smile.

Miss Shaffer turned away from the portraits and gestured that they should catch up with the others. "It is a pity you will never have the opportunity to meet Lady Trafford's children, James and Anne. They were remarkable people."

"Did you know them well?" asked Mary.

"Yes," said Miss Shaffer sadly.

After a moment of silence, Mary realized that it would be appropriate to say something kind in response. But despite the fact that she herself was in mourning, no words came to her. She turned to what her sister Jane would likely say. "It must have been very challenging, for all of their friends and family."

Miss Shaffer nodded, and they caught up with the others at a painting of a vase of flowers.

"This is a piece by Mary Moser," said Lady Trafford. "I like the contrast of the dark background, with the vase and table almost disappearing into it, and the vivid brightness of the light on the flowers."

Mrs. Shaffer leaned her head closer to the painting and then stepped back to take a fuller view of the work. "I think it is admirable when women paint," she said, "but I do not believe that they should sell their paintings. It is better for them to develop their talents to serve their family members and friends, rather than place themselves in the public eye."

"I like the painting," said Mr. Shaffer. "But, like my wife, I do believe it leaves something to be desired."

"I think it is marvelous," said Miss Shaffer. "If I could paint like that, I would try to sell my work."

"I do not doubt that you could succeed," said Lady Trafford.

Mr. and Mrs. Shaffer did not seem pleased with that prospect.

Personally, Mary liked the painting. She herself had no accomplishments that would ever place her in the public eye, but if she did, she wondered if her mother would support her, or if her father would have when he was alive.

"Have you had any news from Charles?" asked Mr. Withrow, changing the subject.

Mrs. Shaffer stiffened.

Mr. Shaffer considered his wife, then spoke. "We recently received a letter, and Charles is doing well."

"Conditions are terrible for the troops," said Mrs. Shaffer.

"At least Charles has not taken ill," said Mr. Shaffer.

"My brother is serving on the continent," Miss Shaffer whispered in Mary's ear.

"I am sorry to hear of it," said Mr. Withrow. "We all

hope something will change soon so this war can end, and the troops can return home."

For most of Mary's life, England had been at war with France. She could hardly imagine what it would be like for their countries to be at peace.

"How is Jacob?" asked Mr. Withrow.

"He is enjoying his studies," said Mr. Shaffer.

"My eldest brother is in London," whispered Miss Shaffer. Mary appreciated how Miss Shaffer provided context so she could feel part of the conversation.

Lady Trafford gestured them forward to another painting. "This painting is not new, but it has been in storage. I thought it time to display it again."

It was a rather striking historical painting depicting John the Baptist's head on a platter. Salome, who had requested his death, stood to the side, smiling. This painting had not been on display when Mrs. Boughton had given Mary a tour of the house a few days before, so Lady Trafford's decision to display it must have been recent indeed.

"It is fascinating to consider the ugly things people will do when they think it best," said Lady Trafford.

"I always find historical paintings very instructive," said Mary. "Particularly those that take, as their focus, religious themes."

Mrs. Shaffer once again stepped closer to the work. "It is well painted," she said decisively.

"I was horrified when I heard of Mr. Holloway's gruesome death," said Lady Trafford.

Mary did not see the connection between Mr. Holloway and their current conversation. Mr. Withrow took one small step back, and all of the Shaffers' faces looked as if they had just come across an unpleasant smell.

"Did you know that Sir Pickering and Colonel Coates think that Mr. Holloway may have been murdered on the eighth?" asked Lady Trafford.

"I had not heard the date," said Mrs. Shaffer.

"Mr. Withrow met with him that very afternoon, here, on our property. Mr. Holloway told him he was headed to Worthing, but no one ever saw him again."

"The eighth?" said Miss Shaffer. "That was the evening Mr. Holloway was supposed to dine with us. He never came."

"Are you sure it was the eighth?" Mrs. Shaffer considered for a moment. "Yes, you are correct, it was the eighth. To think that he might have been murdered while we were halfway through our second course."

Miss Shaffer put her hand on her father's arm. "Father, are you unwell?"

Mr. Shaffer did appear rather pale. "I am fine," he said briskly. "Quite fine."

"Please, take a seat," said Lady Trafford, gesturing to a chair. "I will send for something for you to drink."

"It is unnecessary," said Mr. Shaffer. He turned away from the painting of John's head, but then turned back. "Mr. Holloway and I did not part on the best of terms the last time we saw each other, about a month ago. I had hoped to be able to reconcile with him, but now I will not have that opportunity."

Mary did not think Mr. Shaffer would openly acknowledge a rift between him and Mr. Holloway if he had been involved in the death, but their relationship was worth noting.

"I am so sorry," said Lady Trafford. "There are many things I wish I had said to Anne before she was taken from us so suddenly."

Suddenly, Mary was brought back to her own father's final moments, to the things he had not said, and to the things, in the months and years prior, that she had never said. She was not good at expressing her emotions, and never felt as close to others as they seemed to feel to each other.

"We cannot dwell on regret," said Mr. Shaffer. "We must learn to forgive not only others, but also ourselves."

The conversation moved on to more pleasant topics, and remained that way, all through dinner. After dinner they returned to the drawing room, and Mary sat in a comfortable chair with a book. As Mr. and Mrs. Shaffer spoke animatedly with Lady Trafford next to the fire, Mary overheard Miss Shaffer and Mr. Withrow speaking, almost in a whisper.

"It must have been terrible for you to see Mr. Holloway's body in such a state," said Miss Shaffer.

"I was rather shocked," Withrow admitted. "I had very much come to rely on him. Now, I feel as if I must share the blame for his death." Mary wondered if he, perhaps, had been involved—after the meeting with Holloway, instead of taking care of matters of the estate, he could have gone to Worthing. Yet surely he would not confess such a thing to Miss Shaffer. Mr. Withrow continued, "He would not have been in Worthing if it were not for his meeting with me."

"You cannot blame yourself," said Miss Shaffer. "That is what I keep telling my father. He has kept pacing, back and forth, back and forth in his study, ever since he heard the news yesterday."

Miss Shaffer glanced in Mary's direction, and Mary pretended to be reading her book. Miss Shaffer and Mr. Withrow did not discuss Mr. Holloway again, but Mary had already gathered plenty from this evening's conversations that she could report to Monsieur Corneau.

CHAPTER ELEVEN

"On Saturday, J.F. Spur…underwent a final examination, charged on suspicion of stealing a Bank of England note, for ten pounds, from the General-post Receiving-house….[A] number of letters that had been put into Mr. Miles's receiving house, in Oxford-street, particularly…letters with which the postage had been paid, and which contained bank-notes or bills, had not reached the persons to whom they were directed."

–*The Kentish Gazette*, Kent, Surry, and Sussex,
England, October 22, 1813

Dear Jane,

Thank you for your letter. I am sorry to hear that you are feeling ill. I can only recommend good books as an antidote to your struggles. While they may not resolve physical ailments, they do enrich and uplift the mind, helping people to feel less burdened.

Thank you for informing me that you and Elizabeth have declared an end to the formal mourning period. However, I still feel it important for me, at least, to continue to wear black and not engage in any frivolous behaviour.

I am much recovered from the incident of finding the deceased clergyman on the beach. Do not worry about me on that account. They have yet to find the responsible party.

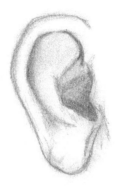

This is Lady Trafford's ear. Can you not see the progress from my letter a few weeks ago? I have drawn features of every single servant in the house and the main stables (there are twenty-two). Lady Trafford even sat for a full portrait. Mr. Withrow is the only person I have not drawn, but I do not think I will ask him.

It is getting cold here, and the wind from the sea makes it feel even colder. We have also had much rain. Both facts are unfortunate because Mr. Linton has prohibited me from doing landscape drawings inside, looking out the window. Most days I am forced out of the castle.

My French is also improving. I can now understand a fair amount of spoken French and speak a fair amount. Twice this past week I met Madame Dieupart in Worthing and was able to practice with other French speakers. Madame Dieupart finally admitted that the years I spent reading French are helping me learn the language faster. She does complain that I sound too much like a book, but there are much worse things than sounding like a book.

Some days I am very tired, but I simply remind myself that it is better to live with a knowledge of one's shortcomings and be able to improve upon them than to continue in ignorance.

I know I mentioned that Lady Trafford seemed a bit unusual. Whenever we have guests, the next day she likes to analyze their word choice and movement. Other times she gives me advice, like moderating how much I speak when someone asks me a question, or asking what she calls reciprocal or counterpoint questions. She has taken several more charity trips, one of them unplanned. It makes her seem a bit eccentric and a little too willing to help people at a moment's notice. None of the trips have been to Brighton, or I would have gone with her and visited Maria.

I hope your illness does not prevent you from enjoying your visit to Pemberley next week. Give my love to Elizabeth.

Faithfully yours,
Mary Bennet

Mary reviewed the letter and, satisfied, she folded it to make it smaller. As always, for the final fold she made sure that the top piece of paper only went halfway down the rest of the letter to leave room for the seal. She melted a bit of wax, savoring the pleasant scent of flame and wax, dripped the wax onto the letter, pressed her seal on it, then wrote out Jane's address.

Lady Trafford, who had been writing her own letter on the other side of the parlor, approached. "I will have someone bring your letter, and my own, to the post office today." She picked up the letter, staring at the seal. "Do you always seal your letters like this?"

"Yes. It is a standard method. My mother taught me." Her entire family used this approach. She had seen Mr. Darcy use a more complicated method once, and at times Mr. Bennet had used more complicated methods as well, but most of the time even her father sealed letters in the same manner she did.

"I would say about six in ten people send letters this way. Thus, you are correct; it is a standard method. But it is not very secure."

Lady Trafford picked up Mary's knife for cutting the wax. She wedged the edge of the knife underneath the sealed wax Mary had just placed on the letter.

"What are you doing?" asked Mary with horror.

"Opening your letter," said Lady Trafford. In a few seconds, the bottom half of the wax popped off that layer of the letter. She showed the letter to Mary. "If you do it carefully, you can avoid ripping the paper. Then you can open the letter," she did so, "read it," she pointedly looked at each page of the letter for long enough that she could read a decent portion, "and then close it again."

Mary swallowed, wondering if Lady Trafford had read the part of the letter written about her.

Lady Trafford held the bottom of the wax seal over the flame, not as close as Mary had done to melt the wax initially, but still close. Then she folded the final flap of the letter back down, pinching the papers tightly together without touching the seal.

"The wax will not be pressed as firmly onto the paper as it was before, since I would not have access to your metal seal to push it down completely, but it will hold, and it is unlikely that anyone would suspect that it has been opened."

"Why would you want to read someone else's letters?"

"Of course I do not want to read anyone's letters. But it is a useful demonstration of why you should send your letters in a more secure fashion."

"I do not send any secrets."

"I am sure you do not possess any secrets, but does that mean you want to allow anyone to read whatever they choose? What if you decide to write something about me to your sisters? Do you want me to know your innermost thoughts?"

Mary's cheeks burned. Lady Trafford had indeed read the portion of the letter about herself.

"Come, sit with me. I will show you another method for sealing your letters."

Mary followed Lady Trafford across the room and sat. The padding on the chair sank beneath her, making the wood at the chair's edge push uncomfortably against her leg. Mary shifted back and forth in her chair but was unable to find a better position.

"It appears that you write your letters on a quarter sheet of paper folded in half, which is good. This allows for four possible writing surfaces—like a four-page book. If you want your letter to be secure, you should only ever write on the front and the two inner pages, as you have done. Some people write on the portions of the back that will be folded into the inside, but I would not recommend it."

Lady Trafford wrote a few nonsense words on each page. Mary cringed at the thought of this quarter sheet of paper being wasted for a demonstration. Why did Lady Trafford not show her on an actual letter? Unless Lady Trafford did not want a single word of an actual letter read.

She passed the fake letter to Mary and then wasted another quarter sheet by making a fake letter for herself. "Now follow along." She folded the letter in thirds, and so did Mary. She folded it in half the other direction. She slid a flat, wooden board under the letter, took a pen knife, and cut a slit through all the layers of paper, about three quarters of an inch from where the edges joined together.

She passed Mary the board and the knife. It was much harder to do than it appeared; Mary had to put the knife into the slit again and again to pass through all twelve layers of paper, and it was not nearly as neat as Lady Trafford's. Clearly that was another skill which required practice, but it was not an accomplishment Mary had heard anyone mention.

"Now, from the same type of paper, I will cut a long, thin triangle—one for each of us. You should use the same type of paper, first, so it matches the letter aesthetically, and second, because this triangle is how we will lock the letter. If someone breaks the lock, it will be difficult for them to make it appear as if the lock has never been broken, for they will need to find the exact same sort of paper."

"I doubt that letter security is an accomplishment taught at the schools for young ladies in London."

"If you choose the correct one, you might be surprised." Lady Trafford continued as if Mary had not voiced any objection. "Now take the thinnest end of the triangle and insert it through the slit you have made through all the layers of paper. Pull the triangle through until it is snug. Yes, like that." Half of the triangle piece protruded from one side of the letter, half from the other side. "Now, though it is not strictly necessary, on the pointy side of the triangle I make a cut from the tip all the way down to the letter."

She did so, passed Mary the knife, and Mary copied. She

had not played with paper this much since she was a young child, and in that case, she was punished for ruining two sheets of her father's paper. She could not remember what the punishment was, so it must not have been dire.

Lady Trafford took the pointy end of the triangle, now cut in two, and folded both pieces so they lay on the letter in opposite directions. "This is the back of the letter." She placed a wooden board under the letter, then melted part of her wax stick, slowly spinning it over the candle flame. Lady Trafford's wax had a stronger smell than Mary's. "I use a more expensive wax, which does more damage to the paper than yours. This is the goal; you *want* to damage your own letter, because it makes it harder for someone to open without leaving evidence."

"If someone really wanted to read a letter," said Mary, "could they break the paper lock, open the letter, and then burn it after reading? There would be no evidence, except for a letter that never arrived."

Lady Trafford smiled. "Very perceptive. Not receiving a letter or reply you know was sent is telling in itself. There is an article in the crime section of today's *Kentish Gazette* describing how a man named Spur stole letters which contained bank notes. It is quite the torrid affair. But we cannot prevent that possibility, and this is something we can control."

She dabbed the hot wax onto the two slit ends of the triangle, then took the end of the triangle sticking out of the front side of the letter, folded it over the side of the letter, and pressed it onto the back side, on top of the cut slits and the still hot wax. She used a tool with a pointed metal end to poke the portion of the triangle on top of the wax. This made indents, and in some places, little holes.

"The indents this creates will extend through many layers of the letter." After blowing on the wax to make sure it was cool, she flipped the letter to the front side. Only about an inch of the triangle paper showed on the edge of this side. "As one final element of security, when I write the address, I make sure that some of the letters are on top of the triangle insert. If someone were to break open the letter and try to replace the triangle—which would be difficult, especially with the wax and the slit and the indents and needing to match the paper— they would also need to perfectly imitate your handwriting for this portion of the address."

Mary finished the final steps for sealing her own letter and was quite pleased with the result. The triangle insert holding the letter together made it look refined and sophisticated.

Lady Trafford gave Mary three more quarter sheets and watched as Mary performed the letter sealing method three more times. Mary cringed each time at the waste of paper, but by the final one, she could do it without any help.

"Now break one of them open, as you would if you were receiving this letter."

Mary pulled on it, but it did not open, so she used the pen knife to slit the folded edge of the triangle insert. She tugged, and after a minute she managed to open the letter.

"I want you to study all the damage that is left by this sealing method. Examine where you see slits and indents and wax remnants. Then try to open the other letters and reseal them without leaving evidence of having done so."

Mary spent over an hour on the task before concluding that it was impossible. As she did so, she wondered about Lady Trafford's methods. Learning how to seal letters in different ways could, admittedly, be useful. But what virtuous woman would instruct someone to practice opening letters without leaving any evidence?

THAT NIGHT, AS Mary was falling asleep, it occurred to her that Lady Trafford might not have told the full truth. She had stated that she did not *want* to read anyone else's letters. But someone could choose to do something, even if one did not want to do it.

Which meant Lady Trafford could have read other letters Mary had sent over the last six weeks. Or letters that Mary had received.

Mary tried to dismiss the thought and fall asleep, but she could not. Instead, she tried to recall every single letter she had written from Castle Durrington, to remember every little detail she had included. Was there any content she would regret Lady Trafford knowing? Not that she could change that now, but at least she could be aware of it and how it might impact her relationship with Lady Trafford. The woman had obviously wanted Mary to know that she might have been reading her letters, and Mary tried to fathom why. She spent hours in her bed, in the dark, her mind busy with remembering her letters and reflecting on Lady Trafford's motives. Fortunately, Mary had reported to Monsieur Corneau only in person, and not sent her reports via post, or Lady Trafford would know what she had been asked to do.

There was a noise outside the house—the whinny of a horse.

Mary immediately went to her window and looked out at the lawn. In front of the house, lit by only a single lantern, was a carriage. Two people descended from it, holding a smaller lantern that they had dimmed by partially covering it with something. Mary could not tell whether the people were men or women, or any further distinguishing characteristics. They hurried to the front door and were immediately let inside the house.

Mary debated staying in her room, but curiosity overcame her. Curiosity could be a virtue, as long as it was properly regulated. She wrapped a shawl around herself for modesty's sake and stepped quietly out of the room. All was silent, and even though this floor currently housed only her and Mrs. Boughton, she trod down the hallway as softly as she could. She descended the smaller, spiral staircase to the first floor and, as she did not know where the visitors had gone, exited to the domed balcony room. She leaned against the balcony railing, looking down at the entry to the house below, but did not see anyone. She wondered if Lady Trafford had been notified of the middle-of-the-night visitors.

She heard footsteps coming down a hall—the hall with Lady Trafford and Mr. Withrow's rooms—and panicked. She felt as if she were in one of Kitty's silly Gothic novels. She had read one of Kitty's novels, only with the purpose of more fully understanding and condemning the pettiness of the world. But now, all the terrible possibilities presented in the novel came to the forefront of her mind.

In Kitty's novel, the main character had been caught eavesdropping on an illicit liaison and been thrown out of the estate in the middle of the night.

Mary could not let herself be seen. She had no way to defend herself and very little money. If she wrote to her family, someone would come fetch her, but it could take several days for her letter to arrive. While Colonel Coates had promised to help her should the need ever arrive, she had no desire to walk to Worthing in the middle of the night and attempt to find him.

She stepped back from the balcony and hid behind a curtain covering one of the decorative alcoves. There was a gap, just large enough for her to fit. She pressed herself flat against the wall panel, and once again found herself wondering at the castle's design and the empty, walled-off space that must exist behind this panel.

She peered around the edge of the curtain and watched as Mrs. Boughton, Lady Trafford, and Mr. Withrow descended the grand staircase, carrying candles. Mrs. Boughton must have let the visitors in and come to fetch Lady Trafford and Mr. Withrow. Mary waited a minute and then followed them down to the main floor.

A faint light shone from underneath the door of the library. She stood in front of it, considering. She had no justifiable reason to barge in, and if she stayed here, she could be discovered. Unlike the domed balcony room above, the circular entryway had no easy place to hide, so she stepped into the parlor next to the library. From here she could still see the entryway but was unlikely to be seen.

Mary pressed her ear against the wall of the sitting room that adjoined the library, but she could hear nothing, so she resigned herself to kneeling behind a sofa, peering out at the entry hall. She recognized the absurdity of the situation, of attempting to spy on her hosts, yet at the moment, spying seemed like the only course of action before her. Ordinary people did not hold middle-of-the-night meetings if there was another alternative. It could be an under-the-table business affair, a plan to defraud someone, an illegal shipping agreement, or countless other clandestine possibilities.

After not more than a minute or two, Mrs. Boughton passed through the entry hall from the direction of the kitchens. She carried a platter of tea and bread and entered the library.

Mary tiptoed back to the circular entryway. The library door was cracked, and she heard voices; they must be seated at the chairs near the entrance.

"We questioned everyone," said a woman's voice, "but it was futile. Either no motive, or, if they had motive, no possible way they could have been in Worthing to perform the deed."

Mary tried to fix the words in her mind, to remember every detail. She could analyze them later.

"I was able to search the parsonage, and I found most of his materials," said a man's voice. He had a slight accent, but Mary could not place it. "Several key notebooks were missing."

"We could lose more than Holloway if we do not recover them." This voice Mary recognized. It was Lady Trafford. They were talking about Holloway's death, as if he were a lost notebook! Mary felt pity for the poor man.

"He must have had them with him," said the man.

Now, Mr. Withrow spoke. "There was nothing on him when Miss Bennet discovered his body, if she is to be believed."

"She would not hide something like that from us," said Mrs. Boughton, and her voice seemed to be getting louder. "She does not have the skill."

Mary backed away from the library door and into the parlor, and not a moment too soon, for she heard the library door shut.

Her heart pounded in her chest. She had almost been caught, almost discovered. At the very least they would accuse her of eavesdropping, though they might take it to the logical conclusion and realize she was spying on them.

She curled up on the sofa, wrapping her shawl more tightly around her, but it did not stop the cold that she felt. Her mind leapt around the snatch of conversation that she had heard. They had searched a parsonage, but she did not know where. It could be here in Worthing, or anywhere really, but if it held Holloway's papers, perhaps it was in Crawley. Questioning people in Crawley made sense as they knew Holloway but would not have been in Worthing to kill him. It surprised her that multiple people could have wanted to kill Holloway—he had been a clergyman—but now that she was involved in a murder investigation, it was time that she ceased to be surprised by such possibilities.

A sound interrupted her thoughts. Perhaps the swinging of a door. She sat up, raising her head just above the edge of the sofa so she could see out into the circular entryway.

Into the entryway stepped Mrs. Boughton carrying a candelabra, followed by Lady Trafford, Mr. Withrow, and their two mysterious guests. They had dark brown skin—though not as dark as Fanny's—a regal air, and fine clothing. The woman appeared to be about Mary's age, and Mary guessed that the man was her father. The woman embraced Lady Trafford and said, "I wish we had time to visit the church. We will on our upcoming visit."

"It is just as well," said Withrow. "At this time of night you would be suspected of grave robbing."

Mary could not hear the response to this statement, or tell from whence it came. The mysterious woman and man exited the house with hardly a sound. Mrs. Boughton locked the front door, and Lady Trafford, Mr. Withrow, and Mrs. Boughton ascended the stairs.

Had these visitors come during the day and not spoken of

a dead man, they would seem like respectable people, the sort of people Lady Trafford might do business with, or who might run in similar social circles. Why meet with them in the middle of the night to share information about Holloway? And what had been meant by the comments about the church and grave robbing? Mr. Holloway had not been buried in Worthing; his body had been sent back to Crawley.

Mary twisted her mourning ring, wondering what her father would think. He would probably find it preposterous that she was skulking about a castle in the middle of the night and offer some justifiable reason for their behaviour. Perhaps they were travelling and could not spare the time for a visit during the day, and of course they were speaking about Holloway—since Mary had discovered his body, it seemed that no one could speak of anything else. Mr. Bennet would likely call her a silly girl. He had always lumped her with her younger two sisters in terms of silliness, which Mary had found rather absurd. But now, here she was, behaving precisely as a silly girl would. Perhaps, in order to be silly, she simply needed the proper opportunity. She stifled a laugh that she felt rising, for silence was still paramount.

Once Mary was certain she would not be caught, she made her way back to her room, trying to decide a way in which to discreetly question Lady Trafford about the visit in the morning.

CHAPTER TWELVE

"Some letters expect that seeing the rapid decline of his reputation, and feeling the necessity of attempting something, however desperate, [Bonaparte] will risk everything in a general battle!

'I have set my life upon a cast,
And I will stand the hazard of the dye.'"

—*The Bristol Mirror*, Bristol, England,
October 23, 1813

F ANNY REMOVED MARY'S nicest black dress from the clothing press and shook it out.

"One of the others will serve me better," said Mary.

"But you are going to town with Lady Trafford," said Fanny.

"I may be going to town, but it is not to display myself." Mary yawned, fatigued from her lack of sleep, in part due to the middle-of-the-night visitors.

"Did you not sleep well?"

"I am a little tired, that is all."

Mary knew Mrs. Boughton was in full confidence with Lady Trafford, but she did not know about the other servants or how strong their loyalties were to their mistress. Of course, whether or not Fanny were involved, she might know something.

"I thought I heard a noise in the middle of the night, perhaps from a horse or a carriage," said Mary.

"The road is not too far from here. Maybe it was a doctor driving to help someone."

The response was not useful. Mary wondered who else she could question without raising suspicions.

Fanny helped Mary out of her nightgown. "Lady Trafford has set aside fabric and other materials for me to make you dresses." She gave a sly smile. "And I would much rather make you dresses than perform some of the less pleasant household tasks."

"I have sufficient clothing for my needs."

"But the fabric will go to waste if I do not use it. Will you let me measure you? I can do it quickly."

Fatigued, Mary did not have the stamina to stand up to Fanny. "I suppose you may make me one new black dress, but it must have no lace, beads, or other adornment, and it should be an example of modesty in all aspects."

"I assume that by the ball you will no longer be wearing black?"

"What ball?"

"Did you not know? Lady Trafford is throwing a ball, in five weeks' time."

"I was never informed." It did not matter whether she was at Longbourn or here; Mary was always the last person to hear about balls.

"If you are still wearing black, it would not be appropriate for you to attend, and as her honored guest for all this time, I can only believe you would want to show her your gratitude by attending rather than shaming her by not."

Fanny was skilled at leaving no room for argument.

"I will stop wearing black by the time of the ball."

"I am so glad. I have such a wonderful plan for your new ball gown."

"I do *not* need a new ball gown," said Mary firmly. "My green dress has served me for many a ball and will serve me for another."

"Maybe you will change your mind," said Fanny. "At least let me take your measurements so I can make you a morning gown."

"Very well."

Fanny began taking measurements and writing down notes. She was efficient and seemed more skilled than others who had measured Mary before.

"Where did you learn this?"

"My mother works for a dressmaker in London. And my father is a tailor. Some day they will open their own shop and make all their own designs."

"I am sure if they are industrious, they will do well for themselves."

Fanny gave a look as if she did not completely agree, but she said nothing.

After a minute of silence, Mary asked, "Do your parents like living in London?" She had only been there for two days with the Gardiners and had not seen much of the city at all.

"They like it well enough. My mother has lived there her whole life. My father was born in Virginia as a slave. He gained his freedom by fighting with the loyalists when the colonies revolted. When we lost the war, he came to London. He misses the weather in Virginia, but not much else."

Fanny finished the measurements and helped Mary into her most plain mourning dress.

"What about you?" asked Mary. "Did you like London?

Or do you like it better here?"

"It does not matter what I like," said Fanny. "This is where I need to be."

ALL THROUGH BREAKFAST, Mary expected either Lady Trafford or Mr. Withrow to say something—anything—about the mysterious visitors, but they did not. Of course, Mary never had told her family about Lady Trafford's middle-of-the-night visit before her father's funeral, so perhaps it was not too surprising.

As Mary rode the carriage to town with Lady Trafford, Mary said, "I trust you slept well last night."

Lady Trafford smiled serenely. "Quite well. And what about you, Miss Bennet? Did you sleep well, or did anything disturb you?"

Now it seemed that Lady Trafford was trying to extract information from Mary.

"I always sleep soundly." The taste of sour milk filled Mary's mouth. She had given a direct lie and felt terrible for it. Honesty, after all, was one of the prime virtues. But what if someone was doing something that might not be honest or straightforward? What then? Should she tell the whole truth? Mary did not want Lady Trafford to know that she had been spying on her. She wanted to find out what Lady Trafford was doing, but without endangering her position at Castle Durrington.

She decided to attempt a different line of questioning that might draw out a reference to the night's events. "Are we expecting any guests?"

"The Mulberrys will be joining us again; they will dine

with us on Sunday. Why do you ask?"

"I enjoy the stimulation of varied conversation which naturally results from having guests at Castle Durrington."

"You will be pleased, then, to know that a number of guests will be staying with us, starting several days in advance of the ball. Did Fanny mention it to you?"

"She did. I look forward to increasing my skills at reading conversations."

Mr. Tubbs, their driver for the day, stopped the carriage on the outskirts of town at a small, dilapidated cottage.

"What are we doing?" asked Mary.

"I have a small gift for the woman who lives here."

They exited the carriage and knocked on the door. It was cracked and warped, and most of the paint had chipped and peeled. It was not the neglect of a year or two, but decades of insufficient time or means devoted to the upkeep of the cottage.

An older woman opened the door. Her clothes were dirty, stained, and even had a few rips and tears. She smelled as if she had not bathed in quite some time. When she saw Lady Trafford, she smiled and the movement of her lips added to the wrinkles on her face, almost threatening to split it in two. She was missing a number of teeth, and of those she had, several were pointed at unusual angles.

"My dear Ruth," said Lady Trafford. She gave the poor woman a shawl, several loaves of freshly baked bread, and a basket of fruits and vegetables, then asked after her family.

"If my son 'adn't gone abroad, I wouldn't be so lonesome."

"Abroad?" asked Mary. "Where does he live?"

"In Devon."

"But Devon is—"

153

"It is so very far away," interrupted Lady Trafford. Mary had been about to say that Devon was only a few counties away, still on the southern coast of England, and not very far at all.

"I heard," said Lady Trafford, "that a new gentleman has taken residence at Edgeworth."

"You 'eard right. It's a Colonel Radcliffe," said the old woman with glee. "He's visited afore, but now he's 'ere for good. He's not with the regiment—he fought a while back, I bluv. And he's in business."

"What sort of business?" asked Lady Trafford.

"Well no one's said, but I knows. Hisn family owns property, in the north. My friend Lucretia works for 'im. She told me all about it."

"What sort of household does he run?"

"Well I'm not one to yabble, but I can tell you a little summat." Ruth told them a story about the sugar running out in the kitchen and then a scandal over missing candlesticks. Colonel Radcliffe had already dismissed two servants due to their behaviour. After at least ten more minutes on Colonel Radcliffe's household, Ruth began gossiping about everyone else in the area. Between those she knew personally and those she knew from the stories of others, she seemed to know absolutely everyone. Mary had always felt that gossip degraded the mind and assisted no one. She found herself growing impatient with both the old woman and Lady Trafford. Mary wanted to continue on to Worthing so she could visit the bookseller. She wondered what benefit this relationship served for Lady Trafford, or if she did it simply out of charity. But if for charity, why not leave the items without holding a long conversation? Or why not give the items to an organization that would distribute them to many people who were in need?

She must take pleasure in the gossip, and this knowledge left Mary disappointed in Lady Trafford, who she had assumed was above such things.

After at least fifteen more minutes of gossip, some of which Mary found difficult to follow because of Ruth's dialect, they returned to the carriage.

"What do you think of her?" asked Lady Trafford.

Mary almost said something cruel that probably would have offended Lady Trafford but stopped herself short. She did not need to be petty, like Lydia sometimes was. She thought for a moment before delivering her response. "She does not have the best grasp of geography."

"It is true," said Lady Trafford. "I hope you will excuse me for preventing you from correcting her. What you were about to say was accurate and might have instructed her in geography. But what would be the advantage of so doing? What would really be gained? You could correct her but at the same time hurt her feelings and make her less likely to talk to you, or to me, again. Unless there are urgent circumstances or a disbelief is causing harm, I attempt to use kindness and an awareness of others and their needs as a guide for what is acceptable conversation."

Lady Trafford might have kind feelings towards the old woman, but her kindness seemed calculated, planned even. Jane's kindness was always genuine and unstudied.

"If you do not think it appropriate to correct her, then why do you always correct me?"

"We have a different relationship, and I want to help you reach your potential." Lady Trafford said it as if she had some distant goal for Mary, some grand vision that she had not chosen to share.

Lady Trafford paused thoughtfully. "I think your father

would have appreciated your observation about her."

"You do?" asked Mary. Besides stating that they had known each other in their younger years and that she respected Mr. Bennet, Lady Trafford had never said anything more about her father.

"Your father and I were once at the same very tedious dinner party. The host spoke for thirty minutes straight without pause. How he managed to breathe, I still do not know. The host told one story about Bicester, Oxfordshire, and every single time he said it as it is spelled, 'Bi-ches-ter,' instead of pronouncing it as it should be, 'Bister.' Finally the man paused for a drink and your father took the opportunity to interrupt.

"'I take it,' said Mr. Bennet. 'That you have been to *Bi-ches-ter* many times?' 'Of course,' said the host. 'At least three or four times.' Mr. Bennet smiled and said, 'I do love *Bister* myself. It has some marvelous old buildings.' The host flushed as he realized his error, and it was all the rest of us could do to not laugh at him."

"That sounds like something my father would say." Despite not necessarily being related to Lady Trafford, Mary had assumed that Lady Trafford must have, in fact, known her father. Why else would she come to view his body or invite Mary as a guest? Yet a part of her must not have truly believed it, for Mary felt great surprise at hearing such a story from Lady Trafford. It was very specific, and on such an insignificant subject matter, that it did not make sense for it to have been fabricated. And it was in line with the way Mr. Bennet often spoke to those he found foolish. "How did you meet my father?"

"Oh, I cannot possibly remember when we met. With relations it is as if you always knew them."

In this Lady Trafford seemed more evasive. But if she actually knew Mr. Bennet, what did she have to hide?

When they arrived in Worthing, Lady Trafford let Mary off on the main street, in front of the bookseller. Mary was about to enter but decided to visit the post office next door first. If she obtained her mail before it arrived at the castle, she could make sure no one read it, even if the sender used only a simple seal to secure it.

Three others were already in the post office: a seamstress and a shoemaker she recognized from church, and a short, well-dressed woman who, like Mary, wore black for mourning. The ribbon on Mary's black bonnet felt tight under her chin, so she pulled out the knot and tied it again as the man at the counter helped the others.

Finally, it was her turn. "Do you have any mail for me?"

"What is your name, miss?"

"Mary Bennet. I am staying at Castle Durrington with Lady Trafford."

The man went to the back room for a minute and returned with a stack of mail. "These two are for you. These others are also addressed to the Castle. Would you like to pay for them as well?"

Lady Trafford probably intended to come to the post office later, or more likely, have Mr. Tubbs do so. But Lady Trafford had given her some money for pocket expenses and had paid for the receipt of all of Mary's letters during the course of her stay at Castle Durrington.

"Yes, please." Another motivation, she admitted to herself, was the chance to see Lady Trafford's correspondence.

The man spent a minute calculating the distances that the letters had travelled. "That will be eight shillings and ten pence."

It was a huge amount—almost half a pound—and Mary almost did not pay it, but she had already agreed, and she was curious to see the stack of letters in the man's hand. She removed the money from the pocket she had brought with her, counted it carefully, and handed it to the postman.

"Do you have anything you need sent?"

"Not today." It occurred to her that rather than sending her mail with one of Lady Trafford's servants, she could deliver it directly to the post office herself or leave it in one of the other post office boxes in Worthing.

She placed the stack of letters in her pocket, then she entered the bookseller's shop. She had told Lady Trafford she would buy a book, and been given ten shillings for it, so despite the expense at the post office, she best spend money here as well. As she browsed, she heard the door to the shop open. The person who entered was none other than Monsieur Corneau; he must have seen Lady Trafford's carriage and come to speak with Mary.

Corneau bowed at another man who was leaving the store. "Ah, Colonel, a pleasure."

"It is a pleasure to meet you again," the man said, and then he was gone. He was not dressed in uniform and was younger than Colonel Coates, so Mary guessed that it must be the new resident Ruth had spoken of, Colonel Radcliffe.

Monsieur Corneau approached Mary, gesturing towards the set of shelves at the very back of the shop. After a moment, Mary followed him there.

"*J'ai plus des choses que je dois vous dire,*" Mary said in a whisper.

"Let us speak in English, Miss Bennet," said Monsieur Corneau, also with his voice low. "It will be easier."

Madame Dieupart's French friends made no complaint

about speaking to Mary in French, and Mary's French had improved to the point that she felt she could hold this conversation in it. Yet perhaps once you had habituated to speaking a particular language with a person, it was too difficult to switch.

In English, Mary told Corneau of the middle of the night visit and the portions of the conversation she had heard. He nodded almost continuously, barely keeping up the pretense of looking at the books on the shelves.

"That is very useful. I will inform Colonel Coates. I am sure he will be very pleased. You do not know the identity of the visitors?"

Mary shook her head.

"If you learn who they are, or if you hear more of these missing notebooks, come straight to me."

"Do you know if Mr. Holloway could swim?"

"I do not. Why do you ask?"

"I was considering his death," said Mary. "The knife wound was not enough to kill him. If Mr. Holloway did not know how to swim, he could have been stabbed anywhere near the water and then thrown in. After drowning, his body could have been washed farther out to sea. Yet if he did know how to swim, then he must have been stabbed on a boat out at sea."

"Colonel Coates and Sir Pickering already searched the boats in Worthing for signs of struggle."

Mary felt her face fall.

"But it is an insightful observation. We have documented seventy-three boats in the surrounding area, from small fishing vessels to large ones that could travel across the sea. I will make sure that none were missed. Do you have anything else to report, or other questions?"

"Did you follow up on Mr. Shaffer?"

"We did," he said. "Mr. Shaffer has a perfect alibi for both the final day of Mr. Holloway's life and the next day. We also went over his boat with great care."

Mary nodded, satisfied on that count. "Who was it you spoke to, as you entered the store?"

"Colonel Radcliffe," said Monsieur Corneau, confirming her conjecture. "He is a new acquaintance. Well, I must go. Thank you for your report."

Mary turned back to the books, and now looked at them in earnest. She chose a nice leather-bound copy of *Practical Piety* by Hannah More. She always found Hannah More edifying and knew she would read the book multiple times, which made it a worthwhile purchase. Also, Lady Trafford did not own a single book by her.

Mary sat down on one of the bookseller's sofas to wait for Lady Trafford to finish her own errands. Instead of opening her new book, she broke open her own letters, neither of which used a secure seal.

The first was a brief note from Kitty, almost terse. Kitty was disappointed that their mother still did not feel well enough for them to travel to stay with Jane or Elizabeth. Strangely, Kitty seemed irritated at Mary. Yet Mary had no influence whatsoever on their mother's health, especially from such a distance. Mary reread Kitty's words and detected a hint of jealously, particularly in a line in which she wistfully asked a question about Castle Durrington. Mary looked up from the letter. She was unused to any of her sisters ever desiring something she possessed that they did not.

The second was a letter from Mrs. Bennet. It rambled on without focus. It did not mention feeling unwell, but it did spend a great deal of time lecturing Mary on what she should demand from Lady Trafford. "Do not allow Lady Trafford to send you away in haste. She is a relative, and by virtue of our relations, do not let her neglect what is owed to you. She should be introducing you to new gentlemen every single week, and you must do whatever you must in order to find a match."

Mary shook her head. Marrying her daughters was the only thing Mrs. Bennet cared about. Mary had liked it better when her mother had assumed that she was not marriageable.

She set aside her letters and examined the others given to her by the post office. There were a handful for the servants, which did not interest her, five for Mr. Withrow, and seven for Lady Trafford. Of all of Withrow's and Lady Trafford's letters, only one was sealed in a non-secure method. The rest were like a textbook on different approaches to sealing letters. Only one used the precise method Lady Trafford had taught her, though two were similar. Others wove paper in a complex method on the edge, were sewed shut with thread, used different types of adhesives than wax, used seals which indented all the paper layers, or used peculiar folds and shapes. Several of the letters were quite heavy, much heavier than any letter she had ever sent.

She examined the postal markings on each of the letters. A number of them came from Brighton, Dover, and London. There was also one from Durham, which was in the far north of England, and one from Bolingbroke. She had no idea where that was, but the letter had passed through London on the way here.

On one of the letters from Brighton it said M. May on the outside. As it was October, it could not be a reference to the date, so perhaps it was someone with the last name of May with a first initial of M.

None of the other letters listed a name or a return address on the outside. It was not that unusual, but it did mean that every single sender assumed that Lady Trafford would pay for the receipt of the letters even without any indication of who had sent them.

Mary did not dare open any of the letters, not here in a shop, where anyone could see her. But she did examine the letter without a complicated closure method a little more closely. The author had folded the letter in a way that left the edges open.

She checked to make sure no one in the shop was paying her any attention, and then separated the edges of the pages. She could only glimpse a few words on the inside, and the cursive was terrible. But she did manage to make out a few words: "I used the money you sent to bribe the—" She could not make out the next portion, but a little later another phrase was clear enough to decipher: "I have confirmed that he has been shipping things illegally to and from France."

Footsteps approached, so she closed the edge of the letter and opened her new book.

"Do you need any refreshment, Miss Bennet?" asked the shopkeeper.

"No. I am quite all right."

That had been too close. She could not risk someone noticing her examining Lady Trafford's mail and then reporting it to her.

As she continued to spy on Lady Trafford and Mr. Withrow, she would need to find concrete evidence, either of their involvement in Mr. Holloway's demise, or, if they were in no way responsible, of whatever nefarious activities they were involved in, for the things she had observed pointed to at least some underhanded behaviour. Lady Trafford's benevolence to Mary was a less important factor than her potential crimes. It was Mary's duty as an Englishwoman to expose Lady Trafford and Mr. Withrow before returning home.

Which meant she truly needed more evidence.

Finding this evidence would require more actions like she had taken last night and today—not things that were wrong, per se, especially as they were morally justified. However, they were things that could put her in an awkward situation should she be discovered by Lady Trafford.

She thought of the words of her father, whenever she struggled to get along with her sisters. "Sometimes, my dear, if you want something, you must allow others to believe they have gotten their way, and that you are doing as they wish." Then he would pause dramatically and say, "It is the only way I have survived your mother all these years."

Mary needed to make Lady Trafford believe that she was doing as Lady Trafford desired, so she would not notice Mary's other actions, or at least be more likely to dismiss or forgive them if she did notice them. She needed to ingratiate herself more with Lady Trafford to guarantee that she would not be sent home before she discovered the truth.

By the time Lady Trafford returned to the shop with the carriage, Mary had decided on a plan. First, she removed the letters from her pocket—except the ones from Kitty and Mrs. Bennet—and gave them to Lady Trafford.

"I took the liberty of collecting your letters."

"That is what the postmaster told Mr. Tubbs," said Lady Trafford. "How very thoughtful of you. Did you receive any letters yourself?"

"Yes, I received one from my sister, Kitty." She did not precisely know why, but she did not want to mention that she had received a letter from her mother. Perhaps it was that her mother mentioned very specifically that Mary needed to demand more from Lady Trafford, but the letter made her feel uncomfortable.

"I have something that I have been considering for the past several weeks," said Mary.

"Yes?"

"When we first met, you said you could train me to be a governess. As I have spent time here, I have realized how much I value independence. I do not want to spend my entire life dependent on the whims of my aunts and uncles, my sisters and their husbands. I would like to make my own way. Would it be possible for you to have me trained in other things beyond French and drawing? I am not completely committed to becoming a governess, but I would like that to be a possibility for my future." All of this was true; she did value independence and would like additional lessons and training.

Lady Trafford smiled. "It is wise to prepare for the future and embrace multiple possibilities."

"So you will help me? I am not...asking too much of you?"

"Not at all. I will plan your course of study myself." She seemed quite pleased.

When they returned to the castle, Lady Trafford led Mary to the library. Mr. Withrow was at work at his desk. He greeted his aunt warmly and gave Mary a "Good afternoon, Miss Bennet" and a polite but lukewarm smile.

Lady Trafford wandered through the library, pulling down a number of books. She handed them to Mary. "To read, for your studies."

Mary read the titles as she carried the books up the stairs. The top one was a book titled *The Complete Book of Manners for Young Ladies*, but there were also books on history, mathematics, and geography. Mary realized she had not asked Lady Trafford about the order in which the books should be read, or if there was anything she should focus on while reading them. She went back down the staircase to ask, but she paused directly outside of the library. Lady Trafford and Mr. Withrow were having a conversation, and the door had not been closed all the way.

"I know that you would have preferred to train her younger sister," came the voice of Lady Trafford. "But while you think Miss Catherine Bennet would have been more suited as a...governess, I do not believe that would be the case."

Mr. Withrow uttered some sort of dissent.

"You may not find Miss Bennet attractive or agreeable, but she may still be useful for our purposes, and you *will* train her, Henry."

Mary put her hand against the wall to steady herself. She noted the pause Lady Trafford had taken before the word governess; clearly, they had something else in mind for her, some sinister purpose that required grand manipulations to get her to come here, to Castle Durrington. What did they want with her?

Yet she could not focus entirely on their plan, instead being struck by Lady Trafford's admission, that Withrow—and probably others—did not find Mary attractive or agreeable. She had never cared much about attractiveness, though she did like to think she was agreeable and pleasant company. She did not care about Withrow's good opinion, yet still the fact of not having it slid down her throat like a bitter drink, settling in her stomach. Perhaps that was why they had chosen her instead of her younger sister; if Mary was not attractive or agreeable, people would care less if something happened to her, if, for instance, she was harmed or injured. Yet Mary was grateful they had chosen her. She would not want Kitty to have been placed in harm's way, and Mary thought that she possessed the intelligence to keep herself out of their plans while gathering enough evidence to reveal them to the world.

Mary turned swiftly away from the library, almost dropping the books as she ascended the spiral staircase. Once in her room, she piled her books on the desk without further consideration. She could not read now, not in the light of the conversation she had heard, and especially not with all that she had learned in the past twenty-four hours.

It had occurred to her that once a letter had been opened, it had no security at all. Anyone who came across it could read it, without leaving any evidence.

She took the letter from Kitty and added it to her packet of letters that she kept on her bedside table. She loosened her hair and then yanked a strand from her head. Then she tucked the hair underneath the string tie and around the corner of the letter, so it appeared as though a piece of hair had simply fallen out and become snagged on the letters. She stared at the positioning of the hair and the exact placement of the letters on the table for several minutes. If someone removed and read any of the letters, she would know it.

She read the letter from her mother one more time. This letter, to Lady Trafford's knowledge, did not exist, so Mary needed to make sure it could never be discovered. She put the letter into the fire and watched until every last fragment of the paper burned.

CHAPTER THIRTEEN

"A second French courier, who has to carry the Emperor's letter bag to Paris, was attacked...by some of General Theilman's partizans. This capture, in a military point of view, is of great consequence. We shall here confine ourselves to publishing some of the letters, in extracts."

—*The Morning Post*, London, October 26, 1813

IT WAS MARY'S first day of lessons with Mr. Withrow, and she was determined not to be intimidated. While Mr. Linton and Madame Dieupart gave her lessons in the parlor, Mr. Withrow had informed Mary that he would provide her with instruction in the library. She tried opening the door, but it was locked. She knocked firmly.

Mr. Withrow unlocked the door, and this time the comforting smell of paper and leather did not lift her spirits. With perfect manners, Withrow invited Mary to sit with him at his desk. He took the large, padded chair and she took a smaller wooden one on the other side.

Fanny followed Mary into the room and took a soft chair in the corner so she could act as their chaperone. She had a basket of bright yellow fabric with some needles and thread to occupy herself.

"At my aunt's request," said Mr. Withrow, "I have agreed to give you a cursory introduction to economics, politics, and mathematics."

"It is my understanding that those subjects are not particularly suited to the feminine mind," said Mary.

"If you are not capable of learning them, then by all means, let us halt these lessons now."

Mary had been questioning their appropriateness, not her own mind. She wished she could say something clever and biting in response as Elizabeth would, but she could only manage, "I am sure I will be quite capable at whatever you choose to teach me."

"We will see," he said, passing her a piece of paper. "You have ten minutes to write an answer to each of these questions."

Mary read the precise, small handwriting at the top of the page. "But I could spend days researching and writing a response for each one."

"I am certain you could, Miss Bennet. But I want your thoughts, not the ideas of others, and I want them to be brief, and I want them immediately. So please begin." He picked up a book on economics and left her to it.

Mary swallowed, wishing she was receiving drawing or French instruction instead. She reread the first question: "What is the ultimate goal in running an estate?" She thought of her father, the late nights he had spent toiling over the estate's ledgers, and the way he had visited each of those he employed and kept himself aware of their concerns. She hoped Mr. Collins continued to do the same. She dipped her pen in the ink and wrote, "To make sure everything and everyone is functioning properly."

Next question: "What are the benefits of charity on the recipient and the giver?" This was easier, for it was addressed by so many of the sermons and books that she read. The hard part of this question was restricting herself to only a few sentences. "Charity lifts the soul, ennobles the less fortunate, and provides relief to the suffering. Ultimately, it is key to gaining the approval of God."

She turned to the final question: "What is at the root of civic unrest, and what is in the best interests of the government?" She knew almost nothing of politics and, despite straining her mind for an answer, could not come up with anything suitable. Mr. Withrow set down his book and said, "Finish whatever you are writing," so in an effort to provide an answer, she wrote a single word, "Peace."

Mr. Withrow reached across the desk, took her paper, and read her responses.

"The real answer to each of these questions is one word: money."

"But—" said Mary.

"Hear me out," said Mr. Withrow. "Your first response is not far off—everything and everyone on the estate must function properly, but that is not the goal, that is the means. The goal is money. If not, everything falls apart: the estate is lost or falls into ruin, the family becomes impoverished and dependent on relatives, all the workers and servants are thrown out into the world, with nothing to support them, often turning to crime and other vices. Thus, the ultimate goal must be money. You and your mother and your sister, who went from having plenty to having little, should know that more than most."

Since her father's death, the lack of funds had plagued them. But the loss of money from the estate was of less importance in her mind than the loss of stability and of her lifelong home.

"In terms of your second response, I will not contest your

lofty ideals, but ultimately, the recipients of charity need money—it is survival; it is life. And those givers of charity maintain their own position through money, and by performing acts of charity maintain the social order and thus their access to money."

His cynicism frightened her. "Whatever do you mean?"

"I mean that charity exists to keep people in their place. It gives them enough to prevent desperation, for desperation causes desperate actions which often challenge the positions of those who give charitably."

Mary rolled her quill between her fingers, unsure if she should take notes on something so antithetical to everything she believed.

"In terms of the third question, I assume you mean that peace is the purpose of government. But let us return to the first half of the question. What is the cause of social unrest? Rebellions rarely happen when people are satisfied with their position, when they have sufficient money for the needs of their station. But when a lack of money, and thus of the necessities of survival, causes suffering, that is when people rise up.

"It is in the best interests of the government to keep the status quo intact. We do not need a bloody revolution like in France, where tens of thousands were killed and the livelihoods of hundreds of thousands were disrupted. Obviously those in positions of authority want to maintain their power and fortunes, and will do whatever it takes—force, propaganda, and a slight redistribution or democratization of power or money when necessary.

"As you pursue this course of study, you must remember that at the root of almost every question or problem, money is a primary, if not *the* primary, motivator."

Mary was appalled. "But there is so much more to life than money. So much of greater worth that motivates people. Paul himself writes that 'the love of money is the root of all evil: which while some coveted after, they have erred from the faith, and pierced themselves through with many sorrows.'"

Withrow exhaled audibly. "It is true that money has caused great sorrow and strife and evil. And there may be individuals with loftier motivations, or who at least believe their motivations are something better. Though more often than not at the root you will find money and self-aspiration."

"That is the most cynical statement I have ever heard uttered," declared Mary.

"You do not have to agree with anything I teach you, but I do expect you to learn it and understand it."

Mary suspected there would be much she would not agree with, but the rest of his lesson focused on very practical, factual knowledge. He was unforgiving of error, but good at answering her questions. At the end of the hour he outlined the planned course of study: estate management, accounting, balance sheets, the political system, the current political parties, the judicial system, the stock exchange, and how to quickly read a ledger and find information in it. The planned lesson schedule would keep her occupied for five weeks, all the way until the ball.

"Why do I need to know all this?" asked Mary.

"When you are a governess to a bunch of little boys, they will need to learn this so they can become leaders in the worlds of business and politics." His words had none of the resistance, none of the doubt she had overheard from his conversation with Lady Trafford.

"Will they not learn these things from their fathers? Or a tutor? Or from school?"

"Eventually, yes; however, *you* will provide the foundation that will give them an advantage. It is never too early to learn essential life skills."

These did not sound like Mr. Withrow's words or sentiments, but rather Lady Trafford's, something he adopted because making the argument suited his purposes. Yet he delivered them in such a manner that if Mary had not spent almost two months in the same household, she would have thought them genuine.

His sentiments on the centrality of money, however, were definitely his own.

WHEN MARY RETURNED to her room, her letter packet was in precisely the same position, but the hair was gone.

Her hand went to the mourning ring and she clutched it tightly, wishing for her father's advice.

She wanted to rationalize the disappearance of the piece of hair: perhaps it had fallen out on its own or come undone when the letter packet was moved for cleaning. But she had secured the hair firmly. And she had placed the packet in a seemingly haphazard position on the table. If someone had moved the packet for cleaning, they would not have placed it back so precisely.

The hair had been secure prior to her lesson with Mr. Withrow, and he had been with her the entire time. Which meant it was not Mr. Withrow, and not Fanny, who had observed their lesson. That left Lady Trafford, Mrs. Boughton, or one of the many other servants. But ultimately, it must be at the direction of Lady Trafford.

She looked hastily around her room. She felt as if she were

being watched, but of course, no one was there. Now that she knew for certain that her letters were being read, she would need to be very careful.

She removed her writing supplies and sat at the table. She needed to gather more information about Lady Trafford and Withrow. Maria Blankenbeckler was in Brighton, and she might be able to help her.

Dear Maria,

I still have no current plans to visit Brighton. It is strange to be so close to you in terms of miles, and yet, for all practical purposes, so very far away.

I have a favor to ask of you. There is some information that I need you to gather for me, but I need you to be discreet. Do not mention me, Lady Trafford, or Castle Durrington in any way. I need you to trust that I need this information without asking why, for I cannot explain why until I see you in person.

I need you to find an M. May that resides in or around Brighton. Who is this person? What do they do? Any information you could provide would be useful.

Second, I need you to find out information about Brighton's Society for Literacy and Improvement of the Poor. Who is in charge of the organization? Who works for it? What exactly do they do? Also, did anything unusual or noteworthy happen within the organization during the week of September the 8th?

I have one final request, which may seem strange, but is of the utmost importance. Do not put your name on the outside of the letter, and do not address the letter with my name. Instead direct it to Mary Woodville, Worthing, Sussex.

Thank you for being my friend, and thank you for helping me with this task. I hope it is not too much trouble for you.

Sincerely,
Mary Bennet

Woodville was the last name of the main character in the only Gothic novel she had ever read—Kitty's novel—so it felt like an appropriate nom de plume. She secured the letter using the paper triangle lock that Lady Trafford had taught her to make.

Then she took a new quarter sheet of paper and addressed her sister.

Dear Kitty,

I am trying to discover more about Lady Trafford's relationship with our father before he died. I desire this information not for any particular cause, but only because I am of a curious nature.

I know that Father's letters were kept after his death. Are there any letters from Lady Trafford to him? Make sure to check both the letter box he kept on his desk and the locked box he kept on one of the top bookshelves, for I know I saw him place letters there as well.

If you could also ask Mother if she had ever heard any mention of Lady Trafford before the funeral.

I suspect someone has been opening my letters before I receive them, but, for various reasons, I do not want to tell Lady Trafford of my suspicion. Because of this, I ask that you do not put your name on the outside of the letter, nor mine—instead address it to Mary Woodville, Worthing, Sussex. I know you will appreciate the name I have chosen. I have never before asked you to keep a secret, but I ask it of you now—please do not tell anyone why you are looking through Father's letters, or that you are sending a letter to me under another name.

Love always, your sister,
Mary Bennet

She used the same, complex method to seal the letter to her sister. She had no way to take the letters to Worthing today, but she would be going tomorrow, so she kept the letters tucked inside her stocking as she went to the sitting room with the pianoforte for her first lesson from Lady Trafford.

The topic was history, and in preparation Lady Trafford had asked Mary to study two chapters on the Wars of the Roses, each from a different history book. Mary came to the lesson prepared, having memorized all the major dates, names, and facts. But Lady Trafford was not at all impressed by Mary's preparations.

"It is not enough to be able to memorize. I want you to think, to analyze, to look at larger theories and trends. Why do you think I assigned you chapters from two different authors on the same subject?"

"I…am not sure."

"They disagree on the primary causes, as well as the results. And what they choose to include as they describe the conflict reveals as much about the contemporary authors and their political viewpoints as it does about the events of the past."

Mary took notes, trying to record all of Lady Trafford's words.

"I want you to reread the chapters, this time with the intent to analyze them. Analyze the Wars of the Roses—their causes, their conflicts, their results. Analyze the differences between the two chapters, and what may be addressed inadequately in each. Analyze the authors themselves, and consider the larger theories they subscribe to. Finally, I want you to consider how these theories apply to Britain's current conflicts on the continent and how these authors would likely write about Bonaparte."

Lady Trafford took Mary's quill and added several additional items to the directions. Mary was unable to suppress a grimace.

"What is the matter?" asked Lady Trafford.

"Nothing is the matter," said Mary, "But I do think that memorizing is much easier than what you expect me to do."

"Yes, but what I am asking you to do will be more worth your while."

Mary considered the list. "Why do you spell his name Bonaparte, instead of Buonaparte?"

"The emperor chose that version from his family history. Buonaparte is a spelling some journalists and writers started using again about a decade ago in order to mock Napoleon and attempt to delegitimize his right to rule France by using the name that sounds less French."

"Would that not be justified, given he is the enemy?"

"Perhaps," said Lady Trafford. "But if you do not treat your enemies with a certain amount of respect, then you will underestimate them and risk losing your own legitimacy."

THE NEXT DAY, after her drawing class, Mr. Parker drove Mary in the carriage to Worthing for her French lesson. It was held in Madame Dieupart's front parlor, which overlooked the sea. Madame Dieupart had invited two other French-speaking ladies for tea, and they spoke with Mary for an hour and a half without a single word of English.

When her lesson was finished, she approached Mr. Parker, who sat idly in the box seat of Lady Trafford's black carriage. "Could you wait for a few minutes?" she asked. "I would like to walk a little around the town before I return to Castle Durrington."

"Of course, Miss Bennet." His mustache twitched. "Would you like me to wait here or to bring the carriage to meet you somewhere?"

"You can wait here. I will not be long."

She walked a little along the boardwalk. She paused for a moment, watching as several boys threw rocks into the sea, making them skip across the water, and then she turned up the main road into town. Unlike at Castle Durrington, here in Worthing it always smelled of the sea.

After a few blocks, she paused in front of a post office collection box. There were several scattered throughout town where you could deposit letters if you did not want to visit the post office itself. Before taking the letters out of her pocket, she looked at those nearby: young ladies fanning themselves as they spoke to an officer, a mother shepherding five young children down the road, a lad carrying a box of fish. None of them paid her any attention, but a block behind her, on the path she had taken from Madame Dieupart's house, someone ducked around the corner. She had seen enough of him to be fairly certain that it was Mr. Parker.

Instead of removing the letters, she walked farther up the road. She tried to keep a measured pace and ignore the pounding in her pulse and her sudden impulse to flee. If Mr.

Parker was following her, she did not want him to realize that she knew it.

In the distance, she spotted Mr. Withrow, speaking with the new arrival in Worthing, Colonel Radcliffe. She had not known that Withrow was in Worthing today. He did not appear to see her, and she wondered if he had instructed Mr. Parker to follow her.

After several blocks, she stepped into the milliner's shop. She examined different ribbons in a way that allowed her to see out of the front window from the edge of her vision without directly facing the window.

Within less than a minute, Mr. Parker passed the shop, glancing nonchalantly at her.

Mary bit her lip and was gripped by fear. She did not want to believe that Mr. Parker meant her any harm—Mr. Parker, who had driven her and Lady Trafford so many times, who took such care with the horses. But there had been a ferocity in his eyes that she had not seen before. He was the fox eyeing the enclosure, and she was the hen trapped within.

She could give herself up, let Mr. Parker follow her and simply not mail the letters, or allow him to see her mailing the letters. But her soul rebelled against that thought, rebelled against giving in and giving up to the wishes and plans of others.

Though she had never particularly liked ribbon, she bought a black ribbon and then did her best to speak as her sister Lydia might.

"There is a gentleman down the street outside that I would rather not talk to," she said. "Do you have another door by which I could leave the shop?"

"We do," said the milliner, "but it is not designed for ladies like yourself."

"Oh please," begged Mary. "He always makes the conversation unpleasant, and speaking to him, alone, by myself, would surely not be proper."

"Very well," said the milliner. He led her through the workroom and to a door that opened into a small, dank alleyway, empty of any people.

"Thank you," said Mary. "Your assistance is much appreciated."

She followed the back alley away from the road and took a side turn at random. As she walked, she heard voices coming from an alcove ahead, so she slowed. She considered turning back, but instead stepped closer.

"I can guarantee the items would be in Chartres within two weeks." Mary could not be certain, but it sounded like the voice of Colonel Coates. From the geography book Lady Trafford had assigned her, she knew that Chartres was not terribly far from Paris. How did Colonel Coates intend to get items to France in war time?

Another man replied, "I would prefer it be earlier."

"If I want to keep my boat unobserved by British and French authorities, it must be on my own timetable. I must do it when the moment is right."

"Then I want to accompany the goods myself."

"That is acceptable," said Colonel Coates. "But the price will be tripled."

"Tripled?"

"Smuggling goods is one thing, smuggling people is quite another. But you do not need to accompany the items. You can ask anyone—even Mr. Shaffer. I do good work."

"I will consider it," said the second voice.

What she had just heard seemed impossible—Colonel Coates, smuggling. Despite the risk, Mary needed to confirm that it truly was him. He was a kind, attentive gentleman, working with Sir Pickering on the murder investigation—it could not possibly be him. Surely there was someone else in Worthing with a similar-sounding voice. And surely he had not just implied that Mr. Shaffer, the clergyman, had used his smuggling services.

Mary peered around the edge of the alcove. It was indeed Colonel Coates, speaking with a merchant she vaguely recognized.

Colonel Coates's head turned in her direction, and she pulled herself back around the corner, then walked briskly down the alley, certain she would be discovered. She hurried past the back of the milliner's shop and down a different path that led back to the main road.

Finally, she came out on the main road, into the sunlight. She breathed in and out, almost panting from the exertion. A woman looked at her reproachfully, so Mary smoothed her skirts and smiled, attempting to mask her inner turmoil.

Colonel Coates was a smuggler. He had a secret boat. Mr. Holloway was likely stabbed on a boat before being thrown into the sea. What if Holloway had discovered the smuggling, and Colonel Coates had killed him for it?

There was no evidence that Colonel Coates had killed Holloway—it could have been someone else who owned one of the other seventy-three boats in the area. Yet it was a possibility, and suddenly Mary did not know who to trust.

With that sobering thought, she returned to the postal collection box. She stopped a few feet away, waiting as a woman sighed dramatically and placed what must be a love letter inside. There was no sign of the colonels, no Mr. Withrow, no Mr. Parker, so Mary removed the letters from her pocket and slipped them into the box.

She walked slowly back to the carriage and waited inside it, outwardly serene, with her hands neatly folded, until Mr. Parker returned.

"Such a lovely day for a walk," said Mary. "A little cold, but quite pleasant. I see you took a stroll yourself?"

"A small one," he said, giving Mary an inquisitive look, but he did not say anything about following Mary, and so she did not either.

CHAPTER FOURTEEN

"There is a tendency in all states to reduce the tiller of the earth to a level with the oxen he yokes to the plough....Were I called upon to estimate the quantity of freedom possessed by any people, I would not enquire under what particular form of government they existed, but by what tenure the land was held by individuals, and into what portions it was divided and subdivided. If the freeholders were few in comparison to the whole population, I should be persuaded that slavery had taken deep root among them, although their political constitution should be of the most admirable construction. History can shew us republics, even democracies, in which three-fourths of the inhabitants are slaves...."

–A letter to the editor by "Agrarius,"
The Liverpool Mercury, Liverpool, England,
November 5, 1813

MARY WORRIED ABOUT Mr. Withrow's soul. Even those willfully acting in error deserved an opportunity to change for the better, so after her next lesson, which had been scheduled for a Friday morning, she handed him a treatise she had painstakingly prepared, entitled "Man is more than money."

Before her French lesson Withrow found her and returned the treatise. "Thank you for allowing me to read this."

"What did you think?" She would not allow him to return it to her with no comment beyond thanks.

"Your paper tended towards the verbose and the sentimental, and took a rather circuitous approach to your subject, but many of your arguments were solid and you cited extensive sources."

A warmth filled Mary's chest; from Mr. Withrow, that was actually a compliment. "Thank you."

"However, I stand by my original position on money."

Mary did not know what more she could do to persuade him. She had done her part in showing him the folly of his ways, and it was his choice of whether or not he would make changes in his own life. Besides, she had other, more urgent ways she needed to spend her time.

After her French lesson she rushed to finish Lady Trafford's assignments, which included both an analysis of two weeks of newspapers and a reading on the science behind mining techniques. In the past week and a half of lessons with Lady Trafford, Mary had discovered that Lady Trafford cared less about a particular subject matter than about an overall approach. They studied history, current events, newspapers, manners, literature, and science, and sometimes, Mary would leave after an hour with Lady Trafford and have no idea what they had studied at all. But regardless of the subject matter, Lady Trafford wanted Mary to come to her own conclusions, to think about the unstated goals and effects, and to consider how the subject impacted daily living.

Yet more important than the time she devoted to any of her lessons was Mary's quest for the truth. It had been a week and a half since she had mailed the letters to Maria and Kitty, which should have given them enough time to receive her correspondence, gather information, and send a reply. The next morning she had several spare hours, so she decided to go to town. It was about a four-mile walk to the post office in Worthing, so that was out of the question, and the last time she had taken a carriage, she had been followed.

She entered the stables and as luck would have it, she found Mr. Tubbs, the man who had driven her to Castle Durrington on her first day. She might have left the stables and postponed her trip for another day had she met Mr. Parker.

"Miss Bennet," said Mr. Tubbs. "Now what can I do for you today?"

"If possible, I would like to ride a horse into Worthing."

"We have plenty of horses you could ride that are used to a side saddle."

She hated to admit her inadequacies, but in this case it was expedient. "I am not a very skilled rider." Of her sisters, Jane was the best horsewoman. Mary was better than Elizabeth, but not by much.

"In that case you should ride Dusty. She is old, but gentle and level-headed."

Mary rested her hand on a smooth wooden post and enjoyed the fresh scent of the hay as Mr. Tubbs prepared Dusty and led her outside. Mary stood on the left side of the horse, swallowing the nervousness she always felt when riding these large beasts. She placed her right hand on the higher pommel of the saddle, also called the fixed head, and raised her skirts a little with her left. Mounting was her least favorite part of riding. She raised her right foot, and Mr. Tubbs supported it with both of his hands. She bent her left knee and sprang up towards the horse, feeling a bit out of control as Mr. Tubbs lifted her right leg and guided her the rest of the way.

Secure on the saddle, Mary breathed a sigh of relief and adjusted her legs comfortably to the left side of the horse, around the two pommels, the fixed head and the leaping head, which made it easier to stay in position and not fall off the horse. She attempted to pull her dress down so it completely covered her ankle and her boot to be more proper, but this was not a riding habit and did not have the extra length, so she could not completely do so. The Bennets had never purchased riding habits for their daughters. Sometimes they did drape a blanket over their legs, but Mary did not want to incur the extra effort of keeping a blanket in place the entire ride.

Mr. Tubbs handed her a riding crop. "When you reach Worthing, stop at the inn and mention that you live at Castle Durrington. They will tie up Dusty, free of charge, and help you mount when you are ready to come home."

"Thank you," said Mary.

"Once you feel ready, start her at a walk."

Mary took a moment to concentrate and then urged the horse forward. Dusty walked, calmly, slowly. The horse followed her directions with only gentle suggestions as she urged her to turn left and then right.

"Now take her at a trot. Yes, like that. Now do not ask her to go any faster than that."

"There is no risk of me wanting to go any faster," said Mary.

After leaving Castle Durrington Mary looked back several times, but it did not appear that anyone was following her. Her ride to Worthing was uneventful, and she did as Mr. Tubbs recommended and left the horse at the inn.

First she stopped at the bookseller where she found a very small writing book, with minuscule sheets of paper bound together. She intended to record her notes and observations on Lady Trafford and Mr. Withrow in order to better notice any abnormalities and transgressions in their behaviour. In case someone saw her in the shop and informed Lady Trafford of her visit, Mary also bought a new piece of music for the pianoforte.

Mary left the bookseller and looked at the post office next door. She could not simply walk in and ask for Mary Woodville's mail; she had visited the post office before, and they might recognize her as Mary Bennet.

Instead she walked farther up the street. She stepped inside a clothing store that catered to the working classes and immediately drew so many startled looks that she knew she could not purchase from such an establishment. She promptly left the shop without even managing a proper apology for her haste.

This would not do—this would not do at all. She needed to return to Castle Durrington before the length of her absence became suspicious, and she needed to check for mail.

In frustration, Mary turned down a smaller side street, and then into an alley. She kicked at the dirt road, and it coated her shoes and turned the bottom of her dress a dusty brown. She stopped kicking the dirt as she passed a raggedly dressed woman sitting on the side of the road, rocking her baby.

A few steps later Mary stopped and turned around. "May I buy your cloak?"

"What you be needin' mine cloak for? Yourn is purty expensive."

"It does not matter what I want it for. I will give you…seven shillings for it."

"I wunt higgle over that," said the woman. She stood and

ripped off the cloak in one quick motion, without setting down the baby.

Mary counted out the shillings and exchanged them for the cloak. It was ragged and smelled like a stall that had not been mucked, but it was very long and had a large hood that would help hide her face.

The woman kissed one of the coins, spit on it, and put it in a pocket, keeping the other coins in her hand. Mary's confusion must have shown, for the woman said, "Tis good luck." She began to walk away with her baby.

"Wait!" said Mary.

She turned around. "You be wantin' mine dress too?" She gave a bawdy laugh and tugged at the collar.

"I do not need your dress," said Mary firmly. "But I will pay you an additional two shillings if you do not tell anyone that you have seen me or sold me your cloak."

"That's mighty suent," said the woman, her hand out-stretched. The baby began to cry.

"Do you *promise* you will not tell anyone I bought this from you?"

"I swear it, on mine baby."

"You should *not* be swearing on your baby," said Mary, concerned that the woman might have done this many times before.

"But I do. I swear on mine baby."

Mary sighed. "Very well." She handed over the extra two shillings. "Please, buy yourself a new cloak before you freeze." The woman hurried off down the alley.

Mary wrapped the cloak around herself and pulled the hood over her head, allowing it to cover part of her face. She did up all the clasps to cover as much of her dress as possible, then smeared some dirt on her hands and her face.

Her disguise ready, Mary entered the post office. A woman holding a large package pulled her two children as far away from Mary as possible, then hurried them out the door. The same man as last time greeted her, but not with the same smile.

"My name's Mary Woodville," she said, trying to imitate the original owner of the cloak's way of speaking. "I'm expectin' two letters."

The man looked in the back room and then returned to the desk. "I do have a letter for you, Miss Woodville."

"Only one?"

"Yes, one. It will be eight pence." The man looked skeptical that she possessed the funds.

As she passed him the money, she realized that this was a rather shoddy disguise. An old cloak and some dirt could not hide her hands that had never seen labor and her well-kept fingernails. And if anyone knew her well, they would still recognize her face. But at least this man did not seem to.

She took the letter. Her name and address were in Kitty's handwriting, which meant there was no letter from Maria, even though Brighton was closer and she should have received the letter faster.

Mary returned to the alley where she had purchased the cloak. She broke the seal and read her sister's words.

My dearest Mary <u>Woodville,</u>

I did not realize that we read the same books. What other secrets have you been keeping from me all these years? This creates all sorts of possibilities. Imagine if we read the same novel every month and then did as we are doing now, attempting to act out the characters through our letters. I think it would provide splendid entertainment.

In terms of what I have discovered, it is for your ears only. Do not show this letter to anyone, or the consequences would be dire! (I think I could make a living writing Gothic novels, and it would oblige me greatly if you agreed.)

In terms of my revelations to you, we shall start from the smallest and move to the largest. First, I asked Mother if she had ever heard of Lady Trafford before Father's funeral. She answered affirmatively, but upon further questioning I have concluded that Mother wishes she could have remembered knowing of Lady Trafford but had never actually heard of or met her before.

Revelation the second. I have gone through the letter box that Father used to keep on his desk. In it I found one—only one!—letter from Lady Trafford, dated January 1809. A lengthy part of the letter discusses the weather and other trivialities. Then she mentions the death of her daughter and calls it "tragic." (I did not know that Lady Trafford had a daughter—you shall have to write me and tell me more of it!) Apparently, her daughter's gravestone was damaged and had to be repaired. Finally, Lady Trafford requests that Father return her request for information. Interestingly, she gives no details on what sort of information she is demanding, which leads me to conclude that she had written him other letters on the subject.

Revelation the third. Prepare yourself to be shocked. The locked letter box that Father kept on the shelf is missing. No one can remember seeing it since before the funeral. We did not bring it with us to the Philipses', and Mr. and Mrs. Collins have not seen it at all. After speaking—discreetly—to an extensive number of people,

I have concluded that the letter box is most definitively gone and probably disappeared within a fortnight of Father's death.

I hope you have a splendid week. There is a public ball, and since I am no longer in mourning clothes, I will attend. It will be my very first ball alone, with no sisters by my side, so I hope you think of me there, and imagine me dancing with as many men as possible.

Yours always,
The Incomparable Kitty Bennet

Mary reflected on Kitty's "revelations." It did not surprise her that Mrs. Bennet would pretend, when questioned, that she had known of Lady Trafford; after all, Lady Trafford was a woman of importance. The second was more interesting. Lady Trafford had indeed known Mr. Bennet, at least well enough that he had kept one of her letters. But if Mary remembered correctly, Lady Trafford's daughter Anne had died in June 1808. Lady Trafford only informed Mr. Bennet of the fact in January 1809. If they had a close connection, the correspondence would have been sent more quickly after the event.

Mary folded Kitty's letter and hid it in her stocking. She removed the beggar's cloak, wrapped it, and tucked it within her own cloak. Then she used her handkerchief to clean her face as well as she could.

She returned to the stable at the inn where she had left Dusty. She saw a reflection of herself in a piece of glass and grimaced. She asked a stable lad for a wet rag and scrubbed at her face and her hands. Once she finished, she was about to ask for help mounting the horse when she paused. How had Mr. Holloway come to Worthing anyway? From the maps she had studied in Castle Durrington's library, she knew it was a lengthy trip, over twenty-five miles. Perhaps he had taken a public carriage, as she had. Or maybe he owned his own horse or carriage.

"Did you know Mr. Holloway?" asked Mary.

"The dead man you foun'?" said the boy. "Course I did."

She did not like being so strongly associated with Mr. Holloway, but it did serve its purpose. "Did he have his own horse or carriage?"

"Oh yes, his own 'orse. I always puts her in the back stall. He wouldn't let us keep her anywhere else."

"The day he came to Worthing and then died—did he bring his horse here?"

"Certain sure he did."

Mary smiled. Her intuition had been correct. "What happened to the horse?"

"Well, the 'orse had been here for most of a week, and we were wonderin' why, but then the magistrate came and got her. I think he sent her back to Crawley."

Mary deflated a little. She felt rather silly about her excitement for her brilliant realization, a realization that had occurred to Sir Pickering weeks ago.

"Did Holloway have any bags with him that day?"

"I dunno. If he did, the magistrate took'm."

It was no use; there was nothing more she could learn here. The horse had been gone for weeks, taken by Sir Pickering along with any other evidence there might have been. But still, she could not resist asking, "Can I see the stall?"

The boy led her back. The stall was empty, but she stepped inside and asked for a moment alone.

This was the stall where Mr. Holloway had left his horse,

an ordinary, smelly stall, with hay and dirt and wooden walls. She had seen Mr. Holloway with Mr. Withrow, and then Holloway had come here, and then he had met with someone, and then he had died.

She found the stable boy again, and he helped her back into Dusty's saddle. As she approached Castle Durrington, she realized she needed to hide her new—well, old—cloak. She would need it again, but with how it smelled, she could not possibly bring it in the castle. She found a hollow in a tree, tucked it inside, and hoped the animals stayed out of it.

After returning the horse she rushed to her room, cleaned herself more thoroughly, and changed into a fresh mourning dress.

Then she practiced her new song on the pianoforte. Playing always helped her relax and brought clarity to her thoughts.

"That is a very nice piece." Lady Trafford had entered the room so quietly that Mary had not realized she was there.

Mary smiled. "I bought it when I went to town today."

Lady Trafford listened for a few minutes and then excused herself to attend to other business.

A part of the song caused Mary to stumble. She stopped, worked out the correct fingerings, and then played those measures ten times in a row to help herself grow more used to the movement. Once she was finished, she started the piece from the beginning. This time, the challenging section did not cause her any trouble.

As she lost herself in the music, she realized that there was one additional point of interest in Kitty's letter: the broken gravestone. It seemed that a private visit to the church was in order.

CHAPTER FIFTEEN

"Wednesday morning, Richard Hucknall, William Hughes, and Thomas Foss, for forgeries; and Joseph Sylvester, for highway robbery, were executed in front of Newgate. Hucknall was formerly a stockbroker and had contrived to elude discovery for a considerable time. The unhappy men met their fate with becoming fortitude and resignation."

–Kentish Chronicle, Canterbury, England,
November 12, 1813

THE CHURCH WAS empty and quiet, and the stillness felt unnatural compared to the fullness it held on days of worship, the constant movement and energy. Mary's steps echoed on the stone floor as she walked through the sanctuary, examining the windows, the paintings, the pews.

The middle-of-the-night visitors had mentioned that they did not have time to visit the church, which implied that there would be reason to do so. Yet Mary could see no secrets in these walls, and unless they had some sort of dealings with Mr. Shaffer and his family, she could not discern a purpose for them to visit.

Of course, Withrow had said that if they visited in the middle of the night they would be suspected of grave robbing. Perhaps it was less the church they wanted than the adjoining cemetery. Which brought her back to Kitty's letter and its mention of the damaged gravestone.

Mary left the building and entered the cemetery. It was a cold day with a strong wind, and soon her feet, her ears, and her nose were chilled. The ground was damp, and as she walked between the rows, mud gathered on her shoes and the hem of her dress. Her eyes scanned the names and dates on each of the headstones, searching for Lady Trafford's children and husband.

In the middle of one row was a patch of freshly turned soil. A recent grave. Maybe even from the last few days. No headstone had yet been placed, no grass yet grew.

This grave was not the purpose of her visit, yet she found herself unable to walk any farther. A few days after her father's funeral, she had visited his grave and it had appeared just like this.

A wave of emotion took her, like the waves Withrow had described which could carry even the strongest swimmer out to sea, and then Mary was drowning, drowning in her sorrow, drowning in her loss. She was back, back to her father's dying words, back to his dying breath. Back to the nights spent keeping vigil over his body, wishing it was not true, willing to trade anything just to see him, speak to him, reassure him that she loved him and hear him express the same for her. Back to feeling his dead cold hand in hers.

Mary sank to her knees, getting mud all up her dress, but she paid it no heed. Her body shook, and it took all her strength just to breathe in the frigid air. What did life mean if it always ended like this, with a body in the ground, subject to worms and decay? What did life mean for those who loved the deceased the most, and were then left alone in the world?

She pictured his hand when it had reached out to her,

weak and pale in its last moments. Then Mr. Bennet coughed, and his hand went not to Mary, but to Elizabeth. But now his hand, decaying and bereft of life, was beneath the ground. She had not even attended his funeral.

She tried to control herself, tried to pull herself back to the present moment, but the more she resisted, the more her emotions dragged her under. So she let them. She submersed herself in the ragged sense of loss until sorrow surrounded her entire being and became every fiber of her.

Gradually, the intensity of it slipped away. The pain was still present, like a fresh bruise, but it no longer consumed her. She removed the mourning ring from her finger and rotated it so the lock of her father's hair faced out. As she slid the ring back on her finger, she realized that Miss Shaffer stood nearby, watching. Mary wondered how long she had been there.

Mary rubbed her face with her hands, certain it was not presentable.

"You must miss your father terribly," said Miss Shaffer kindly as she approached.

Mary nodded.

"It is a hard thing, to lose a family member. I can tell that you loved him dearly."

Mary sniffed, and then tried to stand. Miss Shaffer helped her to her feet.

"Come, walk with me," said Miss Shaffer. She linked her arm with Mary's and led her up and down the rows.

Finally, Mary regained her voice. "I apologize for my behaviour and…"

"You do not need to apologize. The church and these grounds should be a safe place to feel what you need to feel, to express what you need to express."

"Thank you," said Mary. Miss Shaffer made her feel that she did not need to be ashamed.

After a few more minutes of walking, Mary remembered her original purpose. "I know that Lady Trafford's husband and children died not too many years ago. Are they buried here?"

"Yes, they are." Miss Shaffer led her to a secluded spot with three graves.

The largest stone was cut in the form of a cross and was almost Mary's height. Words on the base showed that it belonged to Sir George Trafford. To the left was the headstone for James, and to the right a space, likely reserved for Lady Trafford when her time in this world ended, and then a headstone for Anne, covered with delicate carvings of flowers. There was a long crack which had been repaired near the upper edge of Anne's stone.

"Lady Trafford has been hesitant to talk about their deaths," said Mary.

"She still grieves for them," said Miss Shaffer. "It was one loss after another for her, first her husband, then her daughter, then her son. She seemed lost for quite some time, but now she has found a way to move forward."

"May I ask how they died?"

Miss Shaffer paused, considering, and Mary feared that she would not answer.

"It is simply because I want to avoid doing or saying anything that would offend Lady Trafford or cause her more pain."

Miss Shaffer nodded. "I suppose there can be no harm." She folded her arms against her body and shivered. "Sir George Trafford died of consumption. Anne—" Miss Shaffer wiped a tear from her eye. "Anne was only a year older than I.

She was very ill for an entire year. Finally, she grew healthy and strong and lively again, and then there was the accident."

"The accident?"

"The family was riding horses on a trail. Anne went up ahead with her horse. They were on a rocky ledge and the ground was unstable. Some of it broke under the weight of the horse and Anne and the horse fell. She died in the fall."

Mary could picture it in her mind—a young girl falling, Lady Trafford screaming, maybe her older brother James jumping off his horse and running to her side, and no one, no one able to do anything for Anne.

"That is dreadful," said Mary. "I can see why Lady Trafford does not like to speak of it."

"It was quite tragic. Then with accidental deaths there is always an inquest, and I understand that it was quite hard on Lady Trafford."

Miss Shaffer stared intently at Anne's grave. Five years had passed, yet Miss Shaffer still grieved her friend. Perhaps grief was never easily, neatly resolved.

"Where did the accident occur?" Mary could imagine how hard it must be to pass that same spot again and again, to have the grief brought to the forefront every time.

"It was in Crawley."

"In Crawley?" said Mary. "But that's where Mr. Holloway—"

"Yes," said Miss Shaffer. "Anne's death was actually how Mr. Holloway and Lady Trafford met. Mr. Holloway was one of the local clergymen, and after the accident, he rushed to help and support Lady Trafford. He even personally accompanied Anne's body to Worthing, then stayed for an additional week to be of further assistance."

"Mr. Holloway sounds like he was a good man."

"A good man, and a great one. Truly great. My father has always felt inadequate in comparison to him."

"Mr. Withrow said that he could be rather theatrical."

Miss Shaffer smiled. "Yes, indeed. He could pull a coin out of your ear at a moment's notice, and he liked to hide things in unusual places. He could find nooks and crannies everywhere. When he was younger, he would enter the parsonage, be inside for less than two minutes, and during that time he would have hidden a handful of ribbons around the room. If I found them quickly, I could keep them."

"Hearing of his death must have been hard on you too."

"Yes," said Miss Shaffer simply, and returned her gaze to Anne's grave.

After a few minutes, Mary broke the silence. "What happened to James?"

"He died of convulsions."

There were so many ways to die, so many reasons people died every single day. Yet when death came, it still felt unexpected.

Mary gestured at Anne's headstone. "Was it damaged?"

"Vandals broke into the cemetery. It was not long after the stone was put in place."

"Did they damage any of the other graves?"

Miss Shaffer appeared surprised at this question, as if it had never occurred to her before. "No. I do not believe they did."

It seemed too random for vandals to damage only one grave, the grave of Anne Trafford. The family must have someone who wanted to harm them, but who? And why?

The deaths themselves did not sound suspicious, at least not from Miss Shaffer's account. She wondered who else in Worthing would know more about the grave damage.

Yet she had to take care with whom she asked for stories about Lady Trafford. If someone knew her well enough to know about her past and the mysteries surrounding her family, then they likely had some sort of relationship with Lady Trafford. Mary's questioning could easily be reported to the woman herself. To a certain extent that was unavoidable, but it was one thing for a single person to report back to Lady Trafford, for then it might be dismissed as the fruits of curiosity. But if three or four people reported Mary's line of questioning, it could lead to trouble.

After a few minutes of more mundane conversation, Mary parted ways with Miss Shaffer. She returned to the inn and retrieved the old, smelly cloak, which she had left with Dusty. She prepared her disguise and visited the post office.

A letter from Maria had arrived. With chagrin, Mary noted that Maria had not sealed the letter at all, but simply folded it into itself. After leaving the post office, she found a private spot and read the letter.

Dear Mary,

It feels very unusual to be sending you a letter, addressed to someone else. I cannot imagine why it might be necessary.

I have spent a long time trying to find your information. Admittedly, I did many other things as well. I almost gave up, but then I finally discovered a few things that might be of interest to you.

First, there is no Brighton's Society for Literacy and Improvement of the Poor. At least, there is not now. It was disbanded six years ago, and I could not find any more information on it besides that. There are currently three active societies in Brighton to improve the town.

There are a number of families with the surname May, but I discovered three individuals with the first initial of M. One is Martha May, another is Matthew May, and the final is a Martin May.

I do hope you visit Brighton soon and tell me all about your stay at Castle Durrington.

Your friend,
Maria Blankenbeckler

Mary could not help but be disappointed in Maria. She had provided no information whatsoever about the different Mays, not their ages or occupations or associations. When Mary returned to the castle, she would write Maria another letter requesting more information, though she did not know if Maria would be an effective or efficient source. Kitty had approached her task with much more vigor.

At least, though, Maria had found one useful fact. But if there was no Brighton's Society for Literacy and Improvement of the Poor, then what had taken Lady Trafford to Brighton with such urgency on the day that Mary had arrived at Castle Durrington, the very same day that Mr. Holloway had met his end?

Mary resolved to be more diligent at recording her thoughts and observations in her writing book. Thus far her notes had been sporadic and incomplete, yet with more diligence, perhaps then she could unravel the mysteries around her.

NOVEMBER 10: WITHROW *spends a lot of time managing the estate (though the butler and housekeeper do hire and supervise*

the servants). For an estate this size, I would expect them to employ a steward.

November 11: Lady Trafford went to Worthing to meet with friends. It appeared she brought gifts for the poor old gossip again.

November 12: I went to Worthing so I could report to Monsieur Corneau. I did not directly state that I had overheard Colonel Coates discussing smuggling, but I indirectly referred to it by saying I had heard rumors around town that Colonel Coates might not be dealing completely in forthright ways. Corneau brushed off my concerns, expressed full confidence in Coates, and insisted that Coates's behaviour was completely aboveboard and any rumors to the contrary were unfounded. He then wanted to know who I had heard that from, but I said I did not know who it was. I wonder if Corneau might, in some way, be involved in this venture.

In part to change the subject, I mentioned Anne's damaged gravestone. Corneau said it was unlikely that it had anything to do with the current events. He confided in me that it was an old enemy of Lady Trafford's who had performed the deed, someone that she had framed for a crime, but would not elaborate further. Yet Miss Shaffer said they never discovered the identity of the vandal.

November 13: Lady Trafford disappeared for most of the day and came back from the milliner with a new hat.

November 14: Almost caught. Well, I was caught. Following Withrow. I managed to pretend I had a question for him. I need to keep more distance next time and bring my drawing supplies as an excuse.

November 15: After French, I followed Withrow. He went to the trees in the Roundel. I think he met someone, but I could not get close.

November 16: Lady Trafford cares a great deal that every-

thing be absolutely perfect for the ball. She has given me a large amount of advice on how to act and behave.

November 17: I feel like my sister Kitty—I want to write about the "revelations" I have to share. Perhaps, like Kitty, I should start with the small one first.

Revelation the first. According to the milliner, Lady Trafford did not visit last week. Did not remember the hat I described. Where is the hat from?

Revelation the second. I spent several hours in the lending library in Worthing, searching old newspapers. I believe that I found the event Monsieur Corneau referenced. Two months before Anne's gravestone was damaged, there was a man, half-French, half-English, who was arrested for highway robbery. He claimed he had been framed, though the newspaper did not state by whom, simply stating "by a prominent woman in the community, who had been the one to provide the evidence leading to his arrest." He escaped from prison a week before the gravestone was damaged and was caught a week later. No mention was made in the newspaper that he was the one responsible for the gravestone's damage. I knew that Corneau must have known another way, so I did more research, and I discovered that the arrested man was none other than Corneau's nephew.

As I have reflected back on the day I found Mr. Holloway's body, I have realized that Colonel Coates may have been completely unaware that Corneau asked me to spy for them. Indeed, I wonder if Corneau was reporting what I discovered to Coates at all, or simply gathering the information for his own purposes.

November 18: My letters have been examined again. I think where I am keeping this book is secure (hidden under the bed pressed between the wood and the bed itself).

November 19: Mr. Parker has been absent for a whole week but has now returned. I asked him if he had gone to visit family.

His answer was evasive.

November 20: Two of the servants were let go today. I do not know what happened, but Mrs. Boughton was upset, and Fanny would not speak of it.

November 21: At church, Lady Trafford kept looking at a window that faced the cemetery, but she did not visit the cemetery.

After church, the merchant who had spoken to Colonel Coates about smuggling pulled Mr. Shaffer aside and spoke to him in hushed tones. I was unable to overhear much of the conversation, but I do believe it was about smuggling.

November 22: Withrow went to the Roundel again today to meet with someone, at the same time. Whoever he meets with must enter the Roundel from the south side.

November 23: Lady Trafford left early this morning, unannounced. No word on where she went.

November 24: Lady Trafford is still gone. Withrow was absent the entire day as well. He returned before dinner but ate by himself in his room. I spoke with Colonel Coates, and after telling him that I had never been on a boat but always wanted to, he gave me a tour of his boat. There were no signs that led me to believe that Mr. Holloway was killed on his boat, but there were no signs of smuggling either, and I know, at the least, that Colonel Coates has participated in the latter.

November 25: Lady Trafford came back in time for dinner. Apparently it was a short trip to Chichester to visit a friend.

November 26: I wore my disguise to the post office, and Maria has not replied to the second letter for information that I sent her.

After visiting the post office, I cleaned myself and returned to the stable at the inn so I could ride Dusty back to Castle Durrington. I went back to the stall where Holloway always kept his horse. I remembered that Miss Shaffer said that Holloway liked to hide things, and so I looked to see if there were any good hiding spots. It took several minutes—fortunately, the stable boy was not in the stable at the moment—but I found a board on the side wall that appeared slightly loose. I was able to shift it, and behind it I found one of Mr. Holloway's missing notebooks. I have spent hours reading it. What I have discovered is that it is actually half of a book; it is as if half of his sentences were written in this book and half in another, and in order to understand what is written, you would need both books. Even though Corneau said that if I heard anything about the missing notebooks, I should report to him immediately, I am not going to. He had said I was spying for a worthy cause, but I do not know what cause he is really supporting, and so I will do it for him no longer. Now I seek to find the truth not for others, but for myself.

November 27: Everyone is focused on preparations for the ball.

November 28: Nothing of note. If the pattern holds, tomorrow Withrow will meet with someone in the Roundel. Today I partially completed several landscape sketches there so if I am caught, I have an excuse. I will try to secret myself there tomorrow before the meeting.

THE NEXT DAY, during her French lesson, Mary went back and forth with Madame Dieupart, practicing conversations, a bit impatient the whole time because she knew she would need to cut the lesson short. She felt guilty as this was her last French lesson before the ball; between now and then, there would be no time for lessons due to all the preparations for those who would be arriving early as well as for the ball itself.

But she needed to know with whom Withrow was meeting.

Mary kept watching the clock. Once a full hour had passed, she rubbed her face with her hands, then she tried to look apologetic as she expressed that she was feeling ill. *"Je regrette, Madame, mais je ne me sens pas bien. Pouvons-nous finir notre leçon tôt aujourd'hui?"*

"C'est vrai que tu me parais distraite aujourd'hui. Eh bien! Mais j'espère que tu te sentes assez mieux demain pour continuer notre leçon. Sinon, demande à Madame Trafford d'envoyer un servant me laisser savoir dans la matinée."

Mary felt terrible for feigning illness. Kitty sometimes did this to get out of unpleasant tasks, and Mary wondered if her sister felt this same guilt each time. Yet, despite the guilt, it was surprisingly easy to do. The ease of the act felt like a betrayal to Mary; it should be more difficult to act out a falsehood.

Yet Mary did not call Madame Dieupart back to apologize or stop her from leaving. Her desire to find the truth was stronger than her desire to tell the truth, and though she felt ashamed of herself, she stayed in her room, discreetly watching from the window.

Once her instructor was out of sight, she gathered her drawing supplies and went downstairs. She stood outside the library and listened through the open door; someone, likely Withrow, paced back and forth. Mary exited out the front door, and then took a leisurely, meandering walk, which eventually took her to her destination. She secreted herself inside a large evergreen bush in the middle of the Roundel; this seemed an ideal position from which to spy on Mr. Withrow during his weekly meeting.

After a few minutes, her legs began to hurt. Several branches jabbed into her arms, and pine needles itched her face, but she did not dare push them out of her way. She would stay the course and discover what Withrow was doing.

There was a rustling from one end of the grove, and then from the other, and Withrow and another man met in an open patch of dirt. Withrow smiled and patted the man on the back.

The man wore short black boots, light, whitish trousers, and a large brown overcoat that covered everything else, even his neck. He wore nothing on his head.

The man undid his overcoat and reached for something inside one of its inner pockets. Mary stiffened. Under the cloak, she glimpsed a military uniform. It was white and blue, with a gold gorget around the neck and a white shoulder belt stretching from his shoulder to his waist. From the cut and ornamentation, it was likely an officer's uniform. But it was not the uniform of a British officer—it was the uniform of a French officer from Napoleon Bonaparte's army.

CHAPTER SIXTEEN

"When the war broke out with Russia, the Emperor Alexander wisely packed off the whole tribe of French actors and actresses, that infested St. Petersburgh. Not only is the French drama a powerful instrument in infusing French principles into all ranks of society; but the chief performers, especially the females, have at times been too successfully employed as spies, and agents of political corruption."

—*The Times*, London, November 29, 1813

THE FRENCH OFFICER unfolded the paper that he had removed from his overcoat. Mary wished she had a hiding spot closer to where the French officer and Withrow stood, because she could not make out any details, but it appeared to be a map.

The officer rested the map on a tree stump and moved his hands in different directions along it, gesturing, tapping certain spots, and pausing as Withrow asked him questions. She could not hear a word they were saying, but what she could see was enough. This was much worse than a dubious business deal meant to enrich Withrow and Lady Trafford, much worse than manipulations to bring Mary to Castle Durrington, much worse than a set of stolen mourning rings or searching her parents' bedroom. Much worse than smuggling, and maybe even worse than the murder of Mr. Holloway. Withrow might, at this moment, be betraying his own country.

She shivered in her hiding spot. While she had become more accustomed to going out in the cold, it was more tolerable when one was in motion. It was a particularly bitter day, with a cold wind coming up from the sea, cutting through her cloak.

Her muscles tightened and she involuntarily shifted her body in response. A branch next to her cracked, and a pine needle poked her in the eye. She cut off her cry of pain, clamping her mouth shut and swallowing.

Withrow and the French officer stopped and looked up from the map. They had heard her. The French officer paced around the clearing. As he approached, Mary could see the fine shine on his boots. There was not a single blemish. Beneath his overcoat, attached to his belt, was a sword.

Mary's eye hurt so much that she wanted to let out a sob, but she contained herself, watching, waiting for discovery. The sketches she had brought would not be sufficient excuse if she was discovered, not in this circumstance, hiding beneath a bush.

The French officer passed her hiding spot and returned to Withrow and the map. Yet while she wanted to feel relief, Mary could not. She could hardly breathe out of fear of making another sound.

Finally, the officer and Withrow finished with their conversation. The officer folded his map and placed it in his cloak, which he carefully did up so not a single glimpse of his uniform was visible.

Withrow embraced the man, and as he left, Withrow called out, "Be safe, my friend!" After the man left, Withrow stood for several minutes, waiting, and then he returned to the castle.

AN HOUR LATER, Mary found herself at odds with Fanny. Mary had been playing the pianoforte, trying to calm herself and think rationally about Withrow's meeting with a French officer, when Fanny practically dragged her upstairs to her room.

"Now sit on the bed, right there, and close your eyes," said Fanny.

Mary sat on the bed and gritted her teeth, but did not close her eyes, one of which still hurt from the pine needle.

"Please, close your eyes, just for a moment."

Mary complied, though she wished Fanny would tell her why she had felt a need to interrupt her. At Longbourn, the servants all knew better than to disturb her while she practiced music.

"Now open them," said Fanny.

Mary did so, making her dissatisfaction clear on her face.

Fanny held up two dresses: a cream-coloured morning gown with intricate embroidery and a puce evening gown with copious amounts of lace. Mary was not particularly fond of puce, though Kitty, Lydia, and other fashionable young women adored it.

"What am I looking at?"

"The new clothes I made you, of course. This morning gown will be perfect for your complexion, especially now that your face has perked up from walking, and the evening gown should look stunning by candlelight."

"I did not—"

"But what you will really like is the ball gown." Fanny set down the gowns, turned, and lifted an elaborate, bright canary-yellow ball gown.

Mary sniffed in disdain. It was pretty—she would not deny that—but opulent, like sewing ten-pound notes onto your dress. The neckline was low, both in the front and the back.

"That is *not* what I asked you to make," said Mary.

"Your request did not make any sense," said Fanny. "You asked for another black mourning gown when you are almost done with mourning. So I made you what you need—a new *morning* gown for daily activities, and a new evening gown, especially useful when dining with visitors. And of course, you have no ball gown and we are about to hold a ball. I thought you would be pleased."

"As I told you before, I have worn my green dress to *every* ball I have attended for the past three years. And I intend to wear it to Lady Trafford's ball."

Fanny held the new ball gown up to herself, as if trying it on for size. "And what exactly is wrong with this one?"

"I told you that any new dress had to have no lace, no beads, nor other adornment, and be an example of modesty in all aspects. This dress fails on all counts."

"It's as modest as all the other dresses the women will be wearing at the ball."

"The fact that everyone wears something does not make it modest." Her sisters all wore dresses like this to balls, but Mary would not. She had been profoundly impacted by Fordyce's sermons—they had given her hope when she had felt none, and they helped her understand her place in her family and in the world when she felt lost. James Fordyce devoted an entire sermon to the subject of modesty of women's apparel, and she had memorized a number of its passages. Fordyce warned against the wantonness of fashion; fancy dress could prevent domestic and intellectual and spiritual improvements. He had demonstrated, quite persuasively, that fancy dress was an idol, and that the pursuit of trivial ornament was proof of a trivial mind. Mary was convinced that simplicity and modesty of apparel was the only solution, and over the years, it had become a sort of creed for how she dressed.

The ball gown Fanny had made was anything but simple; it would draw attention to itself and its wearer. Wearing a dress like this once would not stain Mary's character or set her on the wayward path, but doing it would demonstrate a willingness to depart from her principles, and this she would not do. She pushed aside the memory of lying to Madame Dieupart; that had been a necessary evil. But this would be an act of falsehood against her very self.

Fanny set down the ball gown next to Mary on the bed and opened up the clothes press. While Fanny's back was turned, Mary fingered the new dress. It had a soft, creamy feel. It tempted her, just as Fordyce had said it would.

As Fanny turned back around, Mary wrenched her hand away from the fabric. It was bad enough to be tempted by it, but worse if anyone knew.

Fanny held Mary's green dress. She unfolded it, pursing her lips in disapproval. "The fabric is rather faded, and the seams are a little ragged, both here and here."

"I am certain you have the skills to fix the seams."

Fanny shook out the dress. "If you wear this dress, you are letting other people control how you are seen."

"I have always chosen my own clothes, without anyone's input. *I* control how I am seen."

Fanny walked to the window and looked out. "Because of the colour of my skin, people instantly have perceptions of me. But by what I wear, how I speak, and how I hold myself, I can nudge those perceptions in one direction or another." The maid turned to face Mary. "People have perceptions of you too, as a young, unmarried genteel woman with no fortune to speak of."

She picked up the canary gown and held the two dresses side by side. The green dress did look pale and old and ragged in comparison. "You may choose to wear this green dress, but you cannot choose what it means to everyone else—the place and time we live makes those decisions. Now sometimes you may want people to underestimate or ignore or dismiss you, and if so, then of course, wear the green dress. But if you want a different meaning, if you want people to treat you different-ly or think of you differently, you must dress the part."

Mary's hands trembled with anger. She had *never*, in her entire life, had a servant speak to her like this. She pressed her hands firmly against her sides. "People do *not* ignore me or dismiss me or look down on me because of what I wear. People respect me, they enjoy my company, and they admire my many accomplishments."

Fanny arched her eyebrows in a way that Lady Trafford would probably say expressed disagreement, and perhaps even a subtle mocking. "I made you the dresses at Lady Trafford's request."

This gave Mary pause. Why did Lady Trafford want Mary to wear these?

Lady Trafford and Mr. Withrow's behaviour was becom-ing more clear, but still Mary did not quite see what part they wanted her to play in it. Why would Lady Trafford need her to dress in the style of other people? Perhaps her plan was to force Mary into a marriage that would be advantageous in some way to Lady Trafford, and that was why she wanted Mary in these dresses.

If Mary gave Fanny a firm refusal on the clothing, Lady Trafford would surely hear of it and likely force the issue.

"They appear well made," said Mary carefully, considering how Elizabeth might extract herself from this situation, "so I doubt they will require many modifications. I have other matters to attend to at the moment, so perhaps I can try them on another time."

Before Fanny could protest, Mary left the room, closing the door behind her.

Mrs. Boughton was walking down the hallway in her direction.

"Miss Bennet, I have come to request your company. Several of Lady Trafford's guests have arrived. They will be staying at the castle through the ball, and she thought you might like to meet them before you dine."

Mary breathed deeply, trying to calm herself from her altercation with Fanny before responding. "Of course. Thank you."

Mrs. Boughton interwove her fingers together. "I notice there is some…dirt on your dress. Perhaps you would like to change first? And tidy your hair?"

Mary looked down at her skirt. There was indeed some dirt on her dress. It must be from hiding in the bush while watching Withrow and the French officer.

While Mary did not see any need for fancy clothing, she did prefer to be neat and clean. But if she changed, she would have to interact with Fanny again, as the maid still had not left her room.

Mary did her best to brush the dirt off her dress, though

some of it simply rubbed in. "I will be fine as I am."

"Very well," said Mrs. Boughton. As she led her down the two flights of stairs, Mary tried to compose herself. She could not allow Lady Trafford or Mr. Withrow to see her anger or suspicions. She felt like she had gathered most of the key pieces of a puzzle, and she only needed to find a few more before she could fit everything together. She needed to keep up appearances until then.

As Mary entered the parlor, Lady Trafford, Mr. Withrow, and three visitors stood, two women and one man. Their skin was brown, and they wore fine clothing. The man was balding, and what was left of his hair was turning grey. He held himself as one accustomed to being treated with dignity. The older woman wore Indian clothing; the younger woman wore a dress typical of any well-to-do Englishwoman and appeared to be about Mary's age. She had striking features, silky black hair, and a vibrant smile. It took a moment, but then the realization struck Mary. The man and the younger woman were the individuals who had visited the castle in the middle of the night.

Lady Trafford made the introductions. "This is Miss Mary Bennet. Miss Bennet, these are my esteemed guests, Mr. Jeetu Tagore, Mrs. Rebati Tagore, and their daughter, Miss Madhabika Tagore."

Mary curtsied. "It is a pleasure to meet you."

Miss Tagore took Mary's arm and led her to a sofa. Mr. and Mrs. Tagore sat on the other side of the room with Lady Trafford and Mr. Withrow.

Miss Tagore crossed her legs, then set her hands on top of them, as if she were posing for a portrait. "I was ecstatic when Lady Trafford told me that another young lady of my own age was residing at the castle."

People were not normally ecstatic to see Mary. "I am glad you find my presence desirable."

"Of course! Any friend of Lady Trafford is a friend of mine."

"Have you visited Castle Durrington before?" asked Mary.

"Many times. But it has been at least a year."

This was a complete falsehood. While Lady Trafford had not mentioned the middle-of-the-night visitors, even when prodded about how she had slept, she had never lied about it. Yet Miss Tagore seemed to have no compunction about lying.

"How long have you been staying here?" asked Miss Tagore.

"Almost three months now."

"And how has your visit been?"

"It has been generally agreeable."

"Only generally?"

"When you spend a long time with someone," said Mary, "whether it is a family member, a friend, or a new acquaintance, you can hardly expect it to be always agreeable."

"Many of my acquaintances are not honest enough to admit that. Lady Trafford said I would like you, and as always she is correct."

The compliment surprised Mary. She did not tell the truth in order for people to like her.

"And where do you come from, Miss Bennet?"

"I am from Hertfordshire, near Meryton."

"I have passed through Hertfordshire, but never had the fortune to stay."

Any of her sisters would have responded with a standard pleasantry, such as "I hope someday you have the opportunity," but Mary found this sort of small talk dull and could not bring herself to say anything.

"I am from Bengal but have lived in England for a number of years." She leaned in, focusing her eyes on Mary's head. She lowered her voice and whispered, "I do believe you have something in your hair."

Mary patted her head, trying to find the object. "I was outside drawing earlier. Something must have gotten in my hair."

"Try a little higher," said Miss Tagore. "A little to the left—not my left, your left. Now farther back."

Mary removed a small brown twig. Unsure what to do with it, she set it in her lap.

"You must be very diligent in your studies, to be out drawing on a cold day like this one. Why, I almost froze in the carriage, even with fur blankets and a hot rock under my feet."

"I am sorry you were cold," said Mary.

"I have heard it said that this should be a very cold winter."

"I…I really know nothing of the matter."

Suddenly Withrow sat down near them. He had crossed the room without Mary's notice. This disconcerted her, as she normally prided herself on her powers of observation.

Withrow inserted himself into the conversation, talking about some of the new methods used to analyze the weather. Mary felt strangely like Withrow had saved her. She let him and Miss Tagore continue the conversation without adding any further comments. The Tagores, Withrow, Lady Trafford, Mr. Holloway: they were all connected. Their webs wove around her, but like spider webs, they could only be completely seen with the proper light, which she clearly did not have. Mary felt as if the walls of the room were pressing in on her, and her face felt a bit overheated, so she fanned herself with her hand.

"Are you unwell?" asked Miss Tagore.

"No," insisted Mary. "I am quite well."

If Mrs. Bennet were here, she would say that Mary's discoveries had been too much for her nerves and recommend going straight to bed. But Mary would not blame her nerves—they were made of sterner stuff than her mother's—and so she suffered through the conversation.

After a while, Mrs. Boughton led the way upstairs and introduced the Tagores to their rooms. Everyone else was changing into evening apparel, so Mary thought it best to at least change out of her dirt-stained dress. She opened her clothes press and paused.

Fanny had folded the three new dresses and placed them on one of the shelves.

Mary considered trying on the new evening dress. Its purplish-reddish-brown colour was so intense it was almost indecent. Even the name of the colour itself—puce—felt indecent. Perhaps seeing it on herself would rid her of the strange draw she felt towards the dresses. She would see herself in it, and it would become apparent that it was simply fabric with unnecessary opulence.

She almost removed the dress from the clothes press but she stopped herself. It was as likely that the reverse would happen; if she tried it on, she might rationalize wearing it and the other dresses, and it was better to keep desire in check rather than giving it an opportunity to blossom. She had lied to her French teacher, dressed as an impoverished woman, and done a bit of spying, but those were for a good purpose, and she did not want to compromise herself for fashion, especially if doing so would make her a victim of Lady

Trafford's plans, or, even worse, complicit in them.

She took a clean black mourning dress and shut the doors of the clothes press, promising herself not to consider the new dresses again, and feeling quite pleased with herself for standing up to the temptation of fashionable clothing.

DINNER FELT LIKE watching a play. She found herself emotionally detached, her mind returning again and again to the French officer, and wondering if, or how, this was connected to the death of Mr. Holloway. While there were points where she could insert herself into the conversation, she had no will to do so.

Everyone else was so very comfortable with each other, and she found herself mentally playing the matchmaker. Mr. Withrow and Miss Tagore did not seem to be interested in each other romantically, but as dual deceivers they would suit each other well.

Mrs. Tagore was quieter than her husband and her daughter, yet she watched everyone constantly, and when she spoke, everyone listened.

"Miss Bennet," said Mrs. Tagore. Unlike her daughter, who had no accent, and her husband, who had only a trace, her accent was stronger. "What do you like most about it here? And by here, I do not mean the castle. Not your hosts, or your lessons, but more, what do you like most about Worthing and the surroundings?"

Mary thought for a moment, considering. She still felt like she was learning of this place and meeting the people.

"I like that it is different than where I am from. The ocean, the town itself, the people...it is refreshing to be in place that is not one's own. Travel, I believe, may itself be an educator."

"That is a wise answer," said Mrs. Tagore. "To me, Worthing has always been filled with possibilities, with the potential for becoming something new and different."

Throughout the rest of the dinner, Mary considered why Mrs. Tagore had not come for the middle-of-the-night visit. Maybe she did not know of her husband and daughter's visit, yet she seemed the sort of person who would notice every detail.

After the meal, Mary had no desire for more company, so she retired directly to her room. A few minutes later, Lady Trafford knocked. Mary had never even seen the woman on this floor.

Mary let her in, and they both sat in armchairs.

"You were very subdued tonight," observed Lady Trafford.

"I had nothing worth saying." Her heart raced. Had Lady Trafford realized that she had been tracking her and Mr. Withrow? Did she know of the notebook? Would she cast her out of Castle Durrington? Mary would have to walk, in the dark, to Worthing for help. Where had she set her pocket with her money? She would need that to be able to get home. That was, if Lady Trafford even let her go. But before she left, she would need to report everything she had learned about the death of Mr. Holloway, though she could not report it to Coates or Corneau. If only she had a little more time to unravel the many threads she had found.

"Perhaps it is best if you rested more before the ball," said Lady Trafford.

"I think you are right." Mary hoped the topic stayed in safe territory.

Lady Trafford clasped her hands together and considered Mary's face so intently that she wondered if she had spilled food on it during the meal.

"I am in need of your assistance at the ball, Miss Bennet."

Mary rubbed her eye, which still hurt from the branch. "My assistance?"

"Yes. There is a person in Worthing who may be involved in illegal activity, perhaps some sort of smuggling. I have a personal interest in apprehending them, but in order to do so, I need access to a seafaring vessel and a particular set of skills, all in a trustworthy individual, ideally one who does not have a longstanding connection to this region. There is a wealthy merchant who has recently let a house here, a Colonel Radcliffe, who will be attending the ball. I have heard that he might have a new ship, and I believe he may be ideally suited to assist me. Now he has kept his ownership of this ship quiet in order to prevent people from asking him favors, so it would be best not to ask him directly about this, but if it does come up, any details you discover would be appreciated. It would also be useful if you could ask him about the friendships and relationships he has developed in the area."

"Would it not be better for you to speak to Colonel Radcliffe yourself?"

"Some things are best done indirectly."

"I see," said Mary, though she actually did not. It was clear, from the lines of Lady Trafford's letter she had read, and from this conversation, that Lady Trafford had discovered Colonel Coates's involvement in smuggling. Did she also suspect him of being Holloway's murderer? Why was Colonel Radcliffe so essential? How did the Tagores connect to all of this, beyond having searched Holloway's things? And did this have anything to do with Withrow's treasonous conversation with the French officer? Agreeing to help Lady Trafford might provide an opportunity to complete the puzzle.

"Over the past months, during your stay at the castle, I have come to trust your judgment and your skills. Do you think you could do this one thing for me, help me with this one task?"

Mary nodded. "I will do what I can."

CHAPTER SEVENTEEN

"Proclamation addressed by the Russian commander to the inhabitants of the Netherlands.

'Brave Netherlanders!

'It would be an insult to suppose that you require to be reminded of the great deeds of your forefathers. All of you well know how much this unfortunate country has suffered in consequence of its subjugation by the French. The French armies are annihilated; it therefore depends upon your own exertions to rid yourselves of the few Frenchmen remaining in your native country.'"

—Saunder's News-Letter, and Daily Advertiser,
Dublin, Ireland, December 3, 1813

MARY SMOOTHED HER old green ball gown, trying to rid it of its last few wrinkles. Though Fanny had wanted her to wear the new canary gown, she had still fixed the seams in the green dress and it looked quite presentable. She did recognize that her more simple dress contrasted with her surroundings; every inch of Castle Durrington displayed its finery. Expensive vases and fabrics and paintings that Mary had never seen before filled every spare space. Mary had entered the kitchen earlier and had been shocked by the number of additional hired help. The guests had also spared no expense on their wardrobes. People held themselves as if this were the most important night of their lives. Mary had never found it a sacrifice to attend evening engagements—a moderate amount of recreation and amusement was desirable—yet lavish waste seemed unnecessary.

Mary was torn between her many objectives for the evening. She wanted to observe Lady Trafford and, perhaps more importantly, Mr. Withrow. Additionally, the ball would include Colonel Coates, Mr. Shaffer, and endless other townsfolk who either had motive or opportunity to kill Mr. Holloway. The Tagores were surely not here simply for pleasure and friendship, so she should observe them as well. Not to mention that she needed to speak with Colonel Radcliffe in order to fulfill her commitment to Lady Trafford. It seemed impossible to do all these things at once, so Mary decided to start by observing Lady Trafford and her interactions with her guests as they arrived at the ball.

When guests entered Castle Durrington, they gave their cloaks and other items to servants, ascended the grand staircase, and were greeted by Lady Trafford as they entered the large ballroom on the first floor. Mary stood a ways behind and to the side of Lady Trafford, not close enough to be included in the introductions, but close enough that she could hear the conversation between the guests and their host.

Several officers in the militia arrived, friends of Colonel Coates, but Colonel Coates was not among them.

"Where is Colonel Coates?" exclaimed Lady Trafford. "I was very much looking forward to seeing him tonight."

"I despise being the bearer of bad news," said one of the officers, "but Colonel Coates has fallen ill. He sends his deepest regrets."

Mary wondered if Colonel Coates had actually fallen ill, or if tonight was an opportune time for his smuggling operation.

A few minutes later, Sir Richard Pickering arrived, along with his wife, Lady Charlotte Pickering.

"Thank you for coming all the way from Brighton for this occasion," said Lady Trafford.

"It is a terrible night for a ball," said Lady Pickering. "Much too cold."

"I hope that the fires will suffice," said Lady Trafford.

"It is much colder in here than it was in the inn," said Lady Pickering.

"Are you planning to stay at the inn in Worthing to-night?" asked Lady Trafford. "As I have said before, you are always welcome to stay here."

"I would rather be comfortable."

Lady Trafford did not seem offended by this statement, though surely it was meant to give offense. Instead of responding, she turned to Sir Pickering and spoke as if she was taunting a wild animal with a stick. "Still no progress on your investigations?"

"I am hoping that I might discover something of note tonight," said Sir Pickering.

"Please, try not to make the ball unpleasant for *all* of my guests," said Lady Trafford. "You did quite ruin my last."

"I will do what I must," said Sir Pickering. "As the bard says, 'truth will out.'"

Mary wondered what had occurred at Lady Trafford's last ball. Regardless, she felt comfort at Sir Pickering's presence. While she feared telling anything to either Colonel Coates or Monsieur Corneau, Sir Pickering still seemed trustworthy.

The Pickerings stepped farther into the ballroom, and Lady Trafford turned and gestured towards her. Mary pretended not to see, but then she said, "Come here, Miss

Bennet," so Mary was forced to join her.

"Why are you not mingling with the guests?"

She had already prepared an answer to this question, in case it was asked. "I do not want to miss Colonel Radcliffe's arrival, so I thought I would stand near the entrance and listen to the introductions."

"You look conspicuous," said Lady Trafford. "It is better to spend time naturally with the guests, to learn about people, and make connections. I will ensure you are introduced to Colonel Radcliffe."

"Very well." Mary turned to go but Lady Trafford put her hand on her shoulder.

"I thought Fanny made you something new to wear."

"She did, but I much prefer this." Fanny had tried once again, just an hour before, to persuade Mary to wear the new dress. When Mary had absolutely refused, she had left in a huff and Mary had been forced to do her own hair, which was better anyway as it kept it simpler and more in line with her tastes.

"It would be respectful to her if you were to wear that which she labored so diligently to make for you," said Lady Trafford, "and it would please me if you dressed in better apparel. It is not too late to change."

"Yes, it is," said Mary. "Everyone has already seen me in this."

Lady Trafford looked ready to continue the argument, but more guests arrived. Mary slipped away. Now that she had been noticed, she could not stand here, continuing to watch Lady Trafford. She would find and observe Mr. Withrow.

As she passed through a drawing room, Miss Tagore hailed her. As she was also a person of interest, Mary joined her group of ladies and gentlemen.

"This is Miss Bennet. She is a relative of Lady Trafford and has been staying with her for the past several months." In turn, Miss Tagore introduced her to all the others. The topic soon turned to dancing.

"And what about you, Miss Bennet, do you like to dance?" asked one of the gentlemen, a Mr. Franklin.

"My mother took great care to make sure that I learned to dance. She saw it as one of the greatest accomplishments."

"But what do you think? Is it an accomplishment you would like to demonstrate?"

"To me, dancing is one of the most transitory accomplishments. It is not to be used until one is officially out in society. It then becomes useful until one secures a spouse, but then after it is used only sporadically."

"I take it you do not desire to dance?" asked Miss Tagore.

"Being a transitory accomplishment does not necessitate shunning it entirely," said Mary.

The last man she had danced with was Mr. Collins, at the ball at Netherfield, and it had been a pleasant experience. He had been a skilled, attentive dancer. Despite her many goals for the evening, she could spare a few minutes for a dance, should she be invited.

The group dispersed, but before Mary could continue her search for Withrow, Miss Tagore pulled her aside and spoke quietly.

"Did you realize that Mr. Franklin wanted to ask you to dance?"

"No." It had not seemed to her that Mr. Franklin was inclined towards her at all.

"That is why he asked you if you like dancing."

"Oh," said Mary.

"I believe he took your commentary on dancing as a refusal."

"I see." Mary sniffed, trying to hide her surprising sense of disappointment. Yet her main objective tonight was not to dance, and so it should not matter whether a man she had just met invited her to the floor.

They were interrupted by Miss Tagore's partner for the first dance, who led her to the ballroom. Mary followed, a little behind. Miss Tagore and her partner took the position of the first couple; Lady Trafford must have invited Miss Tagore to open the first dance.

Mary walked around the perimeter of the ballroom, stopping once she discovered Mr. Withrow. He was leading his own lady to the dance floor, but her back was turned. Mary stepped a bit closer and waited until the dance began and the woman turned. It was Miss Shaffer, who looked lovely in a cream-coloured gown.

One of the women who Miss Tagore had introduced to Mary came up to Mary and spoke quietly. "Your friend, Miss Tagore. I have heard she stands to inherit her father's entire fortune, three thousand pounds a year. Is that correct?"

"I do not know. I have never discussed it with her." If it was true, it did not surprise Mary. The trouble with having a fortune was that everyone wanted to be your friend, whether or not they were even worth your attention.

"Why have you come to stay with Lady Trafford?"

"In part, Lady Trafford has been training me to become a governess."

The woman's eyes studied Mary's dress, and then returned to Mary's face. "I can see that that is what she believes you are suited for."

Mary bit back a harsh reply. This stranger was not worth

Mary's attention, or her fury. "I hope you enjoy your time at the ball."

"You as well, Miss Bennet."

As the woman walked away, Mary's fists clenched involuntarily, as if she were an angry schoolboy. She spread out her fingers slowly, trying to release the tension in her body. She had thought everyone in Worthing was kinder than those in Meryton, but she had been wrong. She looked down at her dress and its drab green. She hated to admit it, but maybe Fanny had been correct about her clothing. And maybe Fordyce was wrong. Maybe a simplicity and modesty of dress was not the grand moral issue he made it out to be. She certainly would not condemn all the other women here as having trivial minds due to their beautiful apparel. Lady Trafford's dress was the epitome of ornamentation, and yet no one would ever accuse her of a trivial mind. Surely it would not have hurt to wear Fanny's dress for one night.

Mary watched the dance, but she could not rid herself of the tension in her shoulders, or of the self-loathing she always felt, every single time that she was treated this way. Yes, she may have brought the comment on herself, but in some ways, that made it worse, for that made the insult justified. She blinked her eyes and sniffed her nose. The musicians were first rate, and Miss Tagore did a fine job choosing the sets, making them interesting, but not putting too many complex ones in a row. Mr. Withrow seemed attentive to Miss Shaffer, but also a bit reserved. She, on the other hand, was full of smiles and delight. But Mary could not watch more of the dance, could not stand here while the insulting woman stood not far away, glancing occasionally in her direction and laughing. It reminded Mary of her first ball, a public ball she had attended in Meryton when she was fourteen. She was one of the youngest people there—Mrs. Bennet had no desire to make her daughters wait to be out in society—and she had hoped to dance with the vicar's son, Mr. Miles, for he had always been kind to her.

There was only one other girl her age there, a girl who shared the name Mary. Miss Mary Yalden. They had never really been friends, and Miss Yalden's behaviour that night was likely due to Mary always correcting Miss Yalden in Sunday school. Miss Yalden had surely found her overbearing.

At the ball, Miss Yalden had approached her, and, without even giving a greeting, said, "You think too much of yourself."

"I do not know what you mean," Mary had replied.

"I see you watching Mr. Miles. You would not be suited for anyone half as fine as he is."

Just then, Mr. Miles had walked in their direction, and Miss Yalden had said, loudly, "Whatever is that smell?" Then Miss Yalden, with an unpleasant expression on her face, had looked directly at Mary.

Mr. Miles had not asked Mary to dance. And Miss Yalden wore a laughing smile for the rest of the evening.

Mary tried, she tried ever so hard to balance both being herself and being an acceptable member of society. Yet she always failed. Always. Why could she not be different? Why did she always fall into the same traps, the same things that led people to undervalue and mistreat her? Yes, they were autonomous individuals who made their own poor choices in their treatment of her, but there was no reason for her to add to it or incite it. Yet over the years that was what she had always done, and she did not know how to stop. Even though she could hear so many better melodies in her head, this was the only melody she actually knew how to play, and she could not stop playing it.

Her heart pounded, and blood rushed to her head as every snub and insult from the past flashed through her mind. No longer did she feel only the emotions of the moment; she was wading through the muck of every barbed insult she had ever received: all stinging wounds, as fresh as they had been on the days they were given.

Mary found it difficult to breathe. She needed to leave, but Lady Trafford would surely not approve if she fled to her room, and she had much she needed to do tonight. She must find a way to move past this, find a way to set it aside. Instead of fleeing, she walked to her favorite drawing room. Playing the pianoforte could often calm her and help her set aside the judgment and censure of others.

Unfortunately, the pianoforte was occupied. Mary had no compunction about asking someone to let her have a turn, but the lady was at the beginning of what Mary recognized as a very long piece, and Mary thought it most polite to interrupt in between pieces rather than in the middle of a piece.

Perhaps if Mary demonstrated one of her other accomplishments, it would have the same calming effect as playing the pianoforte. Last night, Lady Trafford had instructed her to spend more time at the ball establishing relationships rather than demonstrating accomplishments, yet in situations like this Mary struggled with casual conversation and often found that demonstrating an accomplishment provided for subsequent topics of discussion. Further, after such a demonstration, she was more likely to be treated as a person of worth and value. Mary made her way over to a gathering of older women, along with a handful of younger women who had not been asked to dance, all seated near the side of the room. She knew several of them, including Mrs. Tagore, but even if she had not, at a private ball it was more permissible to speak to whomever you liked.

Introductions were made and, after a few minutes of niceties, Mary informed them that she had memorized several poems in the French language of an inspiring, religious nature, and expressed her hope that they would not mind if she recited one or two.

She pressed her hands together, stood tall, and recited the first poem, making sure her enunciations were precise and raising and lowering the timbre of her voice at the appropriate moments. There was light applause at the end, so she undertook a second poem, after which their compliments were so enthusiastic that she decided to set all advice from Lady Trafford aside and recite a third poem. She had a fleeting thought that she might be indulging in the same bad habits that always led her to trouble, but she pushed it aside.

There was less applause and fewer compliments after the third poem, and she wondered if she should switch to English and recite one of the sermons she had memorized, but before she began Monsieur Corneau approached.

"*Brava! C'est l'un de mes poèmes préférés.*"

"*Je vous remercie*," Mary replied.

He gestured her towards some chairs, and they sat. Mary's recitation had calmed her; it had allowed her to forget most of her troubles, but now, she felt an edge of nervousness. She had been avoiding Monsieur Corneau since her discovery of the newspaper articles about his nephew.

"*Votre français a vraiment progressé, mademoiselle*," he said.

"*Merci*," said Mary.

"It has been a while since we have spoken," said Monsieur Corneau, switching back to English. "Colonel Coates been disappointed not to hear more of your reports."

"I have been so busy with my studies, and I have not discovered anything of note," Mary lied. Her falsehood felt justifiable: asking her to spy for him had been a grand deception on his part, from the very start.

"That is unfortunate," said Corneau. "Sir Pickering seems to think he is close to finding the murderer. With your help, who knows what could be discovered?"

"I will keep watching and listening," said Mary. "That is all that I can do."

Corneau rested his hand on his chin and looked at her thoughtfully. His eyes shifted to where Mrs. Tagore sat with some of the other women. "In one of your reports, you told me of the middle-of-the-night visitors. Did they happen to be the Tagores?"

"No," said Mary, hoping her tone of voice and her facial expression did not give away anything. "The visitors looked quite different than the Tagores."

Mary did not know why she felt she must protect their identity, but now it felt imperative.

Corneau sighed. "Alas, you truly do not have more information for me. Please, let us meet more regularly in the future."

"Of course," said Mary, and she was relieved when he left to converse with someone else.

After a minute or two of steady breathing, she felt ready to return to her self-assigned tasks, so she returned to the ballroom. The music seemed to be drawing to a close, so she positioned herself near where she thought Withrow would be when it stopped. She was not quite correct, but not far off. She followed, at a distance, as he led Miss Shaffer back to her parents and then meandered through the rooms. He was clearly not going to dance the second dance, and while his path seemed aimless, Mary sensed a hidden purpose. She stayed as far behind him as she could without losing sight of him, and stopped several times to smell fresh flowers, purchased from a hot house.

Withrow paused as he entered the smallest drawing room, the final public room on this floor, next to the hall which led to the master bedrooms. He strode in quickly, with purpose.

Withrow placed his hand on Monsieur Corneau's upper arm and led him out a small door behind a potted tree. They had entered Lady Trafford and Mr. Withrow's hallway. Mary stepped behind the same potted tree. They had not completely shut the door; Mary pushed it open a crack farther and peered down the hallway. Withrow used a key to unlock his own door. He gestured to Monsieur Corneau. The Frenchman paused, shrugged, then entered. Withrow followed, closing the door tightly behind them.

CHAPTER EIGHTEEN

"Swiss Confederation.—The war, which was lately far from our frontiers, is approaching our country, and our peaceable dwellings."

—Saunder's News-Letter, and Daily Advertiser,
Dublin, Ireland, December 3, 1813

MARY PRESSED HER ear against the bedroom door. Corneau and Withrow were speaking rapidly in French. With the muffling through the wood, she could hardly understand a word they said, and yet still she stood against the door, trying to make something out.

She glanced down the hallway, praying that all the servants were busy elsewhere and no one found her here, in this position. She tried placing her ear next to the keyhole, but she still could not understand them.

After another minute, she almost gave up and returned to the ball, but then she heard the voice of Monsieur Corneau, louder and more clearly. "*Non. Nous en reparlerons plus tard. Je dis plus tard.*"

She heard the key as it was inserted into the door and dashed back down the hall and into the drawing room. Several people looked at her askance, so she tried to calm her breathing as she walked through the room. She needed to leave the space, for it was likely that Monsieur Corneau and

Withrow would return to this room. If they saw her breathing heavily, they might be suspicious.

She passed through the other rooms, taking a slow, meandering route to the ballroom, rather than going through the domed balcony room to get there more quickly.

Mary repeated the words of Monsieur Corneau in her mind. "*No. We will talk about this later.*" But what would they talk about, and why ever was it so important? Was Mr. Withrow working with or reporting to Corneau in some way?

The couples now danced the second dance. Miss Tagore had a new partner, and though she had opened the first dance, her energy did not seem to flag. Mary wondered if, like Lydia, Miss Tagore would manage to dance the entire night.

Mr. Tagore approached Mary and bowed. "Miss Bennet."

Mary curtsied in reply.

"Dancing is one of the few things my daughter enjoys full-heartedly."

"She is quite skilled at it," said Mary. "And does not seem to lack in partners."

"People see us as a novelty, and often do not take the effort to see us as anything less or more."

"A sign of true character is being able to see past superficialities."

Mr. Tagore nodded. "You are quite correct. And how are you finding the ball?"

"It is quite elaborate," said Mary. "I have never seen the preparations for a ball first-hand. For weeks every single servant has been dedicated only to this event. And the number of additional staff that have had to be brought on for today's event is almost shocking. So much expense has been applied to the music, the decor, and the food, and all the guests have commissioned the finest apparel, and many probably hired a carriage for the evening. I have concluded that rather than hold balls it would be much better to alleviate suffering and help the poor."

By the end of her pronouncement, a number of those standing nearby had turned to listen to her words. She hoped that they would reflect on them even after the ball. Mr. Withrow was nearby—he had returned from his secret meeting with Corneau—and he gave her a hard, cold look, which Mary found completely unwarranted. She only spoke the truth.

Mr. Tagore leaned towards her ear and spoke so only she could hear. "You would do well, Miss Bennet, to show gratitude and loyalty to your hosts, both privately and publicly." His censure felt sudden and fierce, like a burn from touching something hot. Louder, so everyone could hear, he said, "I agree that more should be done to help the poor, but the occasional frivolity has its place, and many of the funds directly pay, and thus help, members of the community."

"You are correct, of course," said Mary quickly. Even though Lady Trafford and Withrow had ordered the theft of her family's mourning rings, even though Withrow had met with a French officer, she was still their guest and did owe them at least a certain amount of outward respect. Furthermore, Mr. Tagore's financial argument had merit.

Sir Pickering approached. "Mr. Tagore, Miss Bennet." He focused on Mary, speaking directly to his point. "It has been a while since we have spoken. Have you recalled anything else from finding the body, or noted anything else since then, which would be useful in assisting my investigation?"

Clearly none of what she had reported to Corneau had made its way to Sir Pickering, or, if it had, not with any credit to her. There was so much she could tell him, so many observations and suspicions. But she could not tell him now, not here, at the ball, not here, with Mr. Tagore at her side and Mr. Withrow a few feet away. She would not cause a scene, especially not when it meant she might prevent the discovery of the rest of the truth.

"Unfortunately, I have nothing more to tell you," said Mary. "How are you finding the ball?"

"Quite capital," said Sir Pickering. "If you will excuse me, I have others I need to speak to."

After Sir Pickering left, Lady Trafford approached with none other than Colonel Radcliffe.

"Mr. Tagore, Miss Bennet, this is Colonel Radcliffe," said Lady Trafford.

Mary curtsied and prepared to speak, but before she could say anything, Colonel Radcliffe turned to Mr. Tagore.

"Mr. Tagore, I heard you work for the East India Trade Company."

"I used to be employed by them," said Mr. Tagore, "but now I work with them, and with other organizations involved in trade."

"I would love to speak to you about it," said Colonel Radcliffe. "Perhaps over cards?"

"I am sure you will have plenty of opportunity to speak to Mr. Tagore," said Lady Trafford. "But first, you must dance."

"I am not much of a dancer."

"But then this is the perfect opportunity, right before supper, when you will be able to rest your feet. The musicians are providing wonderful accompaniment and—"

"I really had not planned to dance tonight."

"I insist," said Lady Trafford firmly. "There are too many women without partners for you to not dance at least one dance. I know for a fact that my dear friend Miss Bennet, who has been my esteemed guest over the past months, had very much hoped to dance tonight."

Lady Trafford gave her a determined look, so Mary said, "I would be most obliged."

Colonel Radcliffe seemed to steel himself, and then he bowed to Mary. "Miss Bennet, would you do me the honor of the next dance?"

"Of course."

"If I may excuse myself, I need to speak to someone, but I will return in a few minutes to escort you to the floor."

Once he had left, Lady Trafford turned to Mary with a knowing smile. "I hope you enjoy your dance and know that I appreciate your efforts." And then she turned to Mr. Tagore. "There are several officers in the militia I should introduce you to."

"Of course," said Mr. Tagore. "It was a pleasure speaking with you, Miss Bennet."

Mary watched the last few minutes of the dance, the musicians took a short break, and then partners for the next dance gathered on the floor, including Withrow, with an older woman whom Mary did not recognize. Mary stood in her spot at the edge of the ballroom, determined not to move. She would not let Colonel Radcliffe out of the dance by making herself difficult to find, as Lydia and Kitty did on occasion when they found their partners undesirable.

The dance began, but still Colonel Radcliffe did not seek her out.

Mary rarely danced at balls, but she had attended plenty, and it was always uncomfortable for a young lady to join the dance floor late, and quite rude on the part of the gentleman.

She turned the mourning ring on her finger. It was her first ball since her father died. He did not always attend balls with the rest of the family, but when he did, he was a source of stability for the whole family, keeping everyone—including herself—within the lines of propriety and respectability. It was an important role, and she missed him for it. She wished that Jane had not ended mourning so early. Mary would rather wear her emotions for her father publicly, so all could see, than keep them hidden inside herself. She had grown more accustomed, now, to the fact of his death, but it was there, ever present, just beneath the surface.

She tried to push her sorrow aside; a ball was not a time to mourn. She would do that later in her own room. For now, she should focus on the task set by Lady Trafford. Of course, in order to succeed she needed the colonel to return.

Mr. Bennet would recommend patience, but she found herself lacking any patience for her partner. She would feel very foolish indeed if the one dance partner who asked for her hand withdrew his offer without even speaking to her first.

Mary counted the couples dancing, and then she began counting the flickering candles in the chandeliers above her.

Colonel Radcliffe approached. He did not look nearly as apologetic as he should.

"My greatest apologies, Miss Bennet. I lost track of the time. Perhaps we could save the dance for—"

"No," said Mary. "We should join the dance now." She had learned from Lady Trafford that sometimes it was necessary to insist upon one's own desires.

"Very well," said Colonel Radcliffe.

He took her gloved hand in his own and led her to the bottom of the floor. After a moment they were able to join.

It was a fast dance with complicated footwork, that even her sisters would find challenging. Soon Mary was out of breath, but she had a task, and she would not be deterred.

"Do you plan to stay"—she executed a short series of complicated footwork—"in the area for very long?"

Colonel Radcliffe smiled agreeably. He did not seem to find the dance complex and was not breathing heavily. "I like change, meeting new people and doing new things. But I do hope to stay here for the foreseeable future."

And now she needed to say something agreeable in reply, as Jane would. "It is a pleasure to have you in the area."

"How long do you intend to stay at Castle Durrington?"

"I am not certain," said Mary.

"Do they treat you well?" said the colonel, and there was something in his tone that gave her pause.

"Yes, very well," said Mary. "It is just that my family has been missing me, especially my mother."

In truth, no one had said anything in their letters about missing her in the slightest, but often such sentiments were difficult to express on paper.

She tried to turn the conversation back to him, to find something about the boat that might be of interest to Lady Trafford.

"Do you run an estate? Or are you involved in business or industry?"

"Nothing I do would be of any interest to you, Miss Bennet."

"I often found my father's work interesting."

"That was probably due to familial connection, then."

The next part of the dance was difficult to talk through, which was just as well, for Mary suspected that were she to talk, she might verbalize her frustration with Colonel Radcliffe.

She could feel her face redden as they took their turn dancing near the fire. Lady Trafford watched her from the edge of the room, and Mary wondered if she knew how miserably Mary was failing her task.

As she raised her leg for a dance step she tripped and almost fell, but she caught herself and continued. She thought she heard laughter from the side of the room, but she did not turn her head to see who it was. Colonel Radcliffe was looking at one of the other women in the dance and did not appear to have witnessed her near fall.

"Have you developed many friendships here, since you arrived?" Mary asked, drawing his attention back to her.

"I have met many people, but it can take time to form strong relationships. Have you made any strong friendships since you arrived, Miss Bennet?"

Mary was taken aback by the question. She knew many people here, but her tutors, Corneau, Miss Shaffer, Lady Trafford, none of them were friends, truly. "Perhaps friendships matter less than the difference we can make in the lives of those around us."

She felt as if she had not discovered any information about any of the things Lady Trafford wanted her to discover. "Have you seen the beach?"

"Of course. It is impossible to miss if you set foot in Worthing."

"Do you like the ocean?"

"I am impartial," he said, but did not elaborate.

"I had never seen the ocean before coming here."

"It is quite large."

"Have you ever been on a boat?" asked Mary.

"Yes."

Elizabeth would know how to draw out a lengthier answer for questions like this, but it did not come naturally to Mary. She began formulating some sort of question or statement, perhaps about a personal desire to ride a boat, but then something hot hit her shoulder.

Immediately her hand went to her shoulder, where she discovered a drop of wax. It must have dripped from one of the candles in the chandelier. It had burned a small spot of her dress, but not entirely through the fabric.

"Are you distressed, Miss Bennet?" asked the colonel.

"No, it was only a small bit of wax."

"Perhaps we should withdraw from the dance and give you time to recover."

Mary's shoulder stung, but she recognized that the colonel wanted any excuse not to dance with her, and she refused to give him one.

"I would like to continue. Besides, the dance is almost complete."

They caught up with their neighbouring couples, and Mary suffered through the final few minutes of the dance. She had lost her train of thought and found herself unable to converse at all.

The dance finally finished, and the couples descended the grand staircase to the dining room. Fortunately, Colonel Radcliffe knew the protocol and that he should sit with Mary at supper, because if she had to force him to do it, she would not know how to make such a request in a polite manner.

Normally Mary would sit at a table that included her family, but none were here. Lady Trafford and Mr. Withrow sat on the far side of the room, and Miss Tagore and her current dance partner sat with her parents and several others. Finally, Mary and the colonel's table filled, with Monsieur Corneau taking the last seat and giving Mary a brief smile.

Colonel Radcliffe helped serve all the ladies their food. He analyzed the dishes and told the woman on his other side about his favorite meals and where they had been served. It seemed to be a purposeful slight, and his easy conversation stood in stark contrast to their conversation during the dance. Almost every new acquaintance this evening had decided to take a strong disliking to her, and she knew that she had only herself to blame.

Despite the delicacies before her, Mary did not eat very much. She wished she had not danced with Colonel Radcliffe, wished that Lady Trafford had not given her such a ridiculous task. She would rather be sitting near Withrow and Lady Trafford and listening in on their conversation than be banished over here. And if things continued as they were, Colonel Radcliffe would pass the entire supper without speaking of anything besides the food.

Mary grew tired of the pretense, of attempting to encourage someone to discuss a subject without mentioning the subject.

"Colonel Radcliffe," said Mary, interrupting his conversation. "I have always wanted to sail in a boat, and I heard you have your own private boat. Do you use it for pleasure trips, or is it strictly business?"

There was a moment of silence, and if she was not mistaken, Colonel Radcliffe flinched slightly. He spared the briefest glance around the table before saying smoothly, "You must have me confused with someone else. I have never owned a boat, and do not much enjoy sailing."

Colonel Radcliffe returned to the previous conversation as if she had not interrupted. He strummed his fingers on the table when he was not eating and glanced occasionally at Mary. He was clearly hiding something; Mary's best guess was that Lady Trafford was correct and he did not want his boat ownership to be publicly known, because of requests from smugglers, or from individuals like Lady Trafford. Or perhaps, like Lady Trafford, he was engaged in manipulations and deceit.

Mary started a conversation with Monsieur Corneau about French poetry. He examined his pocket watch several times, but otherwise seemed engaged. Mary wondered if his meeting with Mr. Withrow was soon.

After the meal they stood. Colonel Radcliffe bowed and thanked Mary for both the dance and the supper. "It was my pleasure," said Mary, because it was the sort of thing one was supposed to say, though in truth it was a lie: she had taken very little pleasure in either activity. Why did mere participation in polite society require telling so many untruths?

The colonel left the room quickly. Perhaps he was avoiding someone, which was suspicious in its own right, but Mary had more important matters to attend to. Withrow lingered, as did Monsieur Corneau, who once again examined his pocket watch. They must be having their meeting soon. She considered trying to secret herself in Withrow's room, but there was no guarantee that they would meet there again, and entering his room would cause a scandal of Lydia-like proportions should she be discovered. It would be better to wait and follow them discreetly, but standing here next to the table was starting to feel conspicuous.

Miss Tagore was about to leave, but Mary touched her on the arm. "I was hoping you would tell me about your dance partners."

"Well, fortunately I am spending the night, so we will be able to analyze them thoroughly in the morning."

Mary bit her lip. "Can you spare me just one moment right now?"

"Anything for you, Miss Bennet. Though it cannot be for

too long—I do not wish to keep my next dance partner waiting." She sighed. "Well, first I danced with…"

Withrow's eyes passed around everyone in the room, lingering for a moment on Monsieur Corneau. Then Withrow slipped away. She decided to wait and follow the Frenchman.

Mary smiled at whatever Miss Tagore was saying. She turned so she was not really watching Monsieur Corneau but would be able to see when he left the room. After a minute he did.

"It would be best if I did not keep you from your partner any longer."

Miss Tagore tilted her head to the side. "Of course."

Mary walked after Monsieur Corneau. He did not go back upstairs to the ballroom or Mr. Withrow's room, but instead entered the sitting room next to the library.

She followed quietly and heard something—perhaps a door. She rushed into the room and saw that the door to the lawn had just closed. She inched it open and was hit by bitterly cold air. She was not even wearing a shawl, but she followed him out onto the back lawn.

He strode rapidly across the frosty grass, away from the lights shining out of the house and towards the Roundel. He carried no candle, and neither did Mary, so it was almost impossible to see him, and even harder not to trip.

As she neared the circular grove of trees, she slowed. She did not want to be seen. She walked as quietly as she could, listening for the voices of Corneau and Withrow. She secreted herself behind a tree at the perimeter of the Roundel where she could hear them clearly.

"I thought we would never escape," said Corneau.

"Did anyone follow?" asked a voice that did not sound like Withrow, yet was also familiar.

"No," said Corneau.

"Where could Miss Bennet have heard about the boat?" asked the other voice, and to Mary's surprise, she realized it belonged to Colonel Radcliffe.

"She has observed a few useful things for me, at my request, but I do not believe she could have discovered your boat on her own."

"She was a most disagreeable dance partner," said Radcliffe. In her opinion, he had been the disagreeable one. "Maybe she heard something from Trafford or Withrow, but I do not know how they would know."

"Withrow claims to be sympathetic to our cause. He attempted to convince me to let him attend one of my meetings."

"I hope you did not agree," said Radcliffe sharply.

"Of course not," said Corneau.

"Good. I do not trust him, or that he would stand with us, no matter what he says."

There was a minute of silence, and Mary worried that they would return to the house and see her on their way. Her heart raced and her teeth chattered so loudly that she feared they would hear her. She clamped her lips shut but tried to keep her upper teeth apart from her lower ones.

"The news in the papers makes our position seem bleak," said Colonel Radcliffe.

"If you read the English papers, yes. It is in their interest to make it seem like their victory is close. However, while there have been setbacks, the Imperial Army is still strong. The emperor needs only one grand victory and then it will be easy for him to gain new recruits and double the size of his army." There was a pause. "His troops are approaching Switzerland. They can no longer remain neutral. That is one front where victory could occur. But many of us believe that here would be better. Consider the statement it would make."

"When you deem that the time is right," said Colonel Radcliffe, "my boat is available to send word to Napoleon."

"That is good," said the Frenchman. "You should also attend our next meeting."

"It is too dangerous. But I will give you more funds." Another pause. "I have found the perfect spot for Napoleon's troops to land without being detected."

Goosebumps covered Mary's arms, and a chill reached her heart. Corneau and Radcliffe's words were nothing less than treason.

CHAPTER NINETEEN

"Bonaparte took exactly twelve years to rise to a height, from which twelve months have been sufficient to precipitate him. In 1799 he was installed First Consul; in 1802 appointed Consul for life; in 1804 Emperor of France; and in 1812, with almost all Europe at his feet, he began that declension at Moscow, which, in 1813, was completed at Leipzic."

–The Morning Chronicle, London, December 3, 1813

MARY STOOD VERY still, realizing, only now, the complete folly of the place where she had chosen to hide. Hiding behind a tree was not in itself a problem, but rather, the fact that she had chosen a tree on this side of the Roundel, so close to them. If she moved, the two men would discover her. If she stayed, the two men would walk directly past her in order to return to the castle. If these men were willing to betray all of England, if they were willing to invite an invasion which would cause death and destruction, they would have no qualms in eliminating one maiden who stood in their way. Furthermore, Colonel Radcliffe was a former soldier; he would know how to kill.

Mary pressed herself against the tree, as much as she was able while wearing this dress. In this, her choice of the old green gown was better than the new, much fuller gown Fanny had made.

"When our plans come to fruition," said Corneau, "you will be well rewarded for your efforts."

"It is not for money or power that I do this," said Radcliffe.

"Of course not," said Corneau. "But if you receive them as happy side effects, you will not complain, no?"

"I suppose not."

There was a rustling. Footsteps. Mary closed her eyes, certain she would be discovered and not wanting to see it coming.

The footsteps passed her, and after a minute Mary turned slightly so she could see the men as they approached the castle. But she saw only one silhouette, not two. Maybe they were walking in perfect alignment, but as Mary watched, that seemed unlikely.

Which meant one of the men was still here in the grove.

Mary's heart pounded with abandon. She tried to still her ragged breath as she once again pressed herself against the tree.

There was more rustling, and this time Mary did not close her eyes. The movement stopped, and as Mary peered into the darkness, she saw the figure of a man, not two feet from her, looking back at Castle Durrington. It was Colonel Radcliffe, and if he shifted his head to the side at all, then the darkness would not be enough to hide her.

If he were to attack her, she could scream, but the Roundel was too far from Castle Durrington. No one would hear her. No one would come to her aid. She was alone.

Her hands trembled. She tried to steady them against the tree, but to no avail. The moment stretched on and on and Mary almost wanted to call out simply to end the suspense.

After a large fraction of eternity, Radcliffe's body moved. This startled Mary, and she bumped her cheek against the tree. She bit back a cry of pain.

To her relief, Radcliffe did not turn, but instead walked back to the castle. She watched until his silhouette entered the same door she had exited a few minutes before.

Mary knew she should return to the house, but she could not move, paralyzed by cold and fear. In one of the many newspapers Lady Trafford had assigned her to read, there had been a description of Bonaparte's soldiers and their savage behaviour towards the city of Smolensk. She could picture it in her mind, but instead of unknown Russians she saw the soldiers attacking the people of Worthing: Madame Dieupart, Miss Shaffer and her parents, the milliner, and the poor woman with her baby.

Her teeth began to chatter again, and this time she could not stop them. They rattled against each other, faster, faster, uncontrollably, until her whole body shook. She forced herself from the protection of the Roundel and walked back towards the castle, but she could not bring herself to return directly to the parlor door. There were so many windows at the back of the castle. Any one of the people inside could look out and see her, including Corneau and Radcliffe.

She kept far from the back of the castle, travelling instead around the side. In front of Castle Durrington, carriages were wrapped around the entire drive, with plenty of people and servants about who could see her. She did not want to enter the front entryway of the castle with its grand staircase. The door to the annex with the kitchen and servant quarters was also on the front side of the castle, but unlike the main entrance, it was not well lit so it would be less likely that someone would notice her. She opened the door, stepped inside, and ran directly into the housekeeper, Mrs. Boughton.

"Miss Bennet!" she exclaimed. "Whatever are you doing here?"

Mary could not muster a response before Mrs. Boughton went on, "You look quite a fright and your cheeks are bright red. Have you been outside?"

"I—" Mary paused, searching for an excuse. "I was overwhelmed by the ball, so I stepped outside. For fresh air."

"Lady Trafford would say it was foolish to not wear a cloak or gloves. You are not even wearing a hat. Here, let's warm you up next to the fire until you are ready to return to the ball."

Mary did not want to be under Mrs. Boughton's care, for Mrs. Boughton had Lady Trafford's confidence and was part of her schemes. Under her scrutiny, she might give something away about what she had done and discovered. "I am too tired to return to the ball tonight. I would like to retire to my room."

Mrs. Boughton pinched her face in displeasure. "Very well."

"I do not want everyone to see me like this. Can I go up by the servants' staircase?"

Conflict waged on her face, but ultimately the housekeeper relented. "Only this one time."

Mrs. Boughton led her to her room and then left to find someone to build up the fire. Mary looked at the canary ball gown, laid out on the bed. She pushed it aside, letting it fall to the floor, and climbed into the covers, not even bothering to remove her old, worn green ball gown.

Mary shivered underneath the blankets. She was so cold. She should not have gone outside without proper clothing for the weather. Surely she would catch a chill from tonight. Her mother had always said that sickness or a chill was acceptable if it was acquired in the pursuit of a man. In fact, she had pursued multiple men tonight, but not in the way that Mrs. Bennet would desire.

In the morning, she would write to Sir Pickering. She considered finding him now, but was too tired and too cold, and even if she found Sir Pickering, there would be too many people for her to tell him everything. It would be better to rest, and act on the morrow.

A few minutes later Fanny entered the room to stoke the fire. Mary pretended to sleep but kept her eyes cracked open so she could watch her. She worked thoroughly, building up a large fire that would stay warm through the night. Then she rubbed her hands methodically on her apron, removing every speck of ash.

Fanny walked to the bedside and picked up the canary ball gown from off the floor. A small tear started to run down Fanny's face, but she wiped it off before it could travel far. Fanny had spent days—no, weeks—working on the dress. For her own sense of self-righteousness Mary had refused to even try it on. On Fanny's face, Mary saw rejection, the feeling of not belonging, that moment when you realize your accomplishments are not valued. Mary had felt all those things so many times before, and now, seeing them writ on Fanny's face, her heart broke for what she had done.

Over the years, others had been cold and harsh and unkind to Mary, and Mary had developed her own coldness in response: rigidity and strictness, correctness and self-righteousness, and further, a shortness of speech. She had built up these behaviours to protect herself from harm, a sort of wall between her and the world, but it was a wall with plenty of fissures that still let harm through. Far worse, it was a wall that caused active harm to others.

She hoped that she could find a way to tear it down.

WHEN MARY WOKE in the morning, Fanny was tending to the fire.

Mary sat up and rubbed her fingers under her eyes.

"Fanny, I have something I would like to speak to you about."

Fanny turned. "Yes, Miss Bennet?" she said stiffly.

"I would like to apologize to you for my behaviour," said Mary. "The way I treated you was inappropriate. I should have worn the dress you spent so much time making, and I should have spoken to you differently. Also, I wanted to tell you that you were correct about how people would treat me based off of my clothing. I hope that you will accept my apologies."

"No," said Fanny.

"What?" said Mary.

"I do not accept your apologies."

"Whyever not?" Mary had never had anyone not accept her apologies before.

"I'm sure that in some way you do feel bad for your behaviour, which *was* highly inappropriate, but you are like every other privileged woman I have met. You're mostly apologizing because *you* want to feel better. You want me to accept so you can feel happy and free of guilt and obligation."

"I...I—" said Mary. But Fanny was correct. Mary's apologies were selfish, and they did nothing to make things better for Fanny.

Fanny walked to the door. "Lady Trafford would like to

see you, in her room, in the next few minutes. I am sure you can dress yourself." She stepped into the hallway and pulled the door shut with a fair amount of vigor.

Mary rubbed her temples. A few months ago, she would have lectured Fanny on the necessity of forgiveness, how it freed the soul and was a divine opportunity to rise above one's troubles and trials. But now, she had no desire for such platitudes. She had hurt Fanny and would need to find something better than an apology to make things right. But what could she do? As she pondered this question, she prepared herself to speak to Lady Trafford.

This was the first time Mary had ever been inside Lady Trafford's room, and Mary could not help but look in awe at the fine, yet tasteful furnishings. Lady Trafford was seated upright in her bed, with a luxurious scarlet duvet, yet she appeared tired, which must be why she had not yet left her room.

"How did you find the ball, Miss Bennet?"

"Larger than some I have been to, but not the largest. I danced more than I normally do at balls." Often, she did not dance at all.

Lady Trafford raised her eyebrows. "Prior to the ball, I asked if you could help me. Were you able to find out anything useful from Colonel Radcliffe?"

Mary bit her lip as she debated whether or not she should tell Lady Trafford what she had learned. Despite all of Lady Trafford's questionable motives and actions, part of Mary still wanted to please the woman. But this was much more than a business deal—this was a matter of great import. She could not possibly share it with someone whose nephew was involved in a similar scheme. She could not share it until she knew who had murdered Mr. Holloway.

"Our conversation was not particularly fruitful," said Mary, and she did not feel guilty because that was the truth. Of course, what she had learned afterwards was fruitful, but Lady Trafford did not know to ask specifically about it.

"That is unfortunate." Lady Trafford disinterestedly stirred her tea, which was set on a stand next to the bed. "Did he say anything of note, or did any of his mannerisms reveal anything about him?"

"He is not a very attentive dancer, but that is all I learned." She thought it best to change the subject before Lady Trafford realized she was hiding things from her. "When will our next lesson be?"

"I am fatigued from the ball. It will take several days for the castle to be put back in order, and even then I will have a great many responsibilities."

This was the sort of response that her family gave her when they wanted to avoid her, so Mary said the sort of thing she would say to her family. "I am glad my parents never put on a ball. Not only is there a high financial cost, but it is a burden on both the servants and their hosts." Too late, she realized how rude this must sound. Despite her resolution to change, she was defaulting to her hurtful behaviours.

"It will be a great relief to you to learn that governesses are generally not expected to attend balls. If ever one of your employers throws a ball, you can stay upstairs in the nursery."

She had forgotten, for a moment, that she had told Lady Trafford that she was interested in becoming a governess.

"Will Mr. Withrow still give me lessons?" On the one hand, she had lost all respect for him. But on the other hand, he still had knowledge she wanted to learn.

"I am afraid he will be much too busy in the coming weeks with matters of the estate and taking several trips."

Mary tried to not let her disappointment show, but it must have, for Lady Trafford said, "Now, now, child. You will still have drawing lessons. And French, once Madame Dieupart returns from her trip. I can also assign you a list of books to read that I am certain you will find very helpful for your future." Lady Trafford pointed at a desk in the corner. "Now fetch me a piece of paper and that quill."

Lady Trafford wrote out a list of five books and then dismissed Mary. As she retrieved the books from the library, Mary noted that each of them had very direct, practical things that could help a prospective governess, much more relevant skills than the instruction she had received from Lady Trafford and Mr. Withrow. One of them, *Moral Tales for Young People* by Maria Edgeworth, contained a story titled "The Good French Governess" which appeared to be a didactic about how to deal with difficult children.

Mary brought the books back to her room but did not attempt to read. Instead, she blocked the door with a chair and removed her letter-writing materials. She was glad that she had not told Lady Trafford what she had discovered, but that was not enough. She needed to act on it, and quickly.

She addressed the letter to Sir Richard Pickering. Writing a letter was better than if she had spoken to him in person, for with a letter, she could remain anonymous. When her concerns were addressed, she did not need her name noised about and made public as involved in the matter; it was enough that her name was had in the community with a connection to a dead body, but a connection to treasonous people, even if she was not one of them, could bring shame to her entire family. She used her left hand to write, which made it agonizingly slow, but also meant no one would be able to match it to her handwriting.

Dear Sir Richard Pickering,

I am writing this letter to you anonymously in order to protect myself and my family. Yet the matter is urgent.

I found myself in a position where I overheard a private conversation between two residents of Worthing: Colonel Radcliffe and Monsieur Corneau. Both of the men sympathize with Napoleon Bonaparte. Corneau seems to be gathering support for an invasion by Bonaparte. Colonel Radcliffe has not been attending the meetings but has been funding Corneau, and has a secret boat that he plans to use to contact Bonaparte when the opportune moment arises. He has also found a place for the troops to land undiscovered, but I do not know the location of it.

Mary twisted her quill in her fingers. What she was about to write felt like a betrayal of her hosts, but it must be done.

In their conversation, Monsieur Corneau mentioned that Mr. Henry Withrow, of Castle Durrington, wanted to join their group. As of the conversation, they had not invited him into their confidence or allowed him to join. However, on a different occasion I saw Withrow with a French officer from Napoleon's army. I did not hear what they said, but they were looking at a map. Perhaps Withrow was gathering information that would help him join Radcliffe and Corneau.

She decided not to mention the things she had learned about Mr. Holloway and the Tagores, Lady Trafford and Mr. Withrow; she did not quite see how everything fit together. But when she discovered the connections, she would report it and see that justice would be done.

> *Thank you for your time in reading this letter. It is my sincere hope that you act promptly on this matter.*
>
> *Sincerely,*
> *An Anonymous Friend*

Mary decided to secure the letter well, but not in the method Lady Trafford had taught her. Instead she used a different method that she had seen on one of the letters Lady Trafford had received. She did not know exactly how it had been executed, but she could approximate it. She folded the letter, sewed the edges together with a needle and thread, and then dripped the wax onto the thread. Instead of using her seal, which someone at the post office might recognize, she pressed a plain square of paper on top of the wax and used a sharp metal point to press three holes in it, which let some of the wax seep through.

She placed the letter in her pocket and visited the stables. Mr. Tubbs once again prepared Dusty for her and helped her mount. When she arrived in town, instead of depositing the letter in one of the post boxes, she checked with the stable boy to see if the Pickerings were still at the inn. They were, so she paid him a few coins to slide the letter underneath their door. She rode back to Castle Durrington, hoping that Sir Pickering would act quickly on the information.

CHAPTER TWENTY

"For a long time back the French government have been endeavoring to cripple our army, by offering inducements to the men to desert; they sent in the following paper among our men, published in English, Spanish, Portuguese, Italian, German, Polish, and Dutch. This is the English copy verbatim:—

"'ADVICE.—The soldiers of all nations, French, Italian, German, Polanders, English, Spanish, and Portuguese, who are in the English service, are advised that the deserters coming to the French Imperial Army, are perfectly well received: they are paid for the arms and the horses they bring with them: none of them is obliged to serve: passports are delivered to them to return to their native country if they choose, or to go to inner parts of France, where they may freely exercise their professions: they are moreover treated with all sort of regard."

—The Suffolk Chronicle, Suffolk, England,
December 4, 1813

WHEN MARY RETURNED from the inn, Castle Durrington was silent and empty, a husk stripped of the sights and sounds and society of the previous days. Mrs. Boughton informed Mary that Lady Trafford, Mr. Withrow, and the Tagores had gone to Worthing to visit the Trafford family graves at the cemetery. The handful of ball guests who had spent the night were still fast asleep in the guest rooms.

Mary considered heading back to Worthing, but with them gone, there might be something more she could discover. She walked up two flights of stairs to the second floor, but instead of going to her own room, she continued down the hallway and around the corner to the Tagores' rooms. She glanced nervously around, but she did not see any servants. She twisted the door handle of Miss Tagore's door. It was locked.

She stepped down the hallway to the next room, the guest room for Mr. and Mrs. Tagore. This time the door opened. She let herself inside and closed the door, leaving a crack so she could hear if someone approached. She needed to work quickly, as they could return soon. She thought of her letter packet and the missing hair; she would need to take care to make sure she left no trace of her visit.

Mary found a letter packet, but it was Mrs. Tagore's, so she did not open it. The Tagores' clothes had been placed in two different clothing presses. There appeared to be nothing unusual inside.

Mr. Tagore had a case, but it was locked, and Mary could not open it.

Besides that, the room was bare, without any indication of the Tagores' presence.

Afraid of being caught, she almost gave up the task as hopeless, but then she thought of how she had hidden her own notebook underneath her bed. She glanced out the hallway to make sure no one was near, closed the door again, and slid under the bed. Secured between the wooden frame and the bed she found a pile of papers and several notebooks. She carefully examined their placement before removing them, and then spread them out on the floor.

Some of the papers were ledgers, from various companies, organizations, and individuals, all written in the same hand. Another paper was a sketch of a map, and another a letter from a member of the East India Trade Company. Mary opened the notebooks. One appeared to be Mr. Tagore's personal diary, and the other—the other was written in a hand Mary now recognized well.

The notebook belonged to Mr. Holloway.

Mary flipped to the end, to the final words he had written in this book before he died. Mary started to read, but then realized she needed her own copy of this—she could not take the book with her and study it the way she needed, or they would realize it was missing.

She dashed down the hallway to her room, gathered her own hidden notebook, a paper, and a pencil, as it would be faster than using a quill, and hurried back to the Tagores' room.

Three quarters of the way through copying the final page, Mary heard horses outside. If Lady Trafford's carriage had returned, someone could enter this room within minutes. But she could not return the notebook and other items to their place until she finished her transcription. Hand shaking, and with quite disgraceful handwriting, she finished the rest of the page.

Mary piled the papers and notebooks back in order, as exactly as she could. She tried not to work too quickly: if she did, things might not appear exactly as they had before. She could *not* leave evidence of her spying.

She heard other sounds, though whether it was Lady Trafford's other guests awaking or the Tagores she could not tell. She slid the items back into their spot between the bed frame and the bed, rushed out of the room, closing the door behind her, and dashed into her own room.

Mary picked up one of the books assigned her by Lady Trafford and pretended to read.

Someone knocked on her door.

"Come in," Mary called.

Miss Tagore pushed open the door. "I am sorry that we missed you in Worthing." She paused. "Are you feeling well?"

"Yes," said Mary. "Why?"

"Your face is a little flushed, that is all."

"Oh," said Mary. "I am tired from the late night."

"We hope you will join us for tea."

"Of course," said Mary. She set down the book and accompanied Miss Tagore downstairs.

After tea, which was agonizingly long, Mary finally had the opportunity to examine her new notes in more detail. She barricaded the door to her room with a chair and set Mr. Holloway's notebook, which she had found in the Worthing stable, next to the page copied from Mr. Holloway's other notebook, which she had found in Mr. Tagore's room.

The page from the notebook in Mr. Tagore's possession read:

the colonel experienced disillusionment keeps his boat here come to Worthing before ship leaves for scouting mission

This seemed to be a clear reference to Colonel Coates. Holloway had been working with Lady Trafford and the Tagores in some capacity and discovered that Colonel Coates was smuggling. Based on this line, Lady Trafford had seen a need for Colonel Radcliffe's boat, in order to apprehend

Colonel Coates. Yet this conclusion did not take into account the second notebook.

Mary turned to the notebook in her possession and read the notes on the final page:

during his service on the continent pays for no record of it but now intends permanence at 3 on the 8th

Mary remembered her previous intuition, that Holloway's notebook seemed but half of a record. She studied the words on the notebook in her possession, examining the spaces between words and what the pressure of the quill on the paper. It seemed as if the words had not been written continuously. She wished she had Mr. Holloway's other notebook, but she dared not return to Mr. Tagore's room for it, so instead she examined the text she had copied from that notebook and how it might fit with the other text.

It took five pages of her notebook and a large amount of frustration, but finally she wrote out a version that combined the two texts in a satisfactory, logical manner, though she had to add punctuation and capitalization for her own sanity:

The colonel, during his service on the continent, experienced disillusionment. Keeps his boat here, pays for no record of it. Come to Worthing before, but now intends permanence. Ship leaves at 3 on the 8th for scouting mission.

When she combined the words, it no longer seemed like Mr. Holloway had been writing about Colonel Coates. For while Colonel Coates had been to France, and obviously visited for smuggling purposes, he served in the militia, not the regulars. He had never served or fought on the continent.

Yet there was another colonel who had served on the continent, and who very well could have visited Worthing before taking up permanent residence: Colonel Radcliffe.

CHAPTER TWENTY-ONE

*"What a sanctuary for the nations of the earth has Eng-
land proved herself to be! With what veneration must not
every inhabitant of every despoiled country look upon an
Englishman! A country which has appeared 'like a rock
standing out of the waters' to rescue every poor mariner,
and every drowning wretch, from the overwhelming
ocean of French rapacity and murder!"*

– The Star, London, England, December 4, 1813

T HE OTHER GUESTS who had spent the night at Castle
    Durrington had finally woken; entertaining them
required everyone's attention, which allowed Mary to slip
back to the stable. Mr. Tubbs helped her onto Dusty, then
Mary rode to Worthing, stabled the horse, donned her
disguise, and went down to the docks to investigate before
taking additional action. In a stroke of luck, the dockmaster
was not in his office, so she snuck inside to search it.

Mary could find no mention of a boat owned by Colonel
Radcliffe, at least not in the official log. Of course, Mr.
Holloway had written that the colonel paid for there to be no
record kept of it, so she should not have been surprised. Yet
everything in the dockmaster's office was so detailed and
meticulous that she had hoped to find something.

With haste, she opened all the drawers in the desk, examining every book and piece of paper. Certain that the dock-master would return any minute, she could not prevent her eyes from glancing at the door.

Finally, she found a loose piece of paper titled with only the letters *CR*. Colonel Radcliffe. It detailed every payment the colonel had made to the dockmaster. She flipped the paper over and discovered a description of where Radcliffe kept his boat.

She heard someone approaching, so she started to put everything back in its place, but realized she was out of time. Instead, she scattered the papers, knocked over a pile of books, and fled from the room, down the hall, and then out, onto the wharf.

Mary walked up the wharf, not rushing or looking back at the dockmaster's building, as either action could lead someone to suspect that she had been in the office. The wind was cold, and Mary was grateful that while the peasant cloak was ragged, it was still adequately warm.

Large military vessels did not land in Worthing, and no huge trading ships made port, nevertheless, it was a sea town and the number of seafaring vessels was numerous. There were endless small fishing vessels, private boats for excursions, and a few mid-size boats. Many of the smaller fishing vessels seemed to be gone for the day. She walked to the third pier, and then all the way to the end, where she found what she hoped was Colonel Radcliffe's boat.

It was not a large boat, perhaps designed for four or five people, and could likely be sailed by a single individual. But it was a large enough boat to cross the channel and send word to Bonaparte, and it was a large enough boat for murder.

When Mary had visited Colonel Coates's vessel, a gang-plank had been lowered and she had walked serenely across, her hand held by Colonel Coates. But here, there was no lowered gangplank, no easy way to climb onto Colonel Radcliffe's boat, if indeed it belonged to Colonel Radcliffe.

The boat was only about two feet from the dock, and the edge of the boat was only two feet above it. She looked around briefly; there were a few others on the docks, but no one was watching her. She leapt over the gap. Somehow, she hit the side of the boat with her stomach, but her arms managed to get over the side. With great effort, she pulled herself over the side and into the boat.

She walked along the deck, looking for evidence. There was some discolouration on the wood, but she could not identify its cause. A door and a short staircase led down to a single, cramped room. Against the far wall was a large chest, which was unlocked but contained only clothing. She examined every other drawer and unlocked container on the boat, but she found nothing, besides several small, locked boxes which she could not open. She even looked for the sort of hiding places Mr. Holloway would have liked, and although she found a few promising spots, there was nothing inside.

She returned to the large chest, this time, going through it more slowly, examining it item by item. It was lined by fabric, but as she pushed down on the fabric and board at the bottom of the chest, she felt them give slightly. She tugged along the edges of the base, found a spot for her fingers, and pulled. Underneath was a hidden compartment.

Inside she found Mr. Holloway's coat. If you had murdered a man, why would you keep his cloak? Mary could not fathom that decision; of course, she could also not fathom the decision to murder a man in the first place. Inside one of the cloak's pockets was another of Mr. Holloway's missing notebooks. If she was not mistaken, this was the notebook she had seen him with that final day when he spoke with Mr. Withrow in the forest. It certainly was in his handwriting and included his notes on various matters, written in a more complete and clear style than the other two notebooks in her and Mr. Tagore's possession. In a different ink, someone else—likely Colonel Radcliffe—had written their own notes and interpretations on top of the pages.

She examined the other objects in the hidden compartment. Tucked inside another man's coat, she found a knife in a sheath. She slid it carefully out. It was longer and sharper than a kitchen knife, and might be the knife that had stabbed Holloway, though if it was, it had been cleaned. There was also a wrapped package that contained papers. She browsed through them, discovering detailed plans of how Bonaparte could attack and subdue this region of England; this was proof of what she had heard the night of the ball. Mary wondered what Sir Pickering had thought of her letter, and if an anonymous letter would be enough for him to take action against Colonel Radcliffe and Monsieur Corneau. She carefully placed all the items back as she had found them and secured the hidden compartment.

She heard voices on the pier. If she was not mistaken, it was the dockmaster and Colonel Radcliffe.

Her eyes darted left and right, searching for a place to hide. She could not swim, and they were on the pier, so she could not leave the boat without them seeing her. But there were no rooms or compartments inside the boat where she might hide herself and remain undiscovered should someone come aboard.

She climbed into the chest and crouched down amongst the clothes, pulling the lid closed on top of herself. She could hardly breathe, and the fabric pressing against her was cold and rough.

The footsteps were above her, and then the door to the staircase creaked open. The men were on the boat.

"I assure you," said the dockmaster, "nothing was taken from my office, nothing was missing. I am sure it was one of the village boys again. I will catch them at it before long."

"Has anyone asked if I own a boat, after the original search?" said Colonel Radcliffe.

"Not at all, sir, not at all."

There was silence, and the footsteps came closer and then stopped, very close, perhaps even next to the chest in which she hid.

Mary was struck, suddenly, by the knowledge that this was how Mr. Holloway had died, this, or a very similar way. He had snuck on board to try to find something, some piece of information. Colonel Radcliffe had boarded, and Holloway hid himself. Radcliffe had sailed off to sea, discovered Holloway, and known that Holloway knew too much. He had then stabbed Holloway and pushed him overboard. The same could happen to Mary. Her body would wash ashore, the truth she knew would be lost, she would be mourned by her family and a few family friends, and then, she would be forgotten.

"I have heard Sir Pickering is still in Worthing, and asking questions," said Colonel Radcliffe. "If events go...unpleasantly...I will need to leave in haste. Make sure my boat is ready for me."

They bid their farewells, but it seemed, from the footsteps and other sounds on the boat, that someone had stayed. After a few minutes, Mary feared suffocation more than she feared discovery, so she cracked the lid of the chest a little for more air. But she did not leave, she could not, not for many long minutes until there were no more footsteps, no more noises.

Mary climbed out of the chest, promising herself that she would never again use such a dreadful, cramped hiding place. In fact, she would prefer if her life went back to normal and she never had to hide anywhere again. Better to embrace the tedium of embroidering to the sound of her aunt's gossip than risk life and limb for the sake of a dead man who had attempted to harm her family.

The boat appeared different than when she had boarded—the sails and ropes were all in different positions. She did not know anything about sailing, but, based on the overheard conversation, she assumed that the boat was now ready for a voyage. She pulled the ragged, smelly cloak tighter around herself, made sure it covered most of her face, and then leapt off the boat onto the pier.

She landed with a thud, and for a moment stayed crouched down, sure she had been heard, but the dockmaster did not come. She stood upright and walked slowly across the dock, and then more quickly once she neared the end of the dockmaster's office.

The dockmaster stepped out and called to her, but she ignored him, hastening her pace.

"Who goes there?" the dockmaster shouted. She glanced back and saw him shake his fist. Then he began to chase her.

In that moment, Mary abandoned everything that she had been taught as a woman of proper breeding: she ran.

She could remember distinctly the last time she had run, at seven years of age. She had been playing a game with Lydia and Kitty, she had tripped and fallen, and after that decided she was too old for that sort of game.

Mary's shoes hit hard on the wooden docks, and then on the stone cobblestones, and still she ran until she was out of breath, ran until she no longer heard the sounds of the dockmaster behind her. Despite the pain in her lungs, her side, and her legs, there was something surprisingly agreeable about running. She looked back and saw no sign of the dockmaster. She did not believe he had seen her clearly, especially with the size of her hood, and hopefully he did not realize that she had been near Colonel Radcliffe's boat, but there was no help for it now, nothing to do but to keep moving on the path she had set for herself.

As she walked down the streets of Worthing, it began to rain. There was a gathering of people outside the inn, so Mary approached.

"What be happenin'?" she asked a woman, remembering to speak in a way that matched her cloak.

The woman stepped back from Mary, eying the cloak with distaste. "It appears that Sir Pickering is inside, speakin' with Colonel Radcliffe."

"What about?" asked Mary.

The woman pretended not to hear her question and walked away. Surely Sir Pickering must be investigating Colonel Radcliffe after reading her letter.

She considered entering the inn and declaring all she knew, but something held her back. She walked up and down the street, examining her motivations. She did feel a small amount of fear, but it was a small fear compared to what she felt earlier, trapped on a boat by herself with a killer. Under further consideration, she realized her true hesitance came from other reasons.

If she took Sir Pickering aside, Colonel Radcliffe would be suspicious, and perhaps take the chance to flee. His boat was ready, and Bonaparte would welcome him with open arms.

She could barge in and make the accusations publicly, but if she did so, then everyone would know that she was responsible, and she might not discover the rest of the truth. For though she knew the identity of the murderer and of the plot to assist Bonaparte, she had more she needed to learn. Beyond a connection with Anne's death, how *was* Holloway connected to Lady Trafford and Mr. Withrow? What were they doing with all their secretive actions? If she revealed herself now, the public knowledge of it could prevent additional spying on her part.

She walked purposely through town, pausing only for a moment next to a fabric shop, with their lovely wares on display, the sort of fabric Fanny might love to own for herself. Maybe she would come back to this shop. For now, she entered one of the alleyways.

Mary found the poor woman not far from where they had met originally. The baby was significantly larger and looked better fed than the first time they had met. The woman wore a cloak just as ragged as the one she had sold Mary, despite the fact that Mary's payment could have bought a substantially better one.

"What is your name?" asked Mary. In their previous conversation she had not asked, but now, since Mary had sought her out intentionally, it seemed important.

"Mine name's Harriet."

"It is a pleasure to officially meet you, Harriet. If it is not too much trouble, I need your help again."

Harriet smiled. "Oh, I like 'elping you." She began to undo the ties on her cloak. "You be needin' another?"

"No," said Mary quickly. "No more clothing. What I need will be a little more difficult." Mary described, in detail, her plan. "Make sure to demand that as many people as possible be there, and make sure to find the hidden compartment, and have the magistrate examine every single item."

"And you say I gets five pound?"

"Yes, five pounds. The reward was in the papers."

"I would give anyone up for five pound. I won't make a boffle of it."

"Now remember," said Mary, "you *must not* mention me, for I am certain they will ask who gave you this information."

"I wunt be druv," said Harriet. It was a common expression in the area, and meant, more or less, *I won't do that*, or *I won't be driven by anyone but myself*. "B'side I don't want to share the five pound with you."

Mary saw an opportunity to add even more motivation for silence. "If you tell them about me, they might decide, since I discovered it originally, to give the entire reward to me."

"I wunt be druv," repeated the woman. "Now don't you be in no gurt fuss about it. I be about my task now." She turned and walked confidently in the direction of the inn.

Mary followed her at a distance. She could not leave Harriet to her own devices and hope that everything happened the way it ought. She had to stay, she had to be a witness that justice was brought to pass.

Harriet entered the inn. From where she stood across the street, Mary heard a fair bit of commotion; Sir Pickering's men came and went, and soon Colonel Coates and several other officers from the militia were gathered, as well as a number of other notable individuals from the community. The only person not present was Monsieur Corneau. Mary assumed that either Harriet had forgotten to ask for him, or he had not been found.

The door of the inn opened again, and this time Sir Pickering and Colonel Radcliffe, Harriet and her baby, exited, followed by a train of other individuals.

"This is ridiculous," said Colonel Radcliffe, gesturing at Harriet. "I have never seen this peasant before in my life. What can she possibly have to say against me?"

"If her suspicions are shown to be invalid," said Sir Pickering, "then this will be very short. Now, Miss Harriet, since you will not tell us the location of your evidence, please lead the way."

Mary joined the end of the procession as they made their way down to the docks. None of the people seemed bothered by the rain; of course, in this area of the country, they had over a dozen words for different types of mud, so a little rain must not bother them. When they arrived at the docks, the dockmaster exited his office and bowed obsequiously to Sir Pickering, not once, but three times.

"I do not own, or have access to any boat," said Colonel Radcliffe loudly.

"That is yet to be determined," said Sir Pickering. "Now, Miss Harriet, I assume you have brought us here to show us a particular boat."

"Yes, he does have a boat." Harriet deliberately looked up and down the wharf.

"Well?" said Sir Pickering.

"There's a good many boats," said Harriet. "But I will remember, I will."

After half a minute, Harriet still stood on the dock, bouncing her baby on her hip rather vigorously, still looking back and forth.

The crowd was rumbling in annoyance, and Mary was about to reveal herself when Sir Pickering turned to the dockmaster.

"Mr. Kempthorne. Perhaps you could tell us."

"I have shown you the records afore," said Mr. Kempthorne. "Colonel Radcliffe has no boat."

"The colonel's paid 'im to keep it off the record," said Harriet, triumphantly repeating what Mary had told her.

"If this is true," said Sir Pickering, "you may be aiding and abetting a murder. That is a very serious crime."

The dockmaster's entire body tensed, and he seemed to make a swift decision to save himself rather than his benefactor. "Colonel Radcliffe does own a boat," he admitted. "And he has paid me to keep it secret."

"Did Colonel Radcliffe come with his boat in the weeks before he took up residence here?"

"Many times," said the dockmaster. "I would need to check my records to be certain of the dates."

"I did not know you had a boat, good chap," said Colonel Coates to Colonel Radcliffe. "We should go sailing together."

The dockmaster led the way to Colonel Radcliffe's boat. Mary lingered at the back of the crowd.

"This is not my boat," insisted Colonel Radcliffe.

Sir Pickering ignored him and gestured for the dockmaster to lay out a gangplank. "Please, join me aboard," said Sir Pickering. Colonel Radcliffe did so, as well as Colonel Coates, two other officers, and Sir Pickering's men.

"Interesting," said Sir Pickering, leaning down and touching the wood. "This is a trace of a blood stain that appears to have been bleached off."

"There's an awmry," said Harriet from where she stood on the pier. "With more you will be findin' useful."

"Where is this…awmry?" asked Sir Pickering.

"It's a… It's inside, inside the boat. Below. And it 'as a secret compartment, on the bottom of it, on the inside." Sir

Pickering—and everyone else—must know that Harriet had never seen either the boat or the chest for herself. Mary could only hope that when pressed for answers, Harriet would not reveal the identity of her informant.

"Bring the chest up here," Sir Pickering directed his men, and after short work they returned with it.

"The chest is labeled C. Radcliffe." Sir Pickering spoke loudly, as if he felt it were important for all in the crowd to hear. "Now let me see if I can find this hidden compartment."

Colonel Radcliffe appeared increasingly uncomfortable. Several of the officers seemed to notice this and kept their hands ready at their swords.

"A coat," observed Sir Pickering. He held it up for display. "Here, in the pocket, is a notebook belonging to Mr. Holloway."

"I do not know how that came to be here," insisted Colonel Radcliffe. "I was not aware of the hidden compartment in this chest, which was a recent acquisition."

Sir Pickering ignored Colonel Radcliffe's protests and continued his examination. "A knife. It is a possible match for the one used to stab Mr. Holloway. Now what have we here?" He did a cursory glance at the papers. "Plans to assist Bonaparte in an invasion…very detailed plans, Colonel Radcliffe, in your handwriting, involving you and Monsieur Corneau."

"I am innocent!" exclaimed Colonel Radcliffe. "Colonel Coates is the one at fault. He is a smuggler."

"I do not know what you are talking about," said Colonel Coates.

"Smuggling is a matter for another day. Today, our topic is murder," said Sir Pickering. "A trial will determine your innocence or your guilt, but the evidence I have found is more than sufficient to arrest you."

Colonel Coates and the other men attempted to grab Colonel Radcliffe, but he stepped out of their grasp and leapt from the boat into the water. He swam for the wharf.

No one seemed keen to jump after him, into the frigid December water. Instead the officers and Sir Pickering's men tried to press through the crowd on the dock, but the people were packed as tightly as on a parade day, and just as immovable.

Colonel Radcliffe had reached the boardwalk, his hands were grasping the planks, yet no one was in a position to stop him. It appeared he would escape.

Mary could not allow that. If no one else would stop him, then she would. Because she had stayed at the back of the crowd, no one was in her path.

She ran across the dock, careful to stay in the centre where she would not risk falling into the water. Her heart seemed to pound in her head, and she wished that her physical accomplishments included more than the pianoforte and locking letters. Colonel Radcliffe heaved himself onto the deck as Mary approached, holding the hood of her cloak tight around her face.

She slipped on the damp wood just as she reached Colonel Radcliffe. He stood. Mary stretched out her leg and tripped him.

He fell on the boardwalk.

Mary scrambled towards him. He pulled himself up, and in desperation, Mary lunged for him, grabbing his legs with her arms. In that moment, she could not help but picture her mother and the other women of Meryton, completely scandalized by the way that Mary held onto a man, in public, no less.

He kicked at her. Mary grunted in pain as his foot connected with her chest, but still she held on, held on, held on, for the few necessary moments until the officers could arrive and secure Colonel Radcliffe.

One of the officers attempted to help Mary to her feet. "I'm fine," she said, pushing him away. She stood, all the while trying to keep her hood tight around her face, and then, as discreetly as she could, she walked away, away from the people, away from the docks. No one stopped her.

"Sir Pickering," Mary heard Harriet say rather loudly. "I knows you owe me five pound."

Mary smiled. Colonel Radcliffe had been arrested for murder, and Harriet would receive her money. Despite what would surely be a bruise from Colonel Radcliffe's foot, Mary much preferred this to all the needlework and gossip that Meryton could offer.

CHAPTER TWENTY-TWO

"SUSSEX—On Saturday a murderer who had been at large for several months was apprehended. Colonel Oliver Radcliffe was a recent resident of Worthing and had previously served on the continent, during which time he defected to the French. His treasonous plans were discovered in September by Mr. Frederick Holloway of Crawley, after which Colonel Radcliffe killed Mr. Holloway. Colonel Radcliffe has been arrested for murder and treason and will soon stand trial. An accomplice of the colonel, a Frenchman named Jules Corneau, has fled from Worthing, and no knowledge is known of his whereabouts."

—*The Times*, London, England, December 9, 1813

I T HAD NOW been six days since the ball, and five days since the apprehension of Colonel Radcliffe, yet still the castle had not resumed a normal rhythm. The Tagores had left the previous day, but her lessons with Madame Dieupart and Mr. Linton had not resumed. But more than that, something had changed, something had shifted between her and Lady Trafford. Before, Lady Trafford had always treated Mary with focused attention. She had sought out Mary's thoughts and ideas, and made her feel central to any gathering. Mary enjoyed their discussions and took pleasure in surprising Lady

Trafford with new insights.

But now Lady Trafford treated Mary the way that everyone else always had. Mary regretted her rudeness to Lady Trafford the morning after the ball, and she had apologized for it a few days before. She still regretted not wearing the dress Fanny had made. But she did not feel that these two transgressions merited a response of this magnitude. Perhaps something else was troubling Lady Trafford and preventing her from giving Mary the same amount of attention.

She had found herself rather bored the past few days, with only books, the pianoforte, and drawing to occupy her, and no murder to distract herself with. In Longbourn, books and her music had always been more than enough for her, but she had become accustomed to a different pace of life, and now it was hard to return to the former. While she was still attempting to find out more about Lady Trafford and Mr. Withrow, she had not made much progress.

Someone knocked at Mary's bedroom door, interrupting her thoughts.

"Come in," she called.

Fanny stepped inside. She had been very distant since the ball and seemed to be avoiding Mary. "You asked for me?"

"Yes," said Mary. "I have something for you."

Mary retrieved the package containing her purchase from the fabric shop. She laid it on the bed, untied the string, and opened the brown paper to reveal the blue fabric.

Fanny's fingers went immediately to the fabric. "What is this?"

"It is silk taffeta. You know that of course," said Mary, wishing for a clarity of speech that she did not often possess. "I thought that since you love designing clothing so much, you might like to make yourself a dress. At the shop they said that this was their newest fabric, and that you really liked it the last time you visited. They said that five yards should be enough, but I bought six to be sure."

Fanny stepped back. She intertwined her fingers and pulled her hands against her chest. "Miss Bennet," she said, "you do not need to, you should not—"

"Yes, I do." Mary picked up the fabric and forced it into Fanny's arms.

"Thank you."

"You do not need to thank me," said Mary. "You do not owe me anything, Fanny. I cannot make things right, I cannot fix what I have done, but at least I can attempt to do something."

Fanny looked as if she might become emotional, and Mary was fully unequipped to deal with emotions, so she rushed out of the room and fled downstairs to the pianoforte. Lady Trafford and Mr. Withrow were already seated in the large parlor, but Mary decided to play anyway.

Mary had begun her second song when Lady Trafford asked her to stop.

"Your music is lovely," said Lady Trafford, "but I was attempting to converse with Henry. Maybe you could do something else right now, and come back and play later, when the room is vacant."

Mary stood abruptly from the instrument. "Have I done something wrong?"

"Not at all, Miss Bennet, but I am rather tired today, and the sound is too loud for me."

Yet Lady Trafford was not like Mrs. Bennet, with very sensitive nerves.

"What is it that I have done wrong?" asked Mary again. "Surely it is more than playing the pianoforte at an inconvenient time." Mary could not help but feel that if she had told Lady Trafford about her role in discovering Radcliffe and Corneau then nothing would have changed: everything good about her stay at Castle Durrington would have remained the same. But she would not tell Lady Trafford, she could not.

Lady Trafford folded her arms across her body and looked at Mary with resolve.

"If you must know, you disgraced me and Castle Durrington at the ball. Despite all the lessons I have tried to teach you, you did not show humility or any manners or breeding. You left without saying goodbye to any of the guests and foolishly went off into the night. And you monopolized too much of the general attention towards yourself."

"I—I was simply attempting to demonstrate my accomplishments," said Mary, unable to address more than the final critique.

"You may have been the most accomplished girl in Meryton, but Meryton is a very small place, and you may find that your accomplishments are not so great when you join a larger company."

Mary felt sick to her stomach and tears began to well up in her eyes, but she would not cry in front of Lady Trafford and Mr. Withrow—she could not let herself do it. Withrow sat, not saying anything, but with a smug look on his face. Mary sniffled, then swallowed, trying to control her emotions.

Lady Trafford's face softened. "I only meant that a bit more humility may be useful in large gatherings, but you truly have shown great progress in many areas over the past few months. I am quite pleased." Lady Trafford paused. "I have been writing to various acquaintants, and I may have found someone who needs a governess not long after Christmas."

Mary used her handkerchief to dab her eyes. She tried to

speak with a level voice. "I am not sure that I am ready to be a governess yet. I still have not decided on that as my fixed course." It had only been an excuse to draw closer to Lady Trafford so she could track her movements. But the last few days she had not even been able to do that, for she had been kept at such a distance.

"It is a rather large decision, perhaps one that is best made in consultation with your family. Speaking of which, it has been quite some time since you have seen them. Your mother must be needing you, and surely you will want to be home well before the holidays."

Now Mary understood the shift in Lady Trafford's mannerisms since the ball. The woman had spent all this time trying to find a way to rescind her invitation for Mary to stay at Castle Durrington. Mary had not expected it to end like this, but she knew when she was no longer welcome.

"I will write my mother at once and make arrangements for my return."

Mary rushed from the parlor. As she reached the hall, tears slid down her cheeks. She had planned to go upstairs and weep in her room, but as she reached the rotunda, wracking sobs shook her body and she collapsed on the floor next to the top of the grand staircase.

She truly had not realized that her actions at the ball had disgraced Lady Trafford, a woman who had done so very much for her over the past months. And Mary had never meant to make a spectacle of herself. Mary's mind ran ceaselessly over Lady Trafford's words, repeating them again and again.

Mary had thought that she recognized her flaws—she knew she could be cold and distant; she knew that she could be rude and too quick to correct. But this was more than just the walls she hid behind. It was as if there was a fundamental defect in her character, something irrevocably wrong with her.

She had to work much harder than other people to behave in expected, acceptable ways. She could never simply interact with the world around her; she had to intentionally process everything and consider how *normal* people would act in any given circumstance. It seemed, over the past months, that Lady Trafford had been trying to teach her to do this better, but despite Lady Trafford's kindness and diligence, and despite Mary's efforts, Mary had failed. And it felt inevitable that Mary would continue to fail.

She could not even hide behind her accomplishments, not any longer. Her perceived accomplishments, the things she had worked so hard to gain, must, in fact, be paltry. This was not Lydia or Kitty mocking her skills at the piano, this was Lady Trafford, a woman of superb taste. If Mary did not have her accomplishments, then what was she left with? She had no beauty, no money, no social competence…she had nothing.

Mary's sobs quieted and her body finally stilled. She twisted the mourning ring on her finger, remembering her father's dying breaths, how he had looked at her but said nothing. Elizabeth might have talked with their father at a time like this. But Mary had not had that sort of relationship with him. She had never had that sort of relationship with anyone. There was no one she could turn to with her emotions, no one who would give her any comfort.

Not a single one of her family members had mentioned Mary returning for the holidays in their brief, occasional letters. Mary had slipped out of their lives and they had hardly noticed. They certainly did not desire her return.

Mary pressed her knees to her chest and wrapped her arms around her legs, grateful that no servants had come upon her when she was like this. There was a mottled light on the sleeves of her dress, and she looked up at the dome above her. Through it shone a cold, weak December light, providing a dreary illumination even at midday.

Footsteps sounded in the hallway, accompanied by the voices of Lady Trafford and Mr. Withrow. She stood quickly; she did not want them to see her tear-streaked cheeks. She considered fleeing up the stairs, but then they would hear her and what if they followed? Instead she stepped behind one of the curtains covering the panels, the same one she had hid behind before, the night of the midnight visitors. She urged herself to be perfectly still and quiet as they entered the rotunda.

"A plan must be decided upon," said Mr. Withrow.

"I need to see the papers myself," said Lady Trafford. "We will discuss this in the library."

Their footsteps echoed as they descended the grand spiral staircase. At least they had not noticed her. She shifted under the curtains, bumping her elbow against the panel behind her. It made an almost hollow sound. She peeked out from the curtain to make sure no one was in the rotunda and proceeded to tap the panel. It was definitely a hollow sound, more like one would expect from a door than a wall. She pushed the panel, but it did not budge, even when she pressed her full weight against it.

She must be wrong, it was only a panel, but she remembered her initial confusion about the castle. This was a circular room surrounded by square rooms. There must be a gap in between.

Mary ran her hands along the intricate, decorative moulding around the edges of the panel. It was difficult to tell what she was feeling in the near darkness, and she could not throw back the curtain in case someone walked by, but it was probably raised and textured leaves and flowers. She did not find anything, so she examined each part again with her fingers, moving more slowly this time.

One section of the moulding drew her attention. It had the same texture and shape as the rest but felt slightly less firm. She fiddled with it for a moment until it loosened, and she discovered a hidden latch. She pulled on it and was able to swing the panel open.

Mary's breath stopped. She had been right! There was something. She peered into the dark space revealed by the panel but could see nothing of note, and she was not keen to stumble around an unfamiliar space blindly, so she pulled the paneling closed, secured the latch, and then walked to her room and lit one of the candles. As she returned to the hidden room, a servant passed her and, staring at the lit candle in her hand in the middle of the day, asked, "Do you need anything, Miss Bennet?"

"No," said Mary, attempting to sound cheerful. "I am perfectly well."

She reached the rotunda, checked to make sure she was alone, and then stepped again behind the fabric curtain, careful not to light it on fire. This time she found and opened the latch easily.

The candle flickered in the darkness, matching Mary's trepidation, and she stepped inside, closing the panel behind her. It appeared to be a storage room. There were a number of small crates filled with old items, and several pig head statues that matched the ones on a rather whimsical section on the estate's castle-side exterior. Mary's hopes sank a little—it was just a storage room, nothing of note. She had hoped for something more, for evidence of Lady Trafford's misdeeds.

She sat on top of one of the crates. Her candle flickered as if there was a slight movement of air, and yet there should not be any draft. She stood and on one wall noted a vent. Air must be coming in from the rest of the house. But what would be on the other side of this wall? She visualized the floor plan she had pieced together in her mind and realized it would be the large drawing room, the one with the pianofor-te.

If air could come through, so could sound. One could sit here and overhear a private conversation happening in the drawing room.

Lady Trafford and her deceased husband had built Castle Durrington. They *must* have known of this space. She pictured Lady Trafford creeping into this room and eaves-dropping on a conversation, and she found that the action seemed in keeping with her character.

Mary paced back and forth around the small space, won-dering if the room held other secrets. Her candle's light flickered on the walls, on the floor. At the edge of one of the crates she noted that some of the floor was wood, not stone. She set down the candle, picked up the crate, which was not too heavy, set it aside, and discovered what could only be a trapdoor.

She pulled it up, as carefully and quietly as she could. It *was* a trapdoor, with a rope ladder hanging down to the space below. A space that must solve the same circle-in-a-square problem downstairs in the main entryway. This space must directly adjoin the library, where Lady Trafford and Mr. Withrow might still be having their private conversation.

Mary's heart raced painfully in her chest. If she were Lyd-ia, she would squeal right now, out of excitement or fear, but Mary kept her emotions contained inside of her.

She set the candle on the ledge and carefully, ever so quietly, climbed down the ladder. It was difficult to do in her dress, but somehow she managed.

She crouched on the floor, close to the wall, and indeed there was another grate, large enough, perhaps, for a small person to pass through. Or voices.

"But who will be his partner?" asked Mr. Withrow. "Surely there is someone else in London who could—"

"It is too late for that now."

"William will not like it."

"Mr. Stanley will do as directed," said Lady Trafford.

There was bit of silence. Mary tried to piece together their conversation but did not know enough context.

Mr. Withrow said, "He should be in Arundel right now. Once he is finished with his work, he will ride directly here. He estimated that he will reach Castle Durrington around three o'clock." He paused. "And before he does, I want Miss Bennet out of the way."

"You were right about her, Henry, you were right. I was too blinded by my hopes to see it. But do not worry, I will get her out of our way."

CHAPTER TWENTY-THREE

"On the day before yesterday, the Emperor [Bonaparte] held a Council of Ministers, and a second Council of Administration of War, concerning the clothing of the troops."

—*The Times*, London, a translation from a
French newspaper report,
printed on December 9, 1813

AFTER WAITING SEVERAL minutes to ensure Lady Trafford and Withrow were finished with their conversation, Mary climbed the rope ladder, her heart racing.

She closed the trapdoor and replaced the crate, careful to make sure it was in the exact position she had found it. She used the inside latch to open the panel, blew out the candle, and peeked behind the curtain. She waited as Fanny walked across the rotunda and used the smaller spiral staircase to go upstairs. Mary waited for a minute more, then left the shelter of the curtain.

Her body felt like it would burst with energy, and she felt a strange urge to run, but she forced herself to walk across the rotunda and up the staircase to her bedroom.

Fanny was just leaving her room. "I was looking for you, Miss Bennet."

"I was...taking a turn about the house." Mary tried to

hide the still hot candle in her skirts.

Fanny appeared not to notice. "Lady Trafford would like to speak to you."

"Can you tell her that I will join her in a few minutes?"

"She requests your presence immediately."

"Do you know why it is so urgent?"

Fanny shook her head.

"Give me just a moment." Mary stepped into her room, leaving Fanny in the hall, and put the candle back in its spot. Then she followed Fanny down two flights of stairs to the library.

Fanny turned to leave, but Lady Trafford directed her to remain. Mary's fingers fidgeted, so she hid her hands in her skirts, fearful of whatever was to come.

Lady Trafford went straight to the point. "I have been considering our conversation from earlier, and I realized that it is not fair to you to keep you in a state of suspension, unsure of your place here, or whether you should become a governess, or when you might have the opportunity of returning to your beloved mother. It would be for the best if you returned home immediately."

"Immediately?" asked Mary, unable to comprehend Lady Trafford's words.

"Yes. I will have you on a carriage to Washington this evening. Then tomorrow to London, and then on to Meryton."

"This evening?" Mary said. Lady Trafford had said she would get Mary out of the way, but Mary had not expected to be thrown out of the house without any warning. She must have something truly dreadful planned with the visitor.

"There is no point in arguing with me, Miss Bennet, once my mind has been firmly set. Now come here, child. You must write a letter to your mother telling of your return. We will send it express so it arrives before you do."

Mary moved like a puppet dragging its feet.

Lady Trafford handed her a quill and a paper. "Now please write the following: Dear Mother," Lady Trafford paused, watching as Mary wrote the words, and then continued, "I am excited to return to see you and my sister in Meryton. Please expect me on the evening of December eleventh. With love, Mary."

Mary finished writing the words and set down the quill.

"Good, good. Brief, but to the point," said Lady Trafford. "I need you to take the horse you always ride and go to Worthing. I will provide you with funds so you can send the letter express, pre-paid. While you are in town, I have a number of items from different shops that I need you to purchase for me."

Lady Trafford passed her a lengthy list, which included items from five different shops. From one shop, she needed to purchase seven different types of parchment paper.

"I am not sure I would be the best person to make these purchases," said Mary. "I would hate to buy something that does not meet your expectations."

"Most of the servants have the day off," said Lady Trafford, "and I cannot spare any of those who remain."

Mary's cheeks burned. She was being treated like a servant. She felt humiliated even though she knew she was only assigned these tasks to keep her away from the castle, so she would not see or meet their visitor, Mr. Stanley. Yet what else could she do besides follow Lady Trafford's orders?

"Very well," said Mary, folding the list. Her eyes strayed to the grandfather clock. It was half past one. Mr. Withrow had stated that Mr. Stanley was expected at three o'clock, which was in only an hour and a half.

"Fanny, please accompany Miss Bennet to her room. She will give you directions about packing her things so they can be ready for her when she returns. Also, since Mary did not wear the new dresses, there is no reason to pack them."

They walked up to Mary's room in silence. As they did, Mary realized there was nothing preventing her from appearing to acquiesce to Lady Trafford's demands and then doing something else entirely. If Lady Trafford did not want her meeting Mr. Stanley, then she would find a way to meet him. She could foresee few negative consequences to avoiding Lady Trafford's assigned tasks; she was already being sent home.

When they reached the room, Fanny asked Mary a few questions about how she wanted things packed, but then stopped. She clasped her hands together and said, "I am sorry that you must leave like this."

Her sincerity almost made Mary cry. "I have been horrible to you, Fanny, yet still you are kind to me. I do not deserve you."

"You have not been horrible."

"Yes, I have. I should have worn the dress you made to the ball, but it was so beautiful, I could not put it on."

"That is a very strange reason to not wear a dress."

"I know, it is. I just…I…I have been overzealous and decided to value simplicity above everything else." Mary paused. "Also, I was afraid, because the dress is beautiful, and I am not."

"A dress is just a dress. I made it to look good on you, not on someone else."

"If I could go back a few days, I would wear it to the ball. I am sorry that I cannot."

"Life is as it is, and there is little you can do to change it."

Fanny seemed resigned to life's whims and caprices.

"Do you *truly* believe that?"

"I suppose not."

"What would you change about life?" asked Mary.

"I want to own my own dress shop and hire seamstresses so I can focus on designs rather than stitching. But that is why I am here. What Lady Trafford offered is enough that I can save for it."

"I hope you get what you want." More than ever, Mary wished she had worn the dress to the ball. "I know that Lady Trafford will not let me keep them, but could I at least try on one of the dresses? Only if it is agreeable to you, of course."

Fanny nodded. "You may, but we need to be quick. Lady Trafford expects you to complete her tasks, and I need to pack for you."

"Thank you," said Mary.

Mary undid her dress as Fanny removed the ball gown from the clothing press.

"Now close your eyes," directed Fanny.

Mary closed her eyes as Fanny pulled the dress onto her, did up the laces, and then led her across the room.

"Now open them."

Mary did so, and despite the fact that she believed gasping should be reserved only for silly females, she gasped. She looked like a maiden from a painting or a play. She looked lovely, maybe even beautiful, and she had never once considered those words in relationship to herself.

She had never worn yellow before, and the canary colour made her feel like someone who both desired and deserved the attention of others. The neckline was swaths lower than any neckline Mary had ever worn before, yet with how Fanny had designed it, it did not feel immodest or revealing. She had not realized a dress could look so flattering on her figure.

Mary swished the dress back and forth, imagining how it would look on a dance floor. "It is stunning."

"Next one," said Fanny, and started undoing the ball gown before Mary could even reply. She seemed to be enjoying herself.

Before she knew it, Mary was dressed in the lacy puce evening gown.

Mary did not normally bestow many compliments, but it seemed the right thing to do. And with Fanny's workmanship, it was easy to be genuine.

"I do not normally like this colour, but I love it on this dress."

"Because I know what to do with it."

"You certainly do. I think even the most intolerable man could not help admiring me. Can I try the last one?"

Fanny smiled. "Of course."

They dressed her in the cream-coloured morning gown. It had intricate embroidery, especially around the bodice, which had the risk of drawing undue attention to that region of her body, a thought which made Mary uncomfortable. Yet it was also her favorite dress. It made her feel that she could go anywhere, do anything, be anyone she wanted to be.

She could lose herself in a dress like this. And do so willingly.

"You are the most amazing seamstress I have ever met."

Fanny smiled in agreement.

"And you designed all of these dresses yourself?"

"I did, Miss Bennet."

Mary lingered in front of the mirror, not wanting to return to her normal clothes and still figuring out how to interrupt Lady Trafford's plans. But she did not have time to dawdle. She needed to fool Lady Trafford into thinking she had gone to Worthing, intercept Mr. Stanley, and somehow trick him into revealing their plans.

It might be easier to succeed if she wore this dress.

"Would it be possible for me to stay in this dress for the next few hours?" Mary asked. And now to say nothing dishonest to Fanny and yet hopefully direct her to the incorrect conclusion. "There is…a man I would like to meet. A man I will only be able to see today. And I would rather him see me in this than in one of my normal dresses."

"Oh, you have a sweetheart in Worthing." Fanny smiled. Though she had no young man, Mary blushed. The sensation felt quite unfamiliar to her. "No wonder you have been so keen to visit these past weeks. Yes, you can wear this dress while you say goodbye to him." She paused. "I would not be surprised if Lady Trafford has me take it apart to use the fabric scraps for something else."

"Thank you," said Mary. She looked again at herself in the mirror, pictured herself intercepting Mr. Stanley, and her face fell. She could wear a beautiful dress, but it would not be enough to change how people saw her or what she was able to accomplish.

"Whatever is wrong now, Miss Bennet?"

"I wish my face and my hair… I wish they matched the dress."

"There is no crime to being plain," said Fanny. "And you are more attractive than you think. But if you want to look different, there may be something I can do."

Fanny left and returned a few minutes later with an array of items Mary had never seen before. "I sent for your horse to be readied, so we don't have much time." She waited, as if expecting Mary to do something. "Sit down," she directed, pointing to a chair. She turned the mirror away so Mary could not watch and proceeded to apply powders and creams to Mary's face.

"I do not want to look like a, like a—" Mary found no other way to say it, so she blurted out the words, "—fallen woman!" Even saying it made her feel unclean.

Fanny did not stop her work. "Well, you would if I put on lip paint or added things to your eyes. But what I am doing will not be obvious—no one will be able to tell I have applied *anything* to your face. I am simply hiding some blemishes."

"But if I can see it, will you take it off?"

"Of course, Miss Bennet. But don't you worry, I have done this many times before."

Mary noted that Fanny possessed a full array of tones, both to match her own skin and a lighter skin like Mary's. Meanwhile, Mary's stomach began to feel uneasy. Maybe intercepting Lady Trafford's guest was not the best plan after all.

Fanny began working on Mary's hair, a process that seemed ridiculous in length. Lady Trafford would be expecting her to leave, and she needed to do so quickly. Mary had always believed that putting energy into one's appearance truly was a waste of time, and this only confirmed it. She drummed her fingers against the arm of the chair.

Finally Fanny finished and turned the mirror towards Mary.

Mary stood in front of it, confused. She did not look like herself. Now it was not just the dress that might capture someone's attention, but her face. Even her neck and her facial structure appeared different, and her skin looked perfectly clear.

"Now pinch your cheeks," said Fanny.

"Pinch my cheeks?"

"To get a little redness in them."

When Mary did nothing, Fanny pinched her cheeks for her, a little harder than Mary thought necessary.

Fanny nodded. "Now walk around the room."

She did not understand the direction, but she followed it.

"You must hold yourself like you belong in this dress."

"I cannot. This is something one of my sisters would wear."

"Then pretend to be one of your sisters."

She pictured herself as Jane, confident, beautiful, almost regal.

"Yes, that is much better," said Fanny.

Mary stopped in front of the mirror. With this dress and the cream and the hair it was like putting on a disguise, becoming someone different. She wondered if her family would even recognize her.

"Please do not tell anyone that I am dressed like this," said Mary. "I do not want Lady Trafford, or anyone else, to know that I am meeting someone."

"I will keep it our little secret. But take good care of the dress."

Mary agreed. She donned her heavy cloak and wrapped it tightly around herself, trying to cover as much of the dress as possible and putting the hood over her head.

Fanny adjusted the cloak slightly, then shepherded Mary through the halls, once hiding her in a closet so the house-keeper, Mrs. Boughton, did not see her.

Finally, they made it out of the house. Mr. Tubbs stood outside, horse ready. He checked the sidesaddle, paying particular attention to the saddle girth straps that ran underneath the horse, then lifted Mary's right foot as she sprang upwards with her left leg.

She adjusted her legs on the left side of the horse, noting that this dress revealed more of her ankles than her normal dress did. She tried to pull down the dress a little more, but it did not make any real difference, so she would need to do her best to ignore it.

From Castle Durrington, she turned east towards Worthing, in case anyone from the house watched her departure. After a minute or two, she looked around to make sure no one was on the road, and then turned the horse north into the forest. She went forward, over branches, around logs, between trees, until, looking back, she could no longer see the road. Then she turned west, travelling at a slow pace until she thought she must be far past Castle Durrington, before turning south and rejoining the road.

Now she travelled west on the road, at a slow trot in the direction of Arundel, which Withrow had mentioned. She passed Patching Pond and the village of Ham-pot, which was only a handful of small houses.

After a few more miles she stopped. If the map she had always looked at in the library was correct, the road would split into two paths, which would both lead to Arundel. Since she did not know which road Stanley would be taking, it would be better to stay and wait for him here, because whichever direction he chose, he would pass by.

She contemplated the next part of her plan, which was not much of a plan at all. Lydia had sometimes managed to introduce herself to men without a formal introduction, but Mary did not want to do anything improper, and she could not simply hail a passing rider on a horse and start a lengthy conversation. Based on analysis she had made from Lydia's accounts, dropping a handkerchief tended to work only about one in four times. Mary needed better odds.

Maybe she could find a reason that she would *need* a gentleman's help. She attempted dropping the reins so she could pretend she could not reach them, but since they had a buckle they fell on the back of her horse's neck and it was easy for her to pick them back up. If she undid the buckle, she could actually lose the reins, but then she might lose control of the horse, and there was no guarantee that she would manage to lose control at the perfect moment, just as the mysterious gentleman approached.

She could fall off the horse and get her foot caught in the slipper stirrup just as she saw the gentleman approaching, but she could not bring herself to do something so idiotic. Finding out what Lady Trafford was up to was not worth risking her neck. She could attempt to get her horse stuck in the mud—if she could find any mud immediately next to the road, but she had promised Fanny she would not get the new dress dirty. She found that despite her father always calling her a silly girl, she could not bring herself to do something genuinely stupid, even if it would provide an excuse to talk to Mr. Stanley.

Maybe she could tangle the horse's reins in some branches. She dismounted the horse—not in the most graceful manner, but there was no one watching—and twisted the reins into a low-hanging tree branch, which was bare of leaves except for a solitary brown one that hung on with all its might.

Mary stepped back to examine her work. This would fool no one.

She tangled the reins into the branches a little more. This time it looked a little better, but still not convincing, and

Dusty pulled herself free. She attempted a third time but gave up. What an ill-conceived idea.

She decided to remount the horse, but then realized that in her entire life, she had never mounted a horse by herself; she had always mounted with a groom or a mounting block. She ran her fingers through Dusty's mane. While the help of a groom must make it easier, she could surely do it on her own.

She raised her right hand up, gripping it on the saddle's fixed head. She used both legs to leap up with all her might.

She did not get anywhere near the needed height.

After several more failed attempts she realized that leaping would not do. She lifted her leg and carefully placed it in the single slipper stirrup on the left side of the horse. She gripped the saddle head with her right hand, leaped with her left leg, and pulled herself up onto the saddle, but as she did so her weight pulled the saddle down, off the top of the horse and onto its left flank. She hung there for a second or two, hand still on the saddle head, until she managed to extract her foot from the saddle stirrup.

It took Mary several minutes to fix the saddle and adjust the girth straps. She had to remove her gloves and her hands grew icy cold.

She tried to mount once again using the slipper stirrup, this time putting less weight on her foot, but once again received the same result. After extracting herself, again, and fixing the saddle, again, Mary stood, contemplating the saddle's design. Men often put a foot into the stirrup of a saddle and mounted, but a man's saddle had a superior design. The girth straps, along with the weight of the stirrup on the opposite side, made it not shift as much during mounting. Even if it did shift, it could shift back easily, by virtue of the man putting one leg on each side of the horse, providing balance. But on a woman's sidesaddle, the woman's weight was almost entirely on the left side of the horse. With the saddle's design, it would be near impossible to ride it like a normal saddle, and that was even if she could get up on it.

The cold bit at Mary's nose, which filled with moisture. She dabbed her nose with her handkerchief, which she then folded and returned to her cloak. What a ridiculous design— to create a saddle that one could not mount by oneself.

She led the horse to a fallen log on the side of the road and attempted to use it as a mounting block, but it was a rather skinny log and did not have the necessary height.

Finally, she sat down on the log, making sure her cloak was positioned to protect the dress. She pressed her gloved fingers against her temples. She supposed she could wait for Mr. Stanley and ask for his help. Warmth bloomed within her chest: she had finally discovered something that required a gentleman's assistance. Of course, she had intended to need his help for something a little more interesting or dire than mounting her horse. If this was one of Kitty's novels, a pack of wolves would attack. But there were no wolves, and really, this would do just as well.

Mary waited for what seemed like a very long time, and as she waited her mood shifted from pleasure at finding an excuse to speak to Mr. Stanley to despair. She did not even know what Mr. Stanley looked like, whether he was tall or short, young or old, whether he came by carriage or by horse. But he certainly did not come, for the road was empty. She wished she had a pocket watch so she would know for how long she had waited in the frigid cold. Her cloak was quality and would have been enough for riding into Worthing, for she would have spent most her time in shops. But it was an unusually cold December, and her cloak was not enough for spending hours outside.

She did some calculations in her mind. Her conversation with Lady Trafford had ended at one thirty. With the time she had spent with Fanny, she probably had not left Castle Durrington until quarter past two. Then she would have spent at least twenty or thirty minutes riding the horse, and a solid thirty minutes first failing to find a reason for needing a gentleman's help and then attempting to mount the horse. She supposed she had spent approximately forty-five minutes waiting, which put the time close to four o'clock. Stanley was meant to arrive at Castle Durrington at three o'clock.

Maybe he was late. She counted aloud to two thousand, growing progressively colder as the numbers grew higher.

Finally, she concluded that Mr. Stanley must have come by a different road, from a different direction, or she had missed him somehow, perhaps when backtracking through the wood. Or maybe when Withrow had said three o'clock, he had not meant today; he could have meant tomorrow.

Mary stood and led her horse back down the road towards Castle Durrington. She regretted riding so many miles, but there was nothing to do for it but walk. She gritted her teeth and tried to maintain a positive disposition. Though she had done more of it in the past few months than in her entire life, Mary did not like walking.

CHAPTER TWENTY-FOUR

"Bonaparte is affecting an air of perfect security and ease. He is hunting, attending the opera, and inspecting manufactures. All this, however, must be merely for stage effect, and we have no doubt that he finds it a painful piece of acting, since it is impossible he can be without apprehensions."

—*Perth Courier*, Perth, Scotland, December 9, 1813

AFTER QUITE SOME time, Mary came across a wooden fence on the side of the road. This reached much higher than the log she had used earlier, and she thought it possible she could use it to mount the horse.

She positioned the horse as close to the fence as possible while still allowing her the space to climb. She was halfway up the fence when she heard a friendly, unfamiliar voice.

"Excuse me, my lady, but may I be of assistance?"

She looked up. Astride a horse was a young man of noble bearing, with a handsome face and a kind smile. She did not know whether or not this was Mr. Stanley, and while her original plan had been to only accept help from him, at this point she would accept help from anyone.

"Why yes, thank you," she said, trying to employ the ease of manners used by her sisters. "I did not bring a groom, as I planned to take only a short ride. Unfortunately, I needed to

KATHERINE COWLEY

dismount, and I have found it quite impossible to get back on."

"It would be my pleasure to serve you," said the man. He dismounted his horse, bowed, and extended a hand to help Mary off the fence. She was not used to men giving *her* this sort of gentlemanly attention, and she wondered if he was this courteous to everyone, or if it were only her dress and her hair that induced this behaviour.

"May I ask your name?"

"I am Mr. Stanley, at your service."

"Mr. William Stanley?" she said with the sort of silly interest Lydia might express. Inwardly she smiled. She had managed to intercept her prey before he arrived at Castle Durrington after all.

"Why yes. Should I know who you are?"

"Not yet, but you soon shall. I am staying with Lady Trafford at Castle Durrington, and we have been expecting you."

"How charming." He raised her gloved hand and kissed it. No gentleman had ever kissed her hand before. "Please, I beg of you, a name."

"Miss Mary Bennet," she said automatically, then realized it might have been better to defer him or give a false name. She reached for more words, something she could ask that might lead him to reveal information, but her mind came up blank. Before she could say anything to prolong the conversation, Mr. Stanley spoke.

"Let me assist you onto your horse, and we can return to Castle Durrington together."

"Of course."

They led the horse away from the fence. Unlike the groom, Mr. Stanley did not check the saddle or the girth straps, but Mary had just done so, so it did not matter. She positioned her right hand on the fixed head of the saddle and raised her skirts slightly with her left. She lifted her right foot, placing it on his hands, and he smiled up at her in a way that led her to wonder if he really was a gentleman.

"Ready?" asked Mary.

"Ready."

She sprang with her left foot and Mr. Stanley lifted up her right foot, but he did it with much greater speed and strength than a groom had ever done. She found herself crying out as she gripped her hand on the saddle head. She tried to land, as she had always done, on the horse, but her posterior never quite connected with the saddle and she felt herself slipping, flying, right over the top of the horse and over the opposite side. She barely had time to register that she was falling before she landed on the dirt on the other side of the horse.

"Miss Bennet! Are you injured?"

The horse made a concerned sort of snort.

For a moment, Mary could not breathe. She blinked, confused by the clouds above her. Finally, she drew in a breath, assessing her situation. She had fallen off the horse and onto her back. Her entire body ached. In particular, her posterior had never been in so much pain in her life, but that was not the sort of injury one mentioned to a gentleman.

In part, she wanted to cry, out of both pain and embarrassment, but she would not betray herself with this sort of expression of emotion. She had already cried once today, and that was more than enough.

Mr. Stanley reached out to grab her hands. "I am ever so sorry," he said as he attempted to help her to her feet. She wanted to push him away, to say something bitter about his lack of competence at performing a basic task, but she stifled the urge. She needed information, and anger was unlikely to draw it out.

She allowed Mr. Stanley to help her to her feet, though it probably would have been easier to do it on her own. As Mr. Stanley continued to apologize, she brushed the dirt off her gloves and her dress, contemplating what she should say as she attempted to ignore her throbbing posterior. Her cloak had come undone, and as she rebuttoned it, she smiled at him.

"No harm done, Mr. Stanley, I am perfectly fine." That was the sort of forgiving thing that Jane would say. And now, ideally, she would say something a bit flirtatious, but not silly, maybe what Elizabeth might say to Mr. Darcy, now that they liked each other. "Though you may be in my debt for a very long time. I will need to decide how to extract payment from you."

"Of course, Miss Bennet. I hope you will give me the opportunity to make it up to you."

The perfect thing to say came to her, based on the fragment she had heard of Lady Trafford and Mr. Withrow's conversation. "I am sure the opportunity will present itself. After all, we will be working together in London, as partners."

Some emotion passed over his face, though exactly what, Mary could not tell. "If you are working with us, then you are not a woman to be trifled with."

She did not understand that comment, so for lack of a better response, Mary smiled again. "You are obviously a man of great strength. Shall we try again?"

He nodded. Mary made a point of checking the saddle. It had shifted slightly, and she fixed it and adjusted the girth straps. Then Mr. Stanley helped her mount, this time without mishap.

Mr. Stanley mounted his own horse—she envied the male

saddle—and started his horse at a trot. But that would not do, not at all. She needed to be able to talk, so she could question him.

"Mr. Stanley! I prefer if we keep the horses at a walk. I am feeling a little stiff from my fall."

"Of course." He stopped his horse and waited to proceed until Mary was beside him.

"How long will you be staying at Castle Durrington?"

"Probably only a few hours, though I will do as Lady Trafford directs."

"And then will you return to Arundel?" That was the village Withrow had mentioned.

"No, back home to Chichester, at least until I go to London," said Mr. Stanley. "What is our assignment? Who are we tracking this time?"

This was the trouble with pretenses: Mary did not have the least idea. Rather than confessing her ignorance she said, "I will let Lady Trafford tell you of it. She will explain it much better than I can."

Her throat felt almost strangled by the fear that he would discover her. Mr. Stanley, Lady Trafford, and Mr. Withrow were clearly part of a large criminal organization, with agents in London, and in France. If he realized that she was not part of the same group, it might not go well for her. She had told no one of her location and she was completely unchaperoned, with a man who was strong enough to throw her over a horse and likely do much worse physical harm.

To Mary's relief, he nodded and did not question her answer.

They were silent for a minute, and then Mary's desire for knowledge overcame her once again. It was like having a book and knowing that it might be dangerous to turn the pages, but turning them anyway, because she could not resist.

"Do you always work with Lady Trafford?"

"Well, she is over this region, so when I am here, I do. Though in London I report directly to Mr. Booth."

She tagged the name in her mind. She wanted to ask for Mr. Booth's first name but thought it would be suspicious, so instead she asked, "Where do you normally stay in London?"

"In my parents' townhouse. We often live there for the season. They do not know many of the things I am really doing; they just want to see me wed, but a search for a bride provides ample reason to attend every social event in town, and my family's investments make visiting places of business and government natural. What about you? Where will you stay?"

"I have an aunt and uncle in London, or my sister and her husband may be staying for the season."

"Who is your sister?"

"Mrs. Fitzwilliam Darcy." He had turned the questions to her, which she did not like, but she felt obligated to respond. Lady Trafford always said that a conversation, to be lively to both partners, must have equal participation and interest on both sides.

They neared Castle Durrington. Lady Trafford might be watching from the front of the house, waiting for Mr. Stanley to arrive. If she rode up with him, she would be discovered.

"I told Lady Trafford I would check on one of her tenants, a woman that is feeling ill, so I will leave you here."

"It was a pleasure to meet you, Miss Bennet."

"And you as well, Mr. Stanley."

She waved to him and rode off on a smaller trail that led through the woods to another part of the estate. Then she rode into the trees, approaching as close to Castle Durrington as she could without being seen.

Lady Trafford, Mr. Withrow, and Mrs. Boughton came out of the house to greet Stanley. Mr. Tubbs took his horse, and they quickly went inside.

Mary tied the reins of her own horse to a tree. She did not want anyone in the house to know she had returned, and if she needed to flee, she could run into the trees and make a quick escape. Of course, she would still need to find a way to mount…if it came to it, maybe she could *climb* a tree.

Staying in the tree cover, she walked as close to the castle as she could. Thankfully, no one was outside, and hopefully those inside were too occupied with a guest to be looking out the windows. She walked quickly across the uncovered space, staying close to the side of the house, crouching as she passed by windows, then made it to the front door.

It was locked.

If she knocked, all would be revealed. She continued on to the east annex and entered the servants' door to the kitchen. It was rather empty, and she only had to hide once, when a servant came for a selection of teas and hors d'oeuvres.

She snuck behind the servant, who rapped on the library door and delivered the food.

Mary slipped up the smaller staircase, made sure no one was in the rotunda, and darted across to the curtained wall. She did not have time to remove her cloak or change her clothes, did not even have time to retrieve a candle. They were in the library, and she *would* hear what they had to say.

She found the hidden latch and pushed open the door, taking a deep breath before she stepped into the dark and shut herself in. She stumbled around in the dark, trying to find the trapdoor. She bumped into the crate covering it, making a small thump. Her heart raced and she stayed as still as possible. Hopefully no one had heard her. She moved the crate and opened the trapdoor. Climbing down the ladder, in this dress, in the dark, was laborious, and she feared that she was missing important things they might be saying, but finally she made it down and sank to the floor next to the grate.

"I am glad your family is doing well," said Lady Trafford. "And now, to matters of business."

"I wish Miss Bennet was joining us for this conversation," said Mr. Stanley.

"Miss Bennet?" said Lady Trafford sharply.

"She is my partner for the job in London, is she not?"

"What on earth are you talking about, Stanley?" asked Mr. Withrow.

"I met Miss Bennet on the road on the way here. She needed my assistance mounting her horse…and I…well…I accidentally threw her over her horse. Our second attempt at mounting worked better, and then we talked a little on the way here. She seemed to know a lot about our plans, and I assumed she was one of us."

"Miss *Mary* Bennet?" asked Mr. Withrow.

"Yes," said Stanley. "She was beautiful and charming and witty. Will someone tell me what is going on?"

"Miss Bennet is a distant relation," said Lady Trafford. "She has been staying with us for the last several months, and I was attempting to train her, but she failed all our tests, and so we did not bring her into our ranks. Please, describe the woman you met."

"She was about this tall," said Mr. Stanley. "With stunning hair, a smooth complexion, and a delicate nose. She had piercing eyes and a regal manner of bearing. She wore a lovely cream-coloured gown."

"That cannot possibly have been Miss Bennet," said Mr.

Withrow. "Someone has been spying on us and has decided to use Miss Bennet's identity to extract information from you."

"Oh God," said Mr. Stanley.

"What did you tell her?" asked Lady Trafford.

"I mentioned where I was from, and when I am leaving. I said that you were the head of this region and…and I mentioned Mr. Booth."

There was a sigh, that sounded like it must be from Lady Trafford. "A woman, waiting for you on the road. She puts you in her debt, and then tricks information out of you. You are supposed to know better than this, Stanley."

"I am so very sorry."

"What is most important right now," said Mr. Withrow, "is finding this impostor. I will have the groom prepare our horses."

"Wait," said Lady Trafford. "If she is still on a horse, she could be miles away in any direction, hiding countless places in the woods."

"We can check all the inns. Get in touch with our contacts."

"We may need to do that," said Lady Trafford. "But first, let us take a moment to think before we act. *Who* could possibly be imitating Miss Bennet, and, more saliently, *how* would this woman know when and where to intercept Mr. Stanley?"

They were quiet, and Mary had a chance to process her thoughts. She had hoped to learn more by eavesdropping, but instead everyone was trying to figure out her identity. She really should not have given her own name—that was a huge mistake. Now they would check to make sure she really had gone to town, and of course, no one would have seen her there.

"Fetch me my tool set, Henry," said Lady Trafford, and Mary leaned closer to the grate to try to figure out what they were going to do. But they said not a word.

A minute later there was a quiet, twisting sound, though she could not tell what it was. Despite the fact that it was quiet, it was very close, as if right outside the grate.

Mary inhaled suddenly. They must know where she was—they must be opening her hiding place.

She stood and grasped for the rope ladder. She climbed as quickly as she could, heedless of the noise it caused. Silence did not matter now.

As her hands reached the top of the ladder there was a creaking noise, and a large, strong hand grabbed tightly onto her ankle.

"Whoever you are, come down here, right now," said Lady Trafford.

"Or I will drag you down." That would be Mr. Withrow.

She could kick and try to force her way up, but Withrow could easily overcome her. Even if she did get out of his grasp, Lady Trafford would know the exit. They would find her; there would be no escaping.

"I will come down," said Mary.

Withrow did not release his grip on her ankle until he had grabbed a hold of her arm. She slowly descended.

The only way out of the space from this direction was a hole near the floor that had held the grate. "Ladies first," said Withrow gruffly. She could not see his face or his expression at all, but she still felt humiliated as she crouched on the ground and crawled through the hole into the library.

Upon exiting, Mary tried to stand tall and composed, with her chin held high as Elizabeth did, always managing to be impervious to the judgment of others.

"Miss Bennet," said Mr. Stanley, and she thought she saw a quick smile.

Mr. Withrow crawled through the hole and leapt up. His face was drawn and angry. His eyes lingered on her face and then moved down her dress. "What have you done to yourself?"

Lady Trafford eyed her appraisingly. She fingered the fabric of Mary's dress, then stepped directly in front of her, examining her face in close proximity. Then, to Mary's great surprise, she laughed, and her laugh was long and buoyant.

CHAPTER TWENTY-FIVE

"From the assembly of military men at Frankfurt...we think it reasonable to prognosticate that some grand operations are on the eve of being undertaken."

—*The Times*, London, December 9, 1813

"WANTED, a Steady, Active, Young Woman...An undeniable character will be required."

—*The Morning Post*, London, December 9, 1813

"TAKE A SEAT, Miss Bennet." Lady Trafford gestured to an armchair. "Stanley, pour her some tea."

Mary sat stiffly in the chair. When Mr. Stanley passed her a cup of the hot liquid, she held it but did not drink.

Lady Trafford poured herself tea and drank. "It is not poison, Miss Bennet."

But still, Mary did not drink. She sniffed, feeling the cold of the room, and wishing this chair were closer to the fire. And then, once she had composed her words in her mind, she spoke.

"I will not let you get away with this. I will write a letter to Sir Pickering. And if you do not let me write, or if you lock me up, Mr. Darcy and Mr. Bingley and my uncles will come looking for me."

"What exactly is it that you think we have done?" asked

Lady Trafford.

Mary stared in her teacup, then finally gave in and drank. The warmth filled her with determination. She set down the cup and stared straight at Lady Trafford.

"You asked Mr. Holloway to steal my family's mourning rings. You tricked me into coming to Castle Durrington because you hoped to use me for your own purposes. We probably are not even related. You lie constantly about your trips and what you are doing. You entertain visitors in the middle of the night. You have been reading my letters. You are one of the leaders of a major criminal organization that is attempting to undermine the people and the government for your own economic gain. And your nephew has been meeting with one of Bonaparte's soldiers."

Mr. Withrow grimaced. When he spoke, his voice was smooth and refined, yet there was something underneath, a negative undertone. "If all of this were true, what makes you think we would give you a chance to share what you know with the world?"

Despite all that Mary had learned, she knew very little of how far they were willing to go to meet their ends. Why would they lock her up or risk her writing a letter when they could simply eliminate her and then tell her family there had been a tragic accident? Colonel Radcliffe might not be the only person willing to murder to keep his secrets. Almost all the servants were gone for the day, nothing could stop them from hurting her, and she was many, many miles from anyone who would know and care what happened to her.

She stood, stepped away from the chair, then dashed to the fireplace and seized the metal poker. Withrow immediately stood and stepped towards her. She pointed the poker in his direction. She would not last long, she knew—three against one, and with them trained criminals, she might as well be defenseless. But she would not suffer injury without at least trying to defend herself.

Mr. Stanley rose from his chair, his hands raised placatingly. "Now Miss Bennet, please set that down."

"This is ridiculous," said Mr. Withrow, taking a few steps closer towards her. "You will hurt yourself."

"We have no intention of harming you in any way," said Lady Trafford.

The poker shook in Mary's hand. "You are going to kill me."

"That would be quite counterproductive," said Lady Trafford. "We do not want to kill you. We want you to work with us."

"I would *never* work with you," said Mary, pointing the poker towards Lady Trafford.

"This has gone on long enough," said Withrow as he approached her, anger in his eyes. "Put the poker down, Miss Bennet."

"No!" She swung the poker at him.

To her surprise, he lunged into her swing. He caught the poker with his left hand and her wrist with his right. His right hand slid up to her shoulder, and suddenly there was pain in her arm and he was twisting her—spinning her faster than in a dance.

He set her on the floor on her back and pressed his knee against her head. She gasped for breath. He stretched her right arm up towards the ceiling, applying pressure in a way that made it so she could not move it. He wrenched the poker from her hand.

"You are quite lucky that I do not intend you any harm, Miss Bennet," Mr. Withrow said in a gruff voice, "or this would have ended much worse for you."

Withrow stepped up and away from her, leaving her on the floor. He kept the poker in his hand and paced a few feet away from her, always keeping his eyes on her. Stanley also stood on the alert, and, despite how he had complimented her earlier, seemed disinclined to do anything to assist her.

Mary stayed there, staring at the ceiling, unwilling and unable to move. Her heart pounded in her chest and her fingers trembled. She had never felt so helpless in her life. She was the mouse, and she had been cornered by the barn cats and stood no chance against them. It had taken Withrow only two, maybe three, seconds to disarm her.

The door to the library opened and then slammed shut with great force as Fanny ran into the room, shouting. "Miss Bennet has been spying us. I found Mr. Holloway's missing notebook in her room. She tricked me, and I think she may have reported Colonel Radcliffe to Sir—"

Fanny stopped as she noticed Mary on the floor and Withrow with the poker in his hand.

"It appears I'm late to this discussion," said Fanny. She walked over to Lady Trafford, handed her Mary's spy book and Mr. Holloway's notebook, and took a comfortable chair, crossing one leg over the other.

"Not too late," said Lady Trafford. She set down the books Fanny had given her and reached out her hands to Mary. "Come, Miss Bennet, let me help you to a more comfortable seat."

Mary resisted Lady Trafford's assistance at first, but Withrow glared at her, so she allowed Lady Trafford to help her to her feet and guide her to a large sofa. Lady Trafford positioned her in the middle of the sofa and sat at her side. Mary felt limp, like an old rag doll, unable to do anything against the capricious nature of its mistress.

"Stanley, more tea," Lady Trafford directed. "This time, chamomile." She set her hand on Mary's knee, but when Mary flinched, she withdrew it.

Mary folded her arms across her chest.

"My dear Miss Bennet, let us start again, as if the past few minutes had not occurred."

Mary did not feel Lady Trafford's remark merited a response and had no interest in what Lady Trafford might have to say.

"I think—yes, a story will be just the thing," said Lady Trafford. "Let me begin at the beginning. Or, perhaps more accurately, my beginning. When I was fifteen years of age, my older brother was killed by the French during the American War for Independence. It was due to faulty information planted by an enemy spy. I was angry, and I wanted to do anything I could to protect our country and our people so others would not lose a loved one the way I had. I spent years writing letters to different members of Parliament, and eventually I was recruited by the government."

At this, Mary looked up.

"The *British* government. I work under King George III and the Prince Regent. Not directly, of course, but as part of—"

"You have said too much," said Mr. Withrow. "She has not sworn an oath of secrecy."

Lady Trafford waved her hand at him in a dismissive manner. "I work as a spy, as part of a network that seeks to fight against those who, knowingly or unknowingly, would undermine our country."

Mary rubbed her neck. Lady Trafford was not the first person to claim to be a spy, or to claim to need Mary's help.

"You are a spy?"

"Yes, the mysterious trips, the midnight visitors, inundating myself with the local gossip—it is all part of my work." Lady Trafford took another drink of tea. "And you, Miss Bennet, are clearly also a spy, but you do not yet have any loyalties."

"That may not be accurate," interjected Fanny. "If you read Mary's book, it appears that Monsieur Corneau recruited her to spy for him, but then she grew to distrust him."

"Is that correct?" asked Lady Trafford.

Mary nodded. "I see no reason why I should trust you either."

Lady Trafford shook her head in disapproval. "I knew Corneau was still angry at me, but I did not believe he would do such a thing." She opened Mary's spy book and spent several minutes reading its pages.

Mary's eyes darted to the door, but with Withrow present, there was no way to escape.

"I can understand your distrust of me," said Lady Trafford. "I did, indeed, ask Mr. Holloway to steal your family's mourning rings. Of course, I had every intention of returning them. I simply wanted to see if you or any of your sisters might be a potential recruit."

Lady Trafford raised Mary's spy book. "I was correct in choosing you. Your investigation was thorough and went undetected by any of us. You orchestrated Colonel Radcliffe's arrest masterfully. I assume it was you in the peasant cloak who tackled Radcliffe when he attempted to escape?"

"Yes," said Mary, confused, for Lady Trafford had not witnessed the events.

"Sir Pickering told me of it. Yes, despite the show we put on of disliking each other, we work together quite closely. In terms of your other accusations and concerns, much of what you have observed me doing in the past months has been my own attempts to solve Mr. Holloway's murder, as well as several other small investigations. For instance, Mr. Tagore and Miss Tagore are also part of my network. They were with us when Anne died, and became friends with Mr. Holloway at that time. Because of their friendship with him, they were well suited to investigate in Crawley. It was impossible for me to do it myself without raising suspicions, especially as Mr. Holloway was found so close to my property."

Lady Trafford waved Mary's notebook like a fan. "Mr. Withrow, would you care to explain your own behaviour to Miss Bennet?"

"Most certainly," said Withrow. "Since it appears you are the individual who wrote the anonymous letter to Sir Pickering, I will address the concern you raised in that letter first. I was indeed trying to establish a better relationship with Corneau. I had my suspicions about his involvement in local anti-government movements and was attempting to infiltrate his operation, with the intent, of course, of stopping him.

"In terms of the French officer you saw me meeting with the in the Roundel, he is actually one of our operatives. He is a French officer with British leanings who has been reporting to us with important information that has aided us greatly in the war effort. He gives me the information, and I pass it along to London."

Mary nodded. If all this were true, it explained their actions, and was in fact a noble effort.

"If you have spoken with Sir Pickering," said Mary, "I am sure you are aware that Colonel Coates is a smuggler. I believe others in Worthing have been working with him. But it does not seem that anything has happened to Colonel Coates or others as a result."

Lady Trafford shook her head. "Half the town is engaged in smuggling in some manner. It would be impossible to arrest everyone, and so Sir Pickering tries to keep the smuggling within certain bounds. French cheeses and fabrics have limited consequence, but when they lead to other crimes, he quickly intervenes."

Mary had always thought of things in very stark terms: good and evil, right and wrong. She would need to ponder on this matter more later.

"I would like to invite you to join us," said Lady Trafford. "Become part of our network. Work for the crown. Help us to defend our country against threats domestic and foreign. You have the spirit for it, the natural talent and propensity. Just think what you will do in service for a greater cause."

"How do I know for certain that you are working for the government, and that this is not an elaborate story meant to fool me?" She had begun to believe Lady Trafford—it made sense, it felt right and true—but, after Monsieur Corneau, she could not be too careful.

"If you demand evidence, evidence you shall have." Lady Trafford stood and walked over to the desk that Mary and Mr. Withrow had used for lessons. She opened a hidden drawer that Mary had not realized was there, then used a small key to unlock a book within. From that, she withdrew a letter which she handed to Mary.

The letter had a complicated paper locking method and an elaborate red royal seal.

"You can break it open. I have several others."

Mary broke the seal and opened the letter. It was penned by the head of the Foreign Office and signed by him and the Prince Regent himself. It expressed that Lady Margaret

Trafford was employed by the British government, though it was vague on any particulars, and granted her immunity.

"I do not know this seal," said Mary. "I have no way to tell if these signatures are legitimate or not. What would prevent you from creating all of this as an elaborate hoax?"

"You are wise to be so skeptical of my story." She looked at Stanley. "You could take a lesson from her on this matter." Lady Trafford thought for a moment. "I do have something that I believe you will find more definitive. Please wait here for me." She turned to Withrow. "I will lock the door."

Once Lady Trafford had left, Withrow set the poker underneath the desk, and then sat beside Mary on the sofa. Mary shifted farther away from him.

"*Never* raise a weapon towards my aunt again. In any circumstance. Do you understand?"

"Yes, I am sorry. I will not do it again."

"Good." Withrow leaned back into the sofa. He crossed his arms and his legs, and looked quite unthreatening, but Mary was not fooled. She rubbed the spot on her head where Withrow had pressed his knee when he had forced her to the ground.

"I really did arrive late," said Fanny. "If the two of you want to recreate your fight, I would love to see it."

Withrow glared at Fanny, but Mary chuckled. Mary would have needed a much larger skill set for it to have been anything resembling a true fight. She picked up the tea and drank. The chamomile's scent and taste were soothing.

The most convincing evidence was their knowledge of Mary's letter to Sir Pickering. He must have shared it with them, and she did not want to believe that this region's magistrate was corrupt.

Lady Trafford returned. In her hands were several loose

letters as well as a letter box. Mr. Bennet's letter box, the one Kitty had written was missing, the one her father had always kept locked and up on a shelf.

Mary set down her tea on the side table, accidentally spilling a little in her haste. "How do you have that?" She approached Lady Trafford, her hands extended, and received the items. Mary sat down again. She set the loose letters to the side and ran her fingers along the ornamental patterns on the metal letter box, along the vines and the animals and the fantastical creatures.

Mary and Kitty had tried to break into the box once. Mary must have been around six years of age at the time, and Kitty five. Their father had taken it away in a kind manner, but firmly impressed it upon their minds that there were some things that were their father's business.

"Your father was also a spy," said Lady Trafford.

Mary's finger halted on the horn of a unicorn. "My father, a spy?"

"That was how we met: an assignment we were both given. We maintained contact over the years, both as friends and as colleagues. When Mr. Holloway visited Longbourn, testing you and your sisters was a secondary purpose. The primary purpose was to retrieve your father's materials related to his work as a spy, including this box." Lady Trafford held out a key. "Mr. Holloway was unable to find the key, which is why you discovered Mr. Withrow in your parents' room."

Mary's fingers trembled as she took the key; she managed to insert it into the keyhole, and, for the first time in her life, opened the box.

Withrow stood and went to his desk. Lady Trafford gestured to Fanny and Mr. Stanley, who both took books off a shelf and began to read. Lady Trafford sat, close enough that she could see what Mary was doing, but not so close as to be intrusive. Mary appreciated the space, for she sensed that everything she knew was about to change.

Mary sifted through the pages, reading through a lifetime of Mr. Bennet's work for the British government. She paused on records, in his own handwriting, of the things he had accomplished. Mentioned were the occasional arrest or unrest in Meryton over the years, and she saw, for the first time, her father's involvement in these events. There were also clippings from newspapers, notebooks with logs of events, much like the one Mary herself had made, and letters—letters from Lady Trafford, letters from people whose names Mary recognized from the newspapers, and letters from many who Mary did not recognize. There were also pages that did not make any sense, which must be written in code.

Mr. Bennet had spent his life doing so much more than running an estate.

"You should read the other letters," said Lady Trafford. "The ones that were not in the box."

Mary picked up the letters, which were written on a fine paper that her father had used only for special correspondence. They had a complicated seal and locking method that had been broken. She opened one and inside found her father's words to Lady Trafford, dated from 1805, when Mary was ten years old. "Dear Lady Trafford," he began. "Your letter on your children puts me in a sentimental mood."

He then described each of his daughters—Elizabeth, Jane, Kitty, Lydia, and Mary.

"Mary is now my greatest reader. She will read any book that is not tied down. She is a very curious and perceptive child, always attempting to figure out the place of things in this world. Sometimes others do not understand her, but that is their loss. Every time Mary sets her mind to something, she succeeds in doing it."

There was a lump in Mary's throat. She swallowed and blinked her eyes, trying to hold back an outward expression of emotion. Her father had written to Lady Trafford about *her*. He had also written about her sisters, but there had always been room enough in his heart for all of them.

She reread his words, the words he used to describe her. If he had had more time in his dying moments, maybe he would have said something of this sort to her.

If she could go back, there were still things she would change. She would do more to express her affection to him, and she would spend more time with him instead of always being caught up in her music and her books. She thought that some regret would always remain. Yet that did not need to overshadow her good memories with her father. For the first time since his death, she felt secure in his love for her. She felt whole.

"May I keep this letter?" asked Mary.

"Yes, you may," said Lady Trafford.

Mary folded the letter carefully and set it aside. She read the other letters that had not been in the box; there were two more personal letters from Mr. Bennet to Lady Trafford. They contained nothing about her or her sisters, but they did demonstrate friendship and trust. Finally, she placed all of her father's papers back in the box, locked it, and handed it back to Lady Trafford. "I believe you."

"Mr. Bennet had no desire to lead or train other spies, as I have done, but he was a great spy. What you saw in that box represents only a small portion of his work over the years."

"Did my mother ever know?" Mary asked, and then she shook her head. "Never mind. I know the answer to that. My mother would never have been able to keep it a secret."

Lady Trafford called the others to attention, then turned back to Mary. "We would like to recruit you to be one of our number. To be a spy working to protect the British people, to preserve our liberties, our government, and our way of life."

"You would make a marvelous spy," said Stanley, who seemed pleased at the chance to put down his book.

Lady Trafford gestured for Withrow to speak.

"I admit that I had no idea that you were spying on us, and that you were quite effective in gathering information." Withrow seemed annoyed at having to make this admission. "I am certain my aunt can find a place for you."

"You would, of course, be compensated for your efforts," said Lady Trafford. "It is not a grand amount, but it is comparable to what you might receive as a governess in a nice home. We can offer you seventy pounds a year. You would also be given funds to cover expenses, a budget for clothing and disguises, money to pay or buy gifts for informants, some who will realize they are informants, others who will not, as well as travel costs."

As she considered the offer, a warmth grew in Mary's chest. This would give her independence, and, more importantly, purpose. No longer did she possess only two options, marriage or remaining a spinster dependent on the generosity of her relations. She could be a part of something greater than herself. While the nature of the work meant she would never be recognized for it, the praise of the world was shallow and fleeting.

"What happens if I turn you down?" asked Mary.

"Ideally, you would return to your home and not share what you have learned with others. If you decide to reveal all that you know, there is the possibility that no one would believe you. If they do believe you and it becomes well-known, it is likely that a number of us will lose much of what we have done as well as our positions. But it will be my own fault for underestimating you all this time."

The response satisfied Mary. She would not undertake a venture such as this if it felt like she was being forced into it.

Mary considered the face of her mourning ring, studying the miniature painting with the weeping willow, the broken column, and her father's name and date of death. She considered spinning the bevel but she did not. She knew the lock of his hair was there, against her finger, without needing to spin it. She considered his hidden legacy, the work he had performed for the government that would never be known to the world.

She wanted to be a part of it.

"I will do it," said Mary. "I will work with you to defend and protect our country and people."

"Excellent," said Lady Trafford.

"And will I, in fact, be working with Miss Bennet in London?" asked a hopeful Mr. Stanley.

"I believe Mr. Booth will need her in London for the season, but he will decide where Miss Bennet's skills will be most useful."

"Send me to London too," said Fanny, suddenly standing.

"Your request for a transfer was denied," said Lady Trafford.

"You don't think Mary can do this"—Fanny gestured at Mary's hair and clothes—"by herself, do you? Besides, there are many places a genteel woman cannot go; a disguise itself is not a substitute for knowledge of how to act within a particular community."

Lady Trafford considered for a moment. "Very well," she said. "You can pretend to be Mary's personal maid. If I publicly announce that I have taken Mary as my ward, it will seem natural for me to give her an allowance and lend a servant."

Lady Trafford turned back to Mary. "Fanny will certainly assist you when a disguise is necessary. But I suspect you will be able to do a great deal simply by being yourself. Not only did Corneau and Colonel Radcliffe underestimate you, but so did Withrow and I. I have spent all this time attempting to mold you into a successful spy, when you had what you needed all along.

"Of course, you will also find that the skills I have taught you can be a useful part of your arsenal. At times you may want people to underestimate you, but at other times you may want to please them and make them comfortable with you, so that you can better extract their confidences. In terms of your accomplishments, it will be your choice of which ones to reveal, and which to conceal. Your knowledge of economics and politics may seem irregular and draw too much attention in some contexts, while it may be useful to display this knowledge in other situations.

"I do need to warn you, Miss Bennet, for almost all the work of a spy is slow and tedious. You speak to people and make connections for days and weeks and months and sometimes you still do not find the information you want or need."

"The things of the greatest worth often require the greatest effort," Mary observed.

"Indeed," said Lady Trafford. "The work we are involved in is worth every effort. I think you will be a great asset to our organization." She reached out her hand to Mary.

"I will do all that I can." Miss Mary Bennet, the newest spy for the British government, shook Lady Trafford's hand.

The End

Historical Note and Acknowledgements

Castle Durrington is inspired by Sir Bysshe Shelley's Castle Goring. (There really is a hidden storage room with pig-head statues, though I took creative liberties with the vents and rope ladder.) With only three exceptions, the epigraphs are real excerpts from newspapers. Like Mary, I learned about letterlocking—letterlocking.org provides numerous resources on the history and art. While historical fiction requires endless research, I relied most heavily on Sue Wilkes' *Regency Spies: Secret Histories of Britain's Rebels and Revolutionaries*, Carolly Erickson's *Our Tempestuous Day: A History of Regency England*, Norma Myers' *Reconstructing the Black Past: Blacks in Britain 1780-1830*, and Susannah Fullerton's *A Dance with Jane Austen: How a Novelist and Her Characters Went to the Ball*.

A veritable spy network of people helped me create this novel. Rebecca Davis translated the French passages, Dena Haynes provided advice on horses, Anna Lunt created the ear drawing, and Richard Johnson repeatedly demonstrated how to disarm someone wielding a fire poker. My Kalamazoo writing group served as insightful first readers—Michelle Preston, Anna Lunt, Marianne von Bracht, Erin Brady, and Meghan Decker. My critique partners pushed the story to greater heights—Sarah Johnson (who read the book half a dozen times), Jeanna Mason Stay, Pam Eaton, Brooke Lamoreaux, Emily Goldthwaite, and Rachel Josephson. Other readers provided expert critiques—Krystyna Hales, Amy Parker, Tiffini Knight, BreAnne Johnson, Whitney Woodard, and Marisa Canova. I could spend pages thanking the countless other friends and writers who have supported and inspired me.

A special thanks goes to my incredible, fearless agent, Stephany Evans, who helped me find the book's true mystery. I am so grateful for my extraordinary editor, Sinclair Sawhney, who helped me dive into the story's emotional heart, and for the rest of the amazing team at Tule Publishing.

And of course, none of this could not have been possible without my family. Endless thanks to my husband, Scott, for his love and support, critiques and marketing advice, and to my three daughters, whose first or middle names all belong to Austen characters.

Also, thank you to Jane Austen. For everything.

If you enjoyed *The Secret Life of Miss Mary Bennet,*
you'll love the next books in….

The Secret Life of Mary Bennet series

Book 1: *The Secret Life of Miss Mary Bennet*

Book 2: *True Confessions of a London Spy*
Coming March 2022!

Book 3: *The Complete Lady's Guide to the Art of War*
Coming September 2022!

About the Author

Katherine Cowley read *Pride and Prejudice* for the first time when she was ten years old, which started a lifelong obsession with Jane Austen. She loves history, chocolate, traveling, and playing the piano, and she teaches writing classes at Western Michigan University. She lives in Kalamazoo, Michigan with her husband and three daughters. *The Secret Life of Miss Mary Bennet* is her debut novel.

Thank you for reading

The Secret Life of Miss Mary Bennet

If you enjoyed this book, you can find more from all our great authors at TulePublishing.com, or from your favorite online retailer.

TULE
PUBLISHING

9 781953 647443